—

**M**ary Beth had never thought she would venture to the underbelly of the West Side, no matter that it was broad daylight and there were cops on every corner.

Then again, she hadn't had to sell her jewelry every day.

It was easier than she'd expected, to pick out which things she could do without, which would not be missed by the wedding guests. She could not, of course, go back to Van Cleef or Tiffany's or the other places where her trinkets had come from; she could not even visit a prominent estate jeweler: Word would spread too quickly that Mary Beth was broke.

Broke!

What a dreadful, startling word that she'd never thought would be associated with an Atkinson, let alone, her.

The cab finally arrived at the address Carla had given her. Mary Beth quickly got out and tried not to look left or right but simply moved straight ahead toward the shop.

She tipped her regal head back. *Act as if it's Tiffany's* she decided.

On stiletto heels she marched into the shop as if she belonged there.

"I have jewelry," she said. "Good jewelry. And I need to sell it."

*Other books by Jean Stone*

# JEAN STONE

—

# TRUST
# FUND
# BABIES

BANTAM BOOKS
*New York Toronto London
Sydney Auckland*

TRUST FUND BABIES
A Bantam Book

ISBN 0-7394-2499-8

Bantam Books are published by Bantam Books, a division of
Random House, Inc. Its trademark, consisting of the words
"Bantam Books" and the portrayal of a rooster, is Registered in U.S.
Patent and Trademark Office and in other countries. Marca
Registrada. Bantam Books, 1540 Broadway, New York, New York
10036.

PRINTED IN THE UNITED STATES OF AMERICA

*To Sisyphus—*

*for his courage*
*and his wisdom*
*and his wit*

# ACKNOWLEDGMENTS

Many thanks to my editor Wendy McCurdy and to my agent Merrilee Heifetz, who came up with this title over lunch and challenged me to come up with the rest.

Thanks also to my supporting cast:
    Jim
    Aunt Lois
    Kathy and Ted
    Cindy and Bob
    Jane and Mike
    Steven and Pierre
    Linda-the-agent

Without all of you, these girls would never have made it.

# TRUST FUND BABIES

# PROLOGUE

———

**L**ester Markham is gone, and so is your trust fund," Carla DiRoma said into the huge, gilt-framed mirror that hung in the half-empty Park Avenue office. She took a slow breath and looked over her shoulder. Twenty-six years, Monday through Friday, nine to five, Carla had worked there as the loyal secretary to the investment banker who'd now disappeared, along with the money of his three trusting clients, the Atkinson cousins.

Mary Beth.

Nikki.

Gabrielle.

Three women who had, from the moment of conception until this late spring morning, had it all.

Carla frowned at her reflection. Little lines creased her low forehead and the corners of her wide mouth. She fluffed the short, curly perm that her mother always had said was "too severe for a woman her age." She stared at her large, forty-five-year-old, faded brown eyes and tried to look sympathetic.

"I'm sorry," she said into the glass, "but you are dead broke."

She supposed that was the best way to tell the three

women: up-front, direct, the way she'd learned from Sister Agnes back in the dusky days of parochial school.

Still, it would not be easy.

A wave of foreboding rolled through her, riding on the fear of the unknown. After all, her life would be different as well, now that the files were empty, now that Lester's long mahogany desk and tall leather chair sat vacant, too.

She leaned against the cool glass and tried not to think of the many times she'd checked her reflection there, trying to look her best for the well-groomed, well-positioned, well-everything-ed man who had been her boss. Though Carla was "attractive enough," as her ex-husband had once said, she knew she did not have the beauty, the confidence, or the innate presence that women like Mary Beth, Nikki, and Gabrielle relished as their birthright. She did not have the breeding to be more than an assistant in Lester Markham's life. She was merely schleppy Carla DiRoma, a working-class single mother of the working-class Bronx, whose ailing mother had died last month, whose two sons were mostly on their own, and now whose reason for rising every morning had suddenly up and gone.

Her eyes traveled the dark-papered walls of the office to the rectangular outlines that marked where the Chagall and the Manet—Lester's prized possessions—had hung.

Like Lester, the paintings were gone.

Adjusting the elastic waistband of her JCPenney skirt, Carla thought about the three women whose lives were about to change. Would they shop at the mall now, instead of Versace or Dior? Would they be content with pizza instead of pâté, the subway instead of stretch limos?

And did any of them have what it would take to survive in the real world, her world?

Soon, Carla would know. But first she would find each of the cousins, one at a time. She would tell them their fate in person, one-on-one, so the blow would be less severe.

It would be the least her mother would have expected.

Slowly, Carla turned from the mirror so she wouldn't see herself smile.

# 1

"I don't care what you say, they must be engraved,"
Mary Beth Atkinson-McNight Roulle hissed into the
phone. She pressed her fingers to her temples. How
hard could it be to etch the date of her daughter's wedding onto six hundred sterling silver bubble wands?
"Tiffany's would find a way."

"You didn't call Tiffany's," snipped the other end of
the line. "You wanted to save money, so you called us."

Mary Beth sucked on a cigarette and blew out the
smoke. "My mistake," she barked, and slammed the
phone into its cradle.

She stubbed out her cigarette and waved her hand in
the air, as if the smoke would dissipate and no one would
know that she'd sneaked a puff. But, God, how could she
not? Not that her family would ever understand the pressure of trying to make Shauna's wedding perfect.

Which, of course, it would be. For openers, it would
not be here in Manhattan but at the family estate on
Martha's Vineyard, where every respectable Atkinson
wedding had been held for three generations. Of course,
it would be a French garden wedding. Water-colored
freesia and roses, lilies, and iris would be woven into

trellises, their fragrance blending with the soft sound of harps. The guests would mingle on the terraced lawn that tiered down to the sea. They would sip pink champagne, and now—with this last-minute, mother-of-the-bride brainstorm—they would also blow shimmering bubbles into the gentle breeze of the ocean-salt air, using sterling bubble wands. That would be engraved.

She would not consider that the sun might not shine, because in summer, on the Vineyard, sunshine was the law. Her mother had once said that, and Mary Beth still believed it, despite years of proof otherwise.

*The wedding,* she thought, her jaw clenching again. Less than six weeks—no, *five*—until the glorious event for which the gilt-edged invitation acceptances were already coming back in the mail.

"Mom?" Her daughter bounded into the second-floor study. She was dressed in Cavalli rhinestone jeans and a silk zebra shirt that had set Mary Beth back more than the bubble wands, with or without the engraving. "Jason's exhausted from finals. We want to go to the Vineyard next weekend."

Jason was Shauna's intended, who had finished his MBA at Harvard, not that he'd need it. Like Mary Beth, Jason's parents flourished on their trust funds. Jason had his own chunk now that he'd turned twenty-five; in the same way, Shauna would have her share of Mary Beth's, if this wedding didn't suck every penny Grandfather Atkinson had passed down. She cleared her throat to ease her bitterness that there would have been more money if she'd listened to her mother twenty-two years ago and not married Eric Roulle, pauper of the free world, nice guy though he was. Eric, the same nice guy who'd asked this morning for twelve thousand dollars for a short trip to Brazil in the name of his coin-collecting bad habit. She often wondered if the coins her husband truly enjoyed were not the rare ones but hers.

"The house isn't open," she told her daughter.

Shauna flopped on the leather chair, tossing her gazellelike legs over the Louis XV tapestry armchair as if it were a bar stool. She flipped back her long copper hair the way Mary Beth might have done in the sixties.

"We don't need the whole house, Mom. We just want a break before the craziness starts."

Mary Beth did not comment that "craziness" was not a very appropriate way for Shauna to refer to her wedding, the wedding over which Mary Beth was breaking her back and neck and pocketbook so it would be perfect. She did not comment, because she knew Shauna was not as obsessed by the wedding as Mary Beth was. Kids today—even her daughter—simply didn't get the importance of protocol and...things. "I hadn't planned to get the house ready until just before the wedding."

"Please, Mom? I want Dee to come, too. We need fittings for our gowns. If you can't get the regular cleaning service, maybe Aunt Nikki knows someone."

Nikki was not really Shauna's aunt, but Dee's quirky mother, Mary Beth's cousin who had once been her friend, before age and attitudes had altered their innocence. Nikki lived on the island estate year-round, in the lighthouse, for God's sake, the family eccentric because every family needed one. Shauna had always adored Nikki, though the woman didn't know Vuitton from Valentino. Or care.

"Don't call Nikki. I'll take care of it." One more thing to add to the list. The never-ending things-to-do list. It occurred to her that it was a good thing she'd never needed a job. There simply would not have been time. "Now leave me alone. I'm trying to find bubble wands."

"Doesn't Tiffany's have them?"

"Well. Yes."

Shauna untangled her legs and stood up. "So what's the problem?"

"The problem is, your flowers alone are going to cost a hundred thousand. I was hoping to save a few dollars here and there."

"What?" Shauna asked, rolling her eyes. "Cut corners on my wedding?" She pressed her hand to her chest as if sliding into a faint.

Sarcasm did not wear well on her otherwise beautiful daughter. Mary Beth wondered if Shauna would be so cavalier if she'd not been born into money, or if she weren't marrying it. Flipping back her hair in her daughter's indifferent manner, Mary Beth said, "Don't be silly, my darling. I only wanted to be sure you were paying attention." She returned to her list and chastised herself for the gross oversight. Jason's family, after all, was so old and so respected, their name had once been hand-calligraphied into the social register. Proof that Shauna was worthy to carry on the bloodline should, indeed, be reinforced with a small turquoise Tiffany box at each place setting. If the box were not turquoise, it simply wouldn't do.

Whatever had she been thinking?


It was nice to know you could still count on some things in this world, like the pristine glass cases at Tiffany's on Fifth Avenue at Fifty-seventh that stretched down the aisles and beckoned with gold and silver and diamonds and pearls and all things that made life worthwhile.

Mary Beth stepped inside, paused, and inhaled the op-ulent scent. It was a habit her mother had taught her; a way of remembering her place in life. She felt a quick ache that Shauna had told Dorothy about the wedding. But how would Shauna—or Mary Beth, for that matter— have expected it would be the one thing that Dorothy had no trouble remembering? Each time Mary Beth went to Harriman House now, her mother insisted she would attend the event. How did one tell a seventy-three-year-old woman that Alzheimer's and reality and God, if there still was one, clearly had made other plans?

"Ms. Atkinson?" A salutational voice obediently called from beside her, as if it, too, knew Mary Beth's place. "Good morning."

She pushed her sorrow back down to her heart, then twirled on her Prada snakeskin pumps, grateful that the clerk had addressed her properly, that she'd had the sense to know that when one's ancestors were Atkinsons, no other name mattered.

"Mrs. LaMonde is waiting for you upstairs."

Mrs. LaMonde, of course, was Roxanne, whose last husband, Jeffrey LaMonde, had international recognition as the steel baron's great-grandson. Hence, Roxanne had kept the name. Mrs. LaMonde was also Mary Beth's best friend, who, surprisingly, had been available when Mary Beth phoned her for shopping reinforcement. Lately their schedules seemed too often to clash, with their chances to share laughter and wine and a few gossipy tales limited to their simultaneous monthly hair-highlighting sessions.

Mary Beth followed the clerk to the inconspicuous elevator tucked around the corner at the front of the store. She adored the tiny lift that brought only prestigious customers up to the private selection rooms, the "upstairs" where Roxanne now waited. On the short ride to Floor Two, she let out a sigh. Once a month with Roxanne was not nearly sufficient time to commiserate about Shauna's small crises (such as needing the Vineyard house opened next weekend) and Eric's ongoing requests (why was it a man with no money had selected numismatics as a hobby?) and the caretaking needs of her mother, God help her. Roxie was the ideal sounding board because she had no children, had been divorced three times, and had no living relatives, except for Lucky, her aging bichon frise.

She slid into the room where Roxanne sat, ogling a crystal decanter.

"I hope that's for my daughter," Mary Beth said, and Roxanne stood and they kissed-kissed.

"Actually, I have my eye on four Elsa Perettis. In sterling, of course." Roxanne was talking about the wonderful silver bone candlesticks that cost over a thousand dollars apiece and would look as timeless and divine in Shauna's home as Roxie now looked in her Anne Klein beige silks—shirt, pants, and cropped jacket to die for. She was one of the few Mary Beth knew on whom off-the-rack looked sublime, aided, no doubt, by her startling red mane of hair. Mary Beth was glad she'd changed into her long black linen pencil skirt and sleeveless turtleneck sweater that set off her blue eyes and taupe-blond hair and made her look nearly as good as Roxanne. Of course, her three-times-a-week, three-hundred-dollar-an-hour personal trainer named Hank deserved some of the credit for keeping Mary Beth in a size four. The two women sat, and Mary Beth looked back to the clerk.

"Bubble wands," she proclaimed. "Engraved."

The clerk smiled. "Individually boxed?"

The mother of the bride nodded.

"What about containers for the liquid? May I suggest a crystal jar, perhaps with a silver cap?"

"Show us some things."

The clerk left them alone. Mary Beth patted Roxanne's arm. "Thanks for coming," she said. "I can't think straight anymore."

"Any excuse to do Tiffany's always works for me." Her slightly puffed lips spread into a smile. Though Roxanne had never admitted it, Mary Beth knew she must have had a tad of collagen injected into her lips. They looked, well, she supposed they looked sexy. Damn good for a woman already past forty. Damn sexy, yes. Mary Beth wondered if she should have hers done as well. Was there time before the wedding? Should she ask Roxie the name of her doctor? Or were some things too private even between them?

"Tell me about the bubble wands," Roxanne urged.

So Mary Beth explained the scenario she envisioned, from the flowers to the harps to the bubbles in the air.

"And they'll float out over the sea," Mary Beth finished. "And it will be magical."

"If I didn't know better I'd say you were a romantic."

Mary Beth merely smiled. Roxanne might have secretive collagen lips, but Mary Beth had a few secrets of her own. Friendship, after all, was only so close, especially when one's basic needs were at stake.

The clerk returned and set three bubble wands on the black velvet tabletop. One was smooth, polished sterling, one had ridges, one was an unusual oval shape.

"The oval is grand," Roxanne said, and, of course, it was, because it was the most expensive. The crystal bottle that matched had a sterling-topped stopper. "Perfect," Roxanne added. "After the bubbles are gone it's a wonderful perfume bottle."

Mary Beth smiled. It felt good to have someone else make a decision. "We'll take them," she said. "Six hundred of each."

The wands and the bottles would cost another small fortune, but Shauna would, hopefully, only marry once, at least to this extreme. Glancing at her watch, Mary Beth realized that if she and Roxanne lunched with a really good Chardonnay, she might have some fun, which might ease the stress of a visit with Mother before going home. As much as she loved Dorothy, lately her mother did not always know who Mary Beth was, so what was the point?

Yes, the wine would help her have fun and prepare her for Dorothy. She'd still have time for a short nap before the cocktail party at the Met. In between, of course, she'd have to write out the check for twelve thousand so her husband, the nice guy, could go to Brazil and have some fun, too.

The courtyard at the fashionably private Harriman House was cool and well tended, a shady refuge from the streets of Manhattan, a country estate behind thick concrete walls. Dorothy had been there since just after Christmas, when Mary Beth could no longer keep her at home because it had become awkward and would only grow worse. For a woman like Dorothy who'd always been dependent, the disease had done little more than exaggerate her need for attention and care—albeit beyond the point Mary Beth was willing or able to go. She'd talked it over with Roxanne, received Eric's encouragement, and delivered Dorothy to Harriman House, where she was among others of her own social standing, not that any of the residents noticed.

Alzheimer's disease.

The diagnosis had given Mary Beth an odd sense of freedom, as if the only responsibility to her mother now was financial. Gone was the need to accompany Dorothy to the Riviera each spring to sit and sip gin on the Promenade des Anglais and listen to the same stories of how grand Nice once was; gone was the duty as cohostess for Dorothy's Vineyard soirées, which meant Mary Beth did the planning and Mary Beth did the work, while her mother entertained on the veranda in a wide-brimmed summer hat and played whist like the southern belle she was not.

None of which meant Dorothy was a prima donna. It was simply the way things always had been done.

Along with the disease came the transfer of her mother's funds into Mary Beth's, though Dorothy's dollars alone were not enough for the support payment of fifteen thousand a month. She could have gone somewhere cheaper, but it would not have been right. Old money was expected to choose Harriman House; it wasn't Dorothy's fault that though her cash would have been ample back in the sixties, it was worth squat in the new millennium.

But relieved of the bittersweet burden, Mary Beth was only too happy to kick in the balance from her own Atkinson trust fund...just one more off-ramp on the superhighway of comings and goings of her inheritance.

Her mother sat on a flower-cushioned rattan chair next to a willow tree. Despite the fact that Dorothy had a full suite with fine furnishings, she preferred open places, where people passed by and nodded and smiled as if they knew she was Dorothy Atkinson-McKnight—society's Deb of 1955. Maybe today, the Deb would recognize her daughter. Maybe, maybe not.

Mary Beth sucked in her breath. "Hello, Mother," she said, and stooped to give her a perfunctory hug. A gentle scent of lavender soap reassured Mary Beth that bringing her mother there had been right, for she was well cared for, she was treated with dignity, as the brochure had promised.

Dorothy blinked but did not reply.

Mary Beth sat on a twin rattan chair and eyed the crisp ruffled robe that looked as sparkly bright as the woman who wore it was not.

"Mother?" she repeated, but Dorothy said nothing. Mary Beth squared her shoulders. Would she ever be able to accept that the woman who looked a lot like her mother was somehow detached from her mind? Lately, however, it was equally startling when Dorothy knew who Mary Beth was. But it was the uncertainty that was most difficult: which personality would emerge in the crisp, ruffled robe today, any day?

She leaned over. "Mother, it's me. Mary Beth. I've come for a visit."

Dorothy looked at her, then looked away. Mary Beth looked in the other direction, trying to ignore the tingle that rose in her throat and threatened to turn into tears.

"I went to Tiffany's this morning," she said, raising her chin, as if they were having a real conversation, as if it were ten years or five or even six months ago, when Mary Beth had shared every drop of life—hers, theirs, and everyone else's—because it entertained Dorothy and, over time, that had become Mary Beth's job. "I bought bubble wands, Mother. They are sterling, of course, and will be engraved..." Her voice had gone flat, stripped of its enthusiasm.

"Nurse," her mother cried weakly.

Mary Beth dared a glance back at Dorothy. A single tear leaked from her eye. "It's okay," she whispered. "I'm not going to hurt you."

Her gaze fell to the five-carat diamond that loosely ringed the blue-veined finger of her mother's right hand, the engagement ring given to Dorothy by Mary Beth's father. He was a faceless man whom Mary Beth had forgotten through her own form of Alzheimer's-for-the-young—a welcome insulation against recollection of all things unpleasant.

"What's the trouble, Dot?" The woman who asked was the occupational therapist Mary Beth had seen often. She was a boxy brunette with red lipstick and drawn-in arches where her eyebrows should have been. She wore a blue smock and reminded Mary Beth of an old-fashioned hairdresser, the kind who smoked cigarettes between bleaching blondes and setting hair in pink rollers. *Cigarettes*, Mary Beth thought. What she wouldn't give for a pack or two now.

"Dot" did not answer the therapist, either. Mary Beth refrained from suggesting that the woman not call her mother Dot. It was bad enough Dorothy often did not know her own name; changing it could only add to the poor woman's confusion.

Then again, she reminded herself, Dorothy—Dot— was no longer her responsibility.

"Did you bring the photos?" It took Mary Beth a second to realize the question was directed at her, not at "Dot."

"No," she replied. "Not today."

The therapist nodded as if she wasn't surprised. Mary Beth smoothed the lap of her black linen skirt, which a short time ago had seemed so couture and now seemed only foolish. Who went to a nursing home, no matter how pricey, dressed for lunch at a Parisian café? The same woman, she supposed, who had forgotten the occupational therapist's suggestion that had come from the doctor to help Dorothy sort through old photographs.

"We encourage residents to get in touch with their past," the gerontologist had said. "Their earlier memories are much stronger than recent ones."

But Mary Beth, of course, had not remembered the

photos because Mary Beth was too busy these days. She swallowed her guilt. "I'll bring them next time."

The therapist threw a steely-eyed stare, as if it were Mary Beth's fault that Dorothy was here in the first place. "Pictures will remind her of home," the woman said with a grunt.

Mary Beth did not mention that except for the rare antiques and pricey bric-a-brac, Dorothy's "home"—the grand apartment on Central Park West—no longer had much left of Dorothy, that her bedroom and dressing room had been converted to a small gym and a steam room. She did not say that because Dorothy might become lucid and might understand that she now was, officially, a ward of Mary Beth's, that her choices were no longer her own.

"I need a dress," Dorothy said suddenly. "When will you buy me a dress for the wedding?"

Mary Beth turned back to her innocent, white-haired mother. "Soon, Mother." There was no reason to tell Dorothy she couldn't go to Shauna's wedding because it would be awkward to have her in public, most of all among friends.

Her mother's pale eyes seemed content with the answer. Then she smiled. "Where is my breakfast?" she asked. "I'd like my breakfast."

Mary Beth stood up. "You ate breakfast hours ago," she replied, then glanced at her watch. "Well," she said, "I have to get going."

The therapist looked Mary Beth up and down, then leveled her eyes with blatant disapproval. "The photos really would help," she repeated.

"All right," Mary Beth said through her teeth. "I said I'll bring them next time." She kissed the translucent skin of her mother's dry cheek, tossed her bag over her shoulder, and marched away, reminding herself that she was the one who paid the fees that paid the damn therapist's salary, and that she must inform the administrator what kind of behavior from the staff was appropriate and what, goddamnit, was not.

When she steamed into the lobby on Central Park West, Mary Beth was still sputtering.

*Damn the paid help who thought they had all the answers.*

*Damn the fact that she needed them and their middle-classness.*

*Damn that all she wanted was to sit down and cry.*

Jonathan, the always-there, gray-white-haired doorman, stepped into her sight, interrupting her angst.

"Ms. Atkinson," he said, tipping his hat. "You have a visitor." She followed his gaze across the huge lobby to the red velvet settee that stood as it probably had since the twenties, yet looked as new and dust-free as the day it had been made. On it sat a woman dressed in one of those hideous all-weather coats from the fourth floor of Bloomingdale's.

Mary Beth looked back to Jonathan, who feigned a slight shrug.

"Her name's Carla DiRoma," he said. "She said she works for someone named Lester Markham."

# 2

Nikki Atkinson crisscrossed string around the thin cardboard box and tied off the ends. "Two wild-berry muffins," she said with a smile to the fifty-something-year-old man on the other side of the counter, who'd often been dubbed a Ted Turner look-alike though he cared little about money and even less about sailing.

"Ah, one of my sins." The man returned the grin, reached into his pocket, and extracted a few bills that were as crumpled as the flannel shirt he wore. She had a fleeting thought that many old-fashioned women might have liked to corral him, to iron his shirts and cook him square meals and trim the silver hair that sprouted over his collar. But no matter how many women had the best intentions, Nikki knew they would have been disap-pointed, because Mack Olson was not needy, he was sim-ply damn comfortable inside and out. She supposed that was part of his unintentional allure.

"No charge," she whispered, then pointed to a color-ful poster tacked to the wall. "It's the least I can do, Mack. You've been trucking all over the island with those." The poster was lettered in finger paints and read "Camp4Kids." Beneath a photo of three laughing children were the words "We Need your Heart. We Need your Hands. This Weekend. Please be there!"

Mack turned back to Nikki. "Maybe the islanders will get the message and show up."

"If they don't, if won't be for lack of publicity. Let's cross our fingers that the weather holds." The end of May on the Vineyard was still an iffy time, when the heavens could open at any moment and decide not to close for a week, sometimes more. But Nikki needed volunteers to help clean and paint and fix up the old campgrounds just outside of Oak Bluffs, the abandoned plot of scrub-oak-covered land sprinkled with neglected cottages and featuring an overgrown pond—all of which she had acquired for Camp4Kids, a summer camp for children with AIDS, her latest attempt to bring love into a world where not enough love could be found.

"Any more word from Town Hall?" It was Mack's way of asking if there would be further protests, if anyone left on the island dared challenge Nikki's mission, as if the kids would corrupt both their morals and their drinking water.

"I think it's history," Nikki replied. "I hope it's history." A few battles begun in the coffee shops had ended in the courthouse, neighbor against neighbor, because ignorance, like AIDS, had not yet been eradicated.

As he'd helped with the posters, Mack had helped solve that, too, his quiet strength more successful than her outbursts of anger. She smiled as she remembered his firm hand as it gripped her elbow and guided her from Linda Jean's restaurant one morning while her anger spewed forth, her senses having forgotten that change was not always welcome and not always good.

Wiping her hands on the apron that covered her long denim skirt, Nikki slipped off the cardigan that always felt too warm when she thought about the AIDS kids and the obstacles they faced. She straightened her black T-shirt and fiddled with her colorful Indian beads. "I guess we'll know for sure this weekend. If folks come with paintbrushes and not picket signs, we might be okay after all."

Mack picked up his bakery box and winked. "The paintbrushes will win, Nikki. You have my word." As he slipped out the door, the small bell tinkled, and she smiled again, because she couldn't do better than Mack Olson's word.

The days were getting longer, long enough so the sun could stretch into her studio at the top of the lighthouse and allow her to paint almost until dinner. Today Nikki appreciated that greatly, for she'd come home from the bakery long past lunchtime to an urgent message from a prominent New York City gallery.

"We need eight more of your portraits," the woman pleaded. "And we need them in time for the Big Apple tourists."

*Tourists.* On-island and off, they had become both the bane and the embodiment of Nikki's life.

She could finish the paintings if she gave up working at the bakery from five A.M. until two. But then when would she have a chance to see people? To talk about life with other islanders, to keep grounded in the real world?

She'd leave the bakery, of course, for the season, to tend to Camp4Kids. But she'd return in the fall, because Nikki was a year-rounder, a supposed misfit who preferred this island to the one of Manhattan.

She stepped back from the easel and examined her progress. A child, a dog, a clown. The child was laughing, hugging the dog; the clown studied the child with a painted smile, yet his eyes were knowing, filled with sorrow.

"Too sad," she said, frowning. For though the children with AIDS inspired Nikki's portraits, she wanted to show courage, not evoke pity. Hope, after all, was what The Rose Foundation was all about. She'd chosen the name Rose in memory of her aunt, who had been fragile and beautiful and who had died much too young.

Like its namesake, the foundation was small. Supported solely by the income from Nikki's trust fund, it supplemented the cost of life-lengthening medication for several hundred young patients. More kids could be helped if Nikki would expand her philanthropic vision into fund-raising on a grand scale. But that reeked too much of charity balls and society soirées, like the world that her cousin Mary Beth worshipped. Or, Nikki could seize the availability of her family connections to trounce on corporate tax write-offs and take The Rose Foundation worldwide. But that would mean succumbing to the influence of her name, and she would not do that, either.

The cell phone rang. Nikki sighed, set down her brush, and took the call. It was Alice Sullivan, the foundation administrator, the one who did the real work.

"There's been another increase in AZT," Alice said. "It's going up ten dollars to a hundred and sixty a week."

Nikki closed her eyes. A hundred and sixty dollars a week. For two pills, three times a day, times the nearly nine hundred infected kids The Rose Foundation served. Some had insurance that had not yet capped, some received a portion from a combination of donor sources, others relied solely on them, on Nikki's money.

*You do the math,* she could almost hear Alice say, but Nikki didn't need to. No matter how it added up, a ten-dollar increase meant a choking hike.

Not without guilt, she reminded herself that of the hundreds of thousands living with AIDS, the kids they served were a drop in the bucket—*a pisshole in the snow*, her mother, Margaret Atkinson, would have called it, if she'd ever had a philanthropic bone in her materialistic body.

"We could try Becker," Alice suggested. It was not the first time Alice had prodded Nikki to take the onus off her. Becker Pharmaceuticals had indicated they could be approached. But the company was part of the conglomerate amassed by Atkinson Enterprises—the frozen-food empire that had earned the Atkinson fortune, the corporate giant led by Nikki's ex-husband, Connor, oil to her water, night to her day.

Becker could assuage the current crisis. Becker could also help Nikki take The Rose Foundation global. Multitudes of AIDS patients could be served from Manhattan to Romania. But in order to make that happen, Nikki would need Connor's support, and she would not be indebted to a man, any man.

"Forget it," she said as much to herself as to Alice.

But guilt made her uncomfortable. In addition to the AZT, now there was the camp. This was the first year; this was a test. Two hundred and twenty-eight of Nikki's nine hundred kids would take swimming lessons and do arts and crafts and learn archery and play softball. And be just like other kids. It wasn't global charity, but it was the best she could do on her own.

She supposed she could ask Mary Beth for a loan, but Mary Beth, like Nikki's mother, had never been open to "sharing the wealth." And other than her cousin, Nikki no longer associated with anyone who might be able to invest.

Opening the door, she stepped onto the tiny walkway that encircled the top of the lighthouse and looked over the sea. "I'll find another way," she told Alice.

But when she clicked off the phone and inhaled the salt air, she knew she was in trouble. Because no matter how many hours she worked at the bakery, no matter how many paintings the New York gallery might sell, it would not be enough to sustain her meager commitment to the world.

When Nikki was a child, she assumed that all kids had an elevator in their house and that families came equipped with cooks and nannies and housekeepers to clean up their messes. She thought of that now as she descended the steep spiral stairs of the lighthouse and went to her makeshift kitchen to prepare dinner. Tonight she would have bread that she'd baked and vegetables she'd grown. And when she was done eating she'd wash and dry and put away her own dishes. Nikki was an ordinary person because it gave her peace.

While slicing the bread, she glanced outside. The familiar red pickup truck was parked next to the small, gray-shingled caretaker's cottage, in front of the ivy that crawled up the stone fireplace. She smiled with the knowledge that someone else was on the estate, that she was not alone. It helped ward off the chill that drifted over the dunes from the gargantuan main residence— "the big house" they'd always called it. The big house, however, stood empty, except when Mary Beth came for the summer. Soon her cousin would be there again, this time bringing insanity disguised as Shauna's wedding.

Nikki shook her head, opened the refrigerator, and removed a pan of leftover pasta. She plunked it on the counter. Would it be cruel if she went off-island and missed the wedding gala?

"Yes, you fool," she said, plucking a large spoon from over the stove. She could not, would not, do that to

Shauna. Though the next generation was not completely unaware of the foibles of the preceding one, Shauna should not have to pay for her mother's transgressions.

*Mothers,* she thought, snapping on the gas jet with more force than she'd intended. She thought of hers again, the grand dame, Margaret Atkinson, who'd been dead ten years yet still seemed to hover. Whenever Nikki needed to make an important decision, there was Margaret, perched on her daughter's shoulder, an unwanted, criticizing conscience, jabbering a nonstop litany, trying to get Nikki to do things her way.

Margaret, the matriarch of the Atkinson legacy, who had supported Connor at the helm of Atkinson Enterprises even after Nikki's divorce because it was "better for the company," the almighty company, as if they still owned it. Nikki's daughter, Dee, being half Connor's, not only held stock but also worked there when she had time, an action that Nikki neither understood nor promoted.

Atkinson Enterprises. The last thing Nikki ever wanted was anything to do with the business. More than once, she had been grateful that her shares of the firm, along with those of her cousins Mary Beth and Gabrielle, had been sold years ago, and the money added to the principal of their trust funds.

*Gabrielle.*

Suddenly, she dropped the spoon. Would it be possible that her estranged cousin was the answer to Nikki's dilemma?

Flicking her eyes outside again, Nikki turned off the gas jet. Then she quickly grabbed her cardigan and headed out the door.

From the small porch of the caretaker's cottage Nikki saw a soft orange glow coming from the fireplace. She'd been inside often enough to know that the square living room/ kitchen combination, the small bedroom, and the bath were meager but sufficient for its lone resident. It was not unlike the lighthouse: a solitary refuge for a solitary soul.

Taking a deep breath, Nikki raised her hand and knocked.

The door opened.

"Hey, Uncle Mack," she said, "Mind if I come inside?"

He neither straightened pillows and magazines nor apologized for the mess.

"I have a pot of two-day-old stew on the stove. Interested?" he asked. He wore the same blue plaid flannel shirt and jeans that he'd worn this morning. His sneakers were parked by the door, and his familiar stride pattered in old wool socks across the worn braided rug.

Nikki shook her head. "No, thanks. But you go ahead."

He shrugged and sat in one of the two overstuffed chairs that cupped the fireplace. He motioned for her to sit in the other. "I get the feeling you're here about something more important."

As she sat, Nikki caught sight of the portrait that hung on the stone wall over the mantel. A vision of Mack, sitting in this chair, pining at the portrait, almost made her wish she'd never painted it. It had been her first, a teenager's amateurish attempt to capture life, the life of her aunt Rose, Mack's wife, namesake of The Rose Foundation. Nikki had painted it many summers ago. In recent years, it had been nothing but unsettling.

He tapped his fingers on the armchair. "If only one person responds to every poster out there, you ought to have a good turnout this weekend."

She pulled her gaze from the portrait, and from the memories of the horrible accident that it evoked.

"But that's not why you've come," he added.

They might have been blood relatives for the way both she and Mack had turned into themselves, the family recluses, the "private" ones. "No," she answered, "I need some advice."

He did not say, "Okay, go ahead," or "What is it?" or anything. He sat and simply waited as she perhaps would have done.

Again, Nikki drew a deep breath. "I need to raise some capital, Mack. I wondered if you might have some suggestions." Slowly, she exhaled; why was this embarrassing?

"I'm a handyman on the Vineyard, Nicole." Mack turned his head back to the fire. "I don't have an investment portfolio. Everything Rose left me I gave to Gabrielle."

Gabrielle's name hung in the air with a presence as powerful as the amateur portrait's. Nikki had not seen her other cousin for a very long time, not since she was a teenager and Gabrielle a little girl. But Mack knew where she was, or at least he'd known several years ago when he went to find her. It hadn't gone well.

Why hadn't she remembered how hurt he had been? What had possessed her to come to him seeking help from the one person he loved more than anyone—or anything—in the world, the one person who denied him that love?

"I...I wasn't thinking of you, Mack." She stammered. She stumbled. She could not mention Gabrielle now or ever. "I wondered if you have any friends, like maybe an island banker or two?"

He laughed. "Friends? Sure, I have friends. A couple of fishermen. And Ben Niles, the builder." He leaned closer to her. "Are you okay, Nikki? Is the foundation in trouble?"

She could have told him about the rise in AZT costs. She could have told him and then he, too, would worry more about the kids he didn't know, and he'd worry about Nikki because he knew how much this meant to her. So Mack would worry, too, and what good would that do?

Nikki stood up. "Everything will be fine," she replied. "There's just a bit of minor juggling I need to do." She said good night and returned to the lighthouse, feeling empty of options, out of ideas, and like an insensitive rat.


*Daffodil yellow,* the clerk had announced when Nikki selected the paint for the kids' cabins. She chose it for its cheerfulness and because it was on sale.

Dipping a wide brush into a bucket of daffodil yellow, Nikki wondered if, at nineteen, her daughter was familiar with either concept.

Fortunately, Dee lived in Manhattan with her father; unfortunately, it seemed she only called her mother when she needed attention or money. Like this morning, when Nikki still was in bed, looking out as the day struggled to grow light, wondering how and where she'd find the money for the mounting foundation costs, and wondering if it would rain. It was easier to dwell on the possibility of rain. Rain would mean that not much work could get done at Camp4Kids. Rain would mean that not many volunteers would show up.

The phone had rung, distracting her from her worries.

"If I were insecure, I'd think you cared more about total strangers than you do about us," Dee had accused.

"Total strangers are often more appreciative than family," Nikki responded. The verbal dance between them had begun when Dee had hit puberty and along with her breasts had developed an Atkinson love of money and of self. Nikki often wondered if Dee were actually Mary Beth's child, if Shauna and Dee had been switched at birth, although they were a year apart.

"I'm calling to see if you'll be there this weekend," Dee asked, as if Nikki might be in Madrid or New Delhi.

Nikki simply answered "Yes," because it was too early in the day for caustic remarks.

"I'm coming with Shauna. We're going to have fittings."

The other shoe that ordinarily accompanied Dee's phone calls suspiciously did not drop.

"Can we have dinner?" Nikki asked, doubtful of a positive response.

"Sure. Maybe. I don't know. I'll see what Shauna has planned."

Of course.

"I'll be at the big house, so you won't have to move the pile of laundry off the bed in your guest room."

Nikki wondered if, before she died, she and her daughter could ever become friends. "Well, I hope I get to see you," she added before ringing off, because she was the adult and Dee was the child, which did not always make it easier to bite back the words she really wanted to say.

Applying a hefty coat to the cabin now, Nikki wondered if there was enough time before the wedding to muster endurance both for her daughter and for the onslaught of society that would invade her backyard and assault her distaste for glitter and glitz.

Then she took a deep breath and tried, instead, to focus on the here and now, on the victories of her day: No vandals had destroyed the cabins; no picketers had greeted the two dozen volunteers who had miraculously showed up this morning and were now scattered around the grounds, blessedly bringing a spirit of hope into the run-down old place.

*Life is good,* Nikki reassured herself, *despite Dee's constant challenges, despite the new wrinkle of added expenses that somehow (please, God) would work itself out.*

But as she reloaded the brush, an unfamiliar voice interrupted her.

"Excuse me. Are you Nikki Atkinson?"

Nikki turned. A middle-aged woman shielded her eyes from the glare of the not-quite-sun. She wore a raincoat and a transparent rain bonnet and carried a collapsible umbrella. The brown leather handbag and matching squarish pumps suggested she'd come from the mainland, that she was not an islander or even a seasoned tourist.

Nikki cleaned off her paintbrush. "That's me. I don't suppose you're a volunteer." She turned back to the cabin, hoping this was not anti-AIDS trouble, a picketer disguised as a librarian.

The woman moved closer until she stood right next to Nikki. "We've never met," she said, "but I feel that I've known you many years." She smiled an odd half-smile, then extended her right hand. "My name is Carla DiRoma," she continued, "and I work for Lester Markham."

# 3

---

Gabrielle closed her eyes and lifted her face to the warm Italian sun. Standing on the hillside in gentle Tuscany, she listened to the stir of the silvery olive leaves and tasted the clean aroma of spring, the promise of black grapes that nestled in the air, the hope of a season that would yield an abundant crop.

Castello di Bonelli needed a good season. It had not had one since 1995. The coolness, the dampness of the recent years had resulted in thin, rotting grape skins, high acidity, tannins that were too hard—and a vineyard that lost more money than it made.

She opened her eyes and looked off toward the estate where Stefano's family had been making wine since the late 1500s. Surely they had weathered cycles of bad climate. They had not, however, had the added liability of an American wife in the household, a nonvintner by birth, a legendary curse on the crop according to Enzio, the "pigheaded foreman," as Stefano often called him.

It was true that Gabrielle had known little about winemaking and even less of growing grapes, that she'd believed the fruits were grown only on vines threaded among arbors, not on tangled, dwarflike trees set in rows across the slopes—trees that needed to be pruned and fertilized and watered sparingly to promote the smallest clusters and the ripest fruits.

She had not known then, but she did know now. She'd learned about the grapes the way she'd learned of patient, truest love.

"Gabriella!" She heard her name called out and knew it was her unsuperstitious husband, the heir to the title "Count Bonelli" that had made her a countess, the man who did not believe she was the cause of his troubles. She turned and smiled, the same way she always smiled whenever she heard him add an "a" to the end of her first name. She'd been smiling for six of her thirty-four years, since they'd met and married, since the birth of little Rosa, the magic of Gabrielle's life.

Stefano raced toward her on winemaker's legs, lean and muscled from traversing the slopes. His dark hair floated in the breeze, his arms were outstretched with the eagerness of a child on his way home from school. He reached her and swept her up, nuzzling his nose into her neck.

She laughed. "What are you doing?" she asked, her Italian accented with a mix of proper British-schooled English and long-since-leftover American. Another annoyance for Enzio.

Stefano kissed her throat in response, then carried her over the hillside, past twisted cypress trees, up to the olive grove and into the cabin, the rest stop for the grape pickers during the autumn harvest.

The small, dark building had been built of boards many decades ago. It was damp inside.

"Stefano..." Gabrielle protested, but he untied the pale blue ribbon that held back her wispy chestnut hair and quickly laid her down on a soft, thick blanket. Then, with the sunlight framing his back, he smiled at her and slowly removed each item of his clothing: his neck scarf, his denim shirt, his jeans. His erection, like the sound of his voice, made her smile.

"We must christen the earth for a crop that is worthy of the great *gallo nero*."

*Gallo nero,* the black rooster. The seal of the *consorzio*. The mark of the finest vintage of Chianti Classico—an honor that had eluded Castello di Bonelli since Gabrielle and Stefano had wed.

She tried to smile in return so Stefano would not think she believed Enzio's curse.

"Besides," he added, his grin widening, "it is time we produced a male heir for the business."

The small smile that she'd managed faded, for she was unsure of his joke. Then he bent down and lifted her long cotton skirt, slid down her panties, and lowered himself onto her. She closed her eyes and pushed aside her doubt. Then she let his welcome scent fill her body and his tender touch caress her heart.

"Mama!" Rosa cried later that afternoon, when Stefano had returned to the spring fertilizing and Gabrielle to the villa, where she prepared sausage, cheese, and fresh-picked porcini mushrooms for their evening meal. She had not heard the school bus rumble up the hill from the village; she had been lost in her world again, where all things were wonderful.

She set down her knife and hugged her daughter. "How was school today, my darling?"

Rosa frowned and when she did, her big eyes saddened. Her hair was dark, but her eyes were big and blue like Gabrielle's, big and blue like an Atkinson's. Gabrielle hugged her daughter again. She was so attached to this tiny being—too attached, perhaps. But she could not fathom life without her. She only wished she could wrap her in a tight, safe cocoon and protect her always, the way that she wished she'd been protected when she was young.

"School was terrible, Mama," Rosa burbled. "The mathematics. Oh. And Cesare Fiore. He stuck his tongue out at me."

Gabrielle stood up and went back to her work. "That boy is no better than a street urchin, Rosa. I don't know why you bother with him." Cesare Fiore was Enzio's nephew, the son of Enzio's sister, whose husband had been killed three years ago when his old truck slid off the dirt road that wound its way up from the village. Cesare's father had been a worker on the vineyard, but not "good enough" for Enzio's sister, Angie, who "should have, would have," married Stefano if Gabrielle hadn't been in Paris, where Stefano went to witness the *consorzio,* if Gabrielle hadn't been waiting on tables in a café on the Left Bank, if Stefano had listened to Enzio's persistent pleas of *Have you lost your mind? She's not one of US!*

"He says now that the pruning's done and school's almost out, his uncle Enzio is going to take him to Florence for three days, maybe four. Will Papa take us, too, Mama?"

Florence. Firenze. A slow, dusty image of leather shops and lovemaking came to Gabrielle's mind. Stefano had taken her to Florence for their honeymoon on their way back from Paris. It was not uncommon for people to make the northward trek from their village south of Siena to the great city, a rite-of-summer rejuvenation. "We will go to Firenze this summer, Rosa. But do not worry. We will not go with Cesare. Or his uncle Enzio."

With pink, full lips that Stefano forewarned might

someday break many hearts, Rosa pouted. She stood on her tiptoes to study the sausage-cutting process. "Well, that would be okay, you know. If we went with them."

Gabrielle laughed and swatted her daughter with a dish towel. "You are so fickle, my little one! First you hate Cesare Fiore. Then you beg me to take you to Firenze with him..."

Rosa turned away. "I did not beg, Mama," she said softly, her small voice cracking.

Gabrielle feared she had made a mistake, that what she'd meant to be playful had instead come out hurtful. Quickly she stooped and took Rosa by her thin arms. "I'm sorry, my darling. I did not mean to tease you. I did not think you liked him."

Rosa shrugged. "I don't," she whispered. "I guess."

Raising her hand under Rosa's chin, Gabrielle slowly lifted it. "It's okay if you do! It's good to like people. I'll tell you what. Let's ask Papa if we can go to Firenze with Cesare and Enzio. We could explore the piazza together. Maybe even visit the museums and the chocolate shops. Would you like that?"

The big, blue Atkinson eyes smiled back at Gabrielle. She hugged her daughter again and reminded herself of her unwavering promise that this child would never, ever suffer the way Gabrielle had suffered, would never, ever wonder if anyone loved her or if she would always be alone.


"I'm with him every day. Why would I want to travel to Firenze with Enzio?" Stefano's words were firm, but his tone was playful.

They had finished dinner in the old stone kitchen of the villa. There no longer was a reason to take their meals in the dining room—the massive teak table was suited for sixteen—and they'd laid off the service people, the cook and the housemaids, three years ago when the bad years had caught up to them. "If I go on holiday, I want to be with my family, not my foreman's."

"It would only be Enzio and Cesare. And Angie, I suppose. If she wants to go."

Stefano rolled his eyes. "And you are not jealous? That Angelina once loved me?"

Gabrielle gestured toward Rosa as she shushed her husband.

Stefano reached across the table, took her hand, and kissed it. "It is no secret, Gabriella. The whole village knows Enzio's sister wanted to marry me, that she wanted to be the Countess Bonelli, the queen of Castello di Bonelli."

Rosa leaned on her elbows. "But you took Mama as your countess, right, Papa?"

They laughed. "Oh, yes, little one. I took Mama as my countess and my queen."

Gabrielle pulled back her hand. "And now the queen requests that we all go to Firenze." As she stood up and carried the dishes to the deep stone sink, she heard a heavy knock on the old wooden back door. It was Enzio, the pigheaded foreman. He was slight, like Gabrielle, and stooped from an added two decades of age. They stood eye to eye, her big blue ones looking into his much smaller black ones. As an afterthought he removed his cap.

"Enzio!" Stefano called toward the door. "We were just speaking of you. I understand you are planning a trip."

Enzio's eyes darted from Gabrielle to Stefano, as if he dared not cross the threshold into the house that was cursed by the American, though she had not lived in

America for twenty-seven years. After a moment's consideration, he stepped inside as if he'd been invited.

"A trip to Firenze, yes. I've heard that the Langones have new presses and a new fermenter. I would like to see them."

"And you would like to taste their wine and maybe visit the *festa* for a few days?" Stefano asked.

Gabrielle began to make coffee, because this had become Stefano's conversation, not hers to interlope. She'd long ago learned that attempting talk with Enzio, small or otherwise, was a futile act. She had, however, heard Stefano speak of the Langones. They owned an enormous vineyard on the other side of Florence and managed to produce *gallo nero* vintages, despite the cool, damp summers. They held two festivals each year—one in spring to bless the growing season, one in autumn after the grapes were harvested. She also knew that among all the Langones, there was not one American.

"Rosa and Cesare might enjoy a trip to see the competition," Stefano added.

"But, yes!" Enzio said as he sidestepped Gabrielle's chair and took a seat across from his boss. "Someday they will be the ones in charge of making the finest wine." He winked at Rosa, who looked at her father and made a face.

"But Papa, I only this year began school!"

Stefano laughed and Enzio laughed and Gabrielle felt like an outsider, as she often did whenever Enzio was in her presence. She scooped dark coffee grounds into the percolator basket and decided that Rosa and Stefano should make the trip without her. It would be a way for Rosa to have fun with Cesare, and a way to encourage the boy to stop picking on her. Besides, Rosa loved Stefano so very much. Perhaps a short time away from the villa—and away from her mother—would be healthy for Rosa. Surely Gabrielle could survive.

She set coffee mugs on the table in front of the two men. "I have an idea," she said. "Why don't the two of you take the children by yourselves? I'm sure they'd enjoy a respite from their mothers."

They went to Firenze, Stefano and Rosa, Enzio and Cesare. And Gabrielle stayed home, as she had become so accustomed. Accustomed to, and loving every minute, each day of her quiet, unassuming life at the villa in the country.

It was odd without Rosa, but she pretended that her daughter was only at school in the daytime, and at night that she was already tucked into her bed.

The morning of the third day that her family had been gone, the sky was the color of blue-lace agate, the smoothly hued gemstone of the ancestral brooch that Stefano had given her, the brooch that she wore at the neck of her high-collared white shirt every Sunday.

But this was not Sunday, and there was work to be done.

Gabrielle hung the bedroom draperies outside to air. She looked up at the house and thought that today, in the sunshine, the place looked as grand as if Stefano's forefathers and foremothers and aunts and uncles and cousins and nieces and nephews still blessed its existence, as if prosperity had never left them, up there on the mount.

Prosperous or not, Gabrielle had found home. Since meeting Stefano, since coming to Castello di Bonelli, she no longer itched like a long-sleeved wool sweater, too hot or too cold, never quite right no matter where she was or with whom.

The "where's" of Gabrielle's life had been few: America—uptown Manhattan and the Vineyard; Salisbury, England, for school from ages seven to eighteen; London, because Aunt Margaret insisted that was where all young ladies went. At twenty-one Gabrielle moved to Paris, because legally Aunt Margaret could no longer control her or stop her.

Though her trust fund afforded Gabrielle a life of leisure, she preferred to squirrel away her money in Switzerland, safe for her future. Then, no matter what or who entered—or left—her life, she would always be free, with the means to move on. Freedom was important to one who had been betrayed.

Gabrielle had trusted no one. As the years passed, her money grew. Certainly there was enough to restore this old villa. Certainly there was enough to weather many, many years of damp, woeful crops.

But she could not save the villa and she could not save the vineyard, for Gabrielle had never told Stefano of her wealth.

If she told him, she would risk losing her financial security.

If she told him, he would be angry that she'd deceived him into thinking she was a bourgeois girl whom he'd "rescued" from a sorrowful existence.

If she told him, it might open the door to other secrets and lies, and Gabrielle couldn't bear that. Her life was too perfect, and Stefano was a proud man.

So instead of telling him, it had been easier to have the administrator secretly wire her income into the Swiss account each month and to pretend that her trust fund simply didn't exist. In return for his silence about her or her whereabouts, Gabrielle had increased Lester Markham's commission.

"Excuse me," a voice called from the front lawn.

Gabrielle turned around. A stranger—a woman—stood beside an old taxi that Gabrielle had not heard arrive. She wore an old-fashioned coat and a friendly smile.

"I'm looking for the mistress of the house," the woman explained as she walked closer, waving her hands toward the villa, as if that would explain what her choppy Italian could not.

Gabrielle immediately identified an American accent. She hesitated, then responded in fluent Italian. "I am the Countess Bonelli."

"Gabrielle?" the woman asked. "Are you Gabrielle of the Atkinsons? From the United States?"

Clouds seemed to gather on the golden-blue sky. A chill oozed from the air and penetrated Gabrielle's clothes, her plain cotton shirt and her plain cotton skirt, clothing of a peasant woman, not of a countess. Not clothing of an Atkinson. Gabrielle did not move. "What is it you want?" Her question was in English; she did not know why.

The woman clutched a large purse. From it spilled papers that looked like brochures, tourist folders, perhaps. Her skin had a pallor of someone who did not often see the sunshine, or who'd lost a night's sleep on a transatlantic flight. Gabrielle said a quick prayer of thanks that Stefano and Rosa were not there.

"My ancestors were Italian," the woman replied as she continued her approach. "My grandfather was from Torino."

Gabrielle could not answer. She could only remain standing, frozen in place, hanging onto the curtains that hung on the line.

The woman moved three steps closer, then she stopped. Gabrielle wanted to back up, but her feet suddenly were cemented to the ground.

"My mother always said someday we'd go to Italy," the woman continued. "And here I am!"

"So it appears." Gabrielle looked down at a small hand with clear-polished, short fingernails that reached out to her.

"I'm from the Bronx," the stranger continued, "New York. My name is Carla DiRoma."

The name was familiar, but distantly vague, like the name of a classmate in the third or fourth form. Gabrielle stared at the hand and wondered what would happen if she refused to shake it, if she turned on her heels and fled into the villa, slamming, then bolting, the large wooden door. Who would know? Perhaps Carla DiRoma was from America, but why should Gabrielle be expected to care?

The woman withdrew her hand before Gabrielle could decide whether or not to shake it.

"I came to find you," she continued. "I know some of your family."

Gabrielle blinked a long, slow blink, as if hoping that by the time her eyes reopened, the woman would have gone back to the taxi and departed for wherever she'd come from. But when her vision returned, the image remained. "My family?" Gabrielle asked, because other than Stefano and Rosa, the word seemed remote.

"Your cousins," Carla said. "Mary Beth and Nicole. They still have the estate on Martha's Vineyard. Isn't that something?"

Letting go of the drapery, Gabrielle slid her hands into the deep pockets of her skirt. She thought of Mary Beth, wearing bright pink lipstick and picking hydrangea in the backyard. She pictured Nikki in cutoffs and sandals, painting a fat white daisy on the hood of her car. She saw them, and she remembered the old ache of wanting to be just like them because they were so grown-up and she was so not. Mary Beth and Nikki. Her family, of sorts. "I haven't seen them in years."

"Yes," the woman replied, "I know."

And then Gabrielle's legs were no longer weighted but instead had grown weak. There was, after all, still one thing that linked her to her "family," a secret she held so close to her heart. "What do you want?" she asked, her voice now as weak as her body.

"Actually..." The woman continued with a grin, "I was wondering if you give out samples of your wonderful wine. Then perhaps we could have a little talk."

# 4

## SUMMARY 1974

This is Mr. Markham," Aunt Margaret said, her lips stiff and bloodless, her blue eyeballs peering over her half-glasses at him, not at them. "He will manage your trust funds."

He was a tall man with soft, blond hair, like Robert Redford, and a suntanned face. He wore a navy blue suit, white shirt, and tie, none of which were wrinkled despite the August Vineyard heat. Aunt Margaret, of course, would not have allowed otherwise.

Mary Beth looked over at Nikki, who sat on the leather sofa paying attention to her mother, Margaret. Margaret was the middle daughter of Grandma Atkinson—whom Mary Beth barely remembered—and Grandfather, who was dead now, too. They'd buried him yesterday, so Aunt Margaret truly was the self-appointed daughter "in charge" because Mary Beth's mother, Dorothy, the eldest, was too flighty and often too tipsy, and because Aunt Rose was too young. So Aunt Margaret ran everything, from the house to the business to all of them, too. Thank God Nikki neither looked nor acted like the stern matriarch who still teased her hair and sprayed it as stiff as an old crinoline slip.

Mary Beth's glance moved to Gabrielle, who played with her Barbie in front of the French doors that led from the library out to the back lawn. The child seemed oblivious to the news that Grandfather had left his money to them, the three granddaughters, the only offspring of his own three daughters.

"Mr. Markham is an important consultant to the business," Aunt Margaret continued, and Mary Beth understood the importance of that comment, because she knew that without Atkinson Enterprises the three granddaughters might not have been raised uptown but in dreadful Brooklyn or Queens, and summers might have meant not ten weeks on Martha's Vineyard, but a day trip to Coney Island. "Now he's going to work for you."

Mary Beth shuddered and sat up straight in her chair. She might be only fifteen, but she knew when to listen.

"In addition to the trust funds, there is the property. Mary Beth, though Nicole is the eldest granddaughter..." —*Only by one* year, Mary Beth wanted to protest, until she noticed Aunt Margaret's lips grow even more rigid— "...you are the only child of your grandfather's eldest daughter. He has therefore left this Vineyard estate and everything on it and in it to you." Her arm swept the room, indicating the leather-bound books, the heavy old furniture, and the paintings on the walls that must be worth something because they were removed to the vault every fall. "There is, however, one stipulation," Aunt Margaret continued. "You must allow lenient 'visitation' to your cousins. And to Rose and Dorothy and me, too, as long as we're alive."

Lester Markham chuckled and Aunt Margaret did, too. Mary Beth supposed she should smile. It wasn't often that Aunt Margaret tried to make a joke.

"The brownstone in Manhattan will remain mine until my death," the woman continued, "at which time it will be turned over to the New-York Historical Society."

That was no surprise. John Jacob Astor had built the place, but it was where Nikki and Aunt Margaret and Aunt Rose, Uncle Mack, and Gabrielle all had lived with Grandfather even before Grandma had died from that awful word cancer.

Patting her bouffant to be sure it was still in place, Aunt Margaret continued. "As for Atkinson Enterprises, I shall run the corporation until a suitable buyer can be found. The money from your shares of the sale will be added to your trust funds at that time."

Lester Markham nodded as if he needed to know that, as if his future were the one on the line. His, not theirs. Not three kids about as unalike as Pat Boone, the Beatles, and, well, Barbie.

Mary Beth was pleased that she'd thought of that—Pat Boone, the Beatles, and Barbie. Her English teacher would have been proud, and might no longer accuse her of being more interested in socializing than in similes, if that were a simile, which, on second thought, she did not think it was.

Then she smiled as she realized she now could tell her English teacher to go straight to hell, because she could buy and sell the whole stuffy, damn school, if she wanted.

Aunt Margaret stood up. Lester Markham quickly rose and helped her with her chair.

"Now, if you'll excuse me," Aunt Margaret said, "I have condolence thank-you's to write."

She dismissed the girls as if she were dismissing Parliament.

Once she'd left and they were alone, Nikki snarled at Mary Beth. "Great," she said, "we're filthy rich. Just what I fucking needed."


Dorothy Atkinson-McNight told her daughter that the least she could do was bring flowers to Grandfather's grave and say a prayer of thanks that he had made her financially set for life. Mary Beth clipped hydrangea blossoms from a backyard bush and knew she no longer could get yelled at for doing so. It was, after all, part of the estate, *her* estate, the "whole kit and caboodle," her mother had called it when Mary Beth had related the news handed down in the library.

She supposed Grandfather had left it to her because he'd felt bad about her father, Glenn McNight, who had turned out to be a drinker, but Dorothy had made her bed and had then had to lie in it. Luck and irony had intervened, however, when Mary Beth was twelve. Surprisingly sober and on his way to the club, Glenn McNight had ironically been killed by a drunk driver, a senior citizen, no less. What would he think if he could see her now, the one who'd inherited the largest chunk because he'd been such a disappointment?

From the second story above her, Mary Beth heard the slow rise of voices.

"Stop it, Mother."

The voice belonged to Nikki, the reluctant, filthy rich heiress.

"Don't smart-mouth me, young lady," Mary Beth heard Aunt Margaret cackle.

Gripping the pruning shears more tightly, Mary Beth almost felt as if she were with them in the tense, airless room.

"This house and the property should have been divided equally, not given solely to Mary Beth."

A small grin curled the edges of Mary Beth's mouth. Though she always hated it when Nikki and Aunt Margaret quarreled, it was somehow satisfying that they were fighting about her; that, for once, the one who was not as old or as smart as her cousin Nikki had actually come out on top.

"I don't want the house, Mother," Nikki shouted back. "I don't even want the trust fund."

"That's the trouble with you. You have no ambition, Nicole. No sense of...class."

Though Mary Beth would never tell Nikki, she really quite agreed. Nikki might be smarter and older than Mary Beth, but the girl did not know how to dress or comb her hair or walk or talk, not in the proper way.

"I do have ambition, Mother. I'm going to be a great artist."

"Ha! And just how would you expect to support yourself if it weren't for your trust fund? Cry all you want about money, Nicole, but it is the most important thing in life."

For a moment there was delicious silence. Mary Beth clipped another blossom.

"You're an asshole," Nikki said.

Mary Beth gulped a gulp she feared might be heard up there on the second floor. She held her breath and listened. Then came the penetrating sound of a loud smack against flesh. Mary Beth jumped as if it were her face that had been slapped.

"Mary Beth? Can I help you pick flowers?"

She spun around and saw Gabrielle. "What are you doing?" she whispered, her heart racing, her cheeks flush. "Where's your mother?" It wasn't that she thought Aunt Rose should or would be with Gabrielle. She asked because the bad thing about eavesdropping was the embarrassment of getting caught. Then she remembered that Aunt Rose was "deep in mourning," Mary Beth's mother had said, and that the "poor thing" had barely left her rooms since Grandfather's funeral.

Gabrielle shrugged. "I don't know where she is. Can I stay here and play with you?"

Quickly, Mary Beth grabbed the child's hand and led

her from the window. As much as she would have loved to stay, she did not want to risk Aunt Margaret finding her and screaming at her, too. Later, if Mary Beth was lucky, Nikki might relate the rest of the story.

The sting on her jaw had been worth it. Nikki stood at her upstairs window looking down on the estate, over the sand dunes, past the abandoned lighthouse, down to Katama Bay, grateful that her mother had stormed from the room with the presumed, misconceived notion that she'd won the battle, that she'd made her point.

But Nikki didn't care what Margaret Atkinson said or thought or did. Money was the god her mother worshipped, and that did not make her a nice person. Her mother could slap her as many times as she needed, but the fact remained Nikki was now the recipient of a sizeable trust fund and that must infuriate the bitch, who would no longer have complete control over her smart-mouthed daughter.

Nikki sighed and pulled back the white-ruffled curtain for a better look out to sea.

Was it any wonder that her father had left when she was only four? Or that he'd taken little but his clothes, and left no forwarding address? A few years after his departure, word had been received: He'd dropped dead of a heart attack at age forty-four, somewhere in Tibet, where he'd journeyed to find peace. She'd hoped that, without her mother, he, at last, had found it.

From the window Nikki could see Aunt Rose. She'd been inside for days, but now strolled the beach with Uncle Mack. Nikki wondered how Rose had hung onto him for so long. Had no one told him of the curse on the men who married Atkinsons? As the couple moved toward the lighthouse, Mack held Rose's arm as if she needed propping up. They stopped at the foot of the lighthouse and Rose sagged against the white concrete pillar, the phallic symbol of seamen, no pun intended, Nikki once told Mary Beth.

Then Uncle Mack lifted Aunt Rose's chin and took her in his arms. Nikki imagined the words he must be whispering.

"It's all right, my darling, I will take care of you now." Though how he would do that remained a mystery because, as part of the curse, the Atkinson women always selected the least prosperous for mates.

A rap-rap on her door was followed by Mary Beth in person, before Nikki could ask *Who is it* or say *It's okay to come in.*

"I've come to set your visitation rights," Mary Beth said as she flopped on the pink-and-red floral cushions of the white wicker furniture that, even as a child, always made Nikki feel like someone she was not. She wondered, now that the house was Mary Beth's, if Nikki could decorate the room the way she wanted. "I insist that you're on the Vineyard every single second I'm here," Mary Beth chattered. "I couldn't stand it without you."

Nikki laughed. "You only want me for my driver's license." There were some benefits to being sixteen, not fifteen, like knowing that the kind of boat-necked jersey and tailored Bermuda shorts that Mary Beth had on today were definitely queer, no matter that they came from Bonwit Teller on Fifth Avenue.

"Very funny." Mary Beth covered her eyes with her hand. "I have a splitting headache. All this talk about money."

"My mother says it's the most important thing in the world."

"Well, of course it is, even though you won't admit it,"

Mary Beth said, and Nikki suspected she'd been listening at doors again, something her cousin was quite fond of.

Nikki looked back to Uncle Mack, who still held Aunt Rose in his arms. "How much will we get from our trust funds?"

"An income forever, to buy whatever we want."

"Well, that's not true, Mary Beth. There will always be limits. Even for us. Besides, how much can we buy?"

Her cousin sat up. "You are such a dolt. I can buy a house on the Riviera, for starters."

"And be friends with Grace Kelly?"

"Well, why not? I have as much money as a princess."

"What about love? Will our money buy love?"

Mary Beth rolled her eyes. "Not according to the Beatles. But they probably wrote that song when they were poor."

"Well, I'd rather have love like Aunt Rose and Uncle Mack than all the money and all the estates in the world. Including on the Riviera." Moving to her vanity, Nikki sat down, brushed her long, mocha-colored hair, then snapped on a beaded headband. "I'm taking a ride to Oak Bluffs. And I hope you don't mind, but I need to go alone."

"Why? Are you going to see...him?"

*Him* was the one person Nikki knew loved her. Hopefully, he would still love her even if he learned her family was so rich, even if he found out she now had a trust fund.

"Why can't I meet him?"

Nikki laughed. "Because you wouldn't like him." She stood up and examined her cutoffs and white peasant blouse. "Stay here and count your money. I'll tell you all about it when I get back." She grabbed her tapestry bag and headed for the door.

"No, you won't!" Mary Beth called after her. "You never tell me the good parts, I just know you don't!"

Just then Gabrielle scampered up the hall. "Mary Beth!" she cried. "Will you comb my hair like Barbie's?"

"Oh, go away," was the last thing Nikki heard Mary Beth mutter before she escaped down the back stairs to rendezvous with *him*.

It was a 1967 Volkswagen Beetle, and though Nikki could certainly afford a newer model of anything, this was hers, the car that she'd put a down payment on with the money she'd made at the Tisbury Fair, selling the lighthouse scenes she'd painted on barnboard. It was her first taste of making money off summer people of which she was one, so it didn't make a lot of sense except that the money was hers to do with as she pleased, and she was pleased to buy the dark green "bug." On the hood, she'd painted a big white and yellow daisy. Her mother had almost had a stroke.

"It's bad enough you have to buy one of those...those hippie cars. But a daisy? Nicole, I forbid you to drive that car until you remove that...*mess*."

Nikki smiled now as she shifted into low gear at the Edgartown intersection, then veered off toward Oak Bluffs. It had been Aunt Dorothy who'd intervened. They were ensconced on the veranda, out of the summer sun. Dorothy told Nikki's mother that the Beetle was perfect for a sixteen-year-old girl and that the daisy was cute. She must have had too many gin and tonics that day, because then she told Nikki's mother to lighten up and stop acting like a dried-up old maid. Nikki had almost laughed out loud. And though Margaret sneered each time she came within sight of the car, the topic, gratefully, never resurfaced.

But as she drove along the beach road now, Nikki wondered if Aunt Dorothy would stick up for her niece if she knew what was really going on in Nikki's life.

"He loves me, he loves me not, he loves me, he loves me not." Gabrielle scowled, hating that she always ended up on the loves-me-not part. Daddy said she should start backward with the loves-me-not, and then it would always end on the loves-me where it belonged. Daddy also said there would be many men to love her, but the lucky man would be the one she loved back.

It all seemed kind of complicated, like the way she knew Mommy was crying right now, even though Daddy sat beside her on the Adirondack chair, holding her hand and whispering stuff Gabrielle couldn't hear because she wasn't supposed to.

It all seemed like adult stuff, like the thing called the trust fund Aunt Margaret had told them about.

Gabrielle set the daisy stem on the lawn. She wondered why Aunt Margaret didn't like kids, even her own daughter, Nikki, and she wondered why she never cried the way Mommy did. Daddy said Mommy cried because she was so sad about Grandfather, but Gabrielle knew it started way before that. One time, back in New York, her mother stood in the doorway of Gabrielle's room and looked in and watched when she thought Gabrielle was sleeping, but she was not. Gabrielle had not opened her eyes, because she could hear her mother crying and she did not want to let her know that she knew.

"Princess?" Daddy called over to her now where she sat on the small checked tablecloth, ready for a picnic with Barbie and Ken. "Where are Mary Beth and Nikki?"

Gabrielle shrugged. "I don't know."

"Why don't you find them? Maybe they'll take you digging for clams."

She picked up Barbie and straightened the bottom of her skirt. There was no sense trying to explain to Daddy that Mary Beth and Nikki didn't have much time for her this summer, that they were always off doing something that did not include a kid. They hadn't said so, but Gabrielle knew, just the way she knew when her mother was secretly crying, and the way she knew that right now was another of those times and that Daddy wanted to get rid of Gabrielle, even though she'd been there first.

If she couldn't go with Nikki she might as well start thinking about her debutante gown. Mary Beth lay on a small part of the eight hundred and twelve feet of beachfront that now belonged to her, only her, flipping through *Bride* magazine. She still had two years until her coming out, but she wanted to start planning now. The world was changing, and Mary Beth sensed that her ball would have to be the grandest of the grand, not at all like those staid, boring things of the sixties and the fifties, like when her mother had been crowned Deb of the Year.

Nikki, of course, had already announced she had no intention of coming out, that she had not become liberated to take three steps back. Nikki claimed she was independent like her father, but Mary Beth wasn't sure if she agreed: She'd been too young when Nikki's father had left. She only remembered being shocked when she learned that Aunt Margaret had taken back her maiden name and given it to Nikki, too, as if there'd never been a man, as if Aunt Margaret never had a husband and Nikki never had a father. Nikki might never admit being one smidgen like her mother, but, as Mary Beth saw it, Aunt

Margaret had been the *liberated* one, long before the word was a topic of discussion.

Rolling onto her back and staring up at the puffy white clouds in the blue Vineyard sky, Mary Beth wondered if she should be liberated, too. There were lots of ways she could do it, like going to her ball in a dress other than white. Could she wear red, white, and blue satin in honor of the nation's bicentennial?

"You'd better put on suntan lotion," a voice beside her said.

She blinked back to the present, and when she did, the hunkiest guy she'd ever seen was standing in front of her. He wore cutoffs and a T-shirt and his sun-streaked hair touched his shoulders and sweat glistened on his chiseled face.

He must be a mirage. She could have asked him if he was, but her mouth had suddenly dried up.

"The ozone layer," he said. "Haven't you heard about it?"

Did mirages talk? She shrugged. "Sure," she said. "Hasn't everyone?" She vaguely remembered hearing Nikki talk about a hole in the sky caused by aerosol deodorant or something like that.

He smiled. His teeth were as white as the lighthouse that stood behind him on their property . . . *her* property.

"My name's Mike," he said.

She would have told him her name, but she had become mute.

"I'm a landscaper up at the estate." He pointed up toward the big house. "Thought I'd take a dip in the water while I'm on lunch break. If that's okay with you."

She shrugged again and wondered if she should sit up and reveal the soft mounds of her too-small breasts that peeked from her bikini top, or if she should keep them covered so he wouldn't think she was a slut. "Suit your-self," she said, and stayed in her position, demurely covered up.

She wished he wasn't standing over her, because in her line of sight was the bulging front of his shorts. She moved a little on the blanket and tried to push away those questions that recurred too often lately, about what a penis really looked like and how it would feel to have it *plunge inside her,* as a romance novel she'd read had said it could do.

She turned back to her magazine with feigned indifference. From the corner of her eye she watched him race down to the water. As he splashed in the waves she thought about Nikki. Was it fair that her cousin had a secret boyfriend and Mary Beth did not? Nikki would not tell her anything, other than that his name was Henry and he was a summer person. The boy in front of her now—Mike—surely must be a townie. Someone who would be here year after year, someone who would wait for Mary Beth to arrive every season because he would barely be able to withstand the winters without her.

Someone who might teach her a few things about life.

Dropping her *Bride* magazine, she stood up. She tugged the bottom of her bathing suit over the firm cheeks of her butt.

"It's up to me, you know," she called toward the water.

He looked in her direction. "What?"

She sauntered to the water's edge. "Me," she said. "I'm the one who says what's off-limits and what's not. My grandfather left me the estate in his will."

Mike looked up the beach in the direction of the house. "Lucky you."

"Yeah," she replied. "Well, just stay away from the rock jetty, it's slippery and dangerous." She did not say

"It's slippery and dangerous *and no place for a girl,*" as Aunt Margaret warned them each day. "And don't get any ideas about camping out in the lighthouse. It's been padlocked for years." She took a few brave steps into the water.

He smiled again. "I promise I'll be good," he said with a wink, and she didn't get the impression he was referring to either the lighthouse or the rock jetty.

As he waded through the water steadily toward her, Mary Beth wondered if maybe she should wear a clingy black sheath to the debutante ball, one that showed off her figure that would, hopefully, be more full by then, with a backside that was round and boobs that were, well, big.

In the meantime, she'd have to learn how to make do.

# 5

Nikki put her peasant blouse back on and drank from a warm can of Tab that sat on the floor by the bed. Henry remained stretched on his back atop the blue-ticked mattress. He lit up a Marlboro and did not smile. "One of these days," he said, "we're going to get caught."

"I don't care," she replied. "I love you." She took a deep drag from his smoke.

He did not answer, but he did not have to. Henry had told her over and over how much he loved her, how much he cherished their moments from the day they'd met at the outdoor tabernacle when she'd sat at her easel painting a picture. He'd asked what she was doing there, because that day was a special service only for colored people, Negroes, or Afro-Americans as they liked to be called that summer.

She stroked his naked black thigh now, and cupped his softened, still-moist penis that, yes, got as big as she'd heard an Afro-American man's could get, bigger, perhaps. And unbelievably good, based on her experience, which was limited to one other penis that belonged to Larry, a white boy back at school, who had *prematurely ejaculated* each of the four times they'd "done it," or attempted to do it. Gently, she squeezed Henry's dark, sumptuous plums. "So what if they catch us? I'm only someone you hired to teach you French over the summer."

It was the lie that they'd fabricated, in case the need arose.

Henry laughed. "Ah, but *ma chérie,* I am going to follow in my father's footsteps, remember? I'm to become a Methodist minister."

Nikki smiled. "Methodist ministers don't fuck?"

"Not when they're eighteen. Not when the girl's sixteen. And white."

"What if she's rich?"

He looked at her and frowned, then inhaled another drag and slowly blew out the smoke. "Are you rich, *ma chérie?*" He did not know of Nikki's family because she hadn't told him, and he'd have no other way of finding out because Oak Bluffs and Edgartown were socioeconomic Grand Canyons apart.

"Filthy rich."

"That would only make things worse. I'd be accused of the ultimate sin of being lured by the white man's devil."

"Well, Jesus, it's not my fault. I could give some money to your father's ministry. Help him build a new church on the mainland." She yanked at the twisted sheet. His leftover sperm leaked from her and spilled onto her thighs. It was no longer warm, yet still it was erotic, as if its sticky presence reconfirmed that they'd made love, that they had joined as one, black and white, rich and poor, whether anyone liked it or not.

Henry smiled and touched her cheek. "We knew when we started this that it couldn't go anywhere. Not beyond this room."

She glanced around "this room" that she'd come to

know well in the past weeks. It was a tiny space, Henry's space, the attic room in a yellow-and-white-trimmed gingerbread house that had red geranium window boxes, a house like so many others that defined the Methodist campground and had been in the family for three or four or more generations. The house to which Nikki had to sneak through the backyards, to enter from the alley.

"Come," he said, extinguishing his cigarette and pulling her down to him. "We have a few minutes before *mon père* gets home."

Nikki wanted to protest, then she saw the heat of the afternoon glisten on his black, solid chest and she felt his hardness rise again. "I cannot get enough of you, Nicole," he whispered. "Do you know that?"

Yes, yes, she knew that. She kissed his full lips and felt his thick tongue as it slid into her mouth and lightly grazed her teeth. Then she rolled on top of him and mounted his pole. She sat up straight, tossed back her hair, ran her hands across her breasts, her belly, and her dark-haired *V*, while his eyes followed her motion, while his lips parted in excitement. Then her hands came to rest between her legs, and she found her clitoris. She touched it just a little and liked that it was wet. Then, with her longest, strongest finger, she rubbed herself with fervor as he thrust himself up, up, way up inside her. She rubbed and rubbed the way that he'd showed her, the way that he liked to watch, the way that made her so hot she thought she might die right then and there and that it would be good.

It came as a big surprise to Nikki that, at the end of the summer, it was not she who'd gotten pregnant, but Mary Beth. And it was Gabrielle who overheard Mary Beth tell Nikki, and who had run off and told her mother.

Maybe because Aunt Rose was neither uptight like

Nikki's mother nor Pollyannaish like Aunt Dorothy, maybe because, at age twenty-eight, Rose was not much older than they were—whatever the reason, both Nikki and Mary Beth were speechless when she came into Mary Beth's bedroom later that day and told them she knew.

Aunt Rose had sat on the white wicker chair next to the posters Mary Beth had hung since Grandfather's funeral—one of Soviet ballet star Mikhail Baryshnikov, the other of tennis ace Jimmy Connors. Nikki stared at the posters and realized how much different Mary Beth's room was from hers, where now the walls were decorated with *Sgt. Pepper's Lonely Hearts Club Band* photos and IMPEACH NIXON bumper stickers.

Nikki sat on the floor and stared at Baryshnikov; Mary Beth sat on the bed and cried.

"I'm not going to ask how this happened, because I know that part," Aunt Rose said quietly.

It was uncomfortable to think about Aunt Rose and Uncle Mack *together,* even though Nikki knew that they were married and had little Gabrielle. It was uncomfortable to think that they, too, had...done it, like she and Henry had, like Mary Beth and...?

"Do you love the baby's father?" Aunt Rose asked.

Mary Beth didn't flinch. "I don't even know his last name."

Aunt Rose nodded as if she understood that, too. The best part was she didn't try to make Mary Beth feel stupid or like a whore or anything. "They're going to make you have an abortion," she said with certainty. "They're going to make you have an abortion. That's what they did to me."

Her voice was so quiet, her demeanor so gentle, that Nikki almost missed what she'd just said. She blinked and so did Mary Beth, and both pairs of their eyes focused on their pretty aunt.

*Aunt Rose?*

"I was seventeen," Rose said. "It happened here, too." She said it matter-of-factly, as if she'd just announced it was time for lunch or time for Gabrielle to go to bed. Then she stood up. A darkness passed over her face, her Jekyll turned to Hyde. "I've never forgiven them and neither will you. But it's what will happen. You will not have a choice."

Mary Beth sniffed. "I could run away. I have my own money now. Or I could stay here if I want. This house belongs to me."

Aunt Rose went to the bed and sat next to Mary Beth. She touched her cheek and smiled a sad smile. "If you run away they will find you. For one thing, you're a minor. More important, you're an Atkinson, and Atkinsons have a responsibility to the world. Or, at least, the Atkinsons think they do." She attempted a small laugh. "It's really quite absurd," she said, "but make no mistake about it. Just because your grandparents are dead, things will not change. My sister Margaret is in charge, and I hate her. I hate them all because I let them get away with it."

She stood again, and Nikki and Mary Beth kept their eyes on her.

"Don't get me wrong," she said, "I love your Uncle Mack and I love Gabrielle. But something will always be missing from my life, a big hole of what might have been." She might have cried right there and then, but her voice was flat, all emotion gone, as if the pain was too great to recall. "The only good thing," Aunt Rose then added, "is that it will be over so fast you'll hardly remember, and they will never tell you if it was a boy or a girl."

With that, she left the bedroom. Nikki and Mary Beth sat very still, and neither of them spoke for what seemed like a very long time.

\* \* \*

Two days later, Mary Beth was whisked off to Puerto Rico for a proper abortion that no one—not Margaret, not Dorothy, or even Aunt Rose—ever spoke of again.

During the few days she was gone, though the sun still shone like summer, it could not break through the sullen cloud that hung over the estate. Even Gabrielle seemed to sense something was wrong, seemed to know enough to sit quietly with Barbie and not say much to anyone.

As for Nikki, she supposed she was afraid. Afraid that the same end could have happened to her. Afraid that she would not have the courage to have an abortion, and then where would she be with a Negro baby to raise? It was then that she realized even all the money in her trust fund could never have saved a baby of hers and Henry's from shame out in the world, out far beyond the safety of Henry's attic room. She knew that for a baby, it would not be fair.

She immersed herself in her art and began to paint a portrait of Aunt Rose, the only one of them who seemed to know what life was really like, the only one with the courage to unearth the San Andreas Fault in the Atkinson bedrock of perfection.

Mary Beth returned to the Vineyard in time for Labor Day weekend, as if nothing had happened. But something had happened, and Nikki could not let it go.

They sat by the lighthouse on that last day of summer, keeping a distance from the traditional barbecue where the Atkinsons served half the residents of Katama Bay. Though Grandfather had died, the show had to go on.

The Atkinson "girls" were, as usual, dressed in lady-like white cotton dresses, adorned with frilly lace for Dorothy, a starched collar for Margaret, and a pale blue ribbon for Rose. Thank God the next generation was not forced into compliance of either clothing or attendance.

"I was so stupid," Mary Beth said, her knees pulled up, her hands clutching them together as if they would remain forever closed, never, ever again to part, even if Prince Charming dropped out of the sky.

"You were no more stupid than me," Nikki said. "I've been making love all summer. The only difference was, you got caught."

"But he wasn't even right, Nikki. He was a gardener, for God's sake."

Nikki did not mention that Henry was the son of a minister. And of African descent. Nor did she confess that, indeed, she had stopped having sex with him when Mary Beth announced she was with child, that reality had crowded too close to her, like last year when a boy in school had a brother killed in Vietnam, and suddenly that black-and-white place on the evening news didn't seem so far away. Nor did Nikki mention that once her good sense prevailed over what she'd thought was love, Henry, sadly, did not seem to mind. *"C'est la vie,"* he'd said, *"n'est-ce pas?"*

Nikki cleared her throat now. "Well," she said, "maybe your mother's right. Once you're back in school you'll forget this ever happened."

Mary Beth was silent. She looked up into the sky; her gaze followed a gull. She did not have to say what Nikki already knew, that being back in school would not change a thing. She'd had an abortion. She'd ended a life that had been half-Atkinson.

Mary Beth stood up and shook sand from her shark-skin shorts, the girl who would not be caught dead in cut-offs and a peasant blouse, but who had made love not war and look where it had gotten her. "Let's go to the party," she said, "and pretend to have fun."

\*    \*    \*

Gabrielle wished she had a sister, someone to play with. She could have wished for another cousin, one her own age, but neither Nikki nor Mary Beth had fathers so she knew that couldn't work. Besides, there was no guarantee that another cousin wouldn't treat her like they did, as if she weren't there. Mommy said to be patient, that it was just because they were so much older than she was. But Mommy didn't really know what it felt like, because everyone loved her, except maybe Aunt Margaret, who made noisy sighs whenever she heard poor Mommy cry.

Sitting under a tree by the caretaker's cottage, Gabrielle listened to the grown-ups laugh and talk and *socialize,* Aunt Dorothy called it, which meant standing and holding a drink that had an olive or a slice of lime floating in the glass.

There weren't any kids there, of course. None of the Atkinson friends seemed to have any, or if they did, they must have kept them locked up in their cellars or in the trunk of an old Dodge like the one the caretaker drove.

*You have such a vivid imagination,* Mommy had said lots of times. She did not understand that making stuff up was the only way Gabrielle could feel she belonged somewhere, even if that "somewhere" did not really exist.

"Princess?"

Gabrielle looked up and saw her father. In his flowered, open-necked shirt and solid gold chain, he looked like a movie star.

"What are you doing out here?" he asked. "Why aren't you at the barbecue?"

"I ate a hamburger. Then I got bored."

He crouched beside her and smoothed one of her pigtails. "You'll be glad to get home, won't you?"

She screwed up her nose because home wasn't much better because that meant going back to school and she'd rather stay home with Mommy. Maybe that would make Mommy feel better, if they could read books and do embroidery and play Chutes and Ladders together.

"Fireworks in less than an hour," Daddy said, checking his watch, then standing up. "Have you seen Mommy?"

Gabrielle shook her head. The look on Daddy's face told her he was worried again. "I'll look upstairs," she said, scrambling upright.

Daddy said, No, he'd already done that. Then he stretched his mouth into one of those fake smiles Gabrielle recognized and said, "She must have gone for a walk."

"I'll go down by the lighthouse," Gabrielle suggested, though when Mommy went off, she always returned but never said where she'd been. She'd been going "off" a lot in the last few days, since Gabrielle had told her about Mary Beth and about the baby that she wasn't really going to have, that her mother had said Gabrielle must have heard wrong because Mary Beth wasn't married and in order to have a baby you had to have a husband. At least she didn't say it must have been just one more thing that Gabrielle made up.

"Okay, princess," Daddy said now. "And I'll look in the woods. We don't want her to miss the fireworks, do we?" He smiled again and went away from the house and the party and into the thick trees. Gabrielle watched him for a minute, then turned and headed toward the lighthouse.


It seemed ridiculous that they were going to have fireworks, what with Grandfather dead and the fog rolling in.

Right now Mary Beth only wanted to get off this damn island and get back to school, where someone other than Nikki would speak to her because they wouldn't know what she had done. She only wanted to be where she could forget this summer ever happened and concentrate on more important things like debutante gowns and après-skiwear for Christmas break. Even if her mother didn't want her to, she could go to Vail; she had her trust fund and God knew she could afford it.

She walked through the dunes where Mike, the gardener boy, had taken her virginity in what had not even been a memorable incident. They'd had sex three times in all, but it had only taken once, and Mary Beth had not known, would never know, if the deed had been done the first or the second or the third time that they'd done it.

As she reached the path by the lighthouse, a small figure darted past her.

Gabrielle.

The child raced from the dunes, bolting past Mary Beth as if she hadn't seen her. Shaking her head, Mary Beth turned down toward the jetty.

It was then that she saw the long blue ribbons fluttering in the breeze. And then that she realized they were the ribbons on the white dress that belonged to Aunt Rose, and that Aunt Rose's body was still in the dress, lying facedown, sprawled on the rocks.

# 6

## LATE SPRING 2001

**C**arla had saved Tuscany for last so she could savor her mother's dream.

"Someday we'll go to Italy," Theresa had said for years, the last time on her deathbed, though she hadn't known it was her deathbed because Carla wouldn't let the doctors tell her. Better that she keep her dreams; better that she close her eyes and envision the old country and die in peace.

"We made it, Mama," Carla said quietly now, patting the side of her carry-on in which she'd carried-on her toiletries and a small, silver-framed picture of Theresa, too. With the photo of her mother always in Carla's bag, "they," indeed, had made it. They had combed the basilicas and the ruins and the small cafés of Rome; they had been awed by the Botticellis and the Titians and the Michelangelos in Florence; they had sipped wine and strolled the countryside and broken thick crusts of bread in Tuscany. Then they had visited Gabrielle.

Six days, five nights, were all her meager savings could afford without dipping into Theresa's life insurance settlement. Yet every waking minute had been filled with wonderment, despite the sad reality that although the picture had been with her, her mother, in actuality, had not.

Looking out the window of the 747, Carla wondered if Theresa was there among the clouds, riding on the wind, smiling with her passport in her hand. Nearly thirty years ago when she'd insisted on getting passports so they'd "be ready," Carla had laughed. Later, when Carla's sons were older, they'd laughed, too. Donnie, the younger one, the comedian, had reminded her that taking the subway across the Bronx to Sunday mass was enough of a challenge for one family and one world. But when Mama moved in with Carla and the boys, she would not give up the church in the neighborhood where her kids were born and raised and had gone to parochial school and where her Sal had been buried.

They had not needed passports for the Bronx. But how could Carla or her mother have predicted that having the vital folder and renewing it each decade would enable her to complete one final task for Lester Markham?

They knew now, all three of the heiress cousins.

Mary Beth had yelled, "Get off my property," though Carla didn't believe the lobby of an apartment building constituted "her property."

Nikki had frowned and slowly nodded as if she were not surprised.

Gabrielle had cried.

With a small sigh, Carla reclined her seat and scolded herself for the secret pleasure she had felt when she'd learned that the women she'd once envied no longer had it all. They were women, after all, not much different from her, except for the money part. Even Mary Beth, for all her high heels and her makeup, had a mother who was sick, and Carla knew what that felt like.

*Envy is a deadly sin.*

Carla had learned her catechism, but sometimes she forgot. She'd have to go to confession as soon as she got home. Then, maybe, she thought as she closed her eyes, this would all be over and Lester would be waiting for her.

The roll of the jet engines lulled her into dreamy sleep and sweet reminiscences of Florence and of Rome and of how much Mama would have loved the trip.

Nikki wanted to go to the police.

"Over my dead body," Mary Beth had yelled into the phone and meant it. There was no way anyone was going to the cops and risk the story of their family situation leaking to the media mere weeks before her daughter's wedding. "Besides," she'd added, "for all we know it's a mistake. Or one of Lester's unamusing practical jokes."

As many years as Mary Beth had known Lester Markham, she had not known him to be a jokester, but Nikki would not know that, sequestered as she was out there on the island.

"Give me a week," she'd pleaded with her cousin, "and I'll have it straightened out."

Nikki had grumbled something about AIDS being more important than a wedding, but she'd backed off when Mary Beth subtly reminded her that the wedding was for Shauna and that Dee was the maid of honor— *their daughters*—and she was only asking for a week, not half a freaking century.

In the end, Nikki had acquiesced, which was why Mary Beth now stood before her mirror one week later, adjusting the clasp on the black pearls and diamonds that everyone at the gallery opening would expect her to wear tonight. The baubles had been Eric's gift for her forty-second birthday, though she'd picked them out herself and simply had the bill sent to the apartment in his name.

Even if they all suspected that the money for the glittering ensemble had come from her trust fund, no one would mention it, not even Roxanne, because no one did that sort of thing and remained on the A-list in New York.

The jewels were perfect with her pewter satin slip dress, perfect for Galerie Renard, perfect for the all-in-good-fun confrontation she expected when she saw Lester Markham, who would undoubtedly be present, because Lester never missed an opportunity to have his picture in *W* or *Town & Country*.

She could have called Lester's office to confirm the absurdity of that woman Carla's visit and her ridiculous message. But Mary Beth had not wanted to embarrass either herself or the man to whom her fortune—her *life*—had been so carefully entrusted. Besides, she'd phoned Lester's office too often in the past year. The cost of clothes and airfare and entertaining had simply escalated, and somehow she'd found that even *her* ends were not quite meeting. And she hated begging for advance payments on something that was rightfully hers. "Have you thought about a budget?" he'd asked once or twice, which, of course, was ludicrous. How was she supposed to know how many clothes she'd need for Greece, or that she couldn't get bubble wands engraved unless they came from Tiffany's?

For the hundredth time that week, she tried to recall if the voice that always answered Lester's phone sounded like that of the woman who had showed up in the lobby.

Leaning closer to the mirror, Mary Beth reassured herself that the woman was probably a disgruntled employee, someone Lester had fired and who was on a quest for revenge. Not that Mary Beth hadn't been startled for a moment. But so far, the world had not stopped turning, nor had Mary Beth's creditors stopped her from buying. Or ordering. Or anything.

Nor had any other threatening visitors arrived at the apartment, the twelve-room, five-bedroom, six-bath apartment that had once been in Dorothy Atkinson's name but had been transferred to her daughter just before the downward slide of Dorothy's mind.

She screwed on the earring backs and wondered if she should have called Lester after all. But why? Lester had been with the family for so long, he was practically one of them. Cheat them? Steal from them? Disappear? No, "family" did not do such things. At least, not to one another.

"Ready, darling?"

Her husband's reflection moved into the vanity mirror. He had the clean, trim look of a male *GQ* model, despite the fact that he would be forty-five in the fall. She stood and smoothed her dress. "Do I look positively divine?"

He took her shoulders and kissed her cheek. "Enchanting. Yes. Divine."

He withdrew his hands and she shivered. "Your fingers are freezing." Layered within his usual wood-musk aroma, the strong scent of gin said the chill was not from the cool evening, but from stirring martinis in the Orrefors pitcher.

Eric stepped away. He checked himself in the mirror. "The Clarkes will be here any minute," he said. "And the Ruddeforths."

Mary Beth hadn't seen either couple since the holiday balls that had cost a pretty penny to attend in the name of charity. The Clarkes (with an "e") and the Ruddeforths wintered at ski resorts; Mary Beth preferred warm climates, like the Greek Isles. Besides, they were Eric's friends, not hers, a group of nouveaux riches whom he'd met on a plane from Houston, where he'd dabbled with another coin collector who'd acquired an Aztec something-or-other. The fact that the Clarkes and the

Ruddeforths had been "bumped" to First Class should have been a clue, but, to Eric, anyone ready for a party was a new friend in his book, and, as Roxanne was known to say, *nouveau* was better than *never*. Mary Beth sighed and adjusted her bracelet. "Your friends will be treated to the debut of my birthday gifts."

"And they will be jealous," Eric said proudly, as if he, indeed, had selected and paid for the jewels. If he weren't so damned charming, he might just piss her off.

Swishing past him with a smile, she retrieved her satin shawl. "Come, darling," she said as she looped her arm through his. "I want to get there early and have a chat with Lester Markham. I have some delicious gossip I cannot wait to share."


"Utter trash," Roxanne whispered in Mary Beth's ear as they stood and stared at the edible sculpture before them. Galerie Renard was famous for introducing outrageous artists to society: this one, Harvé Penfield.

They'd been there almost an hour, and Mary Beth's mission was as yet unaccomplished. She leaned back, one eye scanning the crowd for Lester, the other seemingly interested in the seven-foot-tall marzipan sculpture that stood before her. It was in the shape of George W. Bush. "Too tall," she said. "And he smells like almonds."

Roxanne swayed closer, nearly spilling her champagne, her fifth glass since she had arrived. "They all smell like almonds," she whispered. "Tina Turner. Mike Wallace. Oprah. My God, it's like Madam Tussaud's Wax Museum Almondine."

Harvé Penfield moved within earshot. Mary Beth clutched Roxanne's elbow and steered her away. She surveyed the marzipanned room again for Lester Markham. Instead, she saw her husband positioned next to a statue of former governor Cuomo. Eric was talking with a blonde who wore more diamonds that she'd ever seen around one swanlike neck.

He spotted Mary Beth and gave a happy nod. She turned back to Roxanne. "Lester Markham," she asked. "Where is he?"

Roxanne sipped from her glass. "I have no idea. Should I? Is he still available?" Lester Markham was single—*widowed,* which was better than *divorced* because alimony could not infringe. Though it was well known Roxanne had much more money than Mary Beth, how much was enough had not yet been determined.

Mary Beth sighed. "He's not your type," she said. "He's a self-feeder." She did not have to explain to Roxie that that meant Lester worked for a living, earned a real income, had one of those real things called jobs.

Or at least she'd thought he did.

Her eyes darted around the room once more. Tension gripped her neck. She'd give anything to get Hank, her personal trainer, to travel in her circle so he'd show up, too. Then both her muscles and her mind would be at peace.

Lester. Where was he? Nikki, no doubt, would be on the phone to her in the morning, demanding to know what Lester said, demanding...

Oh, God, Mary Beth thought. Was it just a rotten coincidence that he'd chosen not to show?

*Or...*

"Well, if Lester's on his way, he'd better hurry," Roxanne said. Then she reached over, scooped a fingerful of Mike Wallace's cheek, and popped it into her mouth. "He'd better hurry or the art will be all gone." Then she strutted off, toward a young man balancing a champagne-laden tray.

Mary Beth backed away from the sculpture. She did not know if anyone had seen Roxanne's assault on the journalist. She did not know if anyone would notice the indentation on his jawline, or if the gallery police would stop guests at the door and test their breath for almonds.

And then a headache crashed against the bottom of her neck. Why couldn't she be more like Roxanne—loose and carefree instead of rigid and aware, too aware of everything and everyone and every move around her, teetering on the cusp of what was right and what was not? The right way, the Atkinson way. Every other way, the wrong way.

And Lester Markham knew that. So what the hell had happened? Was the bastard really gone?

"I barely had time with the Ruddeforths," Eric commented as their Town Car—a Lincoln, not a Bentley, a Rolls, or even a Mercedes, because they were so tacky when one had a driver—wove its way through the before-midnight streets and headed uptown.

Mary Beth pressed her finger to her lips to remind her husband not to say anything that could be misconstrued as an argument in front of Charlie, their driver. After all, they shared him with two other families, and God only knew how much he told them, despite the fact that one family was the Lynches who lived mostly on the West Coast and the other was Carlos Diaz from Barcelona who only came to Manhattan in the fall.

But though Mary Beth and Eric had been married over twenty years, sometimes Eric simply forgot. Finesse, unlike charm, was not learned but a birthright. It was why Mary Beth had opted to forgo live-in help for a per diem, don't-get-too-close household staff.

"Let's invite them to the Vineyard for golf next month," she said loudly enough so Charlie would be certain to hear.

Eric winked as if to let her know he finally got it. "When?"

She was too tired to continue with the game. "We'll check our calendar when we get home."

"Well," Eric said, "I'm having breakfast with the Brazilians. I can't confirm my schedule until then."

"Whatever," Mary Beth replied and closed her eyes.

They fell into common silence, Eric perhaps fantasizing about his South American adventure, while Mary Beth tried to fight off a gnawing obsession about Lester Markham and her financial fate.

Tomorrow she would call him. Tomorrow. After her session with Hank, after the knots had been untangled from her neck.


A cool cloud of air stirred the creamy satin sheets, causing Mary Beth to stir before she'd wanted to. She put her hand over her eye mask and waited to feel the warmth of Eric's body leak to her side of the king-size bed. God, ever since his last birthday, her husband made these early morning trips out of bed to the bathroom. If his prostate didn't start getting more considerate, she'd have to ask him to sleep in the room down the hall...*any* room down the hall, because soon Shauna would be married and it would just be the two of them.

And then what would life be like?

The cool air between the sheets warmed up again. That's when she sensed something—a hand? an arm?—move close to her. The urge to cringe came and went quickly as fingers—strong fingers, thick fingers—moved up her side and rested on the rise of her breast that crept out from her nightgown. She smiled. She had not known it was that late.

Her eye mask still intact, she slowly turned onto her back and stretched her arms above her head. The hands moved up the silk, stopping at the line where her nipples had grown stiff and peeked out from the fabric. He moved the thin strap of her nightgown. Had he done that with his teeth? He tugged the fabric, she heard it tear, he pulled it off. Then he was on her nipple with his lips, his mouth, his tongue. She moaned a tiny moan.

He moved above her. She felt his big, hard penis flick across her thighs, a mass of uncontrolled heat awaiting entry to her lair.

His mouth then left her breast and traveled down the hollow of her belly, her taut, tanned, small belly that could have belonged to a twenty-year-old for the firmness of her workouts. With his tongue, he moved aside the narrow strip of hair between her bikini-wax lines. He plunged his big finger into her growing wetness, then nibbled at her throbbing, melting clitoris with those teeth that she knew were big, white, and straight.

She panted and grabbed his head. She shoved it hard against her and humped his face and his tongue and his teeth in rhythm with the pounding of her heart and the...oh, God, the scream of her orgasm that would not stop.

She shuddered and shuddered and felt her peak begin to dissipate. Then he grabbed her buttocks and dove at her again until she went limp, weak and wet and heavenly floating and then he let out a moan of his own and grabbed her hand and pressed it to his penis and together their entangled fingers stroked him back and forth, back and forth until his hot liquid shot across her legs, all creamy and wet, all oozing and oh, so fucking good.

She reached down and smeared his juices over her

body, over her own wetness, her own still-throbbing ache. She rubbed herself, her mound, her place of pleasure, hard, harder, harder, harder until...Jesus...God... it was there...again...again...oh, God...

...oh,

...God...

It must have been a minute that they lay there, maybe more. When the knock came on her bedroom door, Mary Beth had thankfully regained her composure. She pulled off her eye mask and helped Hank roll off the mattress and slide under the bed as Shauna's voice called, "Mother? Are you awake?"

*Mother* was able to get out of bed, slide into her long peach silk robe, and unlatch the door for her daughter without much more than a sliver of concern that the man who had stealthily slipped beneath the bed might be exposed. She'd never felt much guilt about the recent trail of sex men in her life; though she and Eric never, ever discussed it, the physical side of their relationship had long since dwindled into infrequent, unexpected moments that occurred usually after too many martinis on both their parts. Too many martinis and purely physical wants and needs and a feeling of entitlement because they were married, so what the hell.

She'd always had more sex drive than he did anyway. Just as she'd always had more money.

"We were out late last night," Mary Beth said, walking toward her dressing room, steering her daughter from the scene and the scent of her mother's sins. "I just woke up."

Shauna did not seem to care. She sat on a brocade-tufted stool. "Mother," she said, "you know I love Dee, but she's going to screw everything up."

Mary Beth laughed and stepped into the steam room and set the jets on to heat. She turned back to her daughter. "Your cousin does not have the power to screw anything up, darling," she said.

She went to the vanity, brushed out her hair, and snapped a headband around it. Fortunately today was hair day: She was in no condition to appear in public as the glamorous, much-photographed mother-of-the-bride. The thought of photographs reminded Mary Beth that she needed to bring some old photos for her mother before she forgot again.

"Mother, you don't understand," Shauna continued. "She has a chance to go to China, which means she won't be at my wedding."

Shauna, of course, did not know about the supposed disappearances of Lester or the money. She hoped Nikki had had the sense not to mention the situation to Dee, either. "She'll be at your wedding, darling," Mary Beth tried to reassure her. "I shall insist."

"But if she leaves, what will I do? It's too late to ask anyone else to stand up for me...and our gowns are almost finished..."

Mary Beth slapped cleansing cream on her face. "I wouldn't worry about that, darling. First of all, I can think of at least a dozen girls who would be delighted to be in the limelight at an Atkinson wedding."

"I want Dee. She is my cousin. We've always been like sisters..."

The way Mary Beth and Nikki had once been. So long ago, before life directed their pathways toward two different planets.

"Is she going to the Vineyard this weekend with you and Jason?"

"She's supposed to. We're going Thursday. Maybe I'll ask Aunt Nikki to talk some sense into her."

"Ha!" Mary Beth blurted out. "Your Aunt Nikki has sand in her shoes and salt water in her brain. More than likely she hates the whole idea of this wedding in the first place." As soon as she'd said it, she wished that she hadn't.

Shauna blinked back the hurt and shook her head as if she understood her mother and didn't take it personally. "It'll be fine," she said. "I'll figure something out."

She departed as quickly as she had come.

Mary Beth sighed and realized that some days the pressure of being an Atkinson was too much even for her. Then she thought about Lester, and how dare he not show up last night because that meant she'd have to call him this morning before "Aunt" Nikki called out the National Guard and the whole family went to hell in one of those dreary Nantucket handbaskets. She took off her robe and stepped into the shower, reminding herself that when she was done, she really must remember that Hank was still under the bed.

# 7

For the first time since she'd been in Italy, Gabrielle felt suffocated by the countryside.

Who was Carla DiRoma, and was she telling the truth? How had she found her? Had Lester broken his promise? Did her father know where she was? Did her cousins? Would they show up, too?

And dear God, what if Stefano learned that she'd lied?

Her thoughts had pressed together, squeezed like the grapes until their life had gone. She knew she must take some action before Stefano came home.

So she had waited this morning for the postman to trek up the mountain, and she begged for a ride into the village. He said it was against the law for a regular person to ride in the mail car.

But she was a countess, the Countess Bonelli, did he not remember? She offered him money. She offered him wine.

At last he agreed to drop her on the edge of town.

Which was why she walked slowly now, her head high, her gait steady as she tried to look confident so no one would suspect she was trying to hide anything from her husband, the trusting count who'd married the God-forbid-American.

She carried her basket as if she'd come to shop at the market, not to use the public telephone to call Zurich, a call that could not be traced to the villa.

She strolled along the limestone brick street, past pale stone houses that were crowded together, past small in-town gardens where big-faced pansies struggled to keep a last grip on spring, where the sounds of children playing mingled with a dog barking, a mother shouting, an old man cursing.

How Gabrielle loved Tuscany! Her anguish dissipated in the filtered light that rippled through the village street on a dreamlike veil. Aromas of sausage and bread and fresh-picked herbs clung to each delicious breath of air, creating an aphrodisiac that nearly made her forget the reason for her journey.

Finally she reached the piazza, the center of the village, where the stone fountain splayed mountain water from dragon-headed bronze spigots and where the arched arcade gave shelter to an outdoor coffee shop, the newsstand, and, thank God, the telephone. Gabrielle walked toward it with deliberate unhurriedness, passing an old woman who stood behind a cart of cheese wheels and two men who sat at a square table drinking dark wine, despite that the hour was not yet noon.

She fumbled in her pocket and withdrew a piece of paper. On it was the number of the bank in Zurich.

When she reached customer service, she turned from the street and cupped her hand over the receiver. She spoke in English.

"I need to know when the most recent transfer of money was made into my account," she said and gave her name.

"What is your access number?"

"My what?"

"Your access number. The one used for the electronic transfer."

"I don't know that. I don't make the deposits."

"I am sorry, I cannot release any information over the phone without your access number."

"But I have my account number."

"Do you have your last statement?" the woman asked.

"No," Gabrielle replied. She had stopped the statements from coming soon after she'd met Stefano. How could she explain that? "I used to have them sent to my address in Paris. On Rue Galilee."

"But you don't have your access number."

A woman and a young boy exited the newsstand. The boy was laughing. His mother took his hand and smiled down at him. She asked if he wanted a chocolate bar and they went into the arcade.

"Please," Gabrielle said. She set down her basket and rubbed her forehead. "I've been told that the man who managed my funds has disappeared. I need to know how much is in my account, when the last deposit was made, or if this is some sort of hoax." She closed her eyes and fought back tears. "Please help me."

"I'm sorry," the woman repeated. "It's against regulations."

Gabrielle hung her head. "What can I do?"

"You'll have to come here," was the reply. "You'll have to come to Zurich with proper identification."

One ring. Two.

Would Carla DiRoma answer the phone?

Mary Beth tapped her foot.

Three. Four. No answer, no damn answer.

Five. Six.

Not even a goddamn recording.

She checked her watch. Eight-fifty. Was eight-fifty too early for the office to be open? She had no idea. "Standard" office hours had not concerned Mary Beth. She vaguely remembered that a friend once took a job in an office in order to feel "productive." But after a few weeks it had interfered with tennis, so she cut her schedule to three days a week, then two, then none. Mary Beth had not known what time the job had started.

Ring. Ring. How many rings was that?

She huffed a large huff and banged down the receiver, then grabbed the address book again. *Lester Markham. 350 Park Avenue. Suite 2412.*

"Shit," she said softly, with resigned distaste, because there was only one thing left for her to do.

Despite her claims that she needed to be with people, that she liked staying in touch with Vineyarders, one on one, Nikki also could admit to herself that the aroma of baking bread contributed greatly to the seduction of her part-time job. She regretted that she'd have to leave the bakery for the duration of camp, but knew plenty of islanders in need of summer work. All of which, for Nikki, was acceptable, she thought as she hauled another sheet of caraway rolls from the oven. Let the others wait on the tourists; she preferred the peace of off-season.

"That's odd," came a voice from in front of the counter, "I expected to see you kneading peasant bread."

Nikki adjusted the tray on the rack before facing her one and, thank God, her only. "Dee," Nikki said with a grin, because in spite of their differences she did love her daughter. She went around the counter and gave her a hug. "It's good to see you. Do you want a muffin or something?"

"Alice would kill me. I put on four pounds junking out during finals, and she has to let out the waist on my gown as it is."

In addition to being Nikki's right hand, Alice Sullivan was a gifted seamstress, a green thumb with a needle and thread. To Mary Beth's chagrin, Shauna had chosen Alice over Vera Wang to create her one-of-a-kind gown and the gown of her lone attendant. Surveying Dee's very fitted white top and equally tight jeans, Nikki supposed it was possible that four pounds would make a difference. It always amazed her that a daughter of hers was skinny enough to wear such clothes: Connor's lean genes, less of Nikki's full hips and round curves. "Dinner?" Nikki asked.

Dee wrinkled her nose. "Tonight?"

"Great," Nikki said, trying not to add that she needn't force herself. "Can you stay past the weekend?" She would love to shanghai her daughter into volunteering at the camp. Maybe if Dee could see some of the children, see their excitement and feel the good feelings of helping those in need...

"No. Dad needs me at the office."

So much for rescuing her daughter from a capitalist demise, from her father's business-minded, Harvard footsteps.

"Besides, I'm making other plans," Dee continued. "Which is also why I'm here. How would you like to fund a trip to China? I'm dying to go, Mom. Just for a few weeks. I want to study their business acumen firsthand. By myself."

The *by myself* part, of course, meant without Nikki, who had dragged Dee through European museums from Madrid to Dublin every summer in a futile attempt to instill a liberal arts education, until last year, when Dee had chosen to work at Atkinson Enterprises instead.

Nikki tried to smile. She wondered how her daughter would react if she knew there was no longer money for such frivolities as vacations, even when veiled under the guise of studying a *business acumen,* whatever that meant. "Well, you certainly won't go completely by yourself. Will you?" Nikki was stalling for time, trying to come up with a plausible answer other than "Sorry, I'm broke." Apparently word had not yet leaked from Mary Beth to Shauna to Dee that the family fortune, right now, seemed kaput.

"Of course I'm going alone," Dee said. "How much would I learn with a bunch of girls who would only want to shop or to manhunt?"

Nikki refrained from asking what was wrong with that. "What does your father think?"

"He thinks it's inappropriate for a nineteen-year-old woman to travel alone. He said to ask you."

Nikki smiled. She recognized the bait that Dee had flung, that if Connor thought something was "inappropriate," surely Nikki would not. Water and oil. Night and day.

"So he won't kick in any money," Nikki stated. He was paying for her Harvard education in full, because that was not inappropriate. That was for his daughter, his genetically-matched daughter.

"Mom," Dee whined, "it won't cost much. Only a few thousand. Ten maybe. Fifteen."

Nikki did not mention that fifteen thousand dollars could put a couple of kids through camp for the summer. Or take a bite out of this month's AZT cost.

"What about Shauna's wedding?"

"I'll be back in time, no matter what Shauna thinks." She spoke with exasperation, as if her mother were a dolt as well as cheap.

An elderly couple in flannel shirts, worn jeans, and rubber boots came into the bakery. Nikki recognized them as a local man and his wife, who'd been fishing together for sixty years. She doubted they'd ever had discussions about Harvard educations or fifteen-thousand-dollar vacations.

"Excuse me," she said to her daughter, and went to wait on the couple, ignoring the impatience that now radiated from Dee. Nikki built a box and put in two raisin scones and two cranberry-orange muffins, then waited for the couple to decide between the sourdough bread and the whole grain. She kept her eyes on the couple, away from her daughter, who had not moved an inch, awaiting the answer she knew would be yes, because it always had been, which might account for a good part of the problem.

The sourdough won. Nikki tied up the box and rang up the sale. It was not fifteen thousand, only six dollars and thirty-five cents. Not enough for a few weeks in China.

When the couple departed, Dee placed her hands on her too-narrow hips as if to say, "Well?"

Nikki sighed. "I'm sorry, honey," she said, "but it's not a good time. With the camp just beginning, I don't have a clear view of my expenses."

"Mother! I'm not asking for a fucking fortune here!"

Nikki refused to look shocked. "Watch your language, young lady. This is a public place."

"Ha!" Dee spat. "You call this 'public'? Get real, Mother. Rockefeller Center is a public place. LaGuardia Airport is a public place. This is a two-bit bakery on a stupid island! If you don't approve of me going to China, why don't you just say so? Don't pretend you can't afford it. When I turn twenty-five and have my own trust fund, I won't need you at all."

With that, she stalked from the bakery and exerted a great deal of effort in slamming the door, but this was the

Vineyard so it was a screen door and its bang was way less than her bite.


Jonathan had hailed her a cab because Mary Beth couldn't risk Charlie driving and announcing to the social register that Mary Beth had paid a visit to her trust fund manager. One, after all, did not visit one's trust fund manager; one's trust fund manager came to one. Unless, of course, he had disappeared.

Stuffing a few bills into the cabby's rough hand, she gratefully exited from the leftover odor of other people and stepped onto Park Avenue. Then, like a tourist, she looked up at building 350. She counted up twenty-four floors and stared at the glass as if Lester would know she was down there and would come down to street level.

After a moment, when he hadn't showed up, Mary Beth marched into the atrium lobby, ready to take him on. It was ten forty-five—surely he'd be at his desk. Surely, if not he, then that woman named Carla, if she worked there at all.

She went right to the elevators as if she did this every morning, as if she were among the scurry of gray-suited men and women who scrambled into the car in various stages of paper-cup-coffee clutching and tie-adjusting theatrics. Inside the elevator, she followed suit and faced the doors, shoulder to shoulder with the overpopulated middle class.

"Twenty-four, please," she announced in her most pleasant voice.

The couple of looks thrown her way suggested she push the "24" button herself. Her face flushed. She squeezed between two people and pushed number twenty-four.

On the ride up she wanted to close her eyes but did not dare. Instead she stared straight ahead and tried to block out the sounds of her elevator-mates: the cough of an apparent cigarette-smoker (God, what she wouldn't give for a healthy drag right now), the nervous sniff of a young woman with string hair, the shuffle onto one foot then the other of an older man who might have to pee.

She suppressed a smile at that thought. Though she was certain she'd never see these people again, there was no sense in giving the impression that she was a fruitcake—they would step back to avoid brushing her jacket, despite the fact that it was a John Galliano and had cost twenty-six hundred dollars.

They stopped on five, eight, eleven, and sixteen. The cache of worker bees thinned and she slowly exhaled. By the time they reached floor twenty-four, Mary Beth was proud that she was taking control and facing the situation when it would have been easier to pretend it would just go away. Infused with new confidence, she stepped out of the elevator and glanced up and down the hall for suite twenty-four twelve.

The sign pointed right.

Filled with the attitude of a true Atkinson, she click-clicked her high heels on the marble floor that led straight to the solid walnut door. A small brass holder was screwed onto it. It was designed to hold a plate engraved with the name of the occupant. But the brass holder was empty.

She frowned and jiggled the doorknob. It was locked. She glanced back to the number. Was she at the wrong suite?

The old man with the shuffling feet from the elevator suddenly was at her side. "Hey, lady," he asked, "you looking for someone?"

She glanced back at the door, then to the man. "Well, yes. But I must have the wrong suite. I'm looking for Lester Markham."

The man shook his head. "Nope. That was his place, all right. Heard he disappeared. Practically took off in the middle of the night."

Her throat constricted. She touched her fingers on the U-shaped bone at its base and tried to ease open her airway. "Where did he go?" she asked. "Another suite? Another building?"

The old man shrugged. "Who the hell knows, lady? This is New York." With that he waddled off down the hall toward another walnut door that was not Lester's, either.

Mary Beth leaned against the wall and wondered if she'd ever breathe right again and if anyone would notice—or care—if she dropped dead right there.

# 8

M y daughter hates me," Nikki told Alice when Alice arrived at the bakery with the list of bread and rolls needed for the first week of camp— enough to feed forty-two kids and thirty-one adults, including counselors, coaches, teachers, nurses, and two nurse practitioners who were HIV specialists. "Which is fine," Nikki continued as she perused the list, "because most days I'm not too fond of her, either." She looked up at Alice. "Are we going to stiff the Bake Shoppe the way we're stiffing everyone else?"

"We are not stiffing anyone," Alice said with an edge to her voice that Nikki had not expected. "We'll only need to defer payment, until—well, until you decide to get more aggressive. Admit it, Nikki, your cousin is being completely self-centered."

Nikki rang out the register and closed up for the day. "Mary Beth? Self-centered?" She did not laugh because she did not want to bother.

"I finished the latest count," Alice continued. "Three hundred and twelve kids this summer. Starting tomorrow."

Nikki half-nodded. Three hundred and twelve children

would be spread over six two-week increments. Some of them would be lucky and stay for more than one period. Some—oh, God, she thought, hopefully *none*—would have to leave before their time was over, because of their illness or because the money ran out.

*Mary Beth,* she thought, *you can't do this to me...to them.*

She grabbed her bag from under the counter, then realized what Alice had just said. "Tomorrow's only Friday. I thought no one was checking in until Sunday." In a measure to help dodge a problem of Steamship Authority reservations, they had chosen Sunday-afternoon-to-Sunday-morning time blocks, thus averting the dreaded, sardine-squeezed Saturday crossings to and from the mainland.

"We have an early arrival. A little girl. Her dad's bringing her tomorrow. They'll stay with me until then."

Nikki poked the bread list through a metal spike that stood on the counter next to the register. "I have to call Mary Beth," she said. "We have to find Lester."

"There's another small problem, Nikki," Alice said quietly. "We have picketers."

Nikki closed her eyes. "Picketers?"

"When I left the campgrounds today, a small group had formed at the end of the road."

Her dark mood darkened.

"And they were carrying signs that said, 'AIDS patients: Go home for good.' "

Nikki opened her eyes and dropped her chin to her chest. "I hate this day," Nikki said. "I absolutely fucking hate this day." She said it with conviction and without caring that this was a public place and people might hear her. Then she led Alice out, locked up for the day, and headed out to ward off the picketers, those self-proclaimed agitators of nothing right or nothing good.

\*   \*   \*

There were eight of them. Not enough for a full-scale war, but enough to hurt feelings. Kids' feelings. When they saw Nikki's VW turn into the driveway, they scattered. She recognized some faces from the courthouse clamorings.

Quickly jamming the brakes, Nikki put down her window. "Next time, the sheriff comes," she shouted after them. They disappeared so fast, Nikki could not tell if they cared. She sighed and pressed her forehead against the steering wheel, wondering if she could go to jail if she bought a pellet gun and chased them off once and for all.

She wondered if Mack would put up her bail.


"Everyone wants to grow old, but no one wants to be old," Dorothy Atkinson said to her daughter in a lucid moment.

Mary Beth had summoned her courage and gone to Harriman House, armed with the old photos to help prod the woman's mind. "Last in, first out," her mother's gerontologist theorized, an idea that simply meant her mother could remember thirty years ago more easily than yesterday. While new medications might help slow the progression of the disease and alleviate some symptoms, apparently there were few substitutes for things that simply made sense. Perhaps something in the snapshots would trigger Dorothy to remember Lester. Maybe in those murky places of her mind remained a clue about his background. If Mary Beth couldn't call the police, maybe she could find him herself, before Nikki went ballistic or Eric found out.

She aligned rows of pictures by places and by years atop the glass table in the courtyard. "Look, Mother," she said. "I've brought a project."

Dorothy gazed at the stacks of yesterday. She scowled. The Dorothy of the photographs had rarely scowled: She'd been unencumbered by distress, protected by her world of privilege and pampering, and if neither was sufficient there had always been the gin.

Mary Beth pulled up a chair. "Here's a picture of Aunt Margaret in the library at the house on the Vineyard. And look, here's one of all of us. *Summer of 1974,* it says on the back. Remember?" Most of the photos were from the Vineyard, where taking pictures had been what one did in summer, inside the house and out on the grounds, smiling faces—most always female—in sundresses and shorts. The summer of 1974 photo showed them crowded around the lighthouse: Dorothy and Mary Beth, Margaret and Nikki, Rose and Gabrielle. Mary Beth felt no need to mention that 1974 was the summer she'd been pregnant and had that horrible abortion. She slid the photo closer to her mother. " 'The Atkinson Girls,' it says."

"Hmm. It was such a shame about your aunt Rose."

Good! Her mother remembered something, that Rose was her sister and that she was dead. Mary Beth could have reminded her that Rose had fallen on the rock jetty that same Labor Day weekend and was killed instantly. She could have reminded her, but she didn't want to use up Dorothy's fast-depleting brain cells on an incident that might be upsetting.

"Here's one of Grandfather." Mary Beth handed her a faded color snapshot of the old man on a sailboat. He did not look nearly as old as she'd remembered. "He died when I was only fifteen. Imagine that, I was only fifteen."

Dorothy nodded. "He was quite the businessman, wasn't he?"

Mary Beth's hopes raised a little. "Remember the trust funds he set up for Nikki and me...and Gabrielle?"

Slowly Dorothy nodded. "All that nonsense about

money...I was grateful to no longer have to be responsible to see that you had enough."

Responsibility had not been Dorothy's forte, for the need had never arisen. What mattered now, however, was that by some miracle, her mother still recalled the trust funds. "Lester Markham?" Mary Beth asked quickly, afraid to lose the moment. "Do you remember him?"

Dorothy frowned again, and Mary Beth felt an awkward guilt about putting her mother through this. She wished Dorothy could remain oblivious to suffering, as she always had been. She longed for that other, younger mother who had flitted through life, telling Mary Beth things that seemed so important—like that Marjorie Merriweather Post had one special room in her home simply for white gloves, and another for hats.

But the woman at the table no longer wore hats or gloves, and no longer had the need for rooms in which to keep them.

"Let me see that picture," her mother said. Then she smiled. "That was one of my favorite dresses. Do you remember it? It was the palest yellow. I used to think it matched my golden hair."

"Yes, Mother. But we were talking about Lester Markham. Aunt Margaret hired him to handle the trust funds."

"Margaret had on a blue dress. She always said clothes should match your eyes. Critical, she was. She criticized everything I did and said. Rose said Margaret was just jealous because I was more beautiful. She must still be jealous, because she never visits me."

Mary Beth did not explain that it was more likely that Margaret did not come because Margaret, like Rose, was long dead.

Dorothy traced the image of her younger sister in the photo. "Poor Rose. She was so sensitive."

Putting her head down on the table, Mary Beth wished she knew how to bring her mother back to life or, at least, how much she should push. She'd never quite known what was kind and what was not, and Alzheimer's had more greatly blurred the line between. She raised her head again and nodded. "Yes, poor Rose. And you were more beautiful than Aunt Margaret, Mother. Always."

Dorothy smiled again. "I know Lester," she said abruptly. "He sends your checks every month."

Mary Beth sat up straight, afraid, even, to hold her breath, afraid of distracting Dorothy from her train of thought.

"He was a friend of your grandfather's," Dorothy miraculously continued. "Something to do with business, I suppose. Your aunt Margaret admired him, though I had no idea why. She never usually paid attention to such good-looking men." She sighed a tiny sigh. "My goodness, that was a long time ago."

Just then a tall, buxom woman approached the table. She wore a badge that read PATRICIA KENDRICK, ASSISTANT ADMINISTRATOR.

"Excuse me, are you Dot's daughter?"

Mary Beth's jaw tightened into a clench. "I am *Dorothy*'s daughter."

The woman did not smile as she asked, "May I see you in the office?"


She had wanted to tell the woman that she'd see her later, but as she started to say it the woman's eyes narrowed and Mary Beth got the message. She followed PATRICIA KENDRICK from the courtyard into the lushly carpeted, salmon-colored halls, past museum pieces of furniture and gilt-framed old masters.

They entered an office that looked more like a hunt club for its dark green and mahogany, leather, and shiny brass. Mary Beth presumed the decor intentionally re-created familiar surroundings for the old-moneyed guests.

The assistant administrator posed at the hand-carved, rosewood fireplace mantel. "I'm going to come straight to the point, Ms. Atkinson, because that's how we do things at Harriman House."

Mary Beth sat on a silk-covered chair.

"We have not received payment for your mother's care this month," the woman said. "Or last month," she added.

Well, of course they had not received payment this month. Mary Beth had not received her trust fund check. And last month? Oh, yes, the wedding expenses had begun accumulating.... She'd meant to make it up out of the new check, the one that had never come. They were plausible reasons that she could not share because it was no one's business.

She cocked her head. "You haven't received payment? For *two months*?"

The woman did not smile. "I'm sure it's an oversight. But to provide our patients—your mother—with the best possible comfort and care, we have a costly overhead. Perhaps if you speak with your money manager..."

There was no reason to explain that Mary Beth managed her own money and had for the past several years. It was an uncommon practice among people in her "position," but she'd grown tired of hand-slapping by those in control of her checkbook who could not refrain from chastising her about her daily expenses. As if any of them would know the difference between a two-hundred-dollar haircut and the ones they got for eighteen-plus-tip.

Lester, of course, was bad enough. She could fire her check-writers but not her trust fund manager. Aunt

Margaret had ordered it, and even today, her rule prevailed.

"I most definitely will. I cannot imagine what happend." She furrowed her brow into a show of concern. "I've never had problems with the firm."

"Well, things happen. A new employee, perhaps. Some slipshod bookkeeping..."

"Slipshod! Ha!" Mary Beth tipped back her head and laughed. "At their rates you'd think they'd have more than a slipshod bookkeeper overseeing my finances. Oh," she added with a cluck-cluck for effect, "my grandfather would be appalled to know how the ethics of business have slid. It's as if people simply don't care anymore." She leveled her eyes on Ms. Kendrick. "Do you know what I mean?"

"Most definitely. Incompetence is all around us."

Mary Beth stood up. "Well, I, for one, will not stand for it. You have my word. I'll get to the bottom of this immediately."

"As long as we receive payment within the next week, we won't worry about it," Ms. Kendrick said. Then she crossed her arms over her too-ample bosom. "Any later, however, will not be acceptable. You will have to make arrangements elsewhere."

Adjusting the belt of her silk moiré pants, Mary Beth smiled. "You needn't worry, Ms. Kendrick. My mother will be staying right here."

She strutted from the office with the same strut she'd strutted on the way in.


It had been so long since Gabrielle had been in a city she'd forgotten about the noise. Cars and busses and scooters and people clattered and clashed in a cacophony of life. It was not at all like Tuscany, where the music of the air was made up of songbirds and distant cow bells.

She sat in the high-walled, glass reception area of FirstBanc Internationale waiting for an available representative. If the regular transfer had arrived in May, she would know Carla's story was a hoax, that it might be a cruel joke played by Mary Beth or Nikki—Who knew where their lives had taken them? Years ago Gabrielle had seen occasional snippets in the European press about Nikki's philanthropy or Mary Beth's appearances at society events. But Gabrielle had not seen news of them since she'd married Stefano and distanced herself from the world.

Stefano.

By the time he and Rosa returned from Firenze, Gabrielle would be home, and they'd never know that she'd been gone.

She'd once again bargained with the postman for a ride to the village, where she found a taxi driver willing to go to Siena. In Siena she caught a commuter flight to Florence and stayed overnight until the morning flight to Zurich.

And now she sat in the waiting area of FirstBanc Internationale, her small suitcase at her feet, certain she looked like a Tuscan housewife and not at all like a countess, not at all like the heiress whose fortune was tucked in the bank, this bank.

She had no idea what the fortune was now worth. Several million, perhaps. More than a few. She'd learned that money had a way of accumulating if one did not spend it, if one hoarded it in a numbered account poised for the day when one would be abandoned and have to start over.

Tightening the ribbon on her hair, she crossed her

ankles and looked down at her feet. She wore the hand-tooled, black leather flats she'd had made in Florence on her honeymoon. They were still new: Today was only the second time she'd worn them. The first was on their last anniversary, when Stefano had taken her to Pisa for a grape harvest celebration.

A diminutive man approached. His rubber-soled shoes squish-squished on the shiny black tile floor. He wore diminutive wire-framed glasses perched over diminutive eyes. Would she care to follow him?

Gabrielle picked up her suitcase and made her way through the glass reception area down a silver-carpeted corridor lined on both sides with doors. At the third door on the left, the diminutive man stopped. He turned the handle and escorted her inside.

They sat at a square table, just Gabrielle and the man, who introduced himself as Mr. Jahn Hilger, a FirstBanc customer representative. She wondered if he would have called himself *Mister* if she hadn't had the remnants of her accent from the country of her birth.

"I would like to see the current status of my account," Gabrielle stated. Did she appear as nervous as she felt? And why on earth should she be nervous? This was her bank. This was her money. Why did she feel like a criminal?

"When did you receive your last statement?" he asked.

"I stopped my statements six years ago," she replied. An uncomfortable silence elapsed.

"And you have not checked your account in six years?" If he wondered why, he did not ask.

"No," she said so quietly she barely heard herself.

He shuffled some papers, then gave her instructions. She produced her identification, including her passport on which she was not the Countess Bonelli but Gabrielle

Atkinson-Olson. She had never changed her name.
There'd been no need, for she'd not planned to leave.

She signed her name three times for signature verifica-
tion. Mr. Jahn Hilger picked up the documents and left
the room.

Gabrielle folded her hands. She was not surprised to
find they were damp, her fingers wet with angst. It
sounded so bizarre to say she'd not checked her account
for six years, that she'd simply assumed the deposits were
made each month, electronically transferred from the
States, under Lester Markham's trustworthy tutelage,
with the proper taxes withheld, and the proper taxes
paid, all by Lester, of course, the man Aunt Margaret had
put in charge.

She had meant to check her balance once or twice, but
something had always come up, and communicating with
Zurich without Stefano's knowledge had been, well, the
truth was it had been easier not to try.

Even for Mr. Jahn Hilger, who might have seen and
heard more scenarios than even her vivid imagination
could conjure, her behavior must seem weird.

She chewed her lip. She didn't think he could pressure
her into giving a reason for her disinterest—surely that
was against Swiss bank privacy, one of the most attractive reasons why people were customers. If he asked, she
could always say she'd been out of the country, or that
she'd been imprisoned in a mental ward, where she just
might end up if he did not hurry.

The door opened. Mr. Jahn Hilger squish-squished to
the table and set a file in front of her. On top was a
standard-looking bank statement, with columns for deposits, interest, and withdrawals. And the balance.

Gabrielle followed the numbers with her finger. Working backward from the right, she checked the balance

column first. Silently, she gasped. Twenty-three million dollars. More than she'd expected. More than enough to have turned Castello di Bonelli into a successful, competitive vineyard. She pushed her guilt from Mr. Hilger's view and moved her finger to the left.

The withdrawal column was blank. As it should have been.

The interest column was full.

*Cha-ching, cha-ching, cha-ching.* The dollars had, indeed, accumulated. Interest on the income generated by the principal that might no longer be safe, secure, or even there.

Last came the deposit column. She started at the top and ran her finger down until she reached the last deposit. The date read April fourth. There had been no deposit in May.

She sucked in her breath and checked the other dates. Each month the deposit was made at or about the same time. The first week of the month, of every month except last month, and now this month, too.

Her head began to pound. Her eyesight became blurred. "How long does it take to post the numbers?" Could this be wrong? Had the deposits simply not yet been recorded?

"The date is entered as soon as the transaction is received. It's all done by computer. Mistakes rarely occur."

She tried to wet her lips, but there was no moisture left inside her mouth. "One more question, Mr. Hilger."

His small glasses slipped a little as he nodded.

"Is there any way information about me might have been given to anyone?"

His eyebrows raised above the eyeglass frames.

"Could someone here have given my current address to anyone...to the person who makes the monthly deposits, for instance?"

The spine of the man, small though it was, stiffened in defense. "I assure you, your FirstBanc records are totally confidential. No one is ever given information about you. No one. Ever."

He had made his point.

"Besides," he added, retrieving the file and scanning its contents, "it appears we don't have a record of your whereabouts at all. So no one could have been informed. Not even by mistake."

Gabrielle nodded. She took a copy of her statement, folded it neatly, and slipped it in her handbag, the black hand-tooled leather handbag that matched her still-new shoes.

"Thank you for your time," she said. As she picked up the suitcase and left the room, Gabrielle knew what her next step must be. Her money had stopped; but, worse, someone, somehow, had found her in Italy. She knew she must find out how and why before someone else showed up and unlocked the vault that contained her secrets, destroying her marriage and her life. There was, however, only one way to do that. Gabrielle must go back to America, the land that she'd once vowed to herself she'd never set foot in again.

# 9

Later, at the lighthouse, Nikki was too upset to work on the portraits. It could have been the rise in the AZT cost, the fall of her fortune, the stupidity of people, or the fact that she'd tried calling Mary Beth a half-dozen times and heard only the recorder.

Instead of painting, Nikki circled the living room waiting for Dee.

On lap seventeen, as she reached the window, she stopped and squinted outside. But the scrub oaks and cedars were already thick with this season's green leaves, so she could not quite see the big house to tell if Dee was in residence or Shauna and...What was his name? The boy Shauna was marrying?

She turned from the window and hated that her mind sometimes cheated her out of a thought. It was a grave reminder of Aunt Dorothy, Mary Beth's mother, and the state she must be in these days, a state of confusion, in and out, here one moment, gone the next. Nikki wondered, not for the first time, if Alzheimer's was hereditary.

She sat on the end of one of three curved love seats that arced the room. She smoothed her long brown skirt with the beaded bottom, the skirt she'd bought in Santa

Fe nearly fifteen years ago, the same summer she told Connor she wanted a divorce, that she could no longer live with a man who was such a...money-man, despite the fact that it was what her mother wanted, that she was risking the wrath of Margaret Atkinson and maybe her inheritance, too.

The inheritance meant nothing, of course, because Nikki had her trust fund, which was more than enough for her and enough to help others until now.

She detested the idea that she might have to call Connor.

The last time she'd seen him was over the holidays in New York. After the dinner with Dee that they'd had to "be civil," when he'd had too much wine and Nikki too much saki, Connor had asked Nikki to spend the night. Thank God, she'd said no. She'd thought about that on and off over the last few months. It made her remember Connor and the intimacy when they were young and their flesh was warm and their breathing together had been as natural as she had expected within the confines of marriage.

But what about now? If she contacted Connor, would she say no again? Could she say no this time when so many lives depended on her...and on her money? And did one thing really have anything to do with the other?

She eyed the telephone beside the sofa. *When I turn twenty-five and have my own trust fund,* her daughter had said. If Nikki's trust fund was gone, Dee's would be, too. Hundreds of pediatric AIDS patients would suffer if Nikki did nothing. Hundreds of sick kids and her one spoiled daughter.

She'd tried Mary Beth but only got voice mail. Yet still, Nikki couldn't bring herself to call the police. With a swallow of pride, she picked up the phone and dialed the number at the Upper East Side brownstone that she knew too well, for it had once been her home before she'd come to her senses. As the line rang on the other end, she wondered if Mack would think she was being foolish. But Mack didn't know, because she hadn't told him.

The phone rang again and Nikki sensed that the brownstone was vacant of animate things like people, like Connor.

A dignified voice on a dignified message kicked on. *We* were not available at the moment. *We* would be happy to return the call at *our* earliest convenience. The "we" and the "our" referred to Connor and Dee: He'd once told Nikki he no longer had patience for a relationship or love.

*Patience,* she thought. Was that what it took...

*Jason.* The name flashed into her mind. She hung up the phone and bolted upright. Jason was the name of Shauna's fiancé. She smiled, leaned back, and stretched her feet out on the round coffee table crafted of teak from South America, another souvenir from another journey, another time. Then Nikki put her hands behind her head and closed her eyes, safe in the knowledge that her memory was fine, thank you very much; at least, it was fine at this moment.

She awoke to the sound of a loud rumble outside, thunder, perhaps, or a low-flying plane. Nikki stirred quickly—too quickly—and winced with pain. She grabbed the back of her neck.

"Damn," she said, rubbing the muscle that snaked from her head to her shoulder. She looked down at her beaded brown skirt, aware it was morning and that she'd slept all night bent up on the sofa.

The rumble abruptly stopped. It was followed by a growl in her stomach, an unhappy message that she had missed dinner because Dee hadn't showed up.

Nikki stretched out her arm and rolled her shoulder. Her awakening senses warned her that today would be too demanding to allow herself to get stuck in the muck of her daughter's making.

Someone knocked on the door.

*Dee,* she thought, and pulled herself from the couch. In the six or eight feet from the couch to the door, Nikki played out the scenarios of how she would react.

*If that was punishment for China, it did not work,* she'd say.

Or, *Dinner? Gee, I didn't think it was definite.*

Or the truth: *I do not deserve a child as inconsiderate as you are.*

It was not Dee on the step. It was a man who held a shiny black helmet, a sharp contrast to his grayish-blond hair and the matching mustache that was neatly trimmed above his smile. His eyes were so green they looked liquid and jewellike, and his sturdy build seemed appropriate for the Harley-Davidson that stood in the driveway.

The only two questions Nikki had were what he was doing at her front door and why a small child was seated on his motorcycle, weighed down by a helmet that was not black like his, but metallic pink.

"Nikki Atkinson?"

She pulled her gaze from the child and nodded.

"Sam Oliver," he said, extending his hand. "Alice Sullivan sent us. She said you need volunteers at Camp4Kids."

Nikki looked back to the child, then to Sam Oliver. The strength of his hand lingered in her palm after he'd pulled it away. "Well," she said, "yes."

"Oh," he said, stepping aside. "That's my daughter, Molly. She's going to be one of your campers."

The little girl took off her helmet and shook out a clump of springy red curls. She neither smiled nor waved. Nikki stepped out the door and slowly approached the bike.

"Hello, Molly," she said. As she reached her she noticed the child's eyes were as green as her father's. She was fair-skinned and freckled, a beautiful child who could be one of Nikki's portraits. She would look marvelous painted against a rainbow of wildflowers. But, yes, there it was, the quick flash of distance in those magnificent green eyes, the flicker of fear, the knowing that, for her, life was precarious.

"Hello," Molly replied.

"Molly's six years old," her father said.

"How would you like to help?" Nikki asked, quelling her emotion. "Would you like to paint the dock down at the pond?" When Dee was five, she'd loved holding a fat paintbrush and smothering the docks and the fences and the salt-air-weathered cedar everywhere on the property with water repellent. When she was five, she'd even loved her mother.

"Molly's never painted," Sam answered for his daughter, "but I think we can give it a try. What do you say, Peanut?" He ruffled her curls and Nikki felt an ache as great for the parent as for the child.

"Sure," Molly replied. "I can do anything."

Except cure her illness, Nikki thought.


"I can't find the son of a bitch," Mary Beth snarled into the phone as if it were Nikki's fault that Lester and their money had both disappeared.

The morning had melted into afternoon. Looking out the window of the registration cottage, Nikki could see small, eager Molly, helping her father stain a dock, her little forehead crinkled in determined concentration. After trying all day, Nikki finally had reached Mary Beth.

"Enough, Mary Beth. We need to call the police."

"It's only a few weeks until the wedding. Surely we can wait that long."

"No." Nikki did not know the details of Alice's magical financial manipulation, but she knew that when it came to saving kids, every day counted.

"You don't understand, Nicole. I cannot—I *will* not—lose face among my friends."

*All six hundred of them?* Nikki so wanted to say, but knew better than to challenge Mary Beth when her social standing was at stake. She turned from the window. "When are you coming to the Vineyard?" she asked, hoping that, face to face, Mary Beth might be convinced of the importance of finding Lester before more time elapsed.

"I don't know. I'll be in touch."

Her cousin hung up abruptly, as if she'd been interrupted. Nikki set the phone down and decided to call the police. Screw the media, the wedding guests, and the fact her cousin would lose her precious face.


"I hate it when you sneak up on me," Mary Beth said to her husband, as she picked up a brass paperweight in the library and examined it as if she'd never seen it.

"Who was that on the phone?" he asked. "And what son of a bitch is it that you can't find?"

His tone was humorous, because, of course, he did not know. Good old charming yet utterly useless Eric. Perhaps a taste of reality might liven up his life.

"I've run into a tiny situation," she said, setting down the paperweight and crossing to the bookshelves.

"A situation? Oh, dear," he said, following close on her heels. "Did your manicurist leave town?"

There were times when Eric's shallow look at life was

refreshing and fun. This was not one of those times. The fifteen thousand dollars a month—times two, no, times three because it now was *next* month (the month of the wedding, oh, God!)—for her mother's care was important. More important than bubble wands (already on a credit card) or Eric's trip to Brazil in search of old money. She figured there was some irony in that last point, but she was too upset to consider it.

She kept her gaze fixed on the books, some rare, some otherwise. "Actually, it's a bit of a cash flow problem. You won't be going to Brazil."

She would not have been surprised if his cry had been audible. Mary Beth, after all, had never denied Eric money or status. It was part—a great part—of the success of their long-enduring marriage. He did not cry out, but he cleared his throat. "Excuse me?"

"I need the money back," she replied, then turned to see the stillness on his face. "I'm sorry," she added.

"I...I don't know if it's possible. Deposits have been made..."

"I need to pay Harriman House, Eric. I need you to get the money back." It would not cover one month, but might pacify Ms. Kendrick until after the wedding. Or until Lester showed up, whichever came first.

She frowned at herself. How was it that someone with her kind of money could wind up so freaking cash-poor? And how had it happened so damn fast?

"I don't understand," Eric said. "Where is your money?"

At least he said "your" money, not "our" money, as he'd sometimes done in the past. Still, it was not pleasant watching him squirm. "There's some sort of problem with the trust fund administrator."

"Markham?" Eric asked, because he'd made it a point to befriend Lester at the round of gallery openings. The man was, after all, critical to Eric's fiscal health and well-being.

Mary Beth nodded. "I didn't receive my check this month. His assistant came by and said he's left town. Gone. As is my trust fund."

There was an old song from her teenage private-school days, where the music stopped abruptly in the middle of the score, freezing everyone on the dance floor for a beat, maybe two, statues-in-waiting for the next move to be orchestrated. Mary Beth felt that way now. But when sound resumed, it was not musical, and neither she nor Eric was positioned for a dance.

"Jesus, Mary Beth. Haven't you called the damn cops?"

"You sound like my cousin."

"Nikki knows?"

"Her money's gone, too."

He hesitated half a second, then he laughed. "This is a joke, right?"

"No," she said.

"Call the cops."

"I can't."

"Why not?"

"Because of the wedding, Eric. What would our friends think?"

Unlike Nikki, Eric understood.


There were few modern conveniences Gabrielle and Stefano had allowed at Castello di Bonelli. Thankfully, a telephone answering machine was one.

"Hello, my darlings," Gabrielle said from a phone booth at the Boston airport. She'd waited until she arrived on Saturday night, because she'd feared if she called sooner she would have chickened out. "It's Mama. I hope your trip was wonderful, and now I've taken one of my own." She closed her eyes and leaned against the silver wall of the booth. "Everything is fine, but I had to make a trip to America to see my family."

Even as she said the words, she pictured Stefano frowning. When they'd met, she'd told him her parents were both gone, that she only had distant relatives somewhere in the States. She had never told him that her father had found her twice, and that the second time he'd begged her to listen but she would not.

Instead, she had told him to leave and never look for her again.

With any luck now, Gabrielle would find only her cousins; with any luck her father lived elsewhere. Maybe he even was dead.

She sensed someone standing beside her. She opened her eyes. A man waited for the phone. "I shall call soon," she said in quick Italian. "But do not worry! I love you both so very much." She'd added "ciao," in a voice that sounded a bit too cheerful even to her tired ears.

# 10

___

Opening Day. It could have been the Mets and the Yankees or the Giants and the Jets for the lively ruckus at Camp4Kids.

Nikki stood outside the long wooden building that housed the dining commons, supply room, and infirmary. She took a few deep breaths to temper the exhilarating mix of excitement and anxiety that was racing through her.

*It is true,* she told herself. *The camp is finally a reality.* Of the forty-two kids signed up for the first two weeks, there had been three cancellations. One did not want to leave home; two had been hospitalized with complications. Nikki tried to stop the disquiet inside her that said "complications" meant a child was in pain. It was a grim reminder that this was not a summer fun program for the Boys and Girls Club or the "Y." It also further justified her need to find Lester and get her money back.

Yesterday, she'd gone to the police.

She did not tell her friend, Sheriff Hugh Talbott, about the trust funds, only that a business associate was missing.

It wasn't that Hugh didn't want to help. "But this guy is a New Yorker, Nikki. We need the NYPD."

So Nikki had held her breath while Hugh called New

York. As she watched him dial the phone, she told herself over and over that this was the right thing to do. The fact that Connor hadn't been home when she'd called, Nikki decided, had been an omen. Going to her ex-husband was simply not an option. She could not return to that world where she never belonged, no matter how much her mother had demanded otherwise.

She stood on one foot, then the other, while Hugh spoke into the phone. He was discreetly vague. "A missing person... At least two weeks..." He nodded and said "Uh-huh," and "Yes," and made a few other noncommittal remarks while Nikki speculated about whether this would sever her ties with Mary Beth and whether she'd soon need to find a place to live as well.

Finally Hugh said "Thank you," and hung up. "They'll ask around. But if you really think something's wrong, you should go into the city and file a report in person."

Which, of course, had not been possible yesterday, or that day, either, because Camp4Kids was opening and her place was there. She'd said a silent curse that Mary Beth was so self-centered, then vowed to somehow get into New York before another week passed.

Across the campground now, Alice emerged from the registration cottage. With her hair tied back in a bright red bandanna and in her white T-shirt and jeans, she almost looked like a teenager. She scampered off the porch, waving at Nikki. "Crisis," she called. "We have no bus driver."

Nikki took another deep breath and briefly wondered how many more unexpected crises were ahead of them.

"He was fogged in last night at Woods Hole." Alice's words bubbled out in a rush as she reached Nikki. "He's on standby."

There was no need to say more. Like many of the

camp workers, their bus driver was a volunteer. Stuck off-island, he'd be lucky to get a slot for his vehicle by this afternoon. Their safeguard of Sunday-to-Sunday comings and goings had anticipated only the predictable chaos of tourists, not the surprises of Mother Nature.

Most of the kids, however, would arrive this morning. And most had arranged to be picked up at the ferry by the driver who was now stuck on the mainland.

"He can't fly?" Nikki asked. When the traffic got crazy or the ferries were grounded, Cape Air often added extra flights for the twenty-minute vault from Hyannis.

"That's not the problem. The boats are running now, but there's no room for his truck yet, and he needs it here for work tomorrow."

Vehicles and ferries. Too often their schedules did not coincide.

Nikki nodded. "Can't we find another driver?" Just then the rumble of a Harley-Davidson pulled into the lot. Nikki looked at Alice and smiled. She walked over to Sam Oliver.

"Mr. Oliver," she said, once he'd removed his helmet. "You've been such a big help to us already. But I have a question. Do you know how to drive a bus?"


Sooner or later she was going to have to go to the god-damn Vineyard, face her cousin Nikki, and face the last-minute frenzy of the clock that was ticking much too quickly toward this godforsaken wedding.

In the meantime, Mary Beth sat on the edge of her bed, a cache of jewelry spread across the ivory satin comforter, glittering up at her, mocking her for her thoughts.

*How much cash can I get for this stuff, and will it be enough to last through the wedding?*

She didn't dare go to the Vineyard until she could afford

to pay the florist and the tent people and the damn harpists who would not show up unless she met them and showed them exactly what and where everything would go and offered cash in hand, up front. Ungrateful islanders who didn't trust summer residents, never mind that it was the summer folks' money that enabled the rest of them to survive. Thank God she was bringing her own caterer over from the city.

Providing, of course, she could raise the airfare for him and his entourage.

"I've got your money."

Mary Beth blinked, then looked up at Eric, who stood in the doorway. At first she almost thought he meant that he'd found Lester, that overnight her husband had turned from a charming, boyish cad into her savior, her hero at long last. Silly her; she should have known better.

"The check for Brazil," he said, coming forward and dropping an envelope onto the pile of rocks on the bed. "You have no idea how uncomfortable it was."

She grabbed the envelope and looked inside, without mentioning that it might be a bit more uncomfortable to have her mother move back into the house.

"A thousand was nonrefundable," he said flatly.

"I can see that," she replied.

He folded his arms and acted as if he did not notice the jewelry or wonder at its display. "What are you going to do, Mary Beth? About the trust fund? I need to reschedule Brazil. And I'd planned to book Maui for golf. I need to know when I can get back to my life."

Looking over the diamonds and sapphires and emeralds and pearls, Mary Beth was not surprised at Eric's concern for himself. It was, she supposed, her fault. Though their vows had said "for richer or for poorer," she'd known from day one that Eric could not withstand "poorer," any more than he could withstand "sickness" over "health" which, in truth, was the real reason Dorothy had been shipped off to Harriman House, because that, too, had been *uncomfortable* for Eric. Mary Beth supposed that one day she might feel guilty about that, but right now, she was too tired.

"I might, however, have a solution," Eric said suddenly, his bright eyes brightening, the high cheekbones of his GQ looks looking higher and even more GQ. "Let's convince the kids they should elope."

She closed her eyes and tried to pretend she'd not heard what she had heard. "What?"

His hands grabbed her shoulders. "Mary Beth, think about it." Her eyes flew open and she was staring into his face that had somehow moved within inches of her own. "We'll save an absolute fortune," he continued, "and it won't be our fault! No one will know it wasn't simply a whim of two kids who didn't want all the fuss. They'll still get their gifts, and..." He stopped for a moment, his eyelids flashing up and down as he wrestled to think of the next phase of his solution.

"And you can go to Brazil after all," Mary Beth said, filling in the blank space of air. "And Maui. And any-fucking-where you think you'd like to go." She shook free from his grasp and stood up. "I can't believe this, even of you, Eric. You are the father of one daughter, and you would like to screw her out of the most important day of her life."

"It's only a wedding, Mary Beth. Chances are, they'll divorce anyway. Everyone does these days."

She snapped around. "How dare you."

He sighed and stepped toward her. "Look, darling, I'm really sorry, but you must be realistic. You can stop wasting so much time on this damn wedding and start to look for Lester before his trail is cold. Maybe you can even get all of your money back. And no one who matters will ever have to know what really happened."

"And what about Shauna?"

He laughed.

He *laughed,* for God's sake.

"If I thought for one minute this wedding was for Shauna, I might feel different." He spoke with a smile that did not hide his scorn. "But admit it, Mary Beth, it's just another of your grand parties, albeit dressed up in white tulle."

The knot that had formed somewhere in her stomach around the time she'd first brought out her jewels now began to bend and twist and shape itself into a ball. "Get out of this room," she hissed, "before I say something I cannot take back."

He stepped closer to her. She held up both her hands.

"Mary Beth," he said, "think about this. You'll see it's the only answer—"

"Get out," she repeated, closing her eyes again. "Just get the hell out of my face."


The old yellow school bus wasn't full-sized, but it sat a couple of dozen people. It had been donated by Ben Niles, who had used it to transport schoolkids to his Menemsha museum. He'd expanded his programs, so he needed "bigger busses," he'd said, "and a bigger tax write-off." Nikki had lived on the Vineyard long enough to know that a tax write-off was hardly Ben's incentive. He was simply one of the island good guys, without whom the camp would not have been possible.

On the side of the bus, Nikki painted a huge Camp4Kids logo. Alice hadn't thought it was a good idea.

"Not all our neighbors will like it," she'd warned.

But Nikki said screw them if they didn't like it, that most of the protestors weren't Vineyard natives but transplants from places like Boston and New York who seemed to want the island void of all things bad and ugly like reality and disease.

She sat behind Sam Oliver now as he steered the cumbersome ark down the rutty, narrow driveway. She'd decided it was easier to accompany him on his maiden voyage to the ferry than to give him a map and decent directions. She also decided she was glad she'd kept the logo painted on the bus, a badge of her commitment, a symbol of her dream. But when they reached the queue of island taxis and tour busses at the docks, she wondered if Alice had been right.

Standing on the pavement by the disembarkment ramp was a cluster of unhappy-looking people holding hand-painted signs.

IF YOU'RE SICK, STAY HOME, one sign read. It was carried by a woman wearing a yuppie straw hat.

Camp4Kids: FIND ANOTHER ISLAND. The sign held high by a middle-aged man depicted Nikki's camp logo. She wondered if she could sue for copyright infringement as well as gross annoyance.

There were other signs—six, seven, eight in all, enough to make the kids feel what she'd hoped to avoid: different, sick, and unwanted.

Sam shut off the engine.

"Stupid asses," she muttered. "Damn the stupid asses."

Sam nodded but did not say a word.

"I'm sorry, Sam," she said. "I'm sorry you have to see this."

"Ignorance," he said. "We live with it every day. It's not bad enough we have to live with Molly's AIDS, but we have to live with this crap, too."

"The kids will see them when they get off the ferry."

Sam opened the door. "No, they won't." He lumbered off the bus. Nikki followed quietly behind. He marched up to the sign bearers.

"Good morning," he said with a smile as broad and as fake as Nikki had ever seen. He reminded her of Mack when Mack so often intervened. "How you all doing this morning?"

He wove a path between them as if he owned the pier, his eyes fixed on the ferries that chugged across Vineyard Sound, one coming, one going, a sight that was common any time, any day, once winter had passed.

And then he stopped walking and turned back to the protestors. He reached into his pocket and drew out what appeared to be a wallet. He flipped it open and revealed a shiny silver badge. "Lieutenant Samuel Oliver," he proclaimed. "Detective with the New York City Police Department. On special assignment here on Martha's Vineyard."

The picketers did not say a word. Two, then three, lowered their signs.

"I suggest you take your opinions and get off this pier," Sam continued, "before I call out the local authorities."

They stared at him a minute, then looked to one another. Sam coolly replaced his badge into his pocket. By the time the big ferry pulled into the dock, the signs had been removed, the small crowd had been dispersed.

Nikki shook his hand with thanks. "I didn't know you were a police officer," she said, as they waited for their kids.

"One of New York's finest," he replied.

She smiled and turned toward the boat, wondering if good luck was finally moving her way.

\*   \*   \*

The rest of the day was filled with nonstop activity, chatter and clatter, asking and answering questions a dozen times or more. Shauna and Jason had come to help: Nikki was both surprised and pleased. Shauna spent the day with Alice handing out a registration packet and "goodie bag" to each of the kids; Jason hauled suitcases and duffel bags and helped everyone get settled in their cottages. Nikki tried to conceal her disappointment that Dee had left the island without seeing her again, without making an excuse about their missed dinner, without saying good-bye.

By early that evening, Nikki was exhausted. The counselors were holding a get-acquainted party at the dining commons; Sam Oliver had gone to the ferry for the last of the campers; and Nikki had sent the volunteers, including Alice, home for some well-deserved rest.

She was in the registration cottage, sorting through the files of the kids who had arrived. She did not dare put them away, because she feared she'd screw up Alice's system. And "system" was a word that Nikki had always avoided, like "organized" and "practical." The very words that had directed her mother's rigid, ordered life.

As she straightened the files into a stack, her eyes fell on the name of the child who'd been there first—Molly Oliver, Sam's daughter.

She did not have to look inside to remember the background information. Nikki and Alice had sorted through hundreds of applications to Camp4Kids. Every kid had a gut-wrenching story, every kid had a need for laughter, love, and fun. They had tried to select those who were most needy. Their final decision was based on the essays: "Why I want to come to camp." Nikki reached into Molly's file and withdrew the little girl's essay. It was printed like a letter to Santa Claus.

"Dear Nikki and Alice," the letter read. "My name is

Molly Oliver and I am 5 years old." She'd crossed out the "5" and made it into a "6."

"I want to come to Camp4Kids because I have AIDS. My Mommy did, too. I got mine from her. We were in a car accident before I was born, and the blood she got was tinted but nobody knew it."

Nikki pressed her hand to her mouth when she read that. She remembered how she and Alice felt when they'd first read it: *The blood she got was tinted.* Not tainted, but tinted. Perhaps a child's perception of blood that was sick and not the color it should be.

The letter continued. "I want to come and be with the other kids. Daddy says Mommy would want me to. When I was a year old Mommy got real sick. She died two years ago."

Nikki sat silently. She had not, until now, put a face to that letter, the face of the little girl with curly red hair with a father who'd arrived early and donated his time, not just because his child was sick, but because other children were sick, too. A father who was a New York City policeman. As soon as Sam returned tonight, she'd tell him about Lester.

"Nikki?" The voice startled her. Nikki looked up, and there he stood.

"Sam." She quickly slid Molly's essay back into the file, hoping she didn't look like that godawful cat who ate the big, fat bird of embarrassment.

"These are the last of our campers," he said, stepping inside with a round-faced girl who didn't have much hair. Beside Sam was a similar round-faced boy.

"Dennis and Debbie," Nikki said with a wide, welcoming grin, because their files were in front of her and because theirs, too, was a heartbreaking story, a brother and sister from inner-city Philadelphia whose mother was an addict. Debbie, however, was now clean of the virus.

They'd allowed her to come because she'd still been positive when the application had been sent by their caseworker and because, God, hadn't they been through enough?

She reached for the goodie bags—the crayons and coloring books and lightsticks and small toys—as Sam cleared his throat.

"There's someone else I picked up at the ferry, too," he said. "Someone you haven't seen for a while."

It couldn't be Dee, because she had left.

It wasn't Dee.

It was a woman who was pretty and slight and older than Dee. She wore black cotton cropped pants and a short white sweater. She carried a large black bag and a small gray suitcase.

"Nikki," the woman said, "I don't expect that you remember me."

No, Nikki did not.

The woman smiled a cautious smile. "It's me, Nikki. It's your cousin, Gabrielle."

# 11

It was impossible to tell whether Nikki was shocked or pleased or merely unmoved. Maybe Gabrielle could have judged her cousin's reaction better if she were not so nervous, so filled with trepidation that...that what? That Nikki would say "Who asked you to come here?" or "Go away. We got rid of you for a reason."

It was impossible to tell because Nikki simply stood there and stared, and Gabrielle stared back, wondering if she'd have known Nikki on the street or at the market, if she had not been told it was Nikki Atkinson in the flesh.

She was older, of course. Nearly thirty years had lightened her hair and loosened her jawline. Yet she had the blue eyes...they all had the blue eyes...

Nikki moved forward as if in slow motion. Gabrielle clutched her suitcase more tightly, not because she was afraid she'd drop it, but because it was something to hang onto, somewhere to deflect the tremor that had begun in her hand.

"Gabrielle," Nikki said. She was about a foot from her now. She reached up and rested her hand on Gabrielle's cheek. Gabrielle wondered if her skin felt as fiery to Nikki as it felt from the inside out.

"Gabrielle," she repeated. Then she took another step and put her arms around her and said "Gabrielle," again, as if it were the only word she knew.

Gabrielle let out her breath, let go of the suitcase, and hugged her in return, closing her eyes and feeling Nikki's warmth, the warmth of another human being who was connected to her, forever linked by a road map of DNA, whether either of them liked it or not.

When Nikki pulled away, her eyes were wet. With trembling hands—or were those Gabrielle's?—Nikki knitted Gabrielle's fingers through hers. "I can't believe it's you," she cried. "You are so lovely. You are so old!" She paused again and stared. "You look like your mother. You look so much like Rose."

Gabrielle smiled. "Yes," she replied, her voice small and quiet. And then it hit her: Nikki was surprised she was there. Didn't she know about Carla DiRoma or the demise of their trust funds? Should Gabrielle have left things alone?

Suddenly Nikki's expression turned somber. "Lester Markham," she said. "Is that why you're here?"

Gabrielle cast a glance to the doorway where Sam Oliver still stood. It seemed hours ago that the taxi driver at the docks had pointed to the Camp4Kids bus when Gabrielle had inquired for a ride to the Atkinson estate. "If you're looking for Nikki Atkinson," he'd said, "you'll find her at the camp." So she'd approached the bus, whose driver said to "hop aboard."

"Sam?" Nikki asked. "Would you please excuse us?"

Sam smiled. "Sure thing, ladies. I guess my work is done." With a wave, he left.

"We have so much to talk about," Nikki said as she touched Gabrielle's cheek again. "But first I need to get Dennis and Debbie settled, okay?"

In her excitement, Gabrielle had forgotten the two

children who stood off to one side. She quickly moved to an overstuffed chair and sat down, her mind and her heart and her feelings awhirl. Nikki knew about Lester. But she hadn't been expecting her... which must mean she hadn't been the one who'd sent Carla DiRoma; she hadn't been the one who'd known how to find her.

Gabrielle closed her eyes and felt the damp Vineyard air seep into her skin. Then she sank back on the seat and realized that she finally had come home.


They climbed into Nikki's VW—no longer a Beetle, but a Passat. Gabrielle buckled her seat belt and tried to act as if everything were wonderful, as if this were the homecoming of which she had dreamed for so long. She wished it were daylight so she could look out the window and see if she recognized anything—a street corner, a house, the curve of the shoreline.

"Tell me about your camp," she said. It was safer than asking about the future or the past.

Nikki nodded as if she understood. "Somewhere in the nineties, AIDS stopped being a disease and became an issue," Nikki began. "It grew to a crescendo, then I guess people grew tired of hearing about it. The benefits and marches dwindled off. But AIDS is still killing people. Kids. Innocent kids."

Gabrielle's mind was so full that though she heard Nikki, she could not absorb what her cousin was saying. Crescendo... tired... innocent kids. She'd been an innocent kid once. Was death by emotion still considered death if it wasn't accompanied by disease?

"I fund the camp with the income from my trust fund," Nikki continued. "Or I should say I *funded* it with my trust fund. I have no idea what I will do now that the money's gone."

"Without your money your camp will have to close?"

Nikki laughed. "The whole foundation will be defunct," she said, then smiled. "I named it The Rose Foundation, Gabrielle. In honor of your mother."

*The Rose Foundation.* Gabrielle closed her eyes. Nikki had named the foundation for the woman Gabrielle barely remembered from another world, another lifetime. Opening her eyes, she gazed out the window. Signs were vaguely familiar: Pennywise Path, Mariner's Way. She wondered why Nikki was being so kind. Was it out of guilt? She seemed genuinely happy to see her, and yet...

Nikki put her hand on Gabrielle's arm. "I'm sorry," she said, "I'm going on and on like an old fishwife. I haven't asked a damn thing about you. Are you still living in Europe? Have you had a happy life?"

Gabrielle smiled because smiling felt easy. Sitting here with Nikki, riding into Edgartown felt more easy than familiar, as if somewhere in a distant part of her mind, Nikki, this road, and this island had been there asleep, waiting, perhaps, for this night and this time. She thought she should feel angry, but she did not.

"I am happy," she said, and that had been the truth. "I am married to a wonderful man and I have a beautiful daughter, Rosa, who is five. We live in Italy. In Tuscany, where we work a small vineyard that's been in Stefano's family for generations." She did not tell her that Stefano was a count or that she was a countess. She did not say they were poor, except, of course, for the twenty-three million she had stashed in Zurich that she'd made damn sure the man she loved knew nothing about. She did not tell her, because it all seemed so...insane. Nearly as insane as the fact that she was back on the island, the place she'd once loved, then hated.

A green sign with white letters pointed left to

Edgartown Center, right to West Tisbury, Katama, and the airport. They turned right.

"What about you, Nikki? Are you married?"

"Past tense. And I have a nineteen-year-old daughter whom I love from a distance because when we're in the same room we often think of murder."

Gabrielle laughed.

"I'm not sure who I argue with more," Nikki continued. "My daughter or Mary Beth."

"Mary Beth." She said the name and tried to picture what her other cousin must look like. "How is she?"

"The same. Still trying to be her idea of perfect."

"Is she here?"

"Not yet, but any day now. Her daughter's getting married in a few weeks. Here."

The big black-shuttered white houses of Edgartown lined both sides of the street now. They were familiar; they had not changed in twenty-seven years or perhaps in three centuries.

Nikki turned to Gabrielle. "How long will you stay?" she asked quickly. "Will you stay for Shauna's wedding?"

No, she had not planned to stay a few weeks. She could not be gone that long without Rosa! And yet, until she knew more...

"We need to talk about our trust funds," Gabrielle said quietly. "And maybe, at some point, you can tell me why you all abandoned me."

The air between them shifted to a tenuous pause, a gulf that could create irrevocable damage.

"We'll talk," Nikki said softly.

"Well," Gabrielle replied, "I guess that's why I've come."

Nikki turned her head toward her. "For what it's worth," she said, "I'm really glad you're here."

Gabrielle's tears formed again. "Me, too."

Then the VW turned left into the driveway that was still too narrow and still made of dirt. The car bumped over ruts that had been there forever and dodged the scrub oaks that seemed to close in on them. They passed the caretaker's cottage, then came to the clearing. Even in the darkness, Gabrielle could see the outline of the house, the big house up ahead.

Suddenly Nikki stopped the car. "Here's where we get out."

Gabrielle was confused. "Not at the house?"

Nikki pointed to the right. "Home sweet home," she said.

Slowly, Gabrielle turned her head, though she already knew what she would see. It was the stalwart white pillar that looked out to sea, the setting for all of Gabrielle's nightmares, then and now.

"The lighthouse?" she asked. "You live in the lighthouse?" Her voice was small and without much breath behind it.

Nikki placed her hand on Gabrielle's shoulder. "It makes me feel close to her, Gabrielle. To your mother. She was a good person. The best of all the Atkinsons."

But Gabrielle kept staring at the image before her eyes and all she could remember was the horror and the pain.


Mack's red truck wasn't parked in front of the caretaker's cottage. Nikki stood at the window, peering through the light that rose just after dawn, wondering how soon she should tell him Gabrielle was there.

He had, no doubt, left for Chappaquiddick, where he greeted each day with a long walk on Cape Pogue among the cedar thickets and salt marshes and barrier beaches. He'd often told Nikki how he loved monitoring the deer tracks and the osprey nests.

"The mayflowers have all but gone," he'd said only last week, but added that the sanderlings still skipped along the surf's edge, feeding on tiny crustaceans and mollusks left there by the tide, their small white and brown bodies hurrying up the beach ahead of each breaking wave, as if they didn't know that summer had set in and that the tourists were infringing once again.

Mack detested summer and the assault that the season and its people brought upon the land. He was a gentle man who sought gentleness in life. Gentleness and peace.

As much as Gabrielle resembled Rose, she seemed to have much of Mack in her. Perhaps that was why when they arrived last night Gabrielle had said that she would talk better tomorrow, that all she wanted then was to go to sleep.

And now it was morning, and Nikki knew she should tell Mack, before he found out for himself. The risk, however, would be great and maybe, just maybe, Gabrielle would leave as quickly as she'd arrived and then it wouldn't matter.

Would it?


It was so hard not to cry when that was all that you wanted, when you ached from the waist down and the waist up and your guts and your heart and your head all felt as if they were going to explode at the very same time.

Of course, Mary Beth would not cry. Not even to her best friend, Roxanne, who was in the next shampoo stall as part of their regular, once-a-month appointments for highlighting and lunch. She would not cry because she was afraid that once she started she would never stop.

As the warm water trickled through her hair, Mary Beth wondered why she hadn't canceled lunch today. Roxanne would want to talk about the wedding and the what-to-wears and the who-will-be-theres. Mary Beth only wanted to talk about death and how soon it might come.

"All set," the shampoo girl said, interrupting her thoughts with a vigorous towel rub. "Are you having a trim?"

"No, just a blow-dry."

"Lori will be with you shortly."

The shampoo girl left and Mary Beth sat waiting for Lori, the blow-dry expert. She looked into the huge mirror and wondered why mirrors were the mainstay of the beauty salon decor. At the entrance and the exit, perhaps, they'd be appropriate as proof of the *Before* and the *After* of the hundreds of dollars dropped for the *During*. But why would any woman in her right mind want to sit and study her reflection while clad in a shapeless black smock, her face framed by foil packets or by thick, opaque color that leaked around her hairline? Why would any woman want to view herself in towel-dried hair that went this way and that?

"Ms. Atkinson?"

She blinked at the image that had come into the mirror, because in the beauty salon one looked at everyone and everything backwards, right to left. It was not Lori, the blow-dry girl. It was a young woman in black spandex carrying a telephone.

"You have a call," the face in the mirror said and handed over a cordless that appeared in the glass as well as on Mary Beth's lap. She hadn't brought her cell phone today because it did not fit inside her teeny Gucci purse, but she had forwarded her calls in case of an emergency, which, as the wedding loomed closer, seemed inevitable.

She would have preferred to go to a desert island with no phone, fax, or mail, e-mail or otherwise.

*Damn Lester Markham for ruining what should have been the most fun time of her life.*

She picked up the phone and reminded herself that now she'd have to tip the phone-bearer as well as the shampoo girl and the blow-dry girl in addition to Richardo, the highlighting king.

"Mary Beth Atkinson?" She recognized the voice but could not put it with a face. "This is Carla DiRoma. Remember me?"

She quickly turned from the mirror, as if she could not even let her reflection know who was on the phone. Then she brightened. Carla DiRoma! Perhaps Lester had returned!

"Carla!" she said, with much more animation than she had intended. "I hope you have good news."

The line was silent a moment and Mary Beth wondered if Carla was still there.

"Well," the thick Bronx accent finally replied, "I don't know if you'd call it 'news,' but I have something that might help your search."

*Search.* The word meant that Carla had not found Lester, that the money was still gone. She turned back to the mirror and restored her Atkinson demeanor. "What exactly is that supposed to mean?"

The Bronx voice stammered. "Could...could I meet you somewhere? There are some things I could give you..."

Mary Beth closed her eyes. "I don't need anything from you, I assure you, Ms. DiRoma."

"But I have pictures. I didn't think of it until after the police had left...."

Mary Beth sat sharply upright as if she'd just learned Tiffany's was having a sale. "Police? What *police*?" Her eyes quickly flashed around to see if anyone had heard above the running water and blow-dryers. No one—not even Roxanne—appeared. She lowered her mouth to the phone. *"What are you talking about?"*

Carla hesitated again, then said, "The police came to my home this morning. They asked about Lester. They said he'd been reported missing by someone on Martha's Vineyard."

Mary Beth leapt from her chair. *"What the fuck are you talking about?"* She screamed this time; three faces popped around the wall and into her booth: Roxie's, of course, and two shampoo girls.

"I've kept clippings of Lester's pictures...you know, from the newspapers and magazines...from charity balls and gallery openings over the years. You're in some, too. What a coincidence, huh?"

"Where are they?" she asked, wrestling her blood pressure, clenching her jaw, and trying to act as if her entire fucking world was not collapsing all around her right there at the fucking hair salon where everyone would know.

"I have them. I told you. I forgot to give them to the police."

Mary Beth began ripping the foil packets off her newly highlighted hair. "Give me your address. I'll be there right away." She waved at a shampoo girl for a piece of paper and a pen. Carla gave her the address. Indeed, it was in the Bronx.

She quickly disconnected the phone. "Somebody shampoo me and get me the hell out of here!"

Two more girls appeared as if by David Copperfield, all eager and smiling because Mary Beth was known to give a good tip.

"What's going on?" Roxie's voice called out as the back of Mary Beth's head went under water.

"Just some wedding stuff in need of fast attention."

"Does this mean lunch is off?"

Mary Beth steadied her voice. "Sorry, darling, but first things must come first," she said, all the while knowing that missing lunch with Roxanne was probably just as well, because she thought that today was her turn to buy, and what if her VISA was already maxed out?

Gabrielle had slept through the night and most of the morning. She'd been so tired that she'd fallen fast asleep, despite being in the lighthouse, the building that was no longer an abandoned, padlocked shell, but a place Nikki had turned into a cozy home.

Nikki had left a note. "Gone to the camp," it read. "I'll be back for lunch. Make yourself at home."

To Gabrielle, making herself at home on the Vineyard meant a walk along the shore, which is what she did now, treading carefully between sand and stone. She thought about the many picnics they'd once had on the beach and about the walks to Chappaquiddick when the tide was out and the sandbar was intact and they were safely able to avoid the rock jetty. Turning to look back at the wide apron of lawn that stretched up to the house, she could almost picture her mother and father in Adirondack chairs. She could almost feel as if she were on a blanket on the ground beside them, wishing that she were as old as Nikki and Mary Beth and had boyfriends and pretty clothes and someone her own age to talk to.

It was so hard to believe that Nikki and Mary Beth barely spoke anymore. They had been so close once, hadn't they? Or was that just another of Gabrielle's fantasies, like the one that her mother had been so blissfully happy and in love with her father? Or that life had been magical before her mother died?

There had even been a time when she'd imagined everyone had been wrong, that her mother was alive after all. Deceit was an art form Gabrielle had mastered early.

She looked toward the horizon where the fishing boats pushed forward, guided by hardworking islanders, honest people. People whose lives were more simple than hers, people who would not use their skills to deceive their spouse and their child, who did not need to feel guilty for hoarding twenty-three million dollars while her cousin, Nikki, had used up her last dollar trying to help others, *children,* children like her Rosa, but who were very, very sick.

She squinted against the sun. *Oh, God,* she realized. What had she done with her life?

And how would things have been different if she'd been allowed to stay there?

She would not have Rosa; she would not have Stefano.

Shaking her head, she knew she would not stay long. Only long enough to learn what had happened to Lester and the trust funds, long enough to be certain she'd be safe back in Italy, that there would be no more surprise visitors who might expose her secrets and shatter her idyllic life.

No, she would not stay long. Quickly Gabrielle turned up a path that zigzagged between the dunes. When she reached the lighthouse she realized she'd found her way back automatically, as if the memory of the path had remained in her girlhood mind. Memories were like that, she supposed. Even the ones she'd tried hard to forget.

With a sad sigh, she opened the door and went inside. Nikki had returned: She stood in the kitchen, on the telephone.

# 12

I can't believe you called the fucking cops!"

Carla shuffled through the clippings and old photos of Lester Markham, trying to block out Mary Beth, who was standing right there in Carla's kitchen screaming into the telephone at her cousin, Nikki, as if she were a truck driver and not an Atkinson.

Carla was glad Theresa was not alive to witness this dreadful scene, or she'd be saying more Hail Marys than the Pope.

She supposed it was all her fault. She'd been sitting at the table drinking coffee, trying to decide if she'd make new kitchen curtains. The past weeks had been difficult. Her son, Vincent, who was out west fighting fires, had called to say he loved California and he planned to stay. His brother, Donnie, then said that he'd like to join him, and Carla had exploded because she hadn't worked her butt off to put him through junior college to get an associate's degree as a graphic designer so he'd end up a fireman. The truth was, she wanted her sons safe, though she knew that was selfish.

Anyway, her argument didn't work; Donnie had persisted with rebuttal accusations that she wouldn't let him grow up, which she denied, but what else could she do? Besides, with her mother gone, if both boys were out west, how could she be alone?

She'd long since accepted that there'd be no other man who would come into her life. There had been three in all: Carlo Bonginni, the boy next door who'd felt her up when she was just sixteen; her rat-bastard ex-husband whose name she refused to acknowledge, even to herself; and Lester, the one she'd loved in secret, the one she'd loved the most.

So she was sitting drinking coffee and thinking about kitchen curtains because to think about her empty life hurt way too much, especially after the police had come by and asked about Lester in a mechanical way, like he'd never been a person but was merely a statistic, a missing person in a city where "missing" meant too many things and none of them good.

She hadn't thought of it then, but she thought of it later: her collection of pictures, her special box of photos just of him.

Carla had begun saving them years ago, each time Lester's face appeared in newsprint or in one of those glossy magazines. If he were standing beside some woman, sometimes she'd cut the woman's face out and insert a picture of her own, pretending she was the one wearing the red satin ball gown, that she was Baroness von Friedberg from Switzerland or London's Dame Esther Louden or whomever he'd escorted to the glorious event.

She wouldn't show Mary Beth those pictures, of course. But surely she could part with a few that might help the police in their search for Lester, as long as they were searching at black tie, photographed affairs.

*"I don't know when I'm coming!"* Mary Beth was still screaming like in the olden days when long distance phone lines were not much more than static. *"Maybe*

*tomorrow. There are only two weeks left until the wedding, in case you forgot.*" She slammed down the receiver, huffed a small noise, then looked at Carla as if she'd forgotten who Carla was or that she'd been standing in Carla's kitchen making such a ruckus.

"*Well?*" she commanded Carla, as if Carla knew what that was supposed to mean. Then Mary Beth took a huge breath, closed her Atkinson eyes, and said in a more normal tone, "Well, what did the cops say?"

Carla shook her head. "They said they had a call about a missing person. I told them I didn't know where Lester went."

"What about the money? Did you tell them about the money?"

"No. I figured that was your business, Mary Beth. I didn't think it was mine." She did not mention that she'd not wanted the police to think Lester was a criminal.

The Atkinson eyes opened and Mary Beth sighed, and Carla figured that at least she'd done one thing right. "My cousin found a guy who's a New York police detective who might do some investigating on the side. Will you come to the Vineyard with me tomorrow? He wants to question you."

"Martha's Vineyard?" Good Lord, now she'd have been in Italy and on Martha's Vineyard, too, where former President Bill Clinton went back when he was in office. "Well, yes, sure, I guess. How long will we be there?"

Mary Beth slung a small purse around her shoulder. "I don't know. A couple of days. I have to make some last-minute wedding arrangements while we're there." As an afterthought she added, "Bring the pictures of Lester. I don't need to see them now. My driver will pick you up at two o'clock tomorrow." She headed for the back door, then stopped and turned around. "While I think of it, you wouldn't happen to know where I might sell some jewelry? Somewhere... discreet?"

Carla shrugged. "My brother Marcus knows a guy with a pawnshop on the West Side."

"My things aren't cheap."

"Neither is Marcus's friend." Carla scrawled the name of the pawnshop on the top sheet of the magnetic memo pad that was stuck on the refrigerator. She tore off the paper and gave it to Mary Beth, more concerned about what she'd wear to Martha's Vineyard than about the fact that Mary Beth Atkinson wanted to sell the family jewels, and that she'd asked Carla for help.


"God help us, she'll be here tomorrow," Nikki said to Gabrielle after she'd hung up from talking to Mary Beth. "She's upset because I told the sheriff and he called New York, and the police went to Carla DiRoma with questions about Lester. Mary Beth is paranoid that her friends will find out."

"What did you tell her about a detective?"

Nikki shrugged. "Sam Oliver—the one who drove the bus that brought you from the ferry—he's the father of one of our campers. He's also a police detective. New York City."

"Can he find Lester?"

"I haven't asked him yet."

"But you told Mary Beth..."

"This wedding has her more on edge than usual. If she thinks we can find Lester without it being made public, maybe she'll slow down and relax and not make us all crazy."

"So you think he'll help."

"I have no idea."

"So you told Mary Beth just to help her feel better. And I was beginning to think you didn't care about her at all."

"Of course I do," Nikki said with a smile. "She's like you, Gabrielle. She's family."

Gabrielle nodded and poured a glass of iced tea.

Then Nikki said Sam was supposed to leave today, so she'd better hurry back to camp and try and find him. She asked if Gabrielle wanted to go with her.

Gabrielle said no, thanks, but did not know why.

Nikki didn't know how to ask Sam for help—he had done so much already.

Back at Camp4Kids she found him playing third base.

"The team is shorthanded," he said with a laugh, so Nikki patiently waited until the inning was over. Then she convinced him to walk down to the pond.

"Moonlighting," she blurted out, because she decided she had nothing to lose. "Do you ever do it? Private things?"

Sam picked up a stick and etched it through the sand. "No. Can't afford to."

She tried not to be disappointed so quickly. "Couldn't you make more money?"

"Sure. But it's not dependable."

"What if it were just one job... for me?" She did not know how much she should tell him. Though he seemed trustworthy, she still didn't know him. In the back of her mind she imagined Mack would warn her to be cautious, if he knew the story, which he did not.

Sam stopped and seem to consider her question. "I wouldn't have time now, Nikki. I'm putting in all the overtime I can get."

"If you did a job for me, you wouldn't need overtime." Even while she said it, she wondered how she'd pay him.

But Sam was shaking his head. "I finally finished my master's degree, so I'm taking the captain's exam in the fall. I don't want to jeopardize my standing on the force." He looked away from Nikki. "You know that all of Molly's medical expenses aren't covered by insurance."

Yes, Nikki knew. She also knew that without The Rose Foundation, Sam's financial responsibility would be multiplied.

They walked alongside the cattails and past the cove, where a pair of long-throated white swans drifted in peace.

"Did you know that I fund The Rose Foundation with my trust fund?" she asked with a silent hope that Mack would approve of what she was revealing if he knew that the stakes were so high.

Sam shook his head. "I know you're an Atkinson," he said with a laugh, "but I never thought about where the money came from. I guess I figured you raised it from other rich folks like you."

"No," she replied. "It's my money. Or rather, it was. Let's sit down," she added, motioning to an overturned canoe on the beach. Then she told him everything about Grandfather Atkinson, about Aunt Rose's accident, and about Carla DiRoma's appearance at Nikki's door. And at Mary Beth's door. And at Gabrielle's, on the other side of the ocean. She did not tell him about Mack, or the further complications that might arise.

Sam picked up a stick and drew a couple of lines in the sand. "And you don't want to go to the police?"

"I did," Nikki replied. "Well, I asked Hugh Talbott. He's the county sheriff and a good friend. He made a few phone calls, to no avail."

"Why not go into the city? Doesn't Mary Beth live there?"

"We tried. But I didn't want to give details." It was true, after all, that the world knew the Atkinsons, like they knew the Rockefellers and the Vanderbilts. Nikki slid out of her sandals and let the warm summer sand sift through her toes. "We each have our reasons for not wanting to go public, Sam. The bottom line is publicity. The media would love a story like this, wouldn't they? The three Atkinson Enterprises heiresses forced into poverty at middle age?" She did not mention Shauna's wedding, or the fact that Mary Beth would suffer social devastation if her six hundred friends learned of her financial demise.

"It would be gossip for a few days," she continued. "Front page on the tabloids. Then, God help us, someone would write a book. In the meantime, our lives would be turned upside down. And The Rose Foundation...well, we can weather the storm for a little while, but down the road..."

"Yeah," Sam replied. "I understand."

"We could keep Molly in camp all summer if you'd like. Or for as long as it would take you to find Lester." Nikki's eyes moved to the swans. She remembered last fall when she'd come to scout the abandoned campground, to see if she could make it work for the kids. The swans were there then, drifting through the reeds, moving with grace and dignity. Time had not seemed to alter their lives. She wondered if they'd had babies, and if those babies had lived through the unfair diseases that nature often wrought on her unsuspecting young.

"I have some time coming," Sam said, "some personal days. I planned to save them for..." He followed her gaze over toward the swans.

*For Molly,* Nikki knew he was going to say, but he did not.

"I guess this is even bigger than my little girl."

"We'll pay you," Nikki repeated, and she thought of her paintings, the portraits of the kids that needed to be finished. Maybe she could get more orders soon. And Gabrielle and her husband owned a vineyard in Italy, so they must have some money, and Mary Beth must have a way she could contribute.

"I'll need to start with that woman," he said. "The one who worked for him."

"Carla DiRoma," Nikki said. "I thought you might want to. She'll be here tomorrow with Mary Beth."

Sam nodded, then stood up. "Well, Ms. Atkinson, you've got my Molly and now it looks like you've got me, too. Detective Sam Oliver, at your humble service."

She'd gone back to bed, but could no longer sleep. Gabrielle sat in the lighthouse guest room, a patchwork quilt around her, and wondered why she simply didn't leave.

Did it matter to her if they ever found Lester?

No. She had more money now than she would ever need. And Mary Beth apparently didn't know that she was there; Nikki did not seem to know enough about her to blackmail her with her past. If Gabrielle said "Don't be in touch," she thought Nikki would respect that.

She could return to Italy, tell another half-truth, and life could go on as before.

So why was she still there?

Staring out the small window at the sand and sea and the rock jetty, her answer finally came: This was her chance for closure, to clear the clouded memories, if she had the courage.

"It's better this way," Aunt Margaret had said when she'd sent her off to England. "You'll make new friends."

Friends? Yes, but Gabrielle could not, did not, make a new mother. Instead, at seven years old, she quickly blended in at school so no one would know that she was different. She made no time for self-pity; she made no time for loneliness. She made herself go on as if nothing special had happened, because nothing had, had it?

Gabrielle had not let herself remember the image of her mother lying on the rocks. But five years later, on a school trip to Dover, she saw the surf and cliffs and a lighthouse and suddenly there was the memory, crashing toward her like a runaway tidal wave.

She had screamed. She had trembled so hard she thought for sure she'd shake the ground. And just before she passed out, she remembered feeling overcome by pain and fear and overwhelming shame.

At first, Gabrielle had tried to make herself believe her mother was a tragic heroine, who had to die in order to keep a dark family secret, to protect the ones she loved, especially her daughter, especially Gabrielle.

It wasn't long before she knew it had been her father's fault.

"He should not have let her go off alone," Aunt Margaret said. "He was irresponsible. Your mother was fragile. He might as well have killed her."

After the incident at Dover, she had written to Aunt Margaret and asked if she could go home for the summer, go back to the Vineyard. But Aunt Margaret said England was her home now: Her cousins were married and too busy for her; her father had disappeared as well.

For a while Gabrielle tried to find out where he'd gone, but her letters to Nikki and Mary Beth were never answered.

Each year, however, on Gabrielle's birthday, a secret

visitor arrived in a Bentley and took her away for a week. The visitor—her Aunt Dorothy—was usually tipsy, but always brought a bounty of sweets, and they went into London to the ballet and the theater and Harrods because it was such fun. They stayed out late at Piccadilly and Covent Gardens, bought silly paintings and hats and souvenirs, and Gabrielle had to promise never to tell a soul, that this was their secret, between Aunt Dorothy and her.

Once she tried to ask her about Daddy, but her aunt said to let sleeping dogs lie.

When Gabrielle turned eighteen, it was not Aunt Dorothy who came; it was him. Even from a distance, she'd known it was him as he walked up the stone walk toward the dormitory that had been her home for eleven years. The closer he came, the colder she got, and by the time he reached the stairs, she stared into his eyes without saying a word, then went inside before her heart broke in two right there on the steps.

Seeing him in person came as such a shock that all she could hear was Aunt Margaret saying that it was his fault.

Two days later, Gabrielle moved to London to elude him. Six years later he turned up in Paris to say Aunt Margaret was dead. That's when she told him to leave her alone once and for all.

A powerboat sped by now, a parasail riding on its wind, watercolors against the sky, evidence that life went on, a reminder that the ache of tragedy was not meant to last forever.

She dropped her gaze to her small gray suitcase that sat open on the floor. She had not planned to stay, but if she did, she'd need to go to town and buy a few more clothes.

But before that, she must call home. She must hear the voices of Stefano and of Rosa; she must reassure herself that somewhere she was loved.

*    *    *

It was nine o'clock in Tuscany, time enough for Stefano to have finished work for the day. Gabrielle held her breath and placed the call, not knowing where to begin, but hoping the right words would come, that Stefano would not be angry or ask her too many questions.

The phone rang quickly on the other end, as if she'd called Vineyard Haven, across the island, not across the sea.

She was not prepared for that, nor was she prepared to hear a woman answer.

For half a second Gabrielle thought she'd dialed incorrectly.

"*Pronto,*" the woman repeated.

"I'm looking for Stefano," she said in case something was wrong, in case this really was the villa and someone else was there.

"He is on the hillside," the woman said in fluid, smooth Italian, a pure, native tongue.

The sensation that rolled through Gabrielle was like being on an ocean liner in a brewing storm. "This is the Countess Bonelli," she said. "Who is this?"

There was a pause, which could have been a transatlantic thing, though Gabrielle doubted it.

"It is Angelina, Gabrielle. I am making supper for the children. Rosa and Cesare. While the men are on the hillside."

She did not want to picture the woman—*that* woman—in her kitchen, standing at her counter, using her utensils and her plates. She closed her eyes. "It is late," she said. "They are still working?"

"They are covering the new vines. It has been raining for two days."

The ship inside her pitched and swayed. Rain? For two days?

"I shall tell your husband that you called. Is there any other message?"

She leaned against the small stove inside the lighthouse, trying to regain the balance that she'd lost, the composure she'd once felt before she'd realized that the woman who once loved her husband might have moved into her house. "Rosa," she said. "May I speak to Rosa?" She braced herself as if the answer would be, "No. I will not let you speak with your daughter. You left her, now you must suffer."

Instead, Angelina said, "She isn't here. She and Cesare are helping Enzio in the barn."

"She's only five!" Gabrielle blurted out. "How can she help?"

Silence came again.

"You know that when it rains, we all must do our part," Angelina replied.

Without a word, without a hint, huge tears spilled down Gabrielle's cheeks. She did not say she'd call back later. She did not want to call at midnight and hear Angelina's voice again. She did not want to know if the woman had gone home or if she'd stayed there at the villa. There was only so much sickness she could feel in just one day.

# 13

Mary Beth had never thought she would venture to the underbelly of downtown, no matter that it was broad daylight and there were cops on every corner.

Then again, she hadn't had to sell her jewelry every day.

It was easier than she'd expected, to pick out which things she could do without, which would not be missed by the wedding guests. She could not, of course, go back to Van Cleef or Tiffany's or the other places where her trinkets had come from; she could not even visit a prominent estate jeweler: Word would spread too quickly that Mary Beth was broke.

Broke!

What a dreadful, startling word that she'd never thought would be associated with an Atkinson, let alone her.

She tried to shake off the feared whispers of her many friends:

*Mary Beth sold her diamonds?*
*Hmm.*
Nod.
*Tut-tut.*

No, there would be no tut-tutting about her. Not as long as she could keep up appearances.

The cab finally arrived at the address Carla had given her. Mary Beth quickly got out and tried not to look left or right but simply moved straight ahead toward the shop.

It was, of course, locked with a heavy iron gate. So much for retailing on the poor side of town.

A buzzer sounded.

"I need to sell some things," she said into a small speaker on the wall. "Jewelry," she added.

There was nothing for a moment, then the sound of several locks being unbolted, followed by the creak of a door as it slowly opened.

She tipped her regal head back. *Act as if it's Tiffany's,* she decided. *Act as if you belong here because here you are respected.*

On stiletto heels she marched past the man and went into the shop as if indeed, she belonged there, which of course, she did not, at least, she had not, not until Lester Markham had up and flown the coop.

"I have jewelry," she repeated. "Good jewelry."

The man moved behind a counter of dusty glass cases filled with gaudy costume jewelry and worthless watches and a variety of knives, kitchen and otherwise. Yet he was well groomed, with sandy blond hair and a Ralph Lauren shirt. He did not look like her expectation of a seedy pawnshop owner; perhaps this was not pulp fiction after all.

"Good afternoon," he said.

She resisted saying "Carla sent me," and instead placed her large bag on the glass. "I have a few things. I was told you can help me."

He nodded. "What kind of things?"

"Nice pieces. Originals."

He elevated his eyebrows and motioned to the bag.
"In there?"

"Yes," she replied, but did not yet open the bag, as if
she were waiting for another solution to drop from the
sky, like Lester Markham, who would suddenly walk
through the door.

When Lester didn't show, Mary Beth cleared her throat.
"Yes," she said. "Well, I suppose you'd like to see them."

He folded his arms across his Ralph Lauren chest.

She opened the bag. She reached inside and felt the
soft touch of velvet, the warmth of a case that was long
and narrow. She drew in a breath and slowly removed the
case, trying not to think that this contained the diamond
necklace she'd worn to the Kennedy Center four years
ago when they'd been guests of the President—the President!—as a thank-you for her generous check to the national campaign against homelessness, a favorite charity
of the first lady's. It was one of the few times Mary Beth
had been quite so "generous," but she'd been dying to go
to the Kennedy Center as a coveted, much-photographed
guest.

The necklace had been divine with her black crepe de
chine gown, Versace or Armani, she couldn't remember
which. As she opened the case and her eyes fell on the
glitter, she took solace in the fact that diamonds alone
were rather passé now, having bowed to subservience as
mere accents for rubies, sapphires, even for pearls. Surely
by the time they came back into style Lester would return
and this nightmare would be over.

Mr. Whatever-his-name-was (he'd not introduced himself) picked up an eyepiece and began to examine *the
goods,* her goods. He uttered no uh-huhs or uh-uhs, just
examined with great patience each nook and each cranny
as if he were studying the Shroud of Turin.

After what seemed like an hour but maybe was a

minute, he raised his head and announced, "Eighteen hundred."

She tried to keep her chin from dropping to the floor, or at least to her chest, where a strange, tightening sensation was in progress. "That's absurd." She wished she could remember how much the necklace had cost, but money had never mattered so she'd not paid attention. It must have at least been five figures, or she would not have bought it in the first place.

He handed her back the loot. "Sorry," he replied. "But diamonds are passé."

He was so smart.

He started toward his back room, in a well-practiced business tactic, as if he knew about her mother's needs and her daughter's wedding and her husband's distress.

She bit her tongue and took the bait because right now she had no choice. "I have other pieces," she said. "Gold. Silver."

He turned back. "Let's have a look."

For the next thirty minutes, he had "a look." Then he offered twenty-one thousand, total.

"Twenty-five," she argued against her better judgment, which knew the true value was well over two hundred thousand.

"Split the difference. Twenty-three."

Twenty-three was better than nothing. It would pay one month for her mother and give Mary Beth some cash to take to the Vineyard and please the harpists and the tent people and God only knew who else. And it wasn't as if she'd sold everything, or even anything she really liked.

Besides, this debacle couldn't go on forever. Maybe it was just as well that Nikki had hired help.

\*   \*   \*

It was hard to remember how long it took to get from the estate to the center of Edgartown. Gabrielle had walked it many times with Nikki or Mary Beth and remembered stopping often, but she didn't think it was from being tired. They'd stop to feed the seagulls, to sneak through people's gardens, to upset the croquet wickets that had flourished in the seventies when summer people struggled to reinstate propriety amid the hippies who were trying to claim their land.

*Hippies.* She'd loved that word, Gabrielle remembered as she ambled out the driveway and went up toward the road. She'd first heard Aunt Margaret use it, the woman who'd had little patience with anyone, let alone those who did not seem to want to *work for a damn living,* as she'd proclaimed.

At Edgartown Bay Road Gabrielle turned right.

Just then a red pickup truck came up behind her and clamored out the drive. She quickly stepped into the shoulder to avoid getting hit. The truck slowed as if to check that she was all right, then revved off down the street, moving away as quickly as it had come upon her.

She brushed the dust from her left arm. A workman, she assumed. Probably the gardener. A hired hand at the estate, maybe someone making ready for the grand, gala wedding. She wondered if he would have guessed that she was one of them.

Turning the corner, Gabrielle was greeted by the un-shaded brilliance of the sun. She squinted and wished she'd worn sunglasses. Then again, she realized she hadn't packed them: In Tuscany she rarely had need for such accoutrements.

Tuscany.

With every step toward Edgartown, the hurt re-sounded.

If she had never gone to Zurich, Angelina would not be in her house, tending to her daughter, and doing God-knew-what with or to her husband.

If she had never had a secret, she would not have had to go to Zurich.

If Stefano had not married her, the crop of grapes would be abundant, the vineyard would be successful.

She walked and wondered which of these things were her responsibility and which were not. Yet one image that would not leave her mind was the face of little Rosa, her beautiful, small daughter.

She was thinking these things as a VW pulled alongside her. "Gabrielle!" shouted Nikki. "Where on earth are you going?"

Gabrielle shrugged. "Into town. To shop for clothes."

Nikki laughed. "That's almost five miles. Get in the car."

"Five miles?" Gabrielle asked and climbed in. "I didn't remember it was that far."

"We were younger. Even me," she said, and pulled back onto the road.

"Why aren't you at camp?"

Nikki cast her a glance. "I was worried about you. I was going to say that I forgot something, but I try to avoid lying. I'm not good at it."

"Not like Mary Beth," Gabrielle said suddenly, then wondered why. "Good grief, why did I say that?"

"Because Mary Beth always stretched the truth to her advantage. Remember when my mother was furious over the hydrangea bushes? Mary Beth refused to admit she'd cut them down. Chopped them, was more like it."

Gabrielle shook her head. "No, I don't remember." She wished she could remember more.

Settling onto the seat, she realized it was nice that Nikki

had worried about her; it was nice to be the recipient of a maternal gesture. Gabrielle smiled. "Speaking of hydrangea," she said, "a gardener was at the house today. They'll probably be preparing for the wedding soon."

Turning onto Katama Road, Nikki shrugged. "Who knows. I'm just going to try and stay out of our dear cousin's way." She squinted a bit and pulled down the visor. "That's odd, though. The gardeners were just here yesterday. She's probably spending the fortune she no longer has."

"Maybe it wasn't a gardener. But whoever it was almost ran me over in his red pickup truck."

Nikki adjusted the air-conditioning. "A red pickup?"

"Yes. Do you know who it was?"

Nikki fiddled with the visor, though the sun had drifted behind a cloud. "Nope," she replied. "I have no idea."

If Nikki hadn't said she tried to avoid lying, Gabrielle would have bet she'd done just that.


The five miles into Edgartown seemed like fifty after Gabrielle had said she'd seen the truck. Nikki had not known what to say or how.

She could have told her.

She should have told her.

She should have simply said that Mack lived on the estate, that he stayed in the caretaker's cottage as he'd done for years.

She could have told her everything.

Instead, she groped for words, hoping to smooth the rough edge off her lie. "Are you going to buy something to wear to the wedding?"

"I won't be here that long."

Nikki merely nodded.

"What's Mary Beth's daughter like?" Gabrielle asked.
"Is she like her? Is she like your daughter?"

Nikki laughed. "Shauna has a heart. I'm not sure
about my daughter. Or Mary Beth."

"What happened to Mary Beth, Nikki? I remember
she was always, well, more nervous than you. But did
something happen? Something bad?"

"Life happened, kiddo. And other people's expectations. Mary Beth always felt she had to live up to the
Atkinson name. I don't suppose that was her fault. Her
mother was so easily influenced by everyone and everything." And then she told her about Aunt Dorothy and
the Alzheimer's.

Gabrielle began to cry, and Nikki said it was all right,
that Dorothy was in a good place, though it was hard on
Mary Beth, but then again, what wasn't?

She had added the last part to help soften what clearly
was upsetting to Gabrielle.

And then Gabrielle told Nikki that Aunt Dorothy had
secretly visited her in England.

Nikki pulled to the side of the road and stopped. "I
didn't know that."

"You didn't know a lot of things. And I didn't know
why you never answered my letters. Neither you nor
Mary Beth."

"Your letters?" Nikki asked. "I never received any letters. I wrote to you a few times, but my mother said to
stop, that it would only upset you and...and your father."

"My father?"

"We thought he was with you, that he had taken you
away."

Gabrielle turned her head away. "No," she said, "that
was a lie."

Nikki knew that now, of course. Mack had told her

years before. But if she admitted it to Gabrielle, she'd have to tell her about Mack.

"Aunt Margaret tried to keep you from me," Gabrielle said, and Nikki could not disagree. Then she shook her head. "And him," she added. "She told me my father had disappeared." She raised her chin as if trying to keep more tears from leaking out. "There are so many things I don't understand."

There was silence a moment, then Nikki pulled back onto the street. "Sometimes," she said, "I think it's better not to try."

"You sold your *what*?"

They were getting ready for a cocktail party at the Cooper-Hewitt, not that many would be there (it was too close to summer), but they might as well go because you never knew who stayed in the city during the week.

"My diamonds," Mary Beth repeated, with practiced blasé.

"Your *Van Cleefs*?" Eric turned an odd shade of white, and one corner of his mouth curled like the head of an angry king cobra.

She zipped her white silk skirt and hated that she'd had to cancel Hank and his three-hundred-dollar-an-hour, cash-only visits. She blamed the wedding and the Vineyard and, oh, she was just too damn busy (!), so that Hank would not suspect and pass it on. The truth, however, was that she needed his workouts as much as she needed his raw, blissful sex. Ah, perhaps again someday.

"And your diamond-and-pearl ensemble? Is that why you're not wearing it?"

She'd never realized Eric had noticed so much. "It's called survival, my dear," she said, without looking again at his pasty flesh tone. "Someone has to pay attention to the money."

"I canceled Brazil."

As if one lousy trip would cover Shauna's wedding. "The tip of the iceberg, I'm afraid. But not to worry, we have someone chasing our friend Lester down."

"I thought we agreed not to..." he replied. "When people find out..."

Mary Beth sighed. "No one will find out. Now, be a dear and hand me those rings."

He slid a trio of leftover gold filigree bands from the ring holder inside her armoire. He handed them to her and quickly turned away. "I'm going to change my shirt."

"Why? The pale blue is fine."

"I want my French cuffs. In case any word has gotten out, I want to wear my diamond-and-onyx cuff links. No one will question our financial health if they see I still have them."

He was halfway out of the room when Mary Beth called out, "Don't bother. I sold those, too."

Fluffing her hair, she tried, she really did, not to act as devastated as she felt inside. She did not want to ignite his fear more than she already had.

"How dare you," he said in an uncharacteristic voice.

Suddenly her resolve began to crumble. "How dare I?" She closed her eyes, and then she smiled. "Darling, I bought them for you, just as I've bought everything else. That gives me the right to dare as I wish." She adjusted her sleeveless white silk weskit.

"What's going to happen if Lester is really gone?" he asked. "What's going to happen if we're as poor as... this?"

"I have no idea. Perhaps we'll have to get jobs." She was, of course, joking, but this was no time to joke.

Eric stepped forward. "I have other options," he said. "But what about you?"

Mary Beth did not know why that single comment fired straight to her heart, a missile of shock, a surprise attack. After all, she'd always known their marriage revolved around her money, the cog of happiness. *I have other options,* he'd said, as easily as if he'd said the time of day, with no consideration for her feelings or her pride. Her only other option had been Hank, another man whose services she'd paid for, too.

Her voice went low. "Then maybe it's time for you to exercise those options," she said. "Because if you can't take the heat, I truly don't need you in my fucking kitchen."

It might have been half an hour, maybe more, but the next thing Mary Beth heard as she sat on her bed, still dressed in her white silk and staring at the floor, was her daughter's soft voice.

"Mom?" Shauna asked as she entered the room. "What's going on? Why did Daddy just walk out with suitcases in his hands?"

# 14

I f I'm going to have a chauffeur, the neighbors damn
well better see me," Carla said to her son Donnie, who
stood in the doorway of the kitchen looking at his
mother as if she had three heads or none at all. She assumed it was because of the red, white, and blue capris
that she wore, and the matching scarf tied at the open
neck of her white cotton shirt that she'd bought at
Bloomingdale's that morning.

"The neighbors will think you've lost your mind,"
Donnie said, "or that you're going on a Princess Cruise."

That's what she got for having boys, not girls. The
sailor-looking outfit was perfecto for Martha's Vineyard,
the sales clerk had promised. And, Carla's mother would
have loved it. As for her, she'd be a lot more excited if her
obstinate son wasn't giving her such grief.

"Donnie, please," Carla pleaded. "All I'm asking is
that you go outside this afternoon at two o'clock. If you
see any of our neighbors, stall them until my limo ar-
rives."

He moved to the refrigerator, a favorite pastime in the
fifteen or so years since he'd been able to reach the door
by himself. "*Your* limo?" he asked with a hearty laugh.

"I wish Carmine and Nardi were here. They'd love to see *your limo*."

Carmine and Nardi were two of Carla's brothers, the two she barely spoke to because they lived out on Long Island, having married girls from the other side of the subway tracks, the side that would die to be on Martha's Vineyard. But Carla, not them, had been invited.

She smiled. "Well, I just bet they would."

Taking out a half-gallon of milk, Donnie chugged from the carton, then wiped his mouth. "So what am I supposed to say to the neighbors? Stand by, my mother's going to have a photo op?"

Carla straightened her scarf. "I try not to ask much of you, Donnie. Do I ask too much?"

"No, Ma."

"I ask you to round up a few neighbors, that's all. Do I ever ask for anything? I don't even ask you to live here with me. I don't want you to go to California, but haven't I said you should get an apartment with some of your friends?" She did not know why she had turned the focus from the neighbors to Donnie's independence. She supposed it was because it had been on her mind, the sense she was holding him back.

"Yes, Ma."

She sidestepped her guilt. "So when I ask you this little favor, this one teensy little favor, don't you think it would be nice if you did it for your mother? For all the years she had to work for that shit Lester Markham so you and your brother could live in a decent neighborhood and get a good education? This may not be my debutante ball, but it's the closest I've come to society."

Donnie rolled his eyes and took an apple from the bowl on the counter. With horse teeth that came from his father's side of the damn family, he crunched into it. "Stop whining, Ma. I'll do it, okay?"

She tossed the scarf over one shoulder. "You will?"

"Of course. I was just having fun."

"Fun," she said, planting her hands on her round hips. "You boys and your fun." She said it as if Vincent were there, too, her year-apart sons who had kept her alive if not sane all those years that she'd spent on the train schlepping to Manhattan from the Bronx, while Mary Beth and Nikki and Gabrielle had been chauffeur-driven everywhere, thanks to her, Carla DiRoma, who sent their checks out on time.

But this time, the chauffeur was coming for her.

"What are you bringing?" Donnie asked, chomping around the core as if this were his last meal, as if he wouldn't turn around and make another small snack, peanut butter and jelly—pbj, he called it—on white bread, not even whole wheat. Carla wondered if he would eat so much if he had a girlfriend and regular sex.

"What?" she asked. "You mean like a casserole? You think I should bring a casserole?"

He rolled his eyes again and headed for the cabinet where the peanut butter was stored. "I mean like a hostess gift, Ma. Shouldn't you bring a hostess gift?"

A gift. God, she hadn't even thought about that. Well, it wasn't as if she were an invited guest. Not *really* invited, not like a friend of the family or something.

Then she saw him laugh.

"You're teasing me," she said.

"Well, Ma...look at you. You're dressed like you're going to the America's Cup. And you're not being picked up until two, but you are all ready and it's only three minutes past noon."

She looked down at her sailor pants and couldn't help but smile. "You're right," she said. "I'm ridiculous."

He came over and gave her one of his big, wonderful hugs. "No, Ma, you're not ridiculous. You're just being you, and that's okay."

"You sure?"

"I'm sure. And don't worry, I'll go outside. And if nobody's around, I'll start banging on doors until I stir up eyewitnesses to my mother's late-in-life debut."

She hugged him back and thanked the Lord for giving her her boys.

She had shopped with Gabrielle until the shops had closed; she'd taken her to Vineyard Haven for dinner at The Black Dog Tavern. Then they'd stopped by Camp4Kids in time for "lights out." Though Nikki enjoyed her cousin's company, she had, in truth, been killing time until she felt assured that Mack was home asleep, out of the way. In the morning, Nikki checked to be certain Mack's red truck was gone. Then she left Gabrielle sleeping, spent the morning at Camp4Kids, and drove up-island to the coffee shop where she now sat, still without any answers.

Why had her mother cut Gabrielle out of their lives? Why had Nikki and Mary Beth been told Mack took Gabrielle away, while Gabrielle was told that Mack had disappeared?

At one point years ago, Mack told Nikki that during that time he had drifted, getting work when he could, living in run-down hotels, often sitting in the dark, depressed and overcome by his grief at the loss of both his daughter and his wife, earning enough money to make two trips to Europe, both of which had been disastrous and had only added to his sorrow.

Until ten years ago, when Margaret died, when he'd

come back to the Vineyard, when Nikki approached Mary Beth to let him live on the estate grounds.

There were questions Nikki knew would probably remain unanswered, the truths perhaps buried with Margaret Atkinson.

But answers or no answers, Nikki knew she had to tell Mack that Gabrielle was there.

Sitting in the out-of-the-way restaurant where Mack escaped for lunch in tourist season, Nikki could not imagine how she would feel if Dee were taken from her. As strained as their relationship could get, she could not fathom a greater hurt, even under the supposition that it would be for her "own good."

The small bell above the door tinkled and Mack ambled inside.

"Hey," he said, spotting Nikki. "What are you doing here? Not a good advertisement for the food at your dining commons." He pulled a chair out and sat next to her.

"Macaroni and cheese today. I felt like ham." She pointed to the rye bread sandwich on the plate in front of her.

Mack nodded, but she knew he did not believe her for a second or a minute or for all the tea in China, for which Dee had begged money but Nikki had said no.

"I have news," she said. "Some is pretty; some is not."

He folded his arms and looked across the room. "Cup of chicken noodle," he called out to Irma, who stood behind the counter. "And tuna on toasted wheat." His eyes came back to Nikki. "Tell me the not-so-pretty first. I'd rather feel sick on an empty stomach."

She deliberately smiled. "I'm poor," she said. "I have no money."

The corners of his mouth turned up a bit, too. "None?" he asked. "Does that mean I'm buying lunch?"

Mack. Yes, that was Mack. Kind and soft, yet sturdy and strong. She twisted on her chair. "While you're at it, maybe you could throw in a few extra dollars? Enough to support The Rose Foundation for a year or two?"

His eyes grew serious. "What's up?"

And then she told him about her trust fund, adding that Sam Oliver had agreed to help. "But my hopes aren't real high. It's been a few weeks already..."

"That's why you asked if I knew anyone," Mack said. "A banker or someone..."

"Yes," she replied. She would not tell him she'd gone to ask about Gabrielle. His daughter's name would come up soon enough.

Mack ran his hand through hair that should have been thinner for a man in his late fifties, for a man who'd been through so much. "Jesus, Nikki, is there something I can do? Can I help the detective?"

Nikki shook her head. "I don't know, but thanks. You'll be the first one that I'll ask."

He did not mention he had not been the first to know. Reaching across the table, he set his hand on hers. "What's going to happen, Nikki? What are you going to do?"

Irma appeared and Mack removed his hand from Nikki's. The waitress set a cup of soup in front of him.

"I thought you were going to tell me Mary Beth was on her way," he said, and that made Nikki smile again, for it was their trusted pact: Nikki always alerted Mack when her cousin was on-island, sort of like a Doppler radar warning of an impending hurricane.

"Actually, she is."

Mack thought for a moment, then nearly dropped his spoon. "Oh, God," he said, "is her money gone, too?"

"Yes."

He scowled a tiny scowl. "How's she going to swing the wedding? I've always had the feeling Mary Beth spends as much as she gets."

Then his eyes grew solemn again, and Nikki knew that his thoughts had drifted, and she knew where they'd gone. She took a small bite of her sandwich and wished she'd ordered coffee to help wash down the lump that had grown inside her throat. "Yes," she said, without Mack having asked. "Gabrielle has been affected, too."

He looked off toward nothing, then looked back again. "It was her," he replied. "At the estate. I nearly ran into her."

Nikki paused, then she nodded. "It's her," she said slowly, "but she doesn't know about you."

With the check back from Brazil and the money from her jewelry, Mary Beth plunked the fees for April and May on the desk of PATRICIA KENDRICK, financial goddess of Harriman House.

"I'll have the June money in a week or so," she said with deliberate expectation that it would be acceptable. "An error was made, and some of my portfolio was inadvertently diverted into long-term investments." She did not speculate how "long" the term might be.

Ms. Kendrick looked at Mary Beth as if to say we should all have such problems. "And July will be here before you know it," the woman added, because Mary Beth was equipped with neither a calendar nor a brain.

Mary Beth smiled and excused herself. The she checked her watch and went outside to wait for Charlie, who had dropped her off at Harriman House, then had gone to get Carla. She supposed there was time to visit Dorothy, but Mary Beth could not handle that today. The minutes of her own survival were too stressful now, as they swung around the ticking clock toward Shauna's wedding day.

Gabrielle sat in Nikki's studio, talking with Sam Oliver, who'd been sent by Alice to check in on her, or so he'd said. It only took a moment, however, for Gabrielle to realize that he was there to question her, to help him put together the missing pieces of Lester and the trust funds.

To help him determine if she were a suspect.

They sat in the studio, the crow's nest of the lighthouse, because the light up there was better and the view was peaceful, and Gabrielle enjoyed being surrounded by Nikki's wonderful work. She also realized Nikki had been right: Simply being in the lighthouse made her feel close to her mother.

"When was the last time you talked to anyone from the States?" Sam asked.

"Years. Until Carla DiRoma came to my house."

"You never talked to Nikki? Or Lester?"

Gabrielle stared at Sam. "I need to know if this is confidential." She did not want to lie, but if he told the others, then everyone would know.

"It's an investigation, Gabrielle. If you know anything that will help find Lester..."

Could she trust him? Could she trust anyone?

She shook her head. "I hadn't talked to Lester since I was in Paris." That was true. She did not add that was the time she'd set up her account in Zurich, that she'd then arranged for Lester to deposit her money directly, that she'd given him the power of attorney to pay her taxes, that she hadn't seen the statements in many years. She did not add that her husband knew nothing of her fortune.

"So you received your income monthly, as did Nikki and Mary Beth, and you never questioned if things were being handled correctly."

"Aunt Margaret trusted Lester, so I guess we all did." She wondered if Sam noticed the perspiration that had formed across her brow. Turning toward the tiny stretch of jetty that made its way toward Chappaquiddick, Gabrielle said softly, "When I was a girl, the barrier connected this part of the island to Chappy. Except during high tide. I used to love to walk across it...."

Sam was not interested. "What else do you remember about Lester Markham? Did he ever visit you in Europe?"

Gabrielle winced, even though she'd tried not to. Tiny muscles in her jaw and her neck and her fingers began to tingle. Why was he asking all these questions?

"Gabrielle?" Sam asked.

She rubbed the back of her head, hoping it would help her pull an answer together. "Sorry," she said quickly. "I was trying to remember. No, no, Lester never came to see me."

Sam didn't seem convinced, but he got up. "I don't want to upset you any more than I already have, Gabrielle. But if you can think of anything that will help us find Markham..."

She stood, too. "Of course," she replied. "I'll let you know right away." She was so grateful he left she did not say good-bye.

Mary Beth made a cup of coffee and went into the library of the big house on the Vineyard. Her head was utterly pounding inside and out from the senseless chatter of Carla DiRoma. At least Charlie had taken them to LaGuardia so the duration of the trip was shorter than if they'd driven; at least when the island taxi had pulled onto the estate, there appeared to be solitude: The only vehicle around was a shiny motorcycle parked by the lighthouse. Mary Beth wondered with a chuckle if Nikki had taken up with a bad boy, a biker who wore leather and had an armful of tattoos.

She'd told Carla to go upstairs and make herself at home, to pick out a room, any room, except Shauna's, which was the first one on the left. She said they would all meet downstairs for cocktails at seven, though she had no idea if the bar had been stocked or if Nikki was any-where to be found or if that detective was still on the is-land or if he'd gone off looking for Lester.

Then she decided to check the messages on her cell phone, which she'd turned off yesterday to clear her mind and get started on the fast-growing list of what she needed to take care of there on the island and how little she could get away with paying out in cash.

She sat at the desk with her notebook and the phone. Two messages from Shauna; one from Hank; one from Roxanne, was everything okay? And Tiffany's, God bless them, the bubble wands were in, and God bless the fact that they were safely on her credit card. There were also four calls from Phillipe, the caterer.

Four?

There were no calls from Eric.

She decided to tend to Phillipe, because right now, he was the most important, her daughter notwithstanding. "We need to talk about the truffles, darling," his first message said with a tone that was friendly and very much *him*, grand master of *l'art culinaire* at Image de Pomme.

"Truffles, darling," his second message said.

Then, "Get back to me today. Puhhhh-leeeze."

Then there was a hang-up, but it could have been him,

because his next call came this afternoon and was not at all nice.

"Mary Beth. We MUST talk."

She tried to dissect the tone of his voice: It almost was angry, over what, a few mushrooms? As if there weren't more critical things in her life?

She studied the desk, the same desk where Aunt Margaret had sat when she'd told them of their trust funds. Then Mary Beth closed her eyes and considered her options if Lester were never found, if her money had disintegrated into the intangible world of stocks and bonds and not-so-mutual funds.

Would she have to sell the estate? Surely it would bring enough to survive. Yes, it was prime land; yes, it was the Vineyard. But now that the Clintons were in New York, she supposed they would summer at the Hamptons. The Bushes, of course, would be in Maine, leaving island real estate in an unattractive flux.

She might survive, but she would not be rich, not like her friends.

If she kept the old place, it needed work. Eric had promised to take charge of getting it painted in time for the wedding; hardly possible now, even if he were so inclined. She did not, after all, even know where he was so that she might remind him that his daughter's wedding was just days from now.

She could ask Mack to take care of the house, but she hated asking anyone for favors and God knew she couldn't pay him.

With a heart-heavy sigh, she reached for her phone book and looked up Phillipe's number.

The communications journey at Image de Pomme navigated her through a receptionist and two assistants before Phillipe finally came on the line. Mary Beth wondered how it happened that a chef could become so important. She suspected it was connected to the size of his invoice, which she could no longer afford though he didn't know it.

"I'm here," she said. "Now what can possibly be so urgent about truffles?" She tried to sound humorous, but knew she was not funny. In that moment, she reminded herself of Aunt Margaret, an unpleasant thought.

"You want Provençal truffles accenting the soup?" He did not humor her in return.

"You know I do." She picked up a pen and doodled in her notebook. No sense asking if they could economize and eliminate them. The menu, like the bubble wands, was a done deal. What the hell, Mary Beth thought, there was always the chance that Lester would show up in time for the reception. She silently snickered, then hurled her pen over the desk and across the room. Life would be so much simpler if one could live in denial, or at least in Alzheimer's, the world of her mother.

"Mary Beth, we've been friends a long time," Phillipe said.

She did not comment that business associates—hired hands, for God's sake—were not exactly *friends,* but Phillipe had done most of her functions for the past several years. And she certainly deserved credit for throwing other business his way—dozens of weddings, showers, numerous bar and bat mitzvahs, and several New Age debutante balls. Shauna's wedding, of course, would be his most extravagant, and perhaps even earn him yet another assistant.

"What are you getting at, Phillipe?" Though his ego tended to inflate to the size of Manhattan, he should not be so upset that she hadn't returned his calls sooner.

"Money." He blurted the word out so fast that her head quickly reeled.

She opened the desk drawer and fumbled around. Weren't there any cigarettes left in there somewhere? Last year's would do. They'd be dry and tasteless and would burn her throat, but...

*Money?*

She stopped searching for smokes. A slow veil of darkness crept into the room. *No,* she thought, then wanted to wail, *N-o-o-o-o-o-o-o-o.*

"I need money up front."

She snorted a couple of times. She shut the desk drawer. She stared straight ahead to the French doors that led to the terrace that led to the grassy slope that led down to the sea. "Excuse me?"

Phillipe seemed to exhale and haul his bulk from one stool to another. "Mary Beth," he said, "this is difficult. But this is an expensive wedding and I have to protect myself. Ordinarily I wouldn't ask, but, well, there's a rumor going around that you don't have any money. That it's gone. That you're broke."

The fire that crawled up her spine and into her cheeks made the dog days of summer seem cool and refreshing. She tried stretching her neck to unlock the heat. Her vertebrae crunched. "Phillipe," she barked, "what the hell are you talking about?" Barking, she knew, was nothing more than a defense, a thinly veiled mechanism that probably did little to disguise the fact that she did not know what else to do.

*A rumor? What rumor? How the hell had he heard?*

"Please, Mary Beth. I'm willing to settle for half up front, although under the circumstances, I must ask for cash. Or a cashier's check. For seventy-eight thousand, including the truffles."

A white-hot flash of rage burst somewhere inside her. *"Fuck the truffles,"* she shouted. "You'll have your goddamn money within the week, Phillipe, and this will be the last event you do for me or anyone who is anyone, anywhere in Manhattan. I hope that makes you happy." She threw the phone across the room along the same route her pen had just taken. Then she sat there a moment, trying to stop shaking, wondering how she was going to come up with seventy-eight thousand dollars in a week's time and if Shauna's wedding was the beginning of the end of Mary Beth's life.

She looked back toward the French doors and the lawn where the white tents would stand, where the three ladies with harps would be sprinkled among the guests, where the twelve-piece orchestra would play during dinner, where the DJ would set up for later. She looked at the shady spots where the flower-woven trellises would stand; where the huge pots of fragrant blossoms would create summer gardens; where translucent bubbles would float through the air; and where Shauna would emerge, a princess in white; and all would be as it should be, and all would be right.

She'd envisioned this for so long, had planned it so thoroughly, it now seemed like a dream that had already happened, like when she thought about the abortion she'd been forced to have, or when the doctor had said firmly, "Your mother has Alzheimer's." It seemed like a dream that she no longer wanted because it was painful and there was no damn way out.

Then she closed her eyes on the dream and suddenly was aware of one undeniable thing: *It had to be Eric, that cocksucking son of a bitch.*

# 15

There really was a God, and Carla had, at last, found Him. After a lifetime of nothing, she'd finally crossed the tracks and moved up on the hill.

She sat at a round, chintz-covered table in the bedroom, nibbling on a cereal bar that she'd brought from home, trying to absorb all that she'd experienced in the last couple of hours. The ride to the airport had been exciting, even though it was only a Lincoln, not a real limousine. (The driver, however, had held the back door open while no fewer than six neighbors—plus Donnie—had watched from the sidewalk.) Once they'd picked up Mary Beth, Carla had tried to imitate her every move so no one would know she'd never boarded a small plane and flown to the Vineyard like Mary Beth did, with nonchalance that implied she did it every day—which she probably could have, though not anymore, not without her trust fund.

It was all very glamorous, just as Carla had expected. And the house, if not glamorous, surely was impressive.

Taking another bite, she put her feet up on a chair, then leaned back and surveyed her surroundings as if she were an Atkinson, as if she were a goddess, ensconced in her room upstairs in the mansion, or as the family called it, the "big house."

The room she'd picked was big, too, almost as big as her entire apartment at home in the Bronx, including the storage room in the back hall. Surprisingly, the room's only bed was an old-fashioned double kind, but it was a four-poster with plump pillows and a down comforter that must have cost at least five hundred dollars! The wallpaper had giant pink and blue flowers that looked like the ones blooming in the gardens below. Best of all, from the huge picture window, Carla could see the lighthouse and the dunes and the water.

A travel agent would have called this an oceanfront room and would have quoted a premium in-season rate.

So Carla had selected it and hung up her clothes as if she had moved in.

Well, why not? She'd earned the right, hadn't she? All those years of schlepping for Lester, keeping his society life fluid and organized, making sure his attire was proper and dry-cleaned, ordering flowers for his day-after thank-yous—she could have been his wife for the attention she gave him. Could have been, should have been at least a lady for him to escort to the Met or the theater or one of a hundred thousand gallery openings he went to every year.

She took a last bite of her cereal bar and turned to the big manila envelope that she'd put on the table. She held her breath a moment then undid the clasp. Reaching inside, she carefully took out the contents: the newspaper and magazine clippings, some still fresh and visible, some yellow, faded, brittle. Slowly Carla scanned them, the pictures of Lester, in his tuxedo, in his glory. In early photos his wife stood next to him: He held a nondescript cocktail; he smiled. In later photos he appeared more confident, as if his money and position had finally afforded him the kind of life he wanted.

In many photos, of course, he was with her, Carla DiRoma, though her head was often too big or too small for the body that wore it. She bet if she'd had the courage she could give the pictures to her son, Donnie. He'd know how to doctor it on one of those new-fangled computers to make it look as if the baroness or the dame beside him really had been her.

But, of course, she could never ask Donnie; he'd send her to Bellevue without asking questions.

She studied the clippings and realized with sorrow that there would be no more now, not unless they found Lester. She sighed again, then divided everything into two piles: one for the detective, the private ones for her. She slid hers back into the envelope and returned it to her suitcase.

She checked her watch—two hours until "cocktails." She eyed the big bed. Then she took off her navy blue pumps, tested the plumpness of the comforter, and, with a smile, lay on top of the bed to daydream about Lester and the life they could have had if she'd been an Atkinson, and if she had lived there.


It would be harder on Gabrielle if she knew they were lovers as well as best friends. Nikki felt certain that would be the case, though Mack was not agreeing. He, in fact, had not seemed to be listening or thinking or *any-thing* all afternoon. He had merely walked beside her on the boardwalk along Moshup Trail out at Aquinnah where the tourists did not venture too far from the cliffs. Then they'd sat quietly on Philbin Beach, the somber shore where John Kennedy, Jr.'s, belongings had washed up, a private beach only for residents. No one, however, would bother Mack and Nikki. Though they lived down-island, they'd spent a great deal of time there on the beach, their solitude and their love safe from the eyes of those who might think it was wrong.

Today they sat all afternoon.

"She lives in Tuscany," Nikki said at one point. "Did you know that?"

He fixed his eyes on the horizon, where the sky met the water and the line in between separated one from another.

"She has a daughter, a little girl."

He nodded; he had heard that time.

Later Nikki had the courage to say, "Gabrielle is quite beautiful, Mack." But a tightening in her throat and a cauldron of tears that waited to spill out would not let her add, "She looks just like Rose."

Mostly, however, they sat in long silence. They held hands; they listened to the gulls; they watched the small surf. Even as the sun began its slow descent into the west, Nikki could not bring herself to leave this man she loved so much.


*"Where the hell is Nicole?"* Mary Beth shouted into the phone as Carla waited in the doorway. She had followed the sound of her hostess's voice and arrived downstairs in *the drawing room,* she supposed they called it. Pressing her fingers to her temples, Carla was beginning to wonder if being an Atkinson was really so great, and if Mary Beth ever spoke in anything but a shout. *"Well, as soon as you see her, make sure she comes home. And I want to meet that detective tonight, unless he's missing, too."*

At last Mary Beth hung up and looked at Carla. "Alice

claims she has no idea where my cousin is, that she called after lunch and said she'd be gone for a while."

Carla nodded as if she had any idea who Alice was, or why Mary Beth felt the need to confide.

An old clock on the wall struck seven. Mary Beth looked relieved.

"I don't know what's in the liquor cabinet, but I know we have wine." She motioned to a rack that seemed to hold more bottles than the corner liquor store back home.

"Wine is fine," Carla replied. She wondered if Mary Beth noticed that she'd changed into a lavender chiffon caftan, "perfect for a casual dinner overlooking the sea," the clerk had said. She had not showed Donnie the dress, and she was glad, for Mary Beth still wore the same white knit top and khakis that she'd worn on the plane.

Carla accepted a stemmed glass that must have been crystal, just as someone knocked on the front door.

They stayed in the drawing room, Mary Beth and the detective, Sam, while Carla went upstairs and retrieved the news clippings for him. When she returned, she sat and listened, trying to pay attention, all the while peeking into every corner, snapping mental pictures of the furnishings and décor. Especially intriguing was a cherry desk in back that had many tiny drawers. How she'd love to see inside them, just to learn what an Atkinson kept there, like keys to old treasure chests or small pieces of silver.

"How well did you know Lester?" Sam asked, though his question was directed at Mary Beth, which was stupid because Carla was the one who really knew him, not her. "What about family? Did he have family?"

"He had a wife once," Mary Beth replied. "But she died. Cancer, I think."

"Lung cancer," Carla interjected. "She smoked like a fiend."

Mary Beth raised her eyebrows as if she hadn't known that, but Carla knew it well. Until the woman was gone Lester always came to work looking handsome as ever, but always leaving a trail of stale, secondhand smoke that he was lucky hadn't killed him as well.

"Anyone else?" At last Sam was looking at Carla. "No," she replied, then told him that Lester's parents were long dead, his sister had committed suicide years ago, and he and his wife hadn't had any children. Suddenly she had their attention, because she had more answers than the hostess did. She crossed her legs and settled back in the wing chair, sipping from the crystal and feeling like Queen for a Day. She decided not to elaborate that after Lester's wife died he had been "seen" with many wealthy, snobby women, because she did not want to offend Mary Beth. She merely mentioned he had many friends "abroad."

"Did he drink?"

"No. Not that I know of." Well, there had been that one time when he'd kissed her and given her hope. It was twenty years ago—no, twenty-one. A bottle of Dom Pérignon was delivered to the office. It was meant for an attorney down the hall, but the man had recently joined Alcoholics Anonymous so he'd given it to them.

Lester had opened the bottle and they shared the contents, and over by the file cabinet he kissed her and ran his hands over her breasts that he said were so big they must be juicy, ripe melons. She wanted more and told him so, but he turned red in the face and said he had to leave. He never spoke about it and for a long time she'd been convinced there'd been something wrong with her breasts, that he'd felt something foreign or weird or repulsive and that scared him off. She'd stood many nights in front of her mirror touching herself, trying to detect the unpleasantness he'd found, but they felt all right to her.

"Can we talk about him in something other than the past tense?" she asked. "I mean, we don't know that he's dead."

Even Mary Beth grew quiet at that.

"Oh," Sam said softly, "I doubt that he's dead."

"The son of a bitch is living the high life with our cash," Mary Beth said. "Probably in Rio or some European hideaway." She stood up and went to the fireplace, where she tapped her wineglass against the mantel. "This is getting us nowhere. I need my money back. And I need it fast."

"I'm not sure that's going to happen," Sam replied. "At least, I doubt it will happen fast. Chances are, he's covered his tracks."

Carla dropped her chin. "You make him sound like a criminal."

"Excuse me, my dear, but that is what he is." Mary Beth wasn't shouting, but her voice was not pleasant. She turned back to Sam. "Look, why don't you start by going back to New York? Maybe you can trace his last steps or something."

"I have a friend who's already done it. Markham's office is clean; in fact, a new tenant has moved in."

An ache clawed its way into Carla's heart. Someone had already moved into her office? Her and Lester's office?

"His town house is empty; it's not up for sale. It has a huge mortgage. Chances are, he'll let it go to the bank."

Mary Beth swirled the wine around in her glass. "You've been busy," she said with what sounded almost like respect.

"It's my job," he replied.

They were quiet a moment, then Mary Beth sat back down. Sam's presence, perhaps, had a calming effect.

"It's so hard to believe," Mary Beth said. "Aside from the upset about losing the money, it's so hard to believe someone would do such a thing. We all trusted Lester. Hell, my aunt Margaret trusted him, and she didn't like anyone."

"That's exactly what your cousin told me this afternoon," Sam said.

Mary Beth looked up. "Nikki said that? That Margaret trusted him?"

Sam frowned. "No, not Nikki. Your other cousin said it. Your cousin Gabrielle."

Though Mary Beth was holding the wineglass by its stem, the glass tipped to the side, its contents slowly dribbling onto the floor. "Gabrielle?" she asked. "You talked to Gabrielle?"

"Sure," he said. "I have to talk to all of you."

"But where—how—did you find Gabrielle?"

He shrugged and nodded his head toward the door. "She's over at the lighthouse. She's staying with Nikki."

Carla noticed the shock on Mary Beth's face: She had not mentioned that she'd visited Gabrielle in Italy. Carla, after all, was Lester's trustworthy servant even to the end, if this was the end.


It was one o'clock in the morning, Tuscany time, but Gabrielle had not been able to stand another minute of not talking to Rosa. She no longer cared if Angelina answered; she could not have her daughter worried that her mother might have left her.

So she called the phone number of the villa, her home. As the ringing began on the other end of the line,

Gabrielle realized that, despite her determination, she was holding her breath. After three rings, the telephone picked up. But it was not a woman who answered; it was the damn machine.

The answering machine?

At one o'clock in the morning?

There was a phone by the bed. Surely Stefano had heard it. Unless he wasn't there. Unless...

She let out her breath to make room for the pain of the unknown.

"Stefano?" she called out. "Rosa? Honey, it's Mama." But there was only the beep, then silence.

She was still clutching the receiver when the banging started on the door.

"Gabrielle!" a voice shouted. "Open the door, I know you're in there!"

It was Mary Beth. Ready or not.


She looked older than Nikki, despite the blond hair, despite the perfect makeup and the manicured fingernails. She looked older than Nikki because of the lines at her mouth and her eyes and across her forehead—not deep lines of age, but scratches of intensity, small creases of angst.

"It's you," Mary Beth said. "My God, you look just like your mother."

Mary Beth did not look like Aunt Dorothy, because she did not look as happy as Aunt Dorothy always had.

"That's what Nikki said," Gabrielle replied. She waited for a hug that did not come. Instead Mary Beth swept past her and entered the lighthouse.

"I hope she also told you we're keeping this quiet. About the trust funds, I mean. That no one is to know."

Gabrielle laughed, grateful that Nikki had prepared

her for her other cousin's demeanor. "Mary Beth," she said, "is that all you can say? Gosh, I haven't seen you in twenty-seven years."

Mary Beth stopped and turned. "I...I'm sorry. But this is such a shock. I had no idea you were here....How would I know? No one tells me anything."

It took a moment for Gabrielle to notice that Mary Beth was shaking. Then she saw big tears form in her eyes and a small quiver start on her lower lip.

"Oh, Mary Beth," Gabrielle said and went to her cousin and put her arms around her and hugged her until the older woman let go and cried.

"I can't believe it," Mary Beth said. "I never wanted to let myself think of you. All these years..."

"I know, I know," Gabrielle said, though she didn't really know, but was slowly beginning to understand. Margaret Atkinson had wielded so much control over the family that her word and her wishes had never been challenged, and the reasons she'd wanted Gabrielle gone had not been questioned because she had not allowed it. "We'll get through this," Gabrielle said. "We're together again." But as she said the words, she was not thinking of Nikki and Mary Beth, but of Stefano and of Rosa and when—if—she'd be with them again.

# 16

For once it was a blessing that Mary Beth was so self-centered.

When Nikki and Mack finally parted ways—he to his red truck, she to her VW—she headed back to the estate. He had decided to go to the 1802 Tavern in Edgartown. The tavern was owned by his friend Ben Niles's wife, Jill, and had an apartment with a spare bed upstairs that was often used by friends with no explanation needed. Mack hoped he could stay there as long as Gabrielle was on the island.

Nikki hadn't agreed it would be for the best, but knew enough to let Mack be Mack. But when she opened the door to the lighthouse and saw Gabrielle sitting with Mary Beth, her heart seemed to make its way to her throat.

"Mary Beth," she said as if she hadn't expected her, as if her cousin didn't own the property on which they stood and sat, and hadn't said only yesterday that she'd be there today.

"You didn't tell me," Mary Beth accused, "that Gabrielle was here."

Nikki leaned against the wall. She could not tell by the

look on Gabrielle's face if Mary Beth had revealed that Mack lived there. Thank God they'd always been discreet, living in separate quarters though often secretly sharing the same bed at night.

"I wanted to surprise you," Nikki said now, pulling her gaze from Gabrielle, wishing she knew her young cousin better so she could have read in her eyes whether or not she knew that her father lived there.

"Surprise me or give me heart failure?" Mary Beth stood up. "Well, as long as we're here we might as well have dinner together. I've got that Carla woman back at the house, so let's all make nice and not unearth too many family skeletons." She said it in jest, but Nikki half-smiled. Skeletons, apparently, were an Atkinson specialty.

"I'll walk you to the house," Nikki said and quickly led Mary Beth out.

When she shut the door behind them, Nikki put her hand firmly on Mary Beth's arm. "Look, Mary Beth, I don't care what you say or do or do not say or do about this whole mess with Lester. But you are not, absolutely not, to tell Gabrielle that Mack lives here. At some point I might, but only if I think she's ready. In the meantime, Mack is staying in town. That's how it will be, do I make myself clear?"

Mary Beth looked at her blankly. "To be honest with you, Nicole, I'm a bit preoccupied with more important matters, like a wedding in less than two weeks, and a seventy-eight-thousand-dollar bill I must pay my caterer in the next few days. The thought of Mack Olson, quite frankly, had not crossed my mind."

Nikki would have kissed her, but Atkinsons did not do that sort of thing.

\*     \*     \*

Dinner was a noisy, female affair with the three cousins, Carla, and Nikki's assistant, Alice. They ate lobster and fried clams and the catch of the day at the Oceanside Restaurant in downtown Oak Bluffs, and mostly they listened to Mary Beth, who recited every detail of the impending wedding including much of the impressive guest list. Every so often she looked at Gabrielle and said, "I can't believe you're really here."

But she was really there, though she missed being on the hillside in Tuscany, wrapped in Stefano's strong arms, the soft sounds of Rosa asleep in the next room.

In between Mary Beth's banter, Nikki announced that all those years they'd thought Gabrielle had been with Mack she had been alone.

"Except for visits from your mother," Gabrielle said to Mary Beth, who seemed quite stunned.

"You absolutely must stay for the wedding," was all she could reply.

But Gabrielle merely smiled and said she didn't think so, thanks anyway. She glanced at her watch several times and wondered how much longer they would be, so she could get back to the lighthouse and call home again.

When the check arrived, Mary Beth picked it up and paid it with her American Express. As she signed the slip with a flourish she said to Gabrielle, "There's no need for you to stay in that musty old lighthouse. Surely you'd like your old room at the big house."

Gabrielle did not look over at Nikki. "Thanks, Mary Beth, but I'm fine where I am. Besides, I'll probably leave in a couple of days."

"You just got here."

"My family will miss me." She didn't add that they couldn't be missing her too badly if they weren't even at home.

"But we're your family, too. And we've been missing you for years."

It was the nicest thing she'd heard Mary Beth say, the closest thing to heartfelt from a woman whose emotions were locked down—something Gabrielle recognized, because she had learned how to do it, and she'd done it well.

"Well, let's go," Mary Beth announced now and stood up. "I have a busy day tomorrow. One week from Saturday will be here before anyone can say 'sterling silver bubble wands from Tiffany's.'"

Gabrielle looked at Nikki, and Nikki looked at Alice, and Alice looked at Carla, who fell into step behind Mary Beth as she marched out the door.


Gabrielle said good night, then waited in her room until six in the morning, Tuscany time. She crept back downstairs and dialed the villa, but again heard only her own voice-recorded message on the answering machine. This time, she left the phone numbers of both the lighthouse and the camp; tomorrow she would do something to help Nikki, something to distract herself from worrying where Stefano and Rosa were, and if they were all right. As much as she'd like to board the next flight to Italy, Gabrielle sensed that she wasn't ready yet, that her past hadn't yet passed.


In the morning, Camp4Kids was buzzing. As Nikki pulled into the driveway, they were greeted with the welcoming sounds of a boisterous softball game on the makeshift playing field and the heartening laughter of belly flops echoing up from the pond. Gabrielle decided that whoever coined the phrase "bursting with joy" must have been near children and their gleeful innocence.

*Children,* she thought. *Rosa.*

She stuffed down her homesick feelings and followed Nikki into the registration cottage, which was a hubbub of activity. Alice was already hard at work rearranging furniture with the help of a volunteer, and Sam was installing a computer at a makeshift desk.

"A computer?" Gabrielle asked above the scrape of wooden desks across the wooden floor. "There goes our budget."

Sam laughed. "It came from the mainland," he said. "Complete with a law enforcement program to help us people-search the Web. We may need to weed through a few hundred thousand names, but one way or another, we'll find the S.O.B."

Gabrielle knew little about computers, though lately Stefano had said they should get a Web page. *Stefano,* she thought, his name close to her lips. *Stop thinking about him. He will call soon.*

"Actually," Sam said, "I was hoping Carla would be with you. If she worked for Lester she's probably familiar with a computer. I thought she might like to help me out."

"Give her a call at the estate," Nikki suggested.

"I tried. No answer. Do you know if there's a separate phone number for the caretaker's cottage?"

The caretaker's cottage? Gabrielle was surprised. She didn't know there still was a caretaker at the estate; she hadn't seen one since she'd arrived. She vaguely remembered the old man who'd lived in the cottage when she was a kid. But her memory of him was fuzzy, as it was about most of those early years.

Nikki jostled everyone and moved to the computer. "I'll find Carla, don't worry," she said. "Now tell me about this computer. You didn't break the law to get it, did you?"

Sam poked at one key, then another, then fiddled with

the power cord. "It was a gift. We have a new system at the station. The captain offered this relic."

"You didn't tell him—" Nikki began, but Sam held up a hand.

"Not to worry. I only asked if I could use it off-premises."

"And he agreed?" Gabrielle interjected. "On top of giving you time off?"

Sam flipped a switch and, at last, the screen lit up with life. "All the guys have been good to me. My wife and I waited a long time to have Molly...and then there was the accident...and now..." His steady voice cracked a little and he lowered his head. "I know many women don't believe it anymore, but there are a few good men left out there in the world. Guys who care about other people."

Nikki crouched down, put her arm around his wide shoulders, and gave him a hug. "You're one of them, Sam. And I, for one, feel lucky that we can now help one another."

"Yeah," he said, and Gabrielle was so moved she thought she'd cry again. *Molly,* she thought, Sam's sweet, tiny girl, the same age as Rosa, too young to have such pain, too young to have to think about death.

"I'll be on the porch," Gabrielle said and quietly slipped outside so she could be alone, so she could breathe.


After lunch, the kids had their quiet time, "nap" being too childish a word to use on anyone over two, especially for the Camp4Kids kids, who were reminded too often of the differences between themselves and other kids their ages.

Gabrielle went down to the pond, where she skimmed

the water's surface with a cattail, counted her blessings, and hated herself that she took them for granted. Then, she went looking for Molly, who, on top of her illness, had lost her mother at too young an age. Gabrielle did not know what it was like to be sick, but she knew that empty, aching, motherless hole that could not be filled with friends or fun or even with family. When a child lost a mother, there was no Band-Aid. She knew it, because at age thirty-four, she sometimes felt it still.

Molly was stretched out on a towel on the porch of her cottage, wearing pink socks and sneakers, a pink ruffled shirt, and jeans. Gabrielle wondered if Sam picked out her clothes and if Molly told him what she wanted. As Gabrielle drew closer, she saw that Molly was intent on a picture of Barbie in a Mardi Gras costume. She was coloring the costume pink.

"What a beautiful picture," Gabrielle said and sat down next to Molly. "I used to have Barbie. She was my favorite." She did not say she'd had not one, but twelve or fourteen and all the clothes on the market at that time and the accessories, too.

Molly didn't reply.

"Are those feathers on her dress? And is that a mask?"

Molly sat up and pulled back the red curls from her forehead. "She's going to a ball," the little girl said. "In Norlens."

She said "New Orleans" as if someone had taught her, someone with a Louisiana accent who talked Bourbon Street jive. Gabrielle bit her lip to keep from smiling. Molly was so charming, a precocious child of a man with a heart. She wondered if the little girl would be a handful when she got older, and if Sam Oliver would be prepared.

When she got older. If she got older.

"I have a little girl just like you," Gabrielle said and smoothed Molly's hair because she couldn't resist, because the little girl's green eyes were so compelling, and because she missed Rosa so much right now she thought her heart might break.

"Does she have red hair, too? I bet she doesn't. Not many do, you know. Daddy says it's part of why I'm so special."

Gabrielle smiled. "My little girl doesn't have red hair. Or green eyes like you. She has black hair and blue eyes." Atkinson eyes.

"What's her name?"

"Rosa."

Molly looked around her. "Is she here at camp?"

Gabrielle stiffened. She could not say, "No, my child is well, she isn't sick." With a small breath, Gabrielle replied, "No, she's home. We live in Italy. Do you know where that is?"

"Is it close to Norlens?"

"No."

"I live in New York. With Daddy and Grandma Oliver and Uncle Bob. Is Italy close to New York?"

"No. It's on the other side of the ocean."

Molly seemed to consider the answer. She picked out a dark pink crayon and colored the fringe around Barbie's ball gown. "Does she have a Barbie?"

"No," she replied.

"Why not?"

Gabrielle watched Molly carefully color. "I don't know," she replied. She did not explain that there were no Barbies that she knew of in their small village, that they were sheltered from the world, insulated from its influence, the good and the bad. A wonderful place for keeping secrets. Until the world came in. Until reality surfaced.

Gabrielle untied the long ribbon that held her own ponytail. "Would you like me to braid your hair?" she asked.

Molly stopped coloring. She shrugged her small shoulders. "Sure," she said. "Okay."

Molly sat down and Gabrielle pulled back her curls, silky hair like Rosa's, soft curls of innocence so receptive to a bit of love. Slowly she wove them, a bit at a time, wondering when the last time was that Molly had been mothered, and if it would help make her feel better, if only for right now, and if it would help make Gabrielle less lonely for Rosa, if only for this moment, if not the whole day.

When she was finished she tied Molly's braid with the blue ribbon from her hair and wondered what Rosa was doing right then and if she was missing her mama too badly and wondering when she'd be home.

Mary Beth had dragged Carla outside as if she were a servant, or at least someone on the payroll. She ordered her to stand at one end of the lawn with a measuring tape while the man from Tent City made notes on a pad and Mary Beth shook her head this way and that.

"Be a dear and move just a tad to the left," Mary Beth instructed Carla, who did not, of course, mind being a dear because it made her feel part of the party, like one of the invited guests Mary Beth had mentioned last night.

*The Dickinsons of Breckenridge and Palm Beach.*

*The Colrains of Westchester County.*

*The Swedocks of Darien.*

Carla knew the names, of course. She'd seen their faces countless times in the photos where Lester appeared: *Mr. and Mrs. Theodore J. Swedock III enjoy a moment at the Autumn Fest;* or *John and Sally Colrain share hors d'oeuvres with the Matthew Dickinsons.* The captions weren't very clever but the names were always spelled correctly.

"We'll want a smaller tent by the butterfly bushes," Mary Beth announced. "That's where the cake will go."

Carla moved where Mary Beth pointed, toward a long row of bushes with lilac-blue flowers. She wanted to ask why they were called butterfly bushes—did they attract butterflies or had someone thought the flowers looked like butterflies?—but it was apparent that Mary Beth would not appreciate the interruption.

When the tent man was finished, the harpists arrived, followed by the manager and bass player of a twelve-piece orchestra. Apparently, the bass player doubled as a DJ for the after-dinner listening and dancing pleasure of the Swedocks, the Dickinsons, and the Colrains.

After everyone left, Carla asked if they could have some lunch, because it was past three and she might be having fun pretending to be one of them, but it wasn't worth starving to death.

They went into the house, where Mary Beth showed Carla the refrigerator, said to help herself, then picked up her cell phone and started talking again.

Carla sighed and poked through the shelves, coming up with only a package of cheese and a questionable loaf of what looked like last week's bread. She wondered if rich people ever "ate in," unless they had someone to do the cooking, which right now it appeared Mary Beth did not.

When Mary Beth got off the phone, she said to Carla, "Sam wants you over at Nikki's camp. He has a computer and wants to know if you can find things on the Internet. He thinks he might have some software to help track down Lester. Whatever that means."

Closing the refrigerator door, Carla smiled. "Sure," she said, "I know the Internet. Lester paid for me to take a night course." Until now, she'd forgotten about that,

that Lester hadn't been all bad, that he hadn't only used her to pick up his dry cleaning and keep his office together.

Without warning, Mary Beth practically collapsed on the stool by the counter. "Oh, God," she said, "this is exhausting."

Carla nodded. "Planning a wedding," she said. "Yes, it must be."

Mary Beth shook her head. "It's not the planning, it's the paying. I never knew how much I took my money for granted."

Carla didn't know what to say, because she had no idea what that concept felt like.

"What am I going to do, Carla? I spent the rest of my cash today, giving these yahoos deposits so they will show up. I have nothing left. I'm not even sure if I can afford to get back to New York to finish everything on that end. And next week my daughter and God knows who else will arrive and be here until the wedding and I'll have to feed them and keep them in cocktails, plus find seventy-eight thousand dollars for His Highness, Phillipe, and I just don't know how I shall do everything, and do you think we'll find Lester by then?"

Carla just stared at her because she couldn't believe this was Mary Beth Atkinson talking to Carla DiRoma that way. Talking to Carla DiRoma at all! "You used an American Express card last night. It looked like a platinum card. They don't have a limit."

"No limit?"

"Well, that doesn't mean you can use it forever. Sooner or later, you have to pay up."

Mary Beth's eyes quickly brightened. "Sooner or later we will find Lester." Then she waved her hand. "Unfortunately, my caterer is demanding cash."

"What about your jewelry? Weren't you going to sell some?"

Mary Beth laughed. "I did. It was enough to pay for a month for my mother in that home."

Oh, Carla thought, remembering Dorothy Atkinson and how Mary Beth had placed her in Harriman House—the country club of the well-to-do elderly.

"You're poor," Mary Beth said, and Carla did not take it personally. "What would you do if you had to raise money? I just have no idea. I've never done it before."

Carla shrugged. "You own other stuff, don't you? You've got that Lincoln, and your apartment. And you must have some stuff. China, antiques, I don't know, stuff?"

Leaping off the stool, Mary Beth started pacing. "That's it!" she shrieked. "I have some Louis the Fifteenth pieces and Ming vases and Aubusson rugs." She circled the butcher-block island once, then twice. "I could call Sotheby's or Christie's. I could say I'm doing some redecorating, and have decided to do away with some tedious antiques that surely some other family would enjoy." She headed from the kitchen and Carla followed. "Yes! It's done all the time! Besides, it would be good to get rid of some of the junk, the stuff that cluttered my mother's life, the stuff I kept because I thought I was supposed to."

They ended up in the drawing room, where Mary Beth uncorked a bottle of wine. "It's not as if my mother will ever go back there, so she'll never know, right?"

Carla nodded, then shook her head when Mary Beth poured a glass of wine and offered it to her. Mary Beth slugged it down in one gulp.

"You're a genius," she said. "I'll go back to the city tomorrow, if Sotheby's or Christie's can get there that soon.

But first we'll call Nicole and see if someone can pick you up, if you don't mind helping Sam, even if it means you have to stay a few extra days?"

Did she mind? Well, Carla said, as a matter of fact, she did not.

# 17

$\underline{\hspace{1cm}}$

I'd like to see her," Gabrielle said when she and Nikki returned to the lighthouse after dinner at the dining commons—ham and baked beans and lots of happy background music of small voices having fun.

"Who?" Nikki asked, as she turned off the ignition and followed Gabrielle's gaze up to the big house.

"Aunt Dorothy."

Nikki frowned. "I'm not sure that she'd know you."

"I'd like to see her anyway. For me. Before I go home."

"Carla said Mary Beth plans to go back to the city tomorrow. We could go for a couple of days, too. I could see my agent and try to sell more paintings if I ever make the time to get back to work. We could visit with Aunt Dorothy."

Outside the car the crickets chirped while Gabrielle considered the idea. "I'd like that," she said. "I don't know when I'll ever come to the States again."

Nikki hesitated, then added, "For lack of funds, we could stay with Mary Beth, a supreme sacrifice for me, but I'd do it just for you."

Gabrielle laughed. "I think it's all marvelous, except

the part about staying with Mary Beth. She'll be crazy with this wedding. I have some money with me; we can get a hotel room. How about the Plaza?"

"Oh, right," Nikki said with a smile and opened the car door, "I keep forgetting that one of the Atkinsons still has a husband who is solvent." She was pleased to see Gabrielle respond with a grin.

Though it was Ben Niles's wife who owned the 1802, it was her twenty-one-year-old daughter, Amy, who ran it. The tavern, after all, had been in the family for nine generations, now ten, except for a hiatus of a few decades when it was owned by Charlie Rollins, who might as well have been family.

That's how it was on the Vineyard: Most year-rounders knew each other and knew they belonged, a closed society that took care of its own. Which was why later that night, when Nikki went down the alley and in the tavern's back door, Amy spotted her, waved, and said, "Yeah, he's upstairs."

He was sitting at the table, an unread newspaper in front of him, a large mug of coffee that Nikki would have bet was cold.

"I thought you might be lonely," she said, as she bent down and kissed the top of his head.

"That all depends," he said. "Did you bring me clean underwear?"

Nikki laughed and sat down. "You're hardly a fugitive, Mack. But, no, I didn't bring you clean anything. It's bad enough I had to sneak out to see you." She did not add that it reminded her of when she was young, with that boyfriend named Henry who lived in Oak Bluffs. "I told Gabrielle I had to go to camp to juggle the books."

He did not laugh.

"Mack," she said, "are you sure you don't want me to talk to her? Paris was a long time ago."

"And England," he said, dropping his gaze to the mug. "The first time I tried to see her, she was just finishing school. She wouldn't even speak to me then."

"And later in Paris she told you to leave."

Mack simply nodded, as he'd become so adept at doing.

She took his hands in hers. "I am so sorry, Mack. I am so sorry about Rose and so sorry about my mother..."

He cleared his throat.

She squeezed his hands. "Gabrielle and I are going to New York for a few days. She wants to see Aunt Dorothy, and I'm going to try to stir up some more work." She did not mention that Mary Beth would be there as well, that she was going to sell off her belongings to pay for a wedding. "I have a feeling that when we return, Gabrielle will go home."

He did not respond.

"Don't you want me to at least tell her you're here?"

He lifted the mug then set it back down.

"Gabrielle is your daughter, Mack." She tried to keep her voice as gentle as she could.

He stood up and dumped the coffee into the sink, the old cast-iron sink that had probably been forged a century ago, hauled to the Vineyard on an old wooden boat, then installed in the tavern. At some point the old sink made its way to the upstairs. Like most of them of a certain age, it had seen other places but had ended up there.

"Nicole," he said, and she felt herself tense when he called her "Nicole" because it reminded her of her ex-husband, or worse, of her mother. "I made a vow to your mother that I would not interfere with Gabrielle's life."

"You made a vow to my mother? What on earth for?"

"It was between us."

"Well, she's dead."

"It had—it *has*—nothing to do with you."

Suddenly Nikki felt like a child again, a child in the presence of the adults. And as often had happened to Nikki, the child, her defenses quickly took hold. "Gabrielle is my cousin," she said with slow-growing anger. "I never thought I'd see her again. She has suffered terribly because of this family, and I have no idea why. Excuse me for caring."

Mack returned to his chair.

"She killed herself," he said. "Did you know that?"

There was a heartbeat of a pause while his words drifted to her brain, which slowly grasped what he had said. "What?" she asked even then, though the message had been clear.

"Rose. She committed suicide."

The air grew thin inside the room; she felt a bit lightheaded.

"Your mother sent Gabrielle to England as soon as Rose was buried. She said if I told anyone the truth, she would tell the police I'd pushed Rose from the lighthouse, that I had killed my wife for her money. She also said if I went after Gabrielle she'd cut off her inheritance. Gabrielle would not only think her father was a murderer, but she'd also be left without a penny."

Nikki tried to absorb his words. "Rose killed herself?" she asked. "No. She stumbled on the jetty. The rocks were dangerous. . . . It was not an . . . accident?"

"Your mother made everyone believe it was."

Her brain churned again. "But why did she send Gabrielle away? And why did she cut her off from the rest of us?"

"Because Gabrielle knew," he said. "And so did I, because she told me. She saw it happen. My little girl saw her mother leap from the lighthouse and crash onto the rocks. And I was too devastated to do battle with your mother. It's a tremendous guilt I've carried with me all these years."

From the corner of the room, a ship's clock struck twelve bells.

Nikki then spoke. "Aunt Dorothy must have known."

Mack nodded slowly. "As flighty as your aunt Dorothy appeared, she was totally dependent on your mother."

Nikki shook her head. "She visited Gabrielle in England."

Mack was surprised. "Dorothy?"

"Every year on her birthday, while Gabrielle was at school. They secretly spent a week together in London."

A smile of sorts passed over his face.

"I can't believe my mother was so hateful," Nikki added.

"She thought she was protecting the rest of the family."

Nikki folded her arms. "And no one else ever knew?"

"As far as I know, only one other person. Your mother told him so that if I revealed what had happened—even after her death—Gabrielle would be cut off. He was paid very well to be my watchdog all these years."

She did not have to ask to whom he was referring. "Lester," she said, and Mack confirmed it. "But now Lester is gone and so is my mother and so is the money. Can't you go to Gabrielle now, Mack? Can't you tell her the truth and try to start over?"

But his pain seemed to get in the way of an answer.

Black. Who cared if it was June? New York was New York and black always counted.

Nikki folded the long black skirt and shuddered to

think she was actually considering what counted and what did not. But as long as they were going to be in the city, it wouldn't hurt to try to see Dee. She'd love for her daughter to meet Gabrielle; she wondered if Dee would love her the way they'd loved Aunt Rose.

Aunt Rose. It was so hard to believe she had killed herself, even though she had been so sad so much of the time, even though she'd confided about her abortion. But Aunt Rose had had Mack, and she'd had Gabrielle, and why would she have left them?

She shuddered again and tried not to let herself think of that now, but instead to think happy thoughts like the fact that Dee might be pleased to see that her mother actually remembered how to get off-island. For all their differences, Nikki knew she should be grateful that Dee was bright and energetic, and motivated enough to "make something" of herself. Nikki wondered when she would ever stop trying to mold her daughter into her own image, which she clearly was not, and when she would accept that once and for all.

Unlike what her mother had done with her.

Digging into the back of her small closet, Nikki found the perfect New York/Dee top: a black tunic with layers of fringed beads, in case anyone forgot that *she* needed acceptance too, acceptance as an artist first and an Atkinson last.

She stared into her suitcase and wondered if she'd get to see Dee, and if Dee would apologize about the abandoned dinner and if China would be mentioned.

Nikki had been to China, back in the eighties, when she'd gone around the world two or three times, trying to decide if she should stay married to Connor or have the courage to go off on her own. Somewhere between Fiji and the Falkland Islands she realized she was spinning faster than the globe. She disembarked the cruise-ship-of-the-month, hopped a shuttle to Rio, then a jet to New York, and stopped at her attorney's office before going home.

She could have told Dee all about China if her daughter would have listened. But Dee wasn't interested in the sights and sounds and people; she wanted to know their *business acumen,* for God's sake, this daughter of hers.

The positive side of going to New York, of course, was that Gabrielle would be with Nikki so maybe they could have fun. Nikki could show her Manhattan, such as she remembered; they could explore SoHo and the new Times Square. She did not know if she would—could— go with her to see Dorothy. She might be too inclined to harass the woman into an explanation about why Rose had killed herself and why Dorothy had not had the guts to protect young Gabrielle.

And what good would it do to harass poor Dorothy, who probably no longer knew who any of them even were?

Zipping her suitcase Nikki envied Gabrielle her freedom and her life and her home that was five thousand miles away.


Gabrielle carefully wrapped tissue around the aqua tea dress that she'd bought in town. She folded it gently to fit into the suitcase Nikki had let her borrow, because hers was too small for New York. Not for New York, exactly, but for the change of shoes, clothes, and bags that she'd want for two days and two nights in the city, two days and two nights with what was left of the Atkinsons in the place where she'd once lived from September through May.

She checked the shine on the aqua leather pumps and slipped them into felt bags.

*Two days with her family.* She wished Rosa were there, wished she could show off her daughter so that Aunt Dorothy would know that Gabrielle had turned out fine despite all her troubles.

That was, of course, why she'd become obsessed with the notion that she needed to look great, as great and as rich and as...worthy, as surely Aunt Dorothy thought they still were.

In the early years, she had thought of this reunion often, her return to the family that had once cast her aside. As a child, she had dreamed of meeting Aunt Margaret, of knocking a cup of hot tea into her lap. She had dreamed of yelling at Nikki and Mary Beth, shouting *how dare you* and *who needs you, anyway.* She had dreamed of someone—any one of them—wrapping their arms around her and giving her a hug and telling her everything was okay, now that she was home.

That was in the early years. As Gabrielle became a teenager, then was out on her own, it became increasingly clear that she was not welcome. "The pain is too great," Aunt Margaret said in her quarterly correspondence, "but we'll try to get to England this summer for a visit." But it was only Aunt Dorothy who had come. The visits from the others never happened, and more years passed and then Aunt Margaret died and Gabrielle moved on to Paris and hardly dreamed anymore, at least not about them.

Except, of course, her father. Many times she had wanted to ask Aunt Margaret if she knew why he'd disappeared, but she never did. She must have learned at a young age that the question would not be welcome, the way one knows not to walk out into traffic but does not remember being taught.

She'd almost asked Aunt Dorothy once, but was afraid if she did she'd lose her, too. And if it weren't for Aunt

Dorothy, Gabrielle would have felt completely abandoned.

But now she was going to see her, to thank her. So why
did it seem overwhelming?

Nikki walked into the room. "Ready?"

Gabrielle wrung her hands. "I don't know why I'm
nervous."

"It won't be easy to see her, especially if she has no
idea who you are."

"It isn't that. It's me. I feel like a girl fresh out of the
country. I don't know if I'm ready to go back into the
city."

"It's only a city. It's where you were born."

"I have fonder memories of the Vineyard than I do of
New York."

"That's because on the Vineyard there was space.
Space and fresh air. In the city we were squished together—Grandfather, my mother, me, you and your parents..."

Gabrielle nodded. "In that beautiful old brownstone.
You'd think I'd have loved it." She remembered a huge
stained-glass window on the wall of the staircase; she remembered the hand-stenciled moldings that encircled
each of the downstairs, velvet-curtained rooms. She remembered those things, but little else.

"The air in there was always too tense," Nikki said.
"It was because my mother lived there."

Gabrielle sighed and sat down on the bed. Why was
she putting herself through this? Why didn't she just go
back to Stefano, and pretend none of this had ever happened? But a small voice within her said *No, not yet.* "I
do want to see Aunt Dorothy," she replied. "And your
daughter, if she's around. And Mary Beth's."

Nikki sat down beside her. "Wow. All the Atkinson fe

males at the same time. Maybe Mary Beth could arrange a spa day for us."

She laughed. "Nikki, you are so cynical."

"I know. I can't help it." Nikki stood up and picked up the suitcase. "Just remember, we're family, Gabrielle. The past is the past and today is today." She leaned down and kissed her cheek. "Now come on, country girl, we've got a ferry to catch."

Gabrielle stood up and shook out her hair. "That's countess, to you," she replied with a smile and followed Nikki down the narrow spiral staircase and out into the world where she once had belonged.

On the way to the ferry they stopped at the camp. Alice seemed to have everything under control. "Stay forever, if you like," she jested to Nikki. "I have two new assistants and they're a lot less trouble." She pointed to the office, where Carla sorted name tags for the next group of campers. Molly was helping.

"I thought Carla was going to help us find Lester!" Nikki laughed.

"Help is help," Alice replied. "We get it where we can; you taught me that."

Nikki shook her head. "Well, for now I'm headed to New York to try to get some help by selling artwork."

Alice gave her a thumbs-up and Gabrielle bent down and gave Molly a long, wonderful hug, then a kiss on the cheek. Nikki watched with awe, sensing that her cousin had such a loving nature, when of the three Atkinsons, she would have been the one justified in not getting close to anyone, in never being able to open up her heart.

But would kindly, loving Gabrielle forgive Nikki if she

learned of her relationship with Mack? And would she forgive Mack?

They said their good-byes and went back to the car.

"She'll be all right," Gabrielle said, startling Nikki. "Molly," she continued. "I just have a feeling that she'll be all right."

Nikki wondered if Gabrielle recognized a survivor because she'd been one, too.

# 18

She had forgotten it was summer, the worst time to try to escape from the damn island. Mary Beth glanced around the small, crowded airport and hoped the wedding guests had already made their transportation arrangements, as she had recommended back in February. Most, of course, would come in private planes, but, nonetheless, arrangements had to be made.

Strutting to the ticket counter, she thought about Nikki. She couldn't believe Nikki wanted to drive to New York, which would take hours, when all she needed was to hop on a plane. If Gabrielle had the cash to put them up at the Plaza, they damn well could have flown with Mary Beth, who was going to put the airline ticket on her American Express now that Carla said she had no limit.

She supposed they hadn't wanted to fly because Nikki would want her car to traipse around Manhattan and come and go as she pleased without having to depend on taxicabs or planes or subway schedules. Did Nikki know that about herself, that she hated committing herself— hated being *beholden*—to anyone or anything?

And why the hell was Mary Beth concerned about that now?

Maybe Nikki simply detested the puddle-jumper, eight-or-so-passenger planes. Well, the truth was, Mary Beth didn't like them, either, but each time she needed to fly off-island she reminded herself of their safety record and the fact that the silly planes often flew when the ferries would not run, like in forty-mile-an-hour winds, which, thankfully, were not an issue that day.

What was an issue was that she had a wedding in less than two weeks and a houseful of antiques to sell off before then.

At least Sotheby's was doing her a special favor by getting there this afternoon. At least it shouldn't take too long, then she could get back to the business that really was important, like returning to the Vineyard for the final wedding push.

When, at last, she made it to the front of the line, Mary Beth announced, "One-way to New York." No sense making a commitment for the return trip.

Commitment? Ha! She thought of Nikki once again, who had not sustained a marriage because she'd felt so "trapped," who had not seemed to have a relationship, good, bad, or even just for sex in the years since her divorce. While the ticket agent scrolled through her computer, Mary Beth tapped her fingernail on the counter and tried not to wonder about the word *divorce,* and if Eric had returned to his senses yet and if he'd moved back home.

"Sorry," said the ticket agent. "We're all sold out today."

Mary Beth did not move. "You can't be sold out. You're never sold out."

The agent was a young girl in a turquoise polo shirt and jeans who obviously didn't know a thing about either the Vineyard or life. She shrugged.

Mary Beth leaned across the counter. "Put on another plane," she said. "I must get to New York."

"I'm sorry, ma'am, that's not my job."

"Then find someone whose job it is. And I suggest you find that person *now.*" She tried, she really tried, to keep her voice under control, to keep her growing rage from shooting out across the counter in a spray of angry spit.

The girl looked at her, then turned her eyes to the door that led out to the tarmac. The door had opened; a small stream of people sauntered into the terminal. They wore sunglasses and carried tote bags. Among them were two dogs, one black and one golden Labrador retriever.

"Excuse me," the ticket girl said. "I have to attend to these passengers first." She hopped off her stool before Mary Beth could make a lunge for her scrawny neck. "Check back with me in fifteen minutes."

Standing there alone, it took a moment for Mary Beth to realize that she had been abandoned. Perhaps the girl did not know the Atkinson name, or that their money had helped support this island for over half a century.

She slung her bag over her shoulder and looked around for a place to sit and wait out her quarter-hour. But all the chairs were taken by others wanting to escape, and the floor was strewn with baggage, carry-ons and otherwise. She headed out the front door to remove herself from the relaxed vacationers and to have a quiet smoke.


Outside on the sidewalk, she stood and smoked, cursing herself for not anticipating this hold-up and for not riding with Nikki and Gabrielle, who might get there before she did at this rate.

What if she missed Sotheby's? Could they come back tomorrow? Did she have another day to waste?

*Ohhh,* she thought, with a long, mournful exhale, how she hated the drama that her life had become.

Just then the sound of a young man's voice drew her attention. He seemed to struggle with his English as he talked with a taxi driver; his clothes did not resemble anything from L.L. Bean. Clearly he was neither an American nor a tourist; clearly he did not know where he was.

She watched with the idle curiosity of those with nothing else to do, until she distinctly heard the words, "Atkinson. Martha's Vineyard."

Mary Beth knew she should go to the man, but who knew who he was? One of her creditors, perhaps? She dug her sunglasses from her purse, put them on, and turned her head away.

Then she heard him say "Italy, yes. From Tuscany." And then she knew. It must be Gabrielle's husband.

"Good Lord," she said aloud, then crushed out her cigarette and approached him. "You must be Stefano." She extended her hand and removed her glasses. "I'm Mary Beth Atkinson. Gabrielle's cousin."

He had a wide smile that flashed beautiful white teeth. His skin was lightly tinged with the color of the earth and blended with the bronze light of the sun. He shook her hand.

"Stefano," he said. "Bonelli."

It was easy to see what had attracted Gabrielle. But aside from his good looks, Stefano seemed charged with energy, bursting with life. His hand was rough, a laborer's hand, one of strength and countless hours of toil. Gabrielle would like that. Nikki would, too. As for Mary Beth, she preferred the softer touch of a man who didn't work, lucky for her.

"Martha's Vineyard must be small," he said. "I did not expect to meet my wife's relative at the airport."

She laughed. "Oh, it's not so small. But I'm afraid you've missed your wife."

He frowned.

"She left by car this morning. She's gone to New York City with her other cousin, Nikki."

"How far is New York City?"

Mary Beth considered saying he could fly there with her, when the young ticket agent quickly came out the door. "We have one empty seat, ma'am," she said hurriedly. "But the plane is leaving now."

Quickly, Mary Beth scrawled "Camp4Kids" on the back of Stefano's used boarding pass. She thrust it at the taxi driver. "Get him there," she said. "It's in Oak Bluffs." She turned and headed toward the tarmac. "Gabrielle will be back in two days. They'll take care of you until then."

She had no idea if Alice would be pissed off or not, but Mary Beth had no time to make other arrangements. Sotheby's, after all, was doing her a favor by showing up so fast. She could not risk letting this opportunity pass by.


Carla sat at the computer, partly tending to her work, partly thinking about the twelve new campers whose packets she'd help Alice put together, kids with names like Sean Goddard, Marissa Juarez, Moses Thomas. Kids who hadn't been as lucky as her Donnie and her Vincent, even though her boys hadn't been raised like Atkinsons or even like Lester Markham.

Good old Lester. Her thoughts turned to *him* again, as she heard Sam across the room, talking on the phone with the head of the association at the co-op where Lester had lived, asking when had he last seen him and had Lester been doing anything out of the ordinary?

Like what? She wondered. Like carrying a satchel full of money—small bills, not in sequence, like in the old movies she and her mother had loved watching together?

In the old movies, it wasn't hard to find someone, given ninety minutes and two reels of film. But Carla knew it wasn't true in real life. Take her former husband *(please!)* she thought, and was glad she could now muster a smile at the thought of him. Carla had bought the baby food and the diapers, the school uniforms and the base-ball gloves and hockey sticks. Carla had been the one who put both her boys through parochial school and Donnie through community college, no thanks to the rat bastard who had left almost as quickly as he had come. *Pardon the pun,* she told herself with a chuckle that she always chuckled when she remembered that her first baby was born nine months after they had met, and that he'd left right after she became pregnant with the next.

Suddenly, Carla wondered what would happen if she used Sam Oliver's special police-database software to track down the bum, and if she could find him and sue for back child support. She hadn't tried finding him be-fore, because there was some pride in raising the boys herself, and some self-protection in the thought that if he'd paid no money, he could have no claim on them.

It would almost be worth it now, if not for the money, then to see the look on his ugly face.

Still, as the search engine whirred to life, she could not bring herself to type in her ex's name; the reality was that she still hurt because she had been dumped.

And so she typed in: *Lester Markham. New York City.*

Folding her arms, she waited for the magic to happen, for the little people who lived inside the computer to scurry about, opening and closing one file drawer after another, frantically trying to find some hint, some shred of Lester.

Stats popped onto the screen. Quickly, Carla scanned them. His home address, the office. Both locations had been vacated more than a month. Someone, however, had not notified cyberspace.

Delete the city.

*Whirr. Whirr.*

*Your search has found one match.* Only that same Lester Markham of New York City, as if there were only one Lester in the world.

Well, to her, that had been true.

She pondered that a moment, then entered something else: Stanislaus Markham, the name of Lester's cat.

*Whirrrrrrrr.*

*There are no matches for your search.*

This was hopeless. She had worked for the man, practically lived with the man, for twenty-six years. All those years of being like his wife...She'd ordered his food from the market, his airline tickets, his damn theater tickets! She'd R.S.V.P.'d his invitations! She'd—*OH, GOD,* she thought, as the answer came like a bolt from above that shot her upright on the rickety old chair and nearly knocked her off her butt onto the floor.

*How could she have forgotten?* She *had* ordered everything for Lester. By phone, online, and she'd paid his bills—all his personal bills—the same way she'd transferred the money to the cousins each month. The trusted, do-it-all Girl Friday she'd once been called, before sexist terms had gone out of style.

She closed her eyes and tried to slow her excitement to a professional pace. For Carla now knew one piece of information that would endear her to the Atkinsons, and secure her room at the big house, a welcome guest, now and forever more.

"Sam," she said quietly, as soon as he was off the phone. "I have a lead for you. I just remembered: I know three of Lester's credit card numbers and their expiration dates."

"Dee, it's Mom. I'm here at the Plaza with my cousin from Italy. She surprised us with a visit. We'd love to get together and all have lunch or dinner tomorrow...Do you know if Shauna and Jason are around? Mary Beth should be back now, too. Give me a call. Room six-twelve."

She hung up and smiled at Gabrielle. "No expectations that she'll call back."

Gabrielle smiled. "I hope she does. In the meantime, let's go to Times Square. Maybe we can get tickets to a Broadway show."

Mary Beth moved from room to room, making frantic notes on a yellow lined pad of this item and that, the material trinkets of a lifetime, proof that a family had lived and that it had lived well.

A family including Eric, scumbag of all time, whose presence apparently had not found its way back to the West Side of Central Park.

The good news was that Shauna was absent, too, so her daughter would not have to witness the piece-by-piece Atkinson demise. Hopefully, she would not burst through the door at any minute.

But Mary Beth had no time to think of family stuff right now: Sotheby's would arrive in half an hour. She returned to her yellow lined pad and made hurried additions.

And then the call came from Jonathan, the doorman: Ms. Marta Hendersen was there.

On the way into the foyer, Mary Beth paused at the

Federal-period mirror that topped off the list. She straightened her hair and put on her best "I am a very wealthy woman looking for a change" face to eliminate speculation that she might, in fact, be broke. Into her reflection she said a silent prayer that no one in her family would come home right then and there. Then she inhaled a deep inhale and opened the door.

Marta Hendersen wore a tailored navy suit and a detached expression. Behind her was a young man named William Something-or-other—Mary Beth didn't quite get his name, but decided it didn't matter. He seemed to be an assistant to the woman in navy blue.

They began in the library. Slowly, methodically, so precisely that Mary Beth feared she'd scream *Hurry up, for chrissakes.* They worked their way through the sitting room, the dining room, the music room. A few things from one room, a few from another, like plucking chocolates from each layer in the box and hoping no one would notice they were gone. The process took three hours.

By the time they made it to the upstairs study, Mary Beth's eyes darted from her watch to Marta Hendersen. How much longer could this take? Had the woman's calculations reached seventy-eight thousand yet, and would she write Mary Beth a check? "I hate to rush you," Mary Beth said, "but I have an appointment." It was, of course, not true.

Marta Hendersen nodded but did not appear to care.

It was another few minutes before the navy woman peeled the half-glasses from her nose, wiped her forehead, and said, "Of course, it's too late for the fall catalog."

Mary Beth had begun breathing again, apparently too soon. "What do you mean?"

"It's almost the end of June. The fall catalog has been

done for weeks. If we hurry, we can get your items in the winter collection."

"Winter?" Mary Beth asked as if she lived on a desert island and had never heard of such a thing.

"It's the best we can do. I wasn't under the impression you needed to sell the things quickly."

No, of course Marta Hendersen had no such impression. Mary Beth made sure she had not conveyed urgency. Many acquaintances in her social circle dealt with Sotheby's, bought and sold with them regularly. What if any of them found out?

She checked her watch again. "Winter," she repeated. "Well, I guess that will be fine." So much for Phillipe.

Marta Hendersen arranged for the truck to come tomorrow. Then she and William Something-or-other shook hands with Mary Beth and said good-bye. As they got on the elevator, Shauna was getting off.

"Mother," she asked, moving quickly to the front door that was still open, "what the hell is going on?"


Shauna had been raised better than to swear at her mother, or at anyone for that matter. It was not something an Atkinson woman did, unless provoked beyond reasonable means.

Mary Beth supposed that thinking her grandmother's treasures were being sold out from under her might be considered reasonable.

She smiled at her daughter and said, "The cook's not here today. I'll make us tea." It had to be kitchen tea, because the sterling in the dining room had been cataloged and tagged.

"Fuck the tea, Mother," Shauna replied, holding out her hand to stop Mary Beth from escaping to the kitchen and having time to think.

"Excuse me?" she asked, not because she hadn't heard her.

"I think I have a right to know what's going on," she said. Her voice trembled now, her cheeks were pink. "I want to know if what Daddy said is true, if you're selling this apartment because you need the money."

Mary Beth did not know what she wanted more: to know how and when and where Shauna had spoken with her father, or what this nonsense was about selling the apartment.

It did not surprise her that Eric was behind it.

She went into the library and sat on one of the leather sofas. "You're right, honey," she said. "Fuck the tea." She waited for a half-smile from her daughter that did not appear. Then she patted the cushion next to her. "Come here and tell me what happened."

Shauna remained standing as if unsure which way to go.

"Honey," Mary Beth repeated, trying to ignore the nerves that were exploding like tiny fireworks inside her heart. She knew that Shauna loved her father: They'd always had a good relationship, despite his errant-husband ways. Quietly she wondered if she were witnessing the tug-of-war that children of divorce endured and if this were a prelude to her future. "Please," she said, "can't we talk?"

Shauna slowly moved into the room. She sat on the edge of the sofa, not quite ready to offer trust. "Daddy said you don't have any money and that you listed the apartment. He said he heard it from Mrs. Ruddeforth who heard it from Mrs. Clarke who knows someone who handles the estate listings at Guinness and Sloan."

Mary Beth sighed. "I have no idea who told them something so preposterous," she said lightly while wondering, *Guinness and Sloan?* Didn't Roxanne's tennis partner work there from time to time? She made a mental note to call Roxie when she had a chance to see if she had heard the rumor, too. *God*, Mary Beth thought, *as if things aren't bad enough.* "Actually," she said about the crisis of the moment, "maybe the mix-up came because I've just had some people here from Sotheby's. I decided to redecorate. Freshen things up, you know? Maybe someone mistook that for... Who knows?"

"Mother—"

"And we need to talk about your father, darling. I will not allow the fact that he's moved out to interfere with your wedding."

"But Mother—"

Mary Beth held her index finger to her lips. "I don't know what he's told you, and I don't need to know. But the truth is we've been arguing a lot, and though it's all very silly, we decided to live under separate roofs for a short time, take a breather, you know?" She tried to smile. "It's really quite civilized. I shouldn't be saying this on what's practically the eve of your wedding, but after twenty years, well, sometimes both parties need a little break. Who knows. A teeny separation might help us find that spark again. It doesn't mean we don't love each other. And it doesn't mean we don't love you." At least the last sentence was true.

Shauna nodded, but did look her mother in the eye. "I'm not worried about the wedding, Mother. But what about the money? Have you really lost your money?"

No matter what, Mary Beth was damned if she was going to worry Shauna. What if Jason's family learned the truth and canceled the wedding? After all, why would they want their son to marry a girl without a trust fund? A girl who went into a marriage penniless—the way Eric had done?

No matter what, Mary Beth would not let that happen. And she would not have thought that Eric would do that either, not to Shauna.

Then again, she would not have thought he'd have the balls to leave this house and not come back.

"I've had a small situation happen with my trust fund administrator," she said, keeping her tone level and unexcited, a major feat for which she really must remember to thank God. "It's nothing that can't be worked out." She could not tell if Shauna believed her, but she hoped she wouldn't ask for details.

Shauna stood up. "Mother," she said, her lower lip quivering, "I'm going to move in with Jason until we go to the Vineyard for the wedding. I don't know what's really going on between you and Daddy, and I don't care about the money, but I do know I'm getting ready for the rest of my life, and I can't take the chaos of all this turmoil. I'm sorry."

She started for the door, but Mary Beth could not let her leave just yet. "Shauna," she called out. "Please, honey, can you answer me one question?"

Shauna stopped but did not turn around.

"Where is Daddy anyway? Is he living at the club?"

"I have no idea," her daughter said, then left.

And Mary Beth sat there feeling sad about her daughter and angry about Eric, but grateful that Shauna would not be there tomorrow when Sotheby's backed their truck up to the door.

# 19

It was almost as if no one had realized that Carla would be alone in the big house tonight and have the Atkinson estate all to her lonesome self. It hadn't even dawned on her until after lunch that Mary Beth and Nikki and Gabrielle had all left for New York.

Carla DiRoma, mistress of the mansion. Wouldn't her mother have flipped?

She had helped Sam scan the photos of Lester and e-mail them to police stations all over the country; she had continued her computer search, which had so far turned up nothing, though Sam said he had a couple of leads based on Lester's credit card information.

All day, however, Carla thought about how much fun tonight would be, if she would only have the guts to go poking through the house.

Maybe just peek into those little desk drawers in the drawing room? Would that be considered illegal if somehow she got caught?

She'd love to scope out Mary Beth's room. Was her closet packed full of clothes; was her bathroom loaded with expensive makeup and imported perfume; did she have real silk nightgowns and could Carla wear one and

pretend to sleep with Lester, to have rich people's sex under the five-hundred-dollar comforter?

She was checking the clock and looking forward to
leaving camp for the day, when Alice came into the registration office with a dark-haired, gorgeous guy. It was the
same guy she'd seen outside with Alice earlier that day;
she had no idea who he was.

"Carla," Alice said, "this is Stefano Bonelli. Gabrielle's husband."

Gabrielle's husband? What was he doing there?

"Obviously there's been a mix-up and Stefano didn't
realize Gabrielle would be in New York. We've been back
out to the airport, but he can't get to the city today, so he
might as well wait here for her. Unfortunately, my inn is
booked. We've checked all over the island, but it's summer. Our only option is the estate, if you don't mind."

Mind? What right did she have to mind?

"No," Carla replied, "of course I don't mind." There
was, after all, a lock on her door, and she could always
sleep in her clothes. So much for her daydream of big-
house explorations, which was probably just as well. She
went back to work and wondered if she'd ever be able to
stop her foolish daydreams and end up with a real life of
her own.


For one night and a morning, Nikki almost forgot that
another day had passed and they still had not found
Lester, that her remnant funds would soon be scarce and
her kids were still in need.

She and Gabrielle had caught *Les Misérables* and a
late supper: Back at the hotel, a message from Dee
awaited—"How about lunch at one o'clock at Dave
Girotti's Pasta Bar on West Forty-eighth?" Dee did not
apologize for standing Nikki up on the Vineyard. Still,

Nikki smiled at Gabrielle and said, "Hey, you never know. Someday she might like me after all." She should have known Dee had something else on her mind. The morning was clear and sunny; Gabrielle went off sightseeing while Nikki met with her agent, then the cousins met on West Forty-eighth in time for lunch. Not surprisingly, Dee was half an hour late.

"Sorry," she said, without much sincerity. She slid into the booth beside her mother.

"This is Gabrielle," Nikki said, "my cousin."

Dee shook Gabrielle's hand. "Wow," she said, "You're young."

"Just for that, I'm buying lunch," Gabrielle said, and Nikki knew she had probably intended to all along, what with her having money and what with Nikki not.

"I know," Dee said as Gabrielle was watching her. "I don't look like my mother. I look like my father. Do you know him?"

Gabrielle shook her head. "I left the States when I was very young."

"Gabrielle is a countess," Nikki said, and she could tell right away Gabrielle wished that she hadn't. "Can you imagine?" she added, trying to smooth over her bungle, "and we thought Mary Beth was the only royalty in the family."

"The only thing royal about Mary Beth is that she's a pain in the ass," Dee said, and they all laughed, and Nikki felt comfortable with her daughter and very much liked the feeling.

Gabrielle then told Dee about the vineyard in Tuscany and the villa that she lived in and about her daughter, Rosa. Nikki was pleased that Dee was behaving in a civil, pleasant manner, asking questions about Italy and the business of wine-making. But then, halfway through the conversation, halfway through the linguine *olio,* Dee asked Gabrielle, "So you're Uncle Mack's daughter?"

Nikki almost choked. Dee had never seemed to care enough about the odds and ends of the family to pay attention to details; it never crossed her mind that she would mention Mack. Would she reveal that he lived on Martha's Vineyard?

Nikki spoke quickly. "Gabrielle and Uncle Mack haven't seen each other for years. They've decided it's really better if they don't." Fortunately Dee was a smart girl.

"Oh," was all she said, followed by "Sorry." Then she added, "Before I forget, Mom, Dad wants to have dinner with you tonight."

"Connor?"

"Yes," Dee replied, "I believe that's his name."

Nikki ignored her curt response. "I don't know," she said. "I have a full afternoon booked with my agent... we have several galleries to visit... tomorrow morning we're going to visit Aunt Dorothy..."

Dee shrugged. "He said he'll pick you up at your hotel at eight o'clock, unless you call him and say no."

An awkward silence drifted over the booth, a feeling more familiar to Nikki when she was with Dee. Then Dee dropped the other shoe that she often carried. "And speaking of divorce, I want to ask you a question. Is Uncle Eric screwing another woman, and, if he is, do you think Aunt Mary Beth knows?"

Nikki dressed in the black pants with the beaded top. Dinner with Connor would seem odd enough: She didn't want to dress up as if this were a date. It was bad enough Gabrielle had gone out on her own—they'd called Mary

Beth, who'd shrieked, "We're a little busy. Have you checked the calendar?" They mentioned that tomorrow they were going to visit Dorothy before they went back to the Vineyard, to which Mary Beth made no comment, brusque or otherwise.

If Nikki had had more warning she might have made an excuse about tonight, but Gabrielle convinced her there was no reason to say no. Connor had been invited to Shauna's wedding; seeing him tonight might make his presence there more comfortable. Besides, he might want to discuss an issue concerning Dee.

Pinning up her hair so the flecks of silver wouldn't show, Nikki wondered if Gabrielle had encouraged her because she thought there was a chance Nikki and Connor could get back together. Nikki, of course, had failed to mention she was in love with someone else.

Was Eric?

Her thoughts moved to what Dee had said at lunch, that she'd seen Eric at the club, "getting hot with a red-head on the balcony." She hadn't gone too close, but she'd known that it was him. Who else left a trail of woodlike musk and wore those queer gray suits in summer?

Nikki stared into the mirror and wondered if Mary Beth knew. How could she not? Mary Beth made it her business to know everything. But did such ability to control still count when love and trust—and emotion—were figured in the mix?

She checked the back of her hair. It would be nice to have a pretty hair clip. No, she told herself, this was *not* a date. Though she and Mack had never said the word "commitment," it had been implied.

Unfortunately, despite their differences, she and Connor had always had great sex.

Unfortunately, a few million of Connor's dollars would help her life right now. Today her agent had placed another dozen paintings of Nikki's "kids." If Nikki found the time to do them—and *if* the portraits sold—they'd raise around six thousand dollars, maybe seven. Not much to live on for too long, never mind The Rose Foundation and the camp.

She glanced at her watch. Still an hour until he'd be there. On the Vineyard dinner was at six, not eight. On the Vineyard by now she would have either climbed to the top of the lighthouse to study her morning's work, snuggled onto the sofa with an afghan and a book, or retreated to the caretaker's cottage, where she'd be wrapped up in Mack's arms and legs and love.

Instead she sat there, waiting for her former husband, whom, in truth, she might see more often if it wasn't so disturbing.

She knew that even at fifty, Connor still looked good. His dark hair had lightened and thinned on the top, his shoulders were a little more narrow, his waist a little thicker. But he still had a dreamy look in those gray-green eyes that belied his corporate savvy and his total power in the boardroom.

In short, he had the walk and talk and smile and brains that magnetized success. Her mother had seen it when Nikki had first met him at the inaugural ball for Mayor Koch in 1977. She hadn't wanted to go, but Margaret had insisted: "You never know whom you will meet." Two years later, she hadn't wanted to marry Connor, either, but by then he was wrapped up in the business.

And there was the sex.

It was one of those rare times in her life when Nikki decided to please her mother and do something conventional.

It hadn't been a bad marriage, it just hadn't been right.

She tapped her foot and checked her watch again. Only ten minutes had passed. She folded her hands, unfolded them, and touched the back of her hair. Then she stood up, grabbed her purse, and headed for the door. Maybe the shop downstairs had a pretty hair clip, one that didn't cost the fortune that she'd lost.


Tuesday evening on Fifth Avenue in midtown Manhattan seemed as deserted as a tomb in the Valley of the Kings. The shops were closed; the buildings locked up; this part of the city was not Paris or London, where real nightlife didn't start until the wee hours began.

The only places Gabrielle saw open were a couple of restaurants and the church.

She hated dining alone, so she sat in the back of St. Patrick's Cathedral now, waiting until she could return to the Plaza, until Connor would have taken Nikki to dinner.

Inside the massive stone structure it was quiet and cool and softly glowing from the hundreds of candles that burned in the side alcoves, each flame casting hope or thanks or remembrance for people and life lived or lost.

She should light a candle for Rosa and Stefano, for God to keep them safe until she returned. And for them to forgive her, if that were possible.

She should light a candle for herself, to ask God's forgiveness of every wrong she had done, of every secret she'd harbored since she was a child.

Lowering her head, Gabrielle felt a tear run from her eye and drop onto her lap. Most times she'd been able to handle her secrets; most times, she had been able to keep them close to her heart and know they hurt no one as long as they stayed there.

The earliest she remembered was when she was at school, when she'd told the other students that she was an orphan, that the woman who visited every year on her birthday was an eccentric old maid who once had known her mother. She'd never had to explain who her father was because the time he'd come, she'd simply walked away.

When she lived in London she told her roommates she'd been raised in an orphanage and had never known her parents, but that a check came every month from their estate. She didn't know why she said these things. Self-pity? Attention? Perhaps it was only a way to explain the loneliness she felt, the way she always felt poised on the edge of a cry, certain everyone knew, but that they did not care.

In Paris she denounced her wealth to everyone she met, not with words but with lifestyle, waiting on tables, living in a walkup studio on the Left Bank that once had been trendy but by then was just old. She denounced her wealth, and then she'd denounced her father to his face. All to keep her secrets. The way she kept the trust fund from Stefano. And the worst secret of all, letting him believe that Rosa was his daughter, when she was not. Instead, Rosa had been the untimely gift of a brief affair with a very married man who'd wanted neither of them when he'd learned Gabrielle was with child.

She closed her eyes as more tears came. She had come to hate her secrets, had come to feel the pain they could inflict. It was too late for her, but maybe not for Nikki.

Nikki who, starting with The Rose Foundation and working backward, had given all her dollars to those less fortunate. And now Nikki deserved some peace. She deserved the right for her legacy to continue; she deserved to be free of the secret that the money now was gone.

Gabrielle could only hope Nikki would understand why she'd done what she had done.

The bell tower chimed eight-fifteen. She fumbled in her purse and lit several candles on her way out.

"You're beautiful," Connor said as he gazed at her across the candlelit table at Chez Aiglon.

"Ha!" Nikki replied. "You've always been far-sighted." She sipped her wine, unable to decide if she found his words flattering or if they made her squirm.

"I'm serious, Nicole. The Vineyard is good for you. You look so unstressed."

She shrugged. "What's to be stressed about? I have my work, I have my art, I have my—"

"Independence?"

In spite of herself, she smiled. "Yeah. My independence."

He smiled something that looked like a sad smile. He lowered his eyes and straightened his silverware. Nikki felt an urge to reach out and put her hand on his, to say she was sorry for the pain that she had caused.

"Our daughter is turning out a lot like her mother," he said.

She was glad she didn't have wine in her mouth or she would have sprayed it across the room. "I think you have me confused with someone else, Connor. Dee is precise and organized, a very anal business mogul. She is you. She is my mother. She is not me. She is not even close."

"Oh, she's every bit you. She's stubborn and independent—there's that word again."

Nikki straightened. She had never thought Connor was so out of tune that he would not know his own daughter, or his ex-wife. Then again, she thought...stubborn...independent.

No. No way. Dee could not be like her.

"And in every relationship she falls in love with the

idea of being in love. But she does not really fall in love with the person. Did you know that?"

Is that what he thought Nikki did?

She frowned. "I hardly know what Dee looks like any more, never mind how she thinks. Mother and daughter don't communicate real well." She did not mention lunch today because she did not want to talk about Gabrielle or Mary Beth or even Eric, for that matter.

"Maybe if you tried a bit harder to understand, instead of always being braced for confrontation..." He dismissed his words with a wave of his hand. "Enough. You and I can find other things to argue about without talking about Dee." His smile softened his statement.

Nikki tried not to sound defensive. "I assumed that's why we're having dinner. To talk about our daughter."

"No. Not at all."

The waiter arrived with their chateaubriand. As he carved tableside, Nikki dutifully watched and feigned a hearty appetite that surely the filet would cure. But she wasn't hungry. Getting ready for tonight, racing downstairs, finding a black satin hair clip, then pacing until he showed up, and now, hearing him say that dinner was not about Dee, the daughter with whom Nikki was "always braced for confrontation"—Nikki was not hungry. Instead, she was feeling guilty about Mack. Could dinner with her ex be construed as cheating?

The plates were served and Connor dug in with the gusto she did not feel.

"Okay," she said. "So if not to talk about Dee, then why are we here?"

He smiled again. "Can't I invite my ex-wife out for a meal? Was there something about that in our divorce decree?"

She tried to relax. She sliced her carrots.

Then he groaned and set down his fork. "I cannot tell

a lie," he said. "Did you ever make a promise that you couldn't keep?"

She frowned. "Sure. To love, honor, and cherish till death do us part."

The hurt that dulled his face made her regret she'd been sarcastic.

"Anything a little less...dramatic?"

She picked up her wine. "Connor, tell me what's going on. You are terribly inept unless you are being direct."

"You're right," he replied. He slow-blinked his eyes as if taking a deep breath. Then he said, "I know, Nicole. I know that your trust fund is gone."

The white noise of the restaurant rose and fell in natural cadence as if Connor had not just said what he'd said, as if they were discussing the news or the weather or the flavor of the steak.

"Well," she said, as she took her napkin from her lap, folded it, twisted it, then put it back. "I guess that's direct enough."

"I'm sorry," he said. "I know if you wanted me to know you'd have told me yourself."

Yes, she would have. She even might have, until now, until she'd developed an uneasy sense that she'd been duped.

"I need to ask who told you," she said, "only because I need to know who else knows."

"That's the 'promise' part."

She leaned forward. "Fuck the promise," she said. "You already blew it."

He smiled that sad smile. "Your cousin, Gabrielle," he said. "She called me this morning. She's worried about you, Nikki. She's worried about, as she put it, your kids. She's afraid your pride is going to ruin your good work."

Nikki did not answer, because the wine that she'd drunk and the small amount of food that she'd eaten were making their way back up her throat. *Gabrielle? What gave her the right...*

"I can help," he added quickly. "I think you're doing a wonderful thing with the foundation. But please, Nicole. For once, just let me help."

She picked up her napkin again. This time she set it on the table, next to her plate. "This is my fight, Connor, not yours."

"But..."

Nikki stood up. "Please, finish your meal. But I'm going back to the hotel, and I'd rather be alone."

# 20

It was the way she held her head, tilted to one side, chin slightly up, as if awaiting conversation or cause for a smile: That was how Gabrielle recognized Aunt Dorothy, despite the years since she'd seen her, despite the woman's illness.

Gabrielle paused by the entry into the garden and wondered why Nikki would not come this morning. Had Connor told her Gabrielle called him, and if so, what did one thing have to do with another? All Nikki said this morning over coffee was "We'll talk about it on the way home," and "No, I won't be going to see Dorothy."

Smiling a small smile, Gabrielle entered the garden and went to where Dorothy sat.

"Aunt Dorothy," she said, "do you remember me? It's Gabrielle, Rose's daughter."

The slightly tilted head looked up. She did not respond, but seemed to study Gabrielle's face. Pulling a chair from the table, Gabrielle sat and faced the woman. Then she took one of her hands. She was surprised at how brittle the aging skin felt. Was that how skin felt once it had passed seventy?

"Remember when you visited me in England? You

came every year on my birthday, and, oh, what fun we had! You took me to London and we went to Harrods and the theater and the sweetshops..."

"Rose," Aunt Dorothy said, her faded eyes brightening, a light tint of pink rising in her cheeks. "You look wonderful, dear. Just like yesterday."

An aura of slow motion filled the fragrant garden air. Somewhere nearby a songbird chirped a sweet song, but its soft voice was muted by the distance between Gabrielle and her aunt, the distance between reality and remembrance. Gabrielle felt a sudden sorrow, not for Aunt Dorothy, who seemed to sense some delight, but for Mary Beth, who had to witness her mother's slide from the present, who could never bring back her mother as she'd once been.

"This is my sister, Rose," Dorothy said happily, and Gabrielle realized her aunt was speaking to a woman who moved past with a walker, its small rubber wheels traversing the flagstone. "Isn't it nice that she's come?"

The woman with the walker slowed and said, "Hello, Rose," and Gabrielle smiled and said, "Hello" in response.

Though Gabrielle's back was to her, Mary Beth could hear the conversation from where she stood, a few feet from the garden. She had wanted to join them; she had hoped Gabrielle's presence might trigger Dorothy's memories of Lester. But standing there, watching Gabrielle pretend that she was Rose, seeing the gentleness with which Gabrielle held Dorothy's hand, feeling the...*feelings*...Mary Beth knew she needed to leave. After all, she could not stand around in tears when so much needed to be done.

\*     \*     \*

As they drove up I-95, out of the city and back toward the Vineyard, Nikki clutched the steering wheel and leaned into her door as if a black widow spider had roosted on the passenger seat. Gabrielle had tried to make small talk about Dorothy, but Nikki had not wanted to listen.

"I can't believe you betrayed our confidence," she finally said just outside of Stamford, once the skyline of Manhattan had faded far behind them.

"Oh," Gabrielle replied. "He told you."

"Yes, he told me. I was his goddamn wife. I am the mother of his daughter. Yes, he told me." She was not sure what being his ex-wife and Dee's mother had to do with Connor's confession, but it did not seem to matter.

"I'm sorry," Gabrielle said, but added nothing more.

They drove along the Connecticut shore through Westport and Fairfield and the last of the bedroom communities whose tony neighborhoods would once have seemed middle-class compared with the Atkinson fortune.

When they reached New Haven, Nikki spoke again. "You had no right, Gabrielle. No right to interfere with my life."

Gabrielle did not say she was sorry again, but simply, "I didn't see it that way."

The CD did not play; the radio was not on. They rode another hour in silence, each with her thoughts.

The worst part for Nikki was that, in Gabrielle's shoes, she might have done the same thing. It looked so good on paper: Nikki was broke, hundreds of sick kids depended on her income; Connor had piles of money; Connor had once loved Nikki and she had loved him.

What harm in asking?

But Gabrielle didn't know that Nikki loved Mack, that she no longer wanted or needed her ex-husband. "For once, just let me help," he'd said, as if she weren't capable of taking care of things herself, as if he were her mother, who could do a better job.

"I forbid you to leave him," Margaret had shouted when Nikki returned from that fateful world trip. "If you dare disobey me, you will not see one penny more from me or from Connor, I will see to it."

Connor, of course, represented all that her mother—or any of the Atkinson women—had never had: He was a clever businessman who underscored her importance insofar as it looked to the world and who actually put up with her self-important shit.

Clearly, however, her mother had never gotten it, that Nikki didn't want or like the Atkinson money. Margaret's threat to Nikki became one more challenge, yet another vehicle for thumbing her nose.

She went ahead with divorce and took it a step further: It was then that she decided to give away every cent she had, every dime that had been earned, stolen, or invested in the Atkinson name.

Mary Beth thought she was crazy, but she always had. When Nikki asked if she'd let Nikki live in the lighthouse, Mary Beth had laughed.

"Why would you want to? Have you forgotten about the padlock that we thought kept the ghosts inside? My God, Nikki, have you forgotten Aunt Rose died right there on the jetty?"

No, Nikki had not forgotten.

She never challenged her mother's threat about asking for one penny either from her or from Connor. She moved into the lighthouse, gave away the income from her trust fund every month, worked at the bakery, and sold enough of her paintings to afford a meager existence. She had gone on with her life.

She had not been unhappy, even before Mack. From time to time, she was lonely, but she'd not been unhappy.

She hung onto the steering wheel now and did not mean to say out loud, "Dealing with Mary Beth is difficult enough, Gabrielle. I do not need my ex-husband behind the scenes of my life, too."

They crossed the border into Rhode Island. Gabrielle turned her face from the window and Nikki saw that she'd been crying.

"It's worse than you think, Nikki," Gabrielle added. "Mary Beth suggested I tell him. She called our hotel room after you went to meet your agent yesterday. She's in big trouble, Nikki. She really needs money. She convinced me Connor might help her, too, if he knew what was really going on."

Nikki pulled off the highway onto the shoulder. She dropped her face into her hands. "Oh, God, Gabrielle, I can't believe you were fished in by our manipulative cousin."

"I know what she is, and I know who she is. But I also know Mary Beth is the only one of us left with a mother, and she has the responsibility of caring for her. She can't help the way she was raised—any more than we can change the things that happened to us.

"But you're the one who said it, Nikki—we're family. I haven't told her yet, but I've decided to give Mary Beth some money to help keep Aunt Dorothy comfortable. I'd be glad to give you some as well, but I figure you wouldn't accept it.

"I'm sorry if I crossed the line; I was only trying to help make everyone happy. And by the way, Mary Beth thinks your ex-husband still loves you, and she said you might not be such a martyr if you would just get laid."

It was one of those summer mornings when humidity loomed, threatening to suffocate New York as if it were

Alabama. Mary Beth had returned home from Harriman House and wanted to strip off her beige linen dress and put on some shorts. But the Sotheby "movers" had already arrived, and she must look her best, even for them.

Besides, there was always the chance Eric would come home, and she would not let him think she had "let herself go," that she was mourning his ridiculous departure. Let him get down on his knees and beg for her mercy, but let him do it while she was in Donna Karan and not Levi Strauss.

She stood in the library, dabbing her forehead with a fingertip towel, grateful that Shauna was not there to witness the parade of Louis XIV, XV, and XVI marching out the door, or to have to watch the good servant Marta Hendersen studiously checking the list on her clipboard once, then twice.

Mary Beth stood and dabbed and watched the performance, because she did not know what else to do. Should she turn on the air-conditioning? (Could she afford it?) Perhaps she should just sit quietly and thumb through a magazine. She supposed that others in her circle would have left this supervision to the trusted help. But even if Mary Beth had had a live-in, she'd have had to let her go by now, because of the money or lack thereof, of course.

If this were Victorian times, she could sit at her small desk and attend to her correspondence. But her desk, like other things, would soon be in Marta's hands.

So she stood, arms folded, and tried not to think about her mother and about how childlike Dorothy had looked this morning, and how she would feel if she were there, as the wood and silver and china pieces of her life were snugly wrapped, then carted away by muscle boys named Bruce and Pete and Manuel.

At least her mother was safe for another month, maybe

more. But what about after the wedding? Were there things at the house on the Vineyard that no one would miss if Mary Beth were careful and didn't sell too much?

She wiped another line of perspiration that had surfaced on her brow. She could have smoked a cigarette but did not know where she'd hidden her last pack, and besides, it was difficult enough to breathe.

The phone rang. She darted to answer it: Aha, something to do!

It was Beverly McGuire, of the Palm Beach McGuires. "Darling, I have such sad news," Beverly drawled in her slow, Southern drawl. "Lamar has been having some trouble with vertigo again, so I'm afraid we won't be at the wedding. Flying, you know. It's bad for his inner ear."

Mary Beth commiserated as best she could, what with Bruce and Pete and Manuel navigating the hand-carved Georgian chest around her and Marta checking it off the list. She hung up and wondered if she should send bubble wands to the McGuires, as well as the Potters and the Chapmans, who had left messages earlier that they would not be attending after all. Six bubble wands in all—well, why not send them? They could not be returned, on account of the engraving.

She was considering the possibility when the phone rang again. She smiled to herself that at least the Sotheby's contingent would believe the Atkinsons were quite active, not on their way out.

"Ms. Atkinson?" the new caller asked. "This is Melissa DeVane from Guinness and Sloan. Perhaps you're familiar with us?"

It took her a second to realize this was not another invited guest. "Yes, I've heard of you."

Melissa DeVane cleared her throat. "It's come to my attention that you might want to sell your apartment."

Mary Beth did not reply, because she did not want to say "Go to hell, bitch" in front of Marta and her clan.

"I have a client who is very interested," Melissa DeVane added.

Mary Beth turned away from the eyes of Ms. Hendersen. "I'm sorry," she said, "but you've been misinformed." She promised to let Ms. DeVane know if she changed her mind, then hung up with caution so no one would suspect that inside she might explode.

As soon as Sotheby's was finished, she'd go back to the Vineyard. At least there she could immerse herself in last-minute wedding minutia, and be up-to-date on any word of Lester.

God. Every time she thought his name now her blood pressure escalated a dozen or more points.

Struggling for a deep breath, or even for a small one, she decided, yes, she would get out of the city as fast as she could. She would drive, not risk being unable to get a flight. And if there were no car slot on the first available ferry, she'd sit in a bar in Woods Hole and wait until there was one. Anything was better than standing in the smoldering humidity, feeling like a woman who'd once had it all, feeling like it was her fault that her life had taken this hideous U-turn.

"Bingo," Sam said as he hung up the phone, and Carla laughed because she thought only the ladies at St. Michael's said that, on Wednesdays at seven.

"What's bingo?"

"American Airlines, Flight three twenty-six. It seems that our little friend Lester has taken a trip to Punta Cana. And he billed it to his credit card." He leapt off the old chair in the cottage at the camp and said, "I'm going to Alice's to pack a few things. Would you be a good kid and get me on the next flight out of Logan?"

"To Punta Cana? Where is that?"

"I have no idea. But if Lester could find it, I'm sure I can, too."

He raced out the door, and Carla chased after him, reminding him to bring the clippings of Lester, her treasured pictures.


They drove right to the camp so Nikki could check with Alice and be sure things were all right. The conversation they'd had for the rest of the trip had been strained, limited to short takes of questions and answers on safe ground.

"Your daughter, Dee, seems very smart."

"Yes. She takes after her father. She goes to Harvard."

Then later:

"I hope Mary Beth's trip proved to be successful."

"This wedding means more to her than it does to Shauna."

And, as they arrived at Camp4Kids:

"Sam's daughter is so sweet, and he is so nice."

That time, Nikki nodded. "We're lucky to have them both."

As she parked the car, Gabrielle said softly, "Nikki, I'm sorry. I truly am sorry for upsetting you so much."

Nikki shrugged. "It's not your fault, Gabrielle. It's not your fault that you were sent away and you have not been privy to the family dynamics." She got out of the car, but Gabrielle did not follow her. She had decided it was time to go home, back to Stefano. She had seen and done enough and had her fill of closure. The time had come to now go home and face the damage that her leaving might have caused.

She would check on flight availabilities, just as soon as she went down to the pond in search of Molly so she could say good-bye.

Instead of Molly, Gabrielle found someone else.

She could not speak. Her knees grew weak; she leaned against a tree. He walked up from the pond, where he'd been tossing beach balls with the children.

He came close to her and gently lifted a strand of hair that had fallen on her face.

"Gabriella," he said while his eyes roamed her eyes, her cheeks, her nose, her lips. He kissed her mouth.

Her body trembled; tears came quickly.

"Gabriella," he said again.

The trembling grew worse. He put his arms around her and held her while she cried. Then he guided her to the ground to a blanket of soft pine needles. He held her until her tears were gone.

"I have missed you," he said. "Why did you not come home?"

Oh, God, she thought. How had he found her? How long had he been there? Had they told him of her lies?

"I tried to call you. I only got the recording."

"I must have been on my way. I've been here for two days."

They did not speak a moment. Gabrielle watched the children at play, savored their laughter, and wondered if she'd ever been so innocent.

"Rosa?" she asked.

"She is fine."

"You did not bring her?"

"No."

She curled the edges of the cotton belt she wore on her cropped pants. "Is she with Angelina?"

He took her hand. "Yes. There was no one else to take her."

The ache inside her rose again. "There are so many things you do not know," she said. "Enzio was right. You should not have married an American. You should not have married me."

"Because you are so rich?"

The laughter of the children suddenly grew distant, as if she had crossed the time and space between life and death, the purgatory of self-truth. She raised her eyes and looked straight ahead, afraid to meet his gaze.

"You know," she said quietly. He knew about her heritage. He knew about her money. The money that, by rights, should have been not only hers but theirs.

"I have known from the beginning."

She turned to him sharply. "What?"

"I have always known, Gabriella. When we first met in Paris, when I knew I wanted you for my wife, I found out what I needed to know."

She did not move. Her aching turned to stone. "What?" she repeated.

"I learned about your family. I learned about your wealth and about this place called Martha's Vineyard. I don't know why you would not confide in me, but it did not matter, then or now. I love you, Gabriella. Please come home with me."

She could not believe this. He had known all along? "This is a lie," she said. "You are making it up."

He shook his head. "If you do not believe me, ask Enzio. He's the one who found out the information. Because I asked him to."

"You asked him to investigate me?" She did not know if she were more hurt, enraged... or terrified about what might come next. To think that during all those hours of intimacy...to think that he had been checking up on her, deceiving her...

"Gabriella," he said, "please try to understand. My family carries the Bonelli name..."

She stood and shook off his hand that had been clinging to her arm. "Your family carries nothing," she stammered. "Your family is dead and gone, with nothing to show for it but some overworked land and a villa that's falling down." Even as she said the words she knew they were too harsh; she knew Stefano did not deserve this, but still she could not stop, as if her common sense was in fierce battle with her conscience.

"Gabriella," he whispered. "Please..."

She walked to edge of the pond. She felt a little dizzy. She squatted down and leaned against an old rowboat. "You must go, Stefano." She spoke without looking at him, because she could not. "I must straighten things out here. Then I will return to Tuscany for Rosa. She and I will come back to America, where I will not live in such deceit." She was surprised that her heart was not pounding, but was quiet and quite calm, a heart resolved to breaking, as it had been all along.

"You will not take Rosa from me," he answered sternly.

She closed her eyes because she could not fight about this now. She was too weary, she was too full of anguish. "Go home, Stefano," she said again. There would be plenty of time for fighting later, when he learned the rest of her betrayal, when she told him that Rosa was really not his daughter. When she told him Rosa had not been "premature," but had been born on time.

Unless he already knew that, too.

# 21

The day had never ended and the traffic had been deplorable. By the time Mary Beth arrived at Woods Hole, there was a standby line as long as the line at Radio City the week before Christmas. And it was the last boat out tonight.

She had driven the Town Car because Eric had taken the Range Rover and because she couldn't very well ask Charlie to drive her to the Vineyard. How would she explain why she was going alone? And what would she say about the contingent of new people who'd suddenly dropped into her life—Gabrielle, Carla, Sam? It was bad enough Jonathan the doorman had seen Sotheby's at the apartment. Mary Beth couldn't risk further action that might raise eyebrows.

Still, she couldn't believe she'd driven the Lincoln. She'd barely been able to maneuver it through the narrow streets from Falmouth to Woods Hole; if it had pontoons, she could have driven the damn thing across Vineyard Sound and not have had to worry about taking the damn ferry.

Woods Hole, however, was the end of the earth, or at least the end of land as the Upper Cape knew it. Somehow Mary Beth managed to turn around at the docks and head back toward Falmouth to try to find a room on a Friday night.

"Good luck," she hissed to herself, and wondered if she'd simply been born this damn stupid or if she'd turned it into an art form over time, like while Eric was spending her money even faster than she was, or while she'd been making arrangements for Shauna's wedding as if her daughter really were the princess Mary Beth had raised her to believe.

*No Vacancy.*

*No Vacancy.*

*No Vacancy.*

The signs were as predictable as the fog banks that rolled in on the fourth of July just in time to turn thousands of dollars of celebratory fireworks into a blurry, dull mess.

Not for the first time, Mary Beth wondered why she hadn't sold the estate years ago and summered somewhere more interesting like the Hamptons or even Nantucket, which lately had priced itself right out of tourists—but before Lester took off, who would have cared?

*Wait a minute,* she thought, as another *No Vacancy* whizzed by. Did she have enough money to rent a room for the night? Was it true they didn't all take American Express?

She pulled into a parking lot and checked her cash. God, she couldn't believe she had to check her cash. When was the last time she had done that? Had she ever? But now with her other credit cards maxed and her checking account holding God knew what little, Mary Beth was confused. Poor and confused.

She counted once, then double-checked. Two hundred and thirty-one dollars.

Was that enough for a room? Was it enough to take

the car onto the ferry? She didn't know! Christ, she didn't know! She'd been there every summer for forty-two fucking years and she didn't even know how much it cost to get there or how much it would cost if you could not.

Drumming her fingers on the steering wheel, she looked into the parking lot. A convenience store sat there, all lit up as if to greet the passengers who couldn't get on the goddamn boat. She got out of the car and slammed the door, then marched inside determined to find a place to sleep.

"Good luck," a woman with straight hair and crooked teeth said from behind the counter. She rang up four packs of Marlboros for another customer, this one a man in a torn T-shirt and jeans. He did not look like a tourist.

"You don't understand," Mary Beth pleaded. "I got tied up in traffic. I need to get to the Vineyard tonight."

The woman shrugged as if she'd heard the same story a hundred times in the last hour alone.

"Take the paper boat." This came not from the clerk but from the customer with the bag of smokes.

"Excuse me?"

"The newspaper boat. It leaves around two in the morning. Can't get your car on it, but they'll probably take you."

In all her years on the island, she'd never heard of the newspaper boat. She must have been staring at the man because he added, "How'd you think the papers get there so early in the morning? How'd you think *The Boston Globe* and *The New York Times* make it in time for all o' you rich folks to catch up on the news that you went to the island to forget?" Shaking his head, the man laughed and left the store.

Mary Beth looked at the clerk, who shrugged again. "He's right. There is a boat."

Without another word, Mary Beth left the store, con-

vinced more than ever that she'd spent her life removed
from the ordinary world. For the first time, she did not
like that fact.

It was not the smoothest crossing Mary Beth had ever
had. The boat was small and rocked like a buoy on a
stormy night. It smelled slightly of fish and more like wet
rubber and the accommodations were best left unnoticed.
Halfway across, Mary Beth pulled out her cell phone and
called Nikki.

"It is not my goddamn fault that it's the middle of the
night. But I couldn't bring my car across and I need
someone to get me."

She should have known better than to think her cousin
would be delighted that she'd woken her up.

"Well, get our goddamn private detective out of bed,"
she damn well insisted. "Let him earn the money that we
don't have that we're supposed to pay him." She clicked
off the phone, clutched the railing, and stared into the
dark, starless night sky for the rest of the trip, not knowing if anyone would be there, waiting for her, if this goddamn boat ever reached the other goddamn side.

No one was there.

"No cabs at this hour," one of the hired hands announced with a chuckle when they'd disembarked and no
sign of life but the newspaper delivery truck waited on
the pier.

Mary Beth buttoned her short-sleeved cotton jacket
and tried not to think of how hot it had been in the city
this morning or that she was freezing to death now. She
dug into her bag, searching for a pack of cigarettes that,
like her driver, was not there.

"Someone will pick me up," she replied, not at all sure if that were true. She gave up looking for the cigarettes and slung her MCM bag over her shoulder. She strutted past the men who thump-thumped huge bundles of newspapers into the back of the truck, then she marched toward the dark terminal in her high-heeled slides, grateful to be back on land, but not pleased at the prospect of spending the rest of the damn night chatting nonsense with a deckhand. And not pleased to give them any ideas that she was a woman in distress.

Mary Beth Atkinson, of course, did not know the meaning of the word.

She sat on a bench by the terminal, crossed her legs, and wondered if she should call the lighthouse again. Swinging her foot and biting her lip, she tried not to focus on her predicament. What good would it do? Her cousins would be pissed off enough that she'd awakened them, as would Sam, who might not be a cop but an undercover reporter for the *National Intruder,* for all they really knew.

"We can trust him," Nikki had told her. "His daughter is at Camp4Kids. She's only five. And she has AIDS."

Mary Beth shivered now not as much from the chill in the night as from the thought, the inconceivable thought, that a child was sick and a child might actually die. Her world only touched sick children through charities to which she gave generously in order to attend the balls. She did not recall that she'd ever seen a sick child, except when Shauna had had the measles and the mumps. But that was not real sickness; that was not close to being AIDS. She shook her head and wondered how Nikki had come to do this with her life. How. Or why. It seemed like such an odd thing to want to do.

She rubbed her hands together and blew into her palms, realizing that she did not know Nikki much at all.

Perhaps she never had. And now, Gabrielle was back, a damn countess, no less, appearing out of nowhere because her rightful claim had vanished.

Because *all* their rightful claims had vanished.

Well, Mary Beth thought, they might be in this mess together, but was it really possible for the three of them to see it through until the end...or at least until Shauna's wedding was over and done with?

The sound of a motor diverted her attention. She looked up as the newspaper truck lumbered from the docks. Then the boat's motor resumed its chug. A few seconds later, the boat backed from the pier, headed for Nantucket or back to the mainland or wherever it was headed. All Mary Beth knew was that now she was alone on the dark pier in Vineyard Haven, where it was dead-night silent because even the gulls had the sense to be asleep, where the thick scent of low tide oozed from pilings and pier, and where she sat, all alone, by herself, cold as hell.

Kicking off her shoes, she pulled her feet up on the bench. Then she hugged her knees and wondered if this was the first time in her life that she had truly been alone. No husband, no daughter, no mother she could talk to. No driver, no housekeeper, no sales clerk to direct, no best friend to talk to, no personal trainer to fuck. Just Mary Beth Atkinson. Without even a car.

She lowered her head onto her knees. Just as she almost let herself cry, she heard the sound of a Volkswagen rolling into the lot.

"What do you mean he's not here? Did he quit already?"

Nikki was too tired to bother to shake her head. "Carla gave him a lead and Sam is tracking it down. He thinks Lester might be hiding out in Punta Cana."

"Where?"

Nikki sighed. "It's in the Dominican Republic, not that it matters."

"Of course it matters. We've got to go with him! We've got to find Lester!"

"Mary Beth, shut up," Nikki said, pulling out of the lot and steering toward the Shore Road. "We're not going anywhere. I have responsibilities here with the camp. And you have a wedding one week from today."

One week from today? *Oh, God,* she thought. *Only seven days!*

"And while we're at it," Nikki continued, "you might have thought to mention to Gabrielle that her husband was waiting for her on the Vineyard."

"Excuse me, my mistake. I've had a few thousand other things on my fucking mind."

Nikki shrugged. "You managed to concoct a scheme for Gabrielle to get to Connor. And by the way, I will not be taking his money—for me *or* for you—and if there's one thing that I don't need it's to get, as you put it, laid."

Mary Beth looked out the window into the darkness and wished she had stayed on the pier.


She'd once read a magazine article about sabotaging relationships, and Gabrielle had wondered if that pertained to her. But that had been before she'd married Stefano. That had been before she thought she'd learned to trust.

She curled up in the small bed at the lighthouse.

If Stefano had lied about knowing who she was, what else had he lied about?

Was he Angelina's lover?

Had they been lovers all along?

Had he only married Gabrielle because he had known

about her money and that someday the truth would sur-face, and that even if they divorced he would be entitled to . . . to what? Half?

He would never be entitled to Rosa, would he? And could Gabrielle really take Rosa from the man she thought was her father, the man she loved so much?

Nikki had brought her dinner, a peace offering of baked fish and rice and salad. But Gabrielle could not eat: She could not force the food down.

The hours slowly passed. Her head ached and her stomach churned as if she were on a ship, caught in a sea of roiling waves of discontent. She only knew she could not return to Italy, not until she could think clearly. So she'd spent the night awake in the lighthouse, her eyes wide open, thinking about secrets, thinking about lies.

When dawn finally came, she was gifted with sleep that did not seem to last long before she was awakened by the sound of a soft, young voice.

"Gabrielle? Would you like to sleep at the camp? You could sleep in my cottage. We could get another bunk bed."

It was Molly.

Gabrielle reached out and ruffled Molly's curls. The little girl looked pale today. Perhaps she hadn't slept well, either. Perhaps she knew that her mother had died and her father had gone off and perhaps she feared he'd never return. She wondered if Rosa was worried that Gabrielle would never return. A small tear crept into her eye. "What are you doing out here at the lighthouse?" she asked, forcing a smile.

"I came to sit still for Nikki. She's painting my pic-ture."

Gabrielle rubbed Molly's tiny back. "Oh, honey, that's wonderful. Would you like me to braid your hair?"

Molly shrugged. "Maybe later, okay? Nikki said we have to go back to camp now, because it's almost lunchtime."

"Lunchtime?" Gabrielle asked, surprised that it was so late.

Closing her green eyes, Molly said, "Yes, but I could rest here with you until Nikki is ready, if that's okay." Then she crawled onto the small bed and snuggled against Gabrielle, and Gabrielle knew that no matter what, she needed to get home; she needed to see Rosa, no matter what Stefano had or had not done, no matter what she decided to do or not to do.

Mary Beth stared at the phone in the library. She couldn't believe there were sixteen messages in the two days since she'd been gone. How many were from Phillipe? Were any from Eric? And where was her cell phone and why had no one called her on it?

Holding her breath, she pushed the Play button. After all, there was a wedding in the making, and the calls must be important.

"Darling, this is Raven Fitzgerald. As much as we were looking forward to your lovely daughter's wedding, I'm afraid Carl is going to be out of town. So sorry."

*Beep.* Shit. Another cancellation.

"Ms. Atkinson, this is Ertha at Tiffany's. We've shipped your order to Martha's Vineyard today."

Good. *Beep.*

"Mary Beth! It's Lauren James! Must cancel on the wedding. Dad's having surgery in L.A."

Mary Beth frowned. Why was she thinking what she was thinking?

Beep. Thirteen more calls. Two from Phillipe: When could he expect payment? Ten more cancellations.

*Ten?*

The last call was from Shauna.

"MOM! Where is your cell phone? Are you on the Vineyard? I'm at the apartment, and *I think that we've been robbed!*"

Robbed. *Yes*, Mary Beth thought as she slumped on the chair, *we've been robbed, all right*. They'd been robbed of the trust fund, and now Shauna would be robbed of the joy of her wedding if half the people didn't show.


When Gabrielle awoke again, Molly had left and Nikki was gone, as was the VW from outside the lighthouse.

She wished she could talk to Rosa before Stefano got home. But Angelina did not have a telephone; she depended on the one in the piazza when she needed to make a call.

Gabrielle brushed off thoughts of that pay phone, the place where her journey had begun what seemed so long ago. She pulled off her nightgown, slipped into clothes, and went downstairs to use the phone. The lines to Air Italia were busy, would she please try again?

Perhaps a walk would settle her growing agitation.

Out on the sandy path that led down to the jetty, the sea grass was shorter than when she'd been young. Back then the path had seemed like a magic tunnel, with walls on both sides of fine, green straw swaying gently together and a floor of white sand and a ceiling of sky blue.

It was different when she'd found her mother, because it had been almost dark.

Gabrielle caught her breath and tried not to remember, the way she'd tried so many times. She wanted instead to think about Stefano and Rosa, and if she could fix all the wrong that she'd done, and if she could forgive Stefano for what he'd done in return.

She wanted to think about those things, but there on the dunes, the sun and the scent and the sound of the waves that licked the shoreline of Katama Bay mixed together the then and the now and what was real and what was not.

If only she could smell the grapes and hear the cowbells and the rustle of olive leaves. Then she would be away from all of the hurt and she would feel better and life would be good again.

Instead of a cowbell, Gabrielle heard a buoy bell, the low clang at the mouth of the bay, now closed in by the jetty from there to Chappaquiddick, the refuge of birds and berries and all things that had escaped the ravages of time and the intrusion of tourists.

Much like Tuscany, in their little-known, secluded village.

She stopped on the jetty and looked back at the land, at the lighthouse, Nikki's home.

And then she began to cry. Slowly at first, until her vision grew watery and she knew she could no longer hold back. She started to cry, then took a step forward. Her foot caught on a rock. She stumbled. *Stay off the rock jetty;* Aunt Margaret's voice was in the wind. She slid. *It's dangerous, it's dangerous.* She tumbled. Down the rocks where her mother's body had once fallen...

She grasped a rock, she gasped for breath. Sharp edges scraped her palms; her belly bumped against the jetty. She dug her feet into the rock pile just as water lapped her ankles: her footing held. She lay motionless a moment, catching her breath, quieting her shock, thinking only that she was where her mother had been, facedown and cut up, but Gabrielle was not dead, no, not dead.

*Stay off the rock jetty.* But Gabrielle had not.

Then, on quite unsteady legs, she righted herself, brushed small bits of blood and stone from her hands, straightened her sweater, and adjusted her ponytail, each movement a painful reminder that she was very much alive.

Slowly she began to trek back toward the lighthouse. That's when she saw a man up on the shore.

She stopped. How long had he been there? Had he seen her fall?

She turned back toward Chappy. Maybe she should go that way. She was so embarrassed.

But who was that man? And what was he doing on the property? Was he the caretaker? A trespasser? A worker for the wedding?

She turned back to him. He continued to watch her. Yes, he was watching her. And Gabrielle realized she was trapped between him and Chappaquiddick Island, trapped by the puddle of the sea that floated in between.

"Are you all right?" he called out.

She shielded her eyes against the sun. She saw more than his outline that time, more than the shape of him, more than a shadow.

She blinked. "Who are you?" she demanded. "Why are you on our property?"

The man did not move. If he were the caretaker, he could have said so. Instead he said nothing. And then he turned. And as he began to climb the dunes back up toward the lighthouse, an aching chill inched up Gabrielle's spine. And suddenly, she knew. The man who had been standing on the shore was Mack Olson; it was her father.

# 22

The old red pickup was parked at the top of the hill by the caretaker's cottage. Gabrielle stomped toward it, fueled by anger and pain and the ache of betrayal that now balled into rage for the seven-year-old whose mother had died and whose aunt had sent her away, off across the sea, so they did not have to see her, so they did not have to...what? Remember that she lived?

When she reached the truck she was panting and exhausted. Her hands still stung; her stomach was bruised. She pressed against a stitch in her side, then squinted and tried to focus. She did not see him; he was not near the truck.

And then it hit her. *Of course!* He was the one driving the day she'd been walking; he was the one who'd almost run her down. Wouldn't that have been something, she thought, as she yanked the truck door open, if her father had run her over and killed her?

The keys were in the ignition.

She hesitated, then she did not.

Without further thought, she climbed into the truck and turned over the engine.

What was he doing there?

Had he known that she was there?

Had he followed her to the Vineyard and, if so, from where?

She jammed the column shift into gear and started up the driveway, just as she saw movement from behind the curtains in the caretaker's cottage.

*Oh, God,* she thought, and gasped again.

He was the caretaker.

He'd been there all along.

*And Nikki knew.*

She barreled up the driveway. Directions to the camp raced through her mind. The edge of the state forest... between the airport and Oak Bluffs. Go right, go left...

How could she have been such a fool?

What had ever made her think she could fit back into her family?

And why had they been hiding him from her?

Him! Her father! The man whose fault it was that her mother died.

Her breath came in short puffs. She pulled to the side of the road, stopped the truck, rested her head on the steering wheel, and started to sob.

She sobbed and sobbed and sobbed for her mother and for herself, and for all that could have been but had not. She hugged her arms around her stomach and rocked slowly back and forth.

Her mother.

Her father.

Her mother was dead.

Her father was alive.

She sobbed until she ached, until the tears at last subsided in that mysterious ceasing that happens to all tears, as if the pain was gone now, washed out from the soul.

Gabrielle wiped her cheeks and dropped her hands to

the seat. Then she lifted her eyes and ran her palm over the worn seat where her father had sat, up to the dashboard coated with beach dust. There was a cup holder; inside was a cardboard container that held about two swallows of unfinished coffee lightened by cream.

She sat still a moment and stared at the cup. Her hand moved toward it, then abruptly jerked back as if it were too hot, for her father had touched it, had held it with a hand that once held hers, and her father had drunk from it, with lips that once had kissed her cheek.

With eyes misting again, Gabrielle reached over and lightly touched the cup's rim. "Daddy," she whispered. "Daddy, remember me?"

Mary Beth called Shauna and left a message explaining that, no, they'd not been robbed, that she'd said she was redecorating, hadn't she? And by the way, she was sorry she had missed her, and she must have left her cell phone in the car, which was over in Woods Hole because of the damn ferry.

She was about to hang up when Shauna picked up the line.

"Mom?"

Well, who else would have left that message? "Yes, it's me."

"I went there to see if we could talk, but when I walked in half the furniture was missing and so were you." Her daughter sounded odd, as if she'd been awakened from a nap or been taking Valium.

Mary Beth stood up from the chair and tried to circle the old library desk, reminding herself that one of these days she must get a cordless phone, if she didn't sell this place.

"I told you I was going to redecorate," Mary Beth replied. "Did you forget?"

"Mom?" Shauna asked as if she hadn't heard her. "Is your trust fund gone?"

It would be better now if Mary Beth could go upstairs to one of the half a dozen bedrooms, pull the drapes against the sun, and lie down and take a nap. It would be better if this call, this day, this life of hers had never happened. Sadly, it was too late for any of the three.

"The man who administered my trust fund has disappeared," she said. "There is no cash, and I expect that soon there will be no credit. In the meantime, the truth is I had to sell some things to pay for your grandmother's care."

"Can't you find him?"

There was no need to explain that they might have had a better chance if she'd not been so stubborn, so fearful that people would find out, which it appeared they were anyway, what with the wedding cancellations. "We've hired someone, but it may take time."

"We?"

Mary Beth frowned. "Nikki. And my other cousin, Gabrielle."

"He stole their money, too?"

"Well, yes. I assumed that's how you found out. From Dee." But as she said the words, she hated the squishing, squeezing, sickish feeling that was moving from her brain down to her toes.

"So Daddy was right," Shauna said.

*Daddy.* Of course. As she had dreaded and suspected. "When did you see your father?" She sounded calm and in control and wondered why.

"I had lunch with him yesterday."

Mary Beth returned to the chair and sat down. "Did

he mention if he's still planning on coming to your wedding?"

"Well, yes."

"Did he ask about me?"

"No. Not really."

Not really? What the hell did that mean?

"I mean, he asked if you were handling things okay without any money."

The blood crept more quickly to her cheeks than she would have wanted. "And did he happen to mention where he's staying?"

"He, ah..."

She felt the inside of her cheeks suck themselves against her teeth. "He, ah, *what*, Shauna?"

"He didn't have to tell me, Mom. He didn't come to lunch alone."

*I have other options,* he'd said quite plainly, and so apparently he had.

She tried to laugh. "Anyone I know?" she asked as if it didn't matter, as if this happened every day.

Shauna began to cry.

Mary Beth closed her eyes. Oh, God, she thought, and feared that all the courage in the world would not brace her for what Shauna was about to say.

"It's Roxanne," her daughter finally said. "Daddy has moved in with your best friend."

In a perfect world Gabrielle would have taken one look at Mack, and Mack, one look at her, and they would have dissolved into those tears of old movies, flinging themselves into each other's arms, father and daughter, long lost and long loved, reunited at last.

In real Atkinson life, it did not work that way.

Gabrielle drove into the camp and parked the red

truck—Mack's truck—on the lawn. She stumbled from the driver's side; Carla saw her from the window, and called to Alice, who ran down to the dining commons in search of Nikki.

By the time Nikki got there, Gabrielle was sitting halfway up the steps of the registration cottage as if she didn't have the strength to make it to the top.

Nikki sat beside her, took her by the hand, and slowly, very slowly, tried her best to explain.

"It was not his fault, Gabrielle. It was my mother's. God help us, she's the one who hurt you."

Gabrielle did not move. She hugged her hands around her knees.

"I know your mother's death was not an accident," Nikki continued, and put her arm around Gabrielle's shoulders. Though Gabrielle did not comment, neither did she pull away. "That it was suicide," Nikki said, rubbing Gabrielle's shoulder with small, gentle touches. "I only just found out."

They sat quietly, the distant sounds of children the backdrop for their emotions.

"My mother was terrified of a mark against the family name. It's no excuse, but it's how things happened then. She was terrified you'd tell. So she threatened your father. She said she'd have him arrested for your mother's murder, that she would say he pushed her from the top of the lighthouse."

Gabrielle did not even blink. God, Nikki wished that she would blink, move, do something.

"She also said she would cut you off from the Atkinson money, that you would be poor forever."

There was nothing else for Nikki to say except, "I'm sorry, Gabrielle. All those years that we thought you were together, he lived in fear for you. He had no idea my mother would prevent us from being in your life. When he showed up here ten years ago, he wouldn't talk about you. He said the two of you had had a 'falling out.' " She took a deep breath. "That's it," Nikki said. "That's the whole truth. For both of your sakes, please try to forgive him. He thought he was doing what was best for you. He loves you so much, Gabrielle."

Her silence resumed. Gabrielle bent her head to her knees, sitting still for seconds or minutes or hours—time did not matter, it all seemed the same. Finally, she spoke.

"Aunt Dorothy knew my father wasn't with me."

"I think Aunt Dorothy was afraid of my mother. Without Margaret Atkinson to keep her life together, what would have happened to Dorothy?"

Gabrielle gave a small shrug. "Well, we'll never know now." She thought for a moment. "At least she came to see me. At least she didn't let your mother get the last word on everything."

"Even though my mother never knew."

"I think she did."

Nikki was puzzled. "What do you mean?"

"One time in London, I wanted a fur muff. It was so pretty, all fluffy and white. But it was expensive. I said to Aunt Dorothy, 'It costs way too much,' and she went into her purse and took out a handful of money and said, 'Well, Margaret insisted we have a good time, so let's think of this as part of a good time.' I never asked her what she meant."

Nikki shook her head. Did that mean her mother had not been totally malicious? Did that make up for cheating Gabrielle out of her family? For sending her away, alone? Nikki wrestled with her thoughts. Was it time they all worked toward forgiveness, of both the living and the dead?

"I always knew it must have been awful to find your

mother on the rocks," Nikki added, "but to have witnessed her jump from the lighthouse...to have watched her suicide..."

Gabrielle stood up and brushed off her pants. "It was awful, Nikki, but it was not suicide. I don't know how I know, but I will never, in my heart, believe that my mother killed herself."


Carla had spent two nights in a house with a man she did not know. What would Theresa think of that? An *Italian* at that, even though he was married, even though he spent the whole time mooning over his wife until she got back from New York.

Yesterday, however, Gabrielle came back but Stefano did not. Carla did not know if he'd left the island; no one told her and she did not want to ask. If she asked too many questions they might remember she was there and send her off on the next slow boat to the Bronx. She figured she had no business being there any longer, not really, even though she answered the phone when Sam called three times a day to check up on Molly and to report that Lester was still among the missing, though he had been seen once or twice in town. So she talked to Sam and tracked the leads that came over the computer, which so far had been five, though they'd turned out to be zilch.

Mostly she pretended to be busy, like she was doing now, as she tried not to stare at Nikki and Gabrielle on the steps, tried to act as if she weren't listening. But how hard was that! A real Atkinson drama unfolding right there in her presence; it was better than watching those old movies on TV; it was better than rummaging through the old house looking for clues about the way they lived.

She'd called Donnie yesterday to see how he was doing: He asked if they were paying for her time and her
work. Paying her? To live there among them? To be part
of the world she'd only seen from the other side of the
desk? Donnie, however, would not understand. She'd
told him to think of it as a vacation. She did not tell him
that they couldn't pay her even if they were so inclined,
because Lester had taken off with their fortune, and the
least she could do was help. She did not tell him that, because she still felt loyal to the man who'd deserted both
the Atkinsons and her.

Stupid, she knew, but such was her life.

She only hoped she could stay until the Atkinson wedding, though she had no idea what she would wear.

"Carla?"

While Carla had been daydreaming, Nikki had entered
the cottage.

Hell's bells, Carla thought. Had she been caught? She
focused on the computer screen, intent on her work.

"I wondered if you'd do me a favor," Nikki said.
"Gabrielle wants to go home. Would you go to the lighthouse and pack her things? She wants to wait here and I
don't want to leave her. She's upset about a few things."

Carla turned off the computer. "She wants to go
home, like to Italy?"

Nikki nodded. "She went to find Molly; I offered to
make the arrangements."


She didn't take the red truck Gabrielle had come in;
Nikki told Carla she'd take care of it after Gabrielle had
gone.

Carla parked Nikki's car and focused on her mission,
trying not to get carried away that she was going to see
the inside of the lighthouse.

"Her things are in the guest bedroom on the second floor," Nikki had said.

She climbed the spiral staircase, her eyes busily working to absorb everything in the few minutes that she had. For a lighthouse, it wasn't very exciting except that it was round; for belonging to an Atkinson, it was even less... impressive. She might have lived there herself for the lack of expensive-looking stuff, although she didn't know if there were lighthouses in the Bronx.

On the second-floor landing, Carla paused and looked up toward the light, toward the top, from where Nikki said Gabrielle's mother had committed suicide, but Gabrielle said that she had not.

She looked around quickly to see if anyone was there, then carefully climbed the rest of the stairs to the top, quietly, on her tiptoes, one small step at a time.

The first thing she noticed was the canvases all around and the slight scent of turpentine that lingered in the air. She had heard talk about Nikki's wonderful paintings; she had not seen one until now, until the one on the easel that showed a little girl with red curls. Molly! Carla thought. It was Sam's daughter, smiling and bright-eyed and clinging to Barbie. She did not look as if she were sick; she did not look as if she had AIDS and might die.

Then it hit her. Like the time she'd stood up too fast and cracked her skull on an open file drawer, the realization bonked Carla smack on the head. *Lester's paintings,* she thought. *I never told Sam about Lester's paintings.*

*Oh, God,* she thought, smacking her palm against her forehead. Why was she so stupid? And what else should she have remembered about Lester that she'd forgotten?

"Nikki!"

Carla froze in place. This time she'd been caught red-handed, the nosey, unwelcome snoop. Worst of all, the voice belonged to Mary Beth.

"It's not Nikki," Carla replied, but as she got the words out, Mary Beth was halfway up the stairs. She stood in Nikki's studio, looking at Carla.

"What are you doing here?" She didn't sound pissed, just confused.

"I, ah..." If she said she'd come to get Gabrielle's things, Mary Beth would wonder what she was doing there at the top of the lighthouse.

"My cousin, Nicole," Mary Beth said, turning to the portraits as if she'd forgotten the question she'd just asked. "She really is a wonderful artist, isn't she? If only she'd get discovered, she might be able to support all of us now." Then Mary Beth laughed. "But I doubt she wants that; she'd rather sit here in this hovel looking out to the sea." She walked to the window and did just that, looked out to the sea.

"Do you think she did it?" Carla asked even though she shouldn't, but she couldn't help it.

"Do I think who did what?"

"Gabrielle's mother. Do you think she killed herself?"

Mary Beth folded her arms. "Who told you that? It was an accident, down there on the jetty. She slipped on the rocks..." She turned around to Carla. "No," she said, "that's not true. Aunt Rose did commit suicide. My mother told me a long time ago. But how did you know? No one was supposed to know."

Well, it wasn't as if they were trying to talk in seclusion. Nikki and Gabrielle had been outside on the stairs where anyone could have heard. Carla sighed. "I heard Nikki tell Gabrielle that she just found out."

Mary Beth nodded. "I never told Nikki. She loved Aunt Rose so much, I never wanted her to think Aunt Rose had done that."

Carla didn't know Mary Beth very well, but she was surprised at that news. She'd somehow figured Mary

Beth never thought that much about other people's feelings.

"Well, Gabrielle doesn't believe it."

"I wouldn't want to believe it about my mother, would you?"

No, Carla agreed she would not. "Anyway," Carla said, "I came to get her things. She's going home."

"Today? How's she planning to do that? She'll never get off-island on a freaking Saturday. Besides, I need her to stay for the wedding. The guest list is dropping like flies."

Carla shrugged. "Nikki's trying to make arrangements."

"Well, if Gabrielle insists on going, and if Nikki can get her on a flight from Boston, you could always take a ferry with her to Woods Hole where the Lincoln is parked. You could take the car and drive her to Logan. I'd do it myself, but this wedding is driving me insane and Shauna comes tomorrow..."

"I'd be glad to help," Carla said quickly, though Donnie would wonder if she'd be paid for that, too.

# 23

She supposed some people might say she lived in denial, but Mary Beth knew that was far from the truth. No one was more aware of the absurdities and the realities of being an Atkinson than Mary Beth was.

She plunked on the settee in the drawing room with a big glass of wine and a long cigarette, and, for the first time since she'd spoken with Shauna, allowed herself to think about Eric and about Roxanne, and about what this would do to the wedding and to her life. Taking a long drag, she knew she was damned if she was going to let this interfere with the wedding. Only a handful, really, of guests out of six hundred had canceled; perhaps they knew about her money or about Eric or perhaps not. It did not matter. What mattered was that this was for Shauna, no matter what Eric said.

And, no matter what Eric did, the show would go on.

Shauna and Dee and Jason would be there tomorrow, and Mary Beth would be grateful for the activity. Despite the fact that it would be Sunday the cleaning people would start: They'd be there every day from now until then, polishing and shining and getting everything Atkinson-worthy; the gardeners would show up Monday and begin to manicure every inch of the lawn, every flower and tree and every grain of beach sand.

It all would be perfect, because she would demand it. After next week she'd have the rest of her life to figure out how she would pay for it, and for her mother, too.

In the meantime, Sam might always show up with Lester and her millions in tow.

Then again, there was probably a better chance of Dorothy getting back her mind.

Or of Eric leaving Roxanne and coming home to her.

She stood up and went to the window, where outside the orange sunset reflected off Katama Bay. She thought about Dorothy and Nikki and Gabrielle, and she wished someone were around to make her feel less alone. Instead she'd have to rely on the wine and the smokes, and on crawling into bed before it dared turn dark.

Nikki had taken Gabrielle and Carla to the ferry because, as Mary Beth had predicted, there was no other way to get Gabrielle off the Vineyard than to take the ferry as passengers, get the Lincoln, and drive up to Boston. Nikki would have gone, but with a new group of kids arriving tomorrow, there was too much to be done.

Besides, she needed to be with Mack, which was why she had gone to the tavern, dragged him downstairs, and driven out to Philbin Beach, where they now sat alone, watching the sunset and talking through tears.

"I thought you were still in New York," Mack said. "I went home to pick up a few things..." His intentions had been innocent, but when he saw Gabrielle on the jetty, he could not help but stare.

How could he not?

"What's done is done, Mack," Nikki said. "But I told her everything I know now, everything that had been told to Mary Beth and me; everything you've told me since. Maybe in time Gabrielle will understand."

"And maybe I've wasted too many years hoping for that," Mack replied. "Three times now she's turned away from me, Nikki. How much longer should I go on pretending things might be different? When do I stop mourning the loss of my family and get on with my life?"

Nikki frowned. She thought Mack had gotten on with his life. His life on the Vineyard. His life with her. "I don't understand," she said. "I thought you liked your life here." She was careful not to say "our life," because to do so would have broken their unspoken rule.

He picked up a shell and tossed it toward the water. "You think I like living in a caretaker's cottage, hiding from the world, knowing there's a woman I love not thirty feet from me living in a damn lighthouse because she thinks we can't get married and live a respectable life, where we can have friends over for dinner and go out to the movies and once in a while hold hands in public? A life where I can be proud of my wife for the good that she gives to the world, and show that pride to others in more ways than hanging up some lousy posters?"

His words came so fast, his words were so dense, she could not help but think he'd stored them for years, collecting them during those long hours spent in the cottage in front of the fireplace, all that time she'd thought he'd been thinking about Rose.

"Mack," she replied, "I don't know what to say," because she did not.

"Do you know I was only twenty-nine years old when

Rose died? I was still a child, Nicole. Haven't I suffered long enough?"

She took his hand. She kissed it. "I love you," she said. "I love you, but I never once thought you'd want to marry me. I never once thought we could have a real life..."

"Because of Gabrielle? Or because of what people might say? Would that make you any different from your cousin Mary Beth?"

"I don't know," she said. "Maybe I was too afraid myself. Too afraid to let myself be dependent on a man."

"Dependent?" He laughed. "Until a few weeks ago, you were the one with all the money."

She shook her head. "I don't mean financially. I mean emotionally dependent. Until we got together, I too often confused sex with real love. I didn't know how to love, and what was worse was that I knew it. Damn, I knew it."

He took her by the hand and led her down to the shoreline, where the gentle surf of low tide was cool on her toes. Then he stopped and took her into his arms and said, "Nicole Atkinson, will you marry me?" Then he kissed her more deeply than she'd ever known, and suggested they stay there all night on the beach, with only each other and a blanket for their love.


When the telephone rang it was dark outside and felt like the middle of the night. As Mary Beth reached to answer she noticed the clock: one twenty-five. Her heart sped up quickly with the alarm of adrenaline that said something was wrong.

"Mary Beth, it's Alice."

Alice? Who the hell was Alice?

"Where's Nikki? Oh, God, I can't find Nikki. Is she there with you?"

Oh. *That* Alice, the one who ran things for Nikki while Nikki paid the bills, past tense, of course.

"I have no idea where she is." She crawled out of bed and went to the window. "What's wrong, Alice?" She peered out the window: the VW was not parked next to the lighthouse. Nor was Mack's red truck outside.

"It's Molly, Sam's daughter. She's had a seizure. Please, Mary Beth, I need someone's help. Will you come to the hospital? I'll pick you up if you don't have a car."

Mary Beth shook her head. "No, I don't have a car. But what can I do? I don't even know his daughter, do I?"

"She's so sweet, Mary Beth, and she's so scared. We have plenty of medical people, but she needs someone else. Without Nikki or Gabrielle...and even Carla's gone..."

"Oh, all right," Mary Beth said. "But give me twenty minutes to put on some clothes."

"I'll be there in ten," Alice said and hung up.

Mary Beth hung up and wondered if because Sam was away looking for Lester, she was responsible for the welfare of his child.

And, she wondered as she climbed into last night's clothes, where the hell was Nikki, anyway?

She sat in the waiting area of the Emergency Room, wondering if this was a mistake. She barely knew Sam, after all, and God knew she'd never been real good with kids, let alone with sick ones. It was a miracle Shauna had grown into a normal young woman, despite a socialite mother and a social-climbing father.

Eric, she thought, and instantly needed to wash down the vile taste his name brought to her throat.

"Coffee?" she asked Alice, who was stuck to the blue vinyl chair beside her.

Alice turned to her. "I lost my son, you know. To this disease. He wasn't a child. He was gay."

Mary Beth had no idea what to say. How did one respond to that? How could one pretend to understand that kind of pain? "Would you like coffee?" she repeated.

Alice shook her head.

Mary Beth got up and went to the vending machine. She took one out of her remaining dollar bills and indicated coffee, no cream or sugar.

The paper cup thumped down the chute and Mary Beth waited for the spigot to fill it up. Then, looking at the cup, her eyes traveled down to her feet. Her pink high-heeled sandals looked quite ridiculous, out of place in this quiet room where the air was sober and the feeling grim. She glanced around at the others who waited: most were dressed in tourist clothes, shorts and silk-screened T-shirts from golf clubs and resorts in other parts of the country and beyond. A few had cameras that hung from cords around their necks, as if the owners were afraid to leave them in their cars, as if the Nikon thieves would strip them of the photos of their Vineyard vacation while their foreheads were being stitched from their moped accidents.

Then it dawned on her: It was nearly two o'clock in the morning? How long had those people been there? She couldn't wait forever...

"Ms. Atkinson?" a nurse asked. "I'm Eliza. I volunteer at Camp4Kids."

Mary Beth did not recognize her, because she'd had her own problems and hadn't wanted to take on Nikki's, too.

Alice quickly joined them.

"Oh, Alice, I'm glad you found someone." She gestured

toward Mary Beth though Mary Beth did not know why. "As we suspected, Molly had a reaction to her medication. She'll be okay."

"We'd like to see her."

"Right this way."

Alice began to follow the nurse. Mary Beth didn't move. This wasn't her responsibility, was it? Oh, how she wished she had an idea how people in the real world handled such things. If Carla were here, Carla would know. But Carla was in Boston. Like the rest of them, even she'd abandoned Mary Beth.

Then Alice stopped, turned around, and motioned Mary Beth to come. She hesitated a split second, said *what the hell* to herself, then trotted off behind them on her pink high-heeled sandals.

Molly was half asleep. Mary Beth stood at the foot of the bed and watched as Alice kissed the little girl's forehead and smoothed back her curly hair. Mary Beth averted her eyes because she thought she'd cry.

"Hi, honey," Alice whispered. "Everything is okay."

Molly opened her eyes. "Daddy?" Her voice was tiny, her body so little, huddled as it was beneath the starched, white sheet. Mary Beth took a step back. "Is Daddy here?"

"No, honey, but we've called him and he'll see you soon."

"What happened?"

"That darned medication," Alice said with a smile. "They need to fix it again."

Molly's small hand came out from the sheet and searched for Alice's. "Oh, no, not again," she said. "Damn my silly old self."

Mary Beth was startled at the six-year-old's choice of words.

Alice laughed. "You scared Dennis right out of his sneakers."

Whatever she meant, it made Molly giggle. Then her green eyes landed on Mary Beth. "Aren't you Gabrielle's friend?"

Mary Beth cleared her throat. "Yes, Molly. I'm her cousin."

"Gabrielle braids my hair. She's a countess, you know."

Mary Beth smiled. "I know. Isn't that something?" It seemed odd that of the three females in the hospital room, the six-year-old seemed the one with the most confidence.

"Is she coming to see me?"

Mary Beth looked at Alice.

"She went back to Italy, honey," Alice said. "Remember she said good-bye?"

"Oh," Molly replied, her voice growing sad. "I forgot."

A man and a woman, both wearing white lab coats, stepped into the room. With each additional visitor, Mary Beth felt more and more the outsider, unable to contribute, unable to control. She backed up to the wall.

The doctor or nurse or whatever the newly arrived woman was smiled and examined Molly. Then she said she'd like to speak with them in her office about their next course of action.

Molly rolled her eyes. "I hate this part," she said. "This is when the grown-ups talk about you behind your back."

Mary Beth laughed, amused by such gumption in a

child Molly's age. "Grown-ups do it to each other, too, Molly," she heard herself say, and was surprised she had.

Alice looked at Molly and Mary Beth and the woman. She grinned. "I think you can tell us the next course of action right here." She must have known it would be nothing so horrid that she must shield Molly from it. Something suggested to Mary Beth that Alice had been through this before. Many times, perhaps, with her son.

The woman doctor nodded. "Well, I've spoken with Molly's dad and with her doctor in New York. The doctor would like to see her. He thinks she needs a new cocktail, a different combination of medications."

"Oh, no," Molly cried, and the little girl with gumption became a little girl afraid.

Alice squeezed Molly's hand, and Mary Beth felt the tug on her heart.

"They make me sick."

The doctor nodded. "Sometimes that happens, but only for a few days, right?"

Molly slowly nodded.

"Well, then, the sooner you get it, the sooner you can come back to camp, right?" Molly looked bewildered. The doctor looked at Alice and then Mary Beth. "We'd like to airlift her to New York tonight. Her father can be there by morning."

"Airlift?" Mary Beth asked.

"By medevac helicopter."

Alice looked away, and Mary Beth had the feeling she'd known all along, that maybe that was the real reason she'd woken her up, because she needed money. Didn't Alice know that, like Nikki, Mary Beth was broke?

"How much will it cost?"

"I'm afraid it isn't cheap."

Mary Beth closed her eyes. She thought about her

mother. She thought about the wedding. But when she opened her eyes again, there lay a tiny, afraid, little girl.

"Order the helicopter," she said without hesitation. "I will cover the cost." Thank God for unlimited credit lines.

"Mary Beth?" Molly asked. "Will you come with me?"

She stared back at her but did not reply.

"I bet Molly could use a friend," Alice said, and Mary Beth could not say no.

Mary Beth had not been in a helicopter since she and Eric had flown from Nice to Corsica, where the yacht of Emir Sabib awaited their presence for a three-week respite around the Mediterranean. The sheik was an old friend of Eric's coin dealer in London and certain to show them a wonderful time. The walls of that helicopter were lined with soundproofing and adorned with raw silk; the white, butter-soft leather lounge chairs swallowed her up; and the dark-eyed, topless beauty who was their attendant stirred Mary Beth with an uncomfortable excitement.

As she sat now, bent over, next to Molly's bed in the hollow, rattling cabin, Mary Beth felt ashamed of the champagne she'd consumed that week, the thousands of dollars of trinkets she'd purchased in nameless ports, and the lavish food she'd eaten three bites of, then thrown the rest away so she would still look inviting in her cache of bikinis. Not that it mattered, because while the yacht was delightful, Eric was her partner-on-board. The emir might indulge nakedness, but his values were quite moral.

She straightened the IV tube and tucked the blanket under Molly's pale chin. What had the little girl been doing back then? It was two, no three years ago. Had she been diagnosed yet with HIV? Had Sam known that his daughter's future was marred before it had begun?

She thought of him now: Was he sitting in an airport on a Caribbean island, desperately awaiting his flight to the States, sick all inside him, wondering if this time it would be worse?

"Daddy will be there?" Molly whispered, and Mary Beth quickly nodded.

"As fast as the plane can get him there. Faster, I bet, if he has his way."

Molly smiled. "He worries about me more than he should."

It was hard to believe the child was only six. Was grave illness responsible for profound insight?

Mary Beth glanced up to the IV bag to avoid looking at Molly, to help hold back her tears.

"Gabrielle has a little girl," Molly said. "Do you?"

Mary Beth smiled. "Yes, but she's not so little. She's getting married this coming Saturday."

"This Saturday? Is she going to wear a bride's dress?"

*A bride's dress.* There was shameful relief in a topic to which Mary Beth could relate. "Oh, yes. She'll wear a beautiful bride's dress with hand-cut crystals imported from India." There was no need to mention that the materials for the bride's dress had cost fourteen thousand dollars, though Alice was charging only a meager two hundred to put the dress together.

"And she'll have a bouquet?"

"Oh, yes, a huge bouquet of freesia and baby orchids and calla lilies flown in from Chile." Unless, of course, the florist demanded half up front as the caterer had. She straightened the tube again and tried not to think about the seventy-eight thousand that she needed in the next couple of days.

"She will look like a fairy queen," Molly said. "She will be beautiful."

Mary Beth forced a smile. "Yes, she will. She'll look like a fairy queen! And the wedding will be out on the lawn, down near the beach. And all the guests will have silver bubble wands and they will blow fat bubbles in the air, shimmering, glimmering bubbles that will dance in the sunset and make everything perfect."

Molly's eyes had widened, her mouth smiled in wonder. "Oh, it will be like magic. I wish I could be there."

Mary Beth stroked her forehead. "Maybe if you take your new medicine..."

"If I take it I can come?"

With quiet hesitation, Mary Beth replied, "If you take it, perhaps you'll be well enough to come."

"Can I be the flower girl?"

She did not know what to say. It wasn't right to promise something to a child then not have it happen. And yet...Shauna had not planned to have a flower girl... perhaps she would not mind...and it would give Molly something to look forward to.

For Mary Beth, she had looked forward to her debutante ball. If she had not been able to focus on her dress, on how she'd wear her hair, on how the room would look, she might have dwelled on her abortion and killed herself like Aunt Rose did. Distraction, even the most frivolous, could be the most healing.

"Yes," she replied, "you can be the flower girl."

The small face brightened. "Then I'll be there, because I always take my medicine. It keeps me alive, you know."

"Yes," Mary Beth said. "Yes, I know." She took Molly's hand and watched as the child closed her eyes and smiled, dreaming dreams of weddings and blowing bubbles in the air, accepting life for what it was and sidestepping the bad to focus on the good.

Mary Beth traveled the rest of the way without more conversation, but with a new conviction slowly growing in her heart. By the time they touched down on the helipad at St. Francis Hospital, she knew there was something else that she now had to do.

# 24

It was almost noon when Sam arrived, rounding the corner into Molly's hospital room with lightning and urgency directing his feet.

"Daddy!" she cried, and Sam called out, "Peanut!" and she sat up and hugged him as if the hours had not happened, as if she hadn't been watching the clock while trying to be brave.

Mary Beth stayed in the chair at Molly's bedside, where she had been holding the little girl's hand. It surprised her that this time she didn't try to hide her tears.

"God, Mary Beth," Sam said over Molly's shoulder, his own tears staining his sleepless face. "How can I ever thank you?"

The old Mary Beth would have said, "Pay my American Express," or "Find Lester fast." But something had changed in the last several hours, and instead she just said, "No thanks required."

Nikki slouched on the chair at the desk in the administration cottage after Alice had told her what happened.

"I hate that I wasn't here for her."

"It was okay, Nikki. She had the right medical help. And I was here. And Mary Beth."

"Mary Beth. God, I can't believe she went with her."

"I figured if anyone knew how to scrape up the money to get Molly off-island, it would be Mary Beth."

Nikki shook her head, not because she disbelieved Alice, but because she was stunned that her cousin had such compassion, and because she was crippled with guilt that she'd been out at the beach all night making love while Molly, sweet Molly, was in fear of her life.

*This is what happens, so you'd better get used to it,* her inner voice said. *Never forget that these kids are sick.*

But did she truly have the emotional strength to work with them... in sickness and in health?

*Sickness and health, death do us part.*

Mack.

No, she would not think of him now.

Alice spoke softly. "It was easier when you only had the foundation, wasn't it? When you only had to give away your money and not be part of the rest?"

At least a dozen times in the last many minutes since Alice had told her, Nikki had tried to erase a picture of Molly having a seizure, tried to not think of the unfairness of the little girl lying in a big hospital bed.

"I know how you feel," Alice continued. "Before Brian got sick, he had a few friends with AIDS. I helped out at the fund-raisers, but wasn't really 'involved.' "

Nikki had wanted her role in The Rose Foundation to be more than turning over her trust fund and hoping it helped, but she hadn't expected it would hurt this much.

"We have to do more," she said. "We have to help in more ways, and we have to help more of them."

Gesturing toward the files, Alice said, "Starting with the applications we had for camp?"

"We need much more than that."

Alice did not reply.

Nikki drummed her fingers on the old wooden desk. "This needs to be bigger than my trust fund, even if I still had it."

"Finally," Alice said, "you are beginning to understand. Maybe when you ask Connor for the money, you can bring Mack along."

Nikki lifted her head quickly, but Alice simply smiled. "The best part about me," she said, "is I wasn't born yesterday."

The first flight Gabrielle could get to Rome would leave Boston Sunday evening. Carla had wanted to stay at the airport hotel with her, but Gabrielle said no, though not without regret, for Carla had been so nice on the trip up from the Cape, trying to distract her with questions about Italy while Gabrielle was thinking of her father and trying not to cry, thinking of Stefano and trying not to worry.

So she'd told Carla, "Thank you for everything," but that she would be fine.

But she was not fine. Tossing and turning throughout the night, Gabrielle was a jumble of unresolved anger and unresolved guilt, tangled with images of her father and her mother and Stefano and Rosa. Twice, she went into the bathroom and vomited. Once, she considered suicide, like they said her mother had done. But there was Rosa ...she would not leave Rosa.

Around noon she ordered room service. Sipping luke-warm coffee and nibbling a dry croissant sandwich, Gabrielle knew she needed to call Nikki: She needed to give her a message to relay to Mack.

But before she had a chance to say why she had called, Nikki told her what had happened to Molly.

Sitting on a stiff bed in the bleak airport hotel room, Gabrielle cried tears that would not stop, tears for Molly, for all the children, including herself, the seven-year-old who so long ago had seen death too young.

Then she thought of Molly's spirit, so bright and alive, so different from Gabrielle, who had given years to her grief, time squandered while she fought to keep her true self concealed.

Selfish.

Selfish.

She'd heard Aunt Margaret cluck that word at Nikki more than once when they were young.

But it was Gabrielle who'd become the selfish one. Gabrielle and her twenty-three million dollars parked in Zurich and a husband who professed to love her and a daughter who was hers, not his, though he did not know that. Maybe.

All those years she'd thought herself the victim of the family, the abandoned one. True, she'd not heard from Nikki or Mary Beth when she was young. But what had stopped her from contacting them when she was an adult? Had it become more comfortable to dwell in self-pity?

Selfish.

Selfish.

"Nikki," she said, looking out the window at the airplanes lined up on the tarmac, preparing for new places in space and in time. "There's something I need to tell you." A deep breath, then another, helped calm Gabrielle's nerves. "I'm not like you and Mary Beth."

"No kidding. For starters, you're younger."

Nikki was trying to make jokes, but her tone was listless and flat.

"I'm not like you and Mary Beth," Gabrielle quickly said before she lost her nerve, "because I'm still very rich."

The pause wasn't really long enough to be called a pause, just a short hesitation.

Then Gabrielle continued. "I haven't touched the monthly checks from my trust fund for years. Lester—Carla—has deposited them in Switzerland."

The room was quiet for a moment. Gabrielle felt an odd swirling in her head, another slow, upsetting feeling in her stomach.

"Well," Nikki said at last, "good for you."

Gabrielle shook her head. "No. It's good for you, Nikki. I will help out with Aunt Dorothy, and I will keep some in case I ever need it for Rosa and for me. The rest is yours, say twenty million dollars for your kids. Do not say no, because I will not allow it."

"And I can't allow you to do that, Gabrielle. That money is yours."

"It is all of ours, Nikki. It is Atkinson money." She hung up the phone and canceled her flight, then got a seat on a flight bound for Zurich.

It wasn't until she checked out of the room that she realized she hadn't given Nikki the message to give to Mack.


Mary Beth spent the afternoon at home in the city, on the phone with Shauna, who was now on the Vineyard. She'd reviewed the endless list of wedding chores.

*Double-check with the wine merchant about the pink champagne.*

*Call the produce man to be certain they'll have enough strawberries; Phillipe has insisted on an abundance of strawberries.*

*Make sure the tent man shows up tomorrow and that*

*the trellises are in place by Tuesday so the florist can prewire them there.*

*And the chairs! They have to be set up soon so they'll settle on the ground and not go topsy-turvy when the guests sit down.*

"Mom!" Shauna cried at one point, "I'll never do this right. You're the wedding planner in the family, not me."

"Everything will be fine. And if it's not, that will be okay, too."

Shauna paused. "Mom, are you all right?"

Mary Beth laughed. "Never better, darling. But I want to stay in the city a couple more days to be sure Molly's on track." True, there were only six days until the wedding, but Mary Beth now had some other things needing attention. "I'll see you by Wednesday, when Phillipe's due to arrive." She swallowed that stupid lump that quickly rose in her throat. At least the caterer and his assistants were to stay at The Bluefin, an inn owned by old friends who would wait to be paid. "In the meantime, call with any problems."

"Do you have your cell phone?"

"Oh, hell, no, I don't. I must have left it in the Lincoln. Well, call me at the apartment."

After hanging up she tried her cell number, but if Carla was in the car headed back to the Vineyard, she didn't answer the phone, if that was where it was.

She hung up again, then dialed information.

A "Property Associate" at Guinness and Sloan was not available until Monday afternoon. God forbid anyone should speak with her now, despite the fact that it was Sunday. God forbid they should act too eager to list a classic property in a classic building with a classic damn terrace overlooking Central Park. God forbid they should show excitement about the potential commission on the five-plus million it would bring, even in the "economic downturn" everyone was crying about. Ha! She'd show them economic downturn!

She checked the messages—three this time, only two cancellations. Perhaps her luck was turning, or perhaps the rest had decided to come watch the show of the heiress trying to pretend she still had a throne.

The third call was from Carla. "Mary Beth!" she shouted. "I'm in Boston on your cell phone. I dialed the 'One' in your call memory, and I have no idea if you'll get this, but I sure hope you do because all the Atkinson numbers are unlisted." *Well*, Mary Beth thought, *of course they are*. "Anyway," Carla rambled, "I'm on my way to the airport and I had to call and tell you I forgot to tell Sam about Lester's paintings. The Chagall and the Manet. Lester took them when he left." She gave her quick details that Mary Beth jotted down. "Please make sure he knows. It might help him find Lester." Then she hurriedly added, "I'll be gone a few days. I know Sam has a lot on his mind, so I'm chasing down a lead of my own. Happy wedding!"

Mary Beth sighed as Carla said good-bye; finding Lester somehow no longer seemed so urgent.

Then again, she might feel different when Phillipe showed up on the Vineyard with his hand in her pocket, the one with the big hole.

She placed a call to the hospital and Sam gave her the good news that Molly was fine, better than expected, and that so far the new medication wasn't making her sick. He again apologized for the interruption of his search. And again, Mary Beth said Molly was all that mattered, getting Molly better, getting Molly well. Then she gave him Carla's message, only because the woman seemed to think it was important, though Mary Beth doubted it.

"Chagalls and Manets are a dime a dozen these days," she related to Sam. "We had a couple on the Vineyard. In fact, I just saw them in some old photos that I showed my mother."

Then she laughed and said she supposed she'd now have to change her perception of the value of a "dime" and the worth of a "dozen."


Unlike Molly, Dorothy would not be getting better, so Mary Beth visited her in the evening, pored over the pictures again, and talked of the old times and how good they had or had not been to the best of either of their recollections.

It helped that her mother was having a good day, a coherent day.

"Is this where the wedding will be?" Dorothy asked, pointing to the lawn at the Vineyard estate.

"Yes, Mother," she said. "Won't it be grand?"

Dorothy nodded. "There will be champagne?"

"Oh, yes. And bubbles? Remember I told you about the bubbles?"

Dorothy only smiled, so Mary Beth did not know if she remembered or not.

"The sun will shine," her mother said. "It always shines on the Vineyard in summer."

Mary Beth smiled back, her heart breaking a little for the mother she'd once had, for the harmless innocence that belonged only to Dorothy, then and now. She combed back the fine white hair that cupped her mother's face. "You're right, Mother, the sun damn well will shine."

She had already decided that tomorrow, before the Guinness and Sloan agent showed up, she would return to the pawnshop with another bundle of silver and the rest of her jewels. Then she would take a damn bus if she had to, back to midtown. She'd get off at Saks Fifth Avenue, where surely she could find a dress, no, an *ensemble,* at a reasonable cost, because come hell or high fucking water, her mother was going to Shauna's wedding. With luck, Dorothy would be with it for an hour or a moment or even just a heartbeat, long enough to know she'd been there, that she had not been cast aside.

The best part about flying coach was that no one looked at you and wondered if you were someone—a celebrity, a politician, or simply rich. No one but the flight attendants paid any attention, and at that, only when necessary.

Gabrielle picked up a magazine for the third time and wondered why she had bought *Vogue,* when the last thing she cared about right now was fashion. To make matters worse, the issue featured back-to-school wear for young girls, navy wool dresses and happy red sweaters and soft little tams to tilt *à droite.*

If she left Stefano, should she take Rosa to Paris instead of the States? Already fluent in Italian and English, Rosa also could converse quite well in French. Stefano had laughed with good humor when Gabrielle spent endless hours teaching Rosa languages that she'd "have no need for." He laughed, but did not try to stop her, and more than once she overheard him boast of his "trilingual daughter."

He had no way of knowing that preparing Rosa with a classic education was as much protection for Gabrielle as her secret money in the bank in Zurich. Rosa, like Gabrielle, would then be able to carry on with her life, financially, culturally, and every way that she could figure.

She turned another page and realized that the first place Stefano would look would be Paris. It was, after all, where she'd been when they had met. It was where Enzio had rooted out her background. It was where Stefano had pretended he did not know her name or about the money that was behind it. It was where his deception had been as insidious as hers.

No, it could not be Paris.

Leaning her head against the seat back, Gabrielle decided the first important thing right now was to get the money sent to Nikki.

Did it matter that Nikki, too, had deceived her? That she'd known from day one that Mack lived on the estate, yet she'd not told Gabrielle? And why did Gabrielle feel she should contribute any of her money to Nikki's foundation, when all those years...all those years...

*No*, she thought, *it's not her fault*. It was Aunt Margaret's fault, but it wasn't Nikki's fault or even Mary Beth's. She opened her eyes and knew she could not cheat Molly and the children just because she'd been cheated. And she'd save out plenty for Aunt Dorothy and for an income for herself and a small house maybe in the country, in the Loire Valley with its elegant gardens and graceful chateaux.

They could not—would not go to the States now, not to Martha's Vineyard, because it was the past, and it was time to move forward, not back.

A light *ding* overhead summoned an attendant to a seat a few rows ahead. Its sound seemed as tired as Gabrielle felt from traveling through the night, racing toward the sun, away from the West that was stuck in yesterday.

She tried to stretch her feet, but there was not much space. *Coach,* she reminded herself.

Checking her watch, she realized that in less than an hour they would land in Zurich. If everything went smoothly, she'd be in Tuscany tonight, tomorrow at the latest. She would face Stefano and she would hug Rosa, and then she would tell him her last secret, that Rosa was not his. If he could not handle it, she would not stick around. She would wait for the postman, and Rosa would go with her.

"Water?" a voice asked, and Gabrielle turned from the window, where the orange light of morning greeted the silver plane.

But the woman who asked was not an attendant. Standing in the aisle, holding a small water bottle in one hand and a carry-on in the other, was Carla DiRoma.

# 25

**M**y mother always said I'd be happier if I spent less time living other people's lives and more time on my own life," Carla said. "But here you are and here I am, and I kind of thought you'd need a friend." She sat down in the empty seat across the aisle.

Gabrielle was so startled she did not know what to say. "You thought I'd need a friend so you hopped a plane to Zurich?"

Carla smiled, shifting the weight of her carry-on onto her lap. "Not exactly. I thought you were going to Rome."

She unlatched the tray table, pulled it down, and folded her hands on top of it. "Well, then I'm on the wrong plane, because this one goes to Zurich."

"I know."

They were quiet for a moment, their thoughts swallowed by the white noise of jet engines, of sounds muted through headphones, of occasional low talk among the other passengers.

"I know it's none of my business, Gabrielle," Carla said at last, "but are you going to Switzerland to get some money from the bank?"

Gabrielle tented her fingers and examined her manicure. Her nails were short and clear-polished, not long and colorful like Mary Beth's, not stained with oil paint like Nikki's. "You're right," she replied, "it's not your business, Carla."

"Well, I kind of thought it was, because I'm the one who always transferred the money for you. And no offense, I mean you're very pretty and everything, but I know how much goes into that account every month and you sure don't look like you spend anywhere near that kind of money. And on top of that, you're flying coach. Why the heck are you flying coach?"

A tiny smile crept across her lips. "Carla…" she began, but then she shook her head.

Carla leaned across the aisle. "Like I said, I thought you'd need a friend. Plus, I have some of my own business to tend to while I'm there."

Carla DiRoma had a Swiss bank account?

With a heavy sigh, Carla sipped from her bottled water. "The truth is," she said, "when I saw you waiting for this plane I almost had a conniption. I hid behind the others so you wouldn't see me. I used some of my mother's insurance money to buy the ticket to Zurich because of Lester. I remembered that Lester has money in Switzerland. Your aunt Margaret gave it to him to make sure your father stayed away from you."

Another piece suddenly slid into the puzzle of Gabrielle's life. Lester had been her watchdog; Lester had always known where Gabrielle was living, not for her sake, but because he'd been paid to keep Mack from her. "That's how you found me?" Gabrielle asked. "Because Lester always knew where I was?" She reached under her tray table and tried to rub away the queasiness growing inside her.

Carla nodded. "And I bet he's forgotten that I know he has at least one friend in Switzerland. There's a chance he is with them. With her."

"Oh, Carla," Gabrielle replied. She did not know what else to say, because she was unsure how she was feeling.

"I want him to make this right," Carla continued. "I want him to give the money back, and clear up his good name." A small crack came into Carla's voice when she said "his good name."

Gabrielle recognized the sound of tears being held back. She reached across the aisle and touched Carla's arm. "Carla," she asked, "is there something you're not telling me?"

Carla closed her eyes and shook her head, then opened them and nodded. Two tears betrayed her and ran down her cheeks. "All these years," she said. "All these years I loved that man. And now he's gone off with everyone's money and with my dreams, too. It just isn't right."

Gabrielle took Carla's hand. Carla had been in love with Lester? How very dreadful. All those years, in love with the same man, only to have him leave....

"He never cared about me, of course," Carla said. "Not that way. Well, one time I thought he did." She shrugged, then wiped her eyes and patted her carry-on. "I have some pictures. Did you see the ones I gave to Sam?"

Gabrielle shook her head. "No."

"But you remember Lester, don't you? How handsome he was, especially a long time ago."

"I don't remember him, Carla. I was very young, and I only saw him that last summer. Show me your pictures." Poor Carla DiRoma. As if her life did not seem dreary enough. Gabrielle smiled and leaned a little closer, trying to act interested in photos of the man who had been Aunt

Margaret's accomplice, the man who'd stolen their money, hurting Nikki and the kids and stripping Mary Beth of the life she'd had and the security for Aunt Dorothy.

Carla took out a big white envelope and poked through the contents. Then she selected one large news clipping and handed it to Gabrielle. "This one's my favorite," she said. "A close-up of him at that Black-and-White Ball in 1978."

Gabrielle took the clipping and snapped on the overhead light. Then she looked down at the picture in her hand.

And then it all came back.

It came back in a rush, a tidal wave like the one that had hit her in Dover when she'd been in school, the one where she remembered seeing her mother fall from the lighthouse with the blue ribbons floating up behind her.

It came back with the same force, the memory of it all. She saw them both now: her mother and Lester Markham, at the top of the lighthouse.

What were they doing up at the top? In order to be there, they had to have been inside, but no one was allowed inside; the door was always padlocked, wasn't it?

But there they were: Lester and her mother. And Gabrielle clearly saw his face as he raised his arms and grabbed her mother's shoulders; she saw her mother struggle; she saw him push her over the top of the railing, and then she saw her mother fall onto the rocks.

Her mother had not committed suicide, as Gabrielle had somehow known all along. She had not killed herself. Lester Markham had murdered her.


Life was about choices, Nikki knew that: to live here or there, to marry, to have children, to paint or to prosper.

She remembered reading a comment attributed to Clint Eastwood in which the actor supposedly said, "Every decision I ever made seemed to be the right one at the time I made it."

She understood now that life really could be that simple. Accepting the results, however, was what could be difficult.

Never, no way, could Nikki take the money from Gabrielle, when her cousin did not know that Nikki was in love with her father. It would seem like cheating, and Gabrielle had been cheated out of enough.

Early in the morning Nikki stood in her studio, inhaling the salt air that came in the open window, and surveying her work as it leaned against the walls, awaiting critique: seven portraits were complete, one to go. Twelve more yet unstarted. She'd been stuck on number eight, the portrait of Molly. Without the little girl around, Nikki could not summon her muses to get it finished.

She could wait for Molly to return, but that might not happen. Mary Beth had called last night and said Molly was much improved, but who knew, who knew.

Standing back from the portrait, Nikki could see that the hair color was wrong, too brownish-red, not enough orange, not enough playfulness for a six-year-old. She folded her arms and stared at the picture, wishing that a daub of yellow or a touch of magenta could restore the child's spark and bring back her health.

But Nikki could not mend Molly's health with paint, any more than Nikki could accept Gabrielle's dollars, twenty million of them though there were. She could not take Gabrielle's money, but she could no longer deny the rights of the children.

And if that meant not marrying Mack, not being his wife, not living a "respectable life" as he'd called it, then that was her choice, and she'd have to accept it.

With a last look at the paintings, she left her studio and went down the spiral staircase and out into the sunshine.

It wasn't easy to get to the big house. Nikki wove between a bevy of pickup trucks and vans and SUVs stacked up in the driveway, surrounded by hedge trimmers and garden shears and lawn edgers and mowers. Perhaps there was going to be a lawn party for the Queen of England or at least Hillary and Bill. George and Laura. Whoever.

She let herself into the house, where the clutter in the foyer was worse than that in the yard. From the bottom of the stairs, Nikki called out Shauna's name. It took a minute, but there came the bride, in jeans and old T-shirt, clutching a clipboard and a pen. She was worn out and frazzled looking, although it was only eight o'clock.

Taking one look at Nikki, Shauna burst into tears. "I can't do this, Aunt Nikki. I can't handle everything!"

Nikki hugged her niece. "Oh, dear, it's overwhelming, isn't it?"

"Oh, you have no idea the *details* my mother coordinates. It's no wonder she's crazy most of the time. And now, the money! How can she pay for this?"

So Shauna now knew about Lester and the trust fund. Nikki pulled away and put her finger to her lips. "I don't think it's a good idea to make that public information."

"Am I considered 'public,' too?"

Shauna and Nikki both turned their heads toward the direction of the voice. At the top of the stairs stood Dee, hands plunked on her narrow hips and wild anger in her eyes.

"Oh," Nikki said. "Honey."

"Don't 'honey' me, Mother." She marched down the

stairs, nearly knocking down a woman carrying a dust mop. In this place and in this moment, Nikki was struck by how much Dee walked and talked like Margaret and like Mary Beth. "Why haven't I been told? Don't I have a right to know?" Oh, yes, Nikki thought. Margaret and Mary Beth. She might look like Connor and have his business smarts, but she had inherited the Atkinson attitude.

With a quick scan of the cleaning people busying themselves in the foyer, Nikki said, "Let's go into the library, girls, and get this straightened out."

She sat behind the desk where her mother had always sat giving orders and directions to anyone who would listen, which almost always had been everyone but Nikki.

Shauna closed the door behind them and the girls sat. Nikki thought that if Gabrielle's daughter had been there, too, the picture would not have been unlike the day Margaret had told them of their trust funds: three daughters not quite of age, being told they had inherited a fortune.

The difference was that Nikki was not Margaret and the fortune now was gone.

"Shauna," Nikki said, "I don't pretend to know how your mother intends to pay for your wedding. But I've known her all her life and, believe me, she will find a way. Nothing has ever stood in the way of something my cousin wants."

Tears rolled down Shauna's cheeks. "I don't want this, Aunt Nikki. I don't want all this...commotion. This is supposed to be a happy time."

Nikki leaned across the desk. "And it will be, dear. Just let it happen. Let your mother do as she wishes.

Then you'll be married, and from then on you can tell her to go to hell, if that's what you want."

Shauna jerked her head up, saw Nikki's smile, then laughed. "Oh," she wailed. "Will any of us survive this wedding?"

"Your mother will," Nikki replied. "Make no doubt about that." Then she turned to Dee. "As for you, my darling daughter, you were not told about the missing money because I wanted to protect you. I had hoped the money would be found: We have a detective searching for Lester. But for what it's worth, I'm sorry you learned from someone other than me."

Dee would not raise her eyes to look at Nikki. "It's not as if I need the money, Mother. I mean, Daddy has plenty—" Then her eyelids shot up. "Doesn't he?"

Nikki winced at the reaction of her material-minded girl. "I'm sure your father will see that you're provided for," she said, and could not help it that the words sounded rather cold. "But for now, for Mary Beth's sake, I'd appreciate it if you didn't let this get around. She'd be devastated if anyone else found out before the wedding. I'm sure both of you understand."

"I told Jason," Shauna said. "As well as Dee." She flicked her gaze to her maid of honor then back to Nikki. "Jason's cool with it. He even said his parents won't care. Their money is so old mine wouldn't have held a candle to it, anyway. But I'm sorry I told Dee, Aunt Nikki. I just assumed she knew—"

"Ha!" Dee snorted.

"I should have been up-front and said that's why you couldn't go to China," Nikki said to her daughter. "In the meantime, however, I do need to speak with your father. Do you know when he plans to arrive for the wedding?"

Dee shrugged. "He's here already."

Nikki sat back in the chair. "He is? Where?"

"He's on the island. In Gay Head, at the inn out there."

"Aquinnah, Dee," Shauna interjected and Nikki was glad because it gave her a moment to compose herself. "It's not called Gay Head anymore."

"I just saw him the other day," Nikki said. "He didn't mention he'd be coming early."

Dee shrugged again and stood, her attitude back in place, as if she had never been a normal person the way she'd been at lunch with Gabrielle, even if that "normalcy" had simply been a cover-up to her other agenda, which had been to shock Nikki with gossip of Eric and his lover. "Some people have a way of not confiding in others," Dee commented now, and left the room in a huff.

Nikki watched her daughter depart, then she shut her eyes in exasperation.


Gabrielle made it off the plane with Carla, through immigration, and into the city to the famous Bahnhofstrasse, where the banks were aligned between high-priced, glitzy shops, where the railroad station sat at one end, and the lake shimmered at the other.

Then she made it into FirstBanc Internationale, where she and Carla went into separate boxlike rooms with separate representatives.

She made it thus far without her legs buckling, without breaking down or crying out *Oh, God, my mother was murdered and I saw it happen.*

She did not know why, but she sensed that Mack would have been proud that she'd maintained her composure. Neither did she know why she had told him she saw her mother jump—a child's denial? A child's misunderstanding? She did not know, would perhaps never know the answer to that, but she did know that the truth had erupted with one newspaper clipping.

And it was the truth. She knew it as clearly as she knew that what she was doing now was the absolute right thing.

Twenty million dollars seemed a nice, round figure to transfer into The Rose Foundation. Gabrielle did not waver when she saw the entry in the withdrawal column. She thought of it as catharsis for the years of her despair, for her mother, who had been killed by Lester, and for her aunt Margaret, who had been the one responsible for Gabrielle being turned into an orphan, and for her father, who had allowed it so she would be hurt no more. The twenty million would be Gabrielle's memorial to all of them, her rite of letting go.

And a few hundred thousand for Aunt Dorothy and to help Mary Beth traverse her hurdles.

Sitting in the private room, awaiting the final paperwork, Gabrielle decided not to call Nikki or Mary Beth until after the wedding. Most likely, there was enough chaos on the island with the festivities at hand; she did not want to steal the attention from the bride or the groom.

And then there was Sam. Neither Gabrielle nor Carla knew if he still hunted Lester...the murderer and thief.

When she had finished the paperwork, Gabrielle stepped outside to wait for Carla. She sat on a park bench between Movado and Bulgari, achingly aware of every muscle in her body, realizing how exhausting truth could be. Perhaps that was why she hadn't faced it before.

And still, she had one more truth to share, to reveal to Stefano, to prepare for his despair.

Carla came out of the bank and walked to her. "I have some news," she said. "Let's go down to the lake."

Gabrielle was too tired to stand and too tired to talk. Yet she got up and walked because it seemed easier than saying no.

"He's really gone," Carla said as they approached the water. "His account was closed six months ago."

Gabrielle stopped. She shielded her eyes against the sun that reflected off the water. "Six months ago?"

Carla nodded. "He transferred the cash by phone."

"Transferred it where?"

"Into your accounts. Yours. Nikki's. Mary Beth's."

"But why?"

Carla sighed. "Apparently Lester didn't steal your money. He lost it months ago through simple mismanagement. He used his own money to try to cover his tracks. I guess he thought the stock market would make a grand comeback."

Gabrielle sat down on the ground, on grass as green as the sweeping green lawn where she'd once sat and played with Barbie and Ken while her mother and her father held hands in Adirondack chairs and where life had been perfect, or had seemed that way.

Zurich, however, was a long, long way from Martha's Vineyard, and mismanaging funds was the least of Lester Markham's sins.

"Oh, God," was all Gabrielle replied, because suddenly she simply wanted to move on with her life and did not want to know or care what happened to the money or why Lester had done all the things he'd done.

But something told her that would not be possible.

# 26

I'm going to sell the apartment," Mary Beth said to Sam, the stranger who'd become her friend since she'd brought Molly from the Vineyard. A stranger who wasn't interested in her money, other than in doing his job to find that jerk Lester.

Monday had flown by.

Mary Beth had gone back to the hospital Sunday night after seeing her mother: She and Sam had shared a toast of chocolate milk when the doctor said "So far, so good," then they'd taken turns reading to Molly, joking with Molly. Mary Beth tried to braid her hair the way Molly said Gabrielle had done, but she was lousy at it, and they all laughed at that.

She'd fallen asleep in the high-backed chair in Molly's room and did not wake up until the middle of the night. At first she'd thought a nurse had covered her with a blanket, but later learned it had been Sam, who'd slept on the other side of Molly's bed on a narrow roll-away.

On Monday morning, the pink returned to Molly's cheeks. Mary Beth kissed her quickly, ran home, and showered, then traveled to the pawnshop, where she netted another sixteen thousand—not what Phillipe wanted, but sixteen thousand, nonetheless. He could accept it as her "up front" payment, or he and his truffles could go to hell.

After the pawnshop she went up to Saks, where she found a lovely sky-blue sundress and short jacket that would make Dorothy Atkinson feel like the million none of them had. Shoes and a purse, even costume jewelry that looked like diamonds and aquamarine completed the look and added up nicely on the American Express.

Last, Mary Beth met the real estate agent, who set the price at five million three. The "interested party" was, in fact, looking at it that minute, while Mary Beth and Sam sat in the hospital cafeteria, having grilled cheese sandwiches and orange gelatin squares for dinner.

"I'm nervous," she said to Sam, "and excited, too. I don't know what's going to happen, but for once that's okay." She picked up her spoon and jiggled the gelatin. "I have no idea why it seems okay now."

Sam laughed.

Around them, the clatter of trays and utensils and the *ching-ching* of the cash register continued undisturbed, life in its ever-forward motion, despite the pain that some were in, despite the loss some were enduring, or were expected to endure. Mary Beth thought of her mother and knew that, while the situation was sad, it was nothing like Molly's, who was just a child. "I don't know how you do it," Mary Beth added quietly, and they both seemed to know what it was she meant.

"I do it because I have to," Sam said. "I do it because I love her."

Yes. Love. Whatever that was. She set down her spoon and took a bite of her sandwich.

"Can you sell the apartment without your husband's

permission?" Sam's question came so fast it took her quite off guard.

"My husband's name is on nothing," she said defensively. They had, after all, been married before prenuptial agreements were fashionable, and greedy Eric had never complained, for even though his name was nowhere, he probably figured he'd be entitled to something if they divorced. She hadn't considered that. "His name is not on the real estate, not on the furnishings. Not on the crystal or the art collection we've amassed over the years." But even as she spoke she began to worry.

"Oh, God," she suddenly said and returned the grilled cheese to her plate. "Will he be entitled to half of the equity?"

Sam shrugged. "I don't know. Maybe."

"But the apartment's *mine*. It was my mother's." A whine had crawled into her voice, a whine she unfortunately recognized because it came from her. She balled her fists and tried to think of Molly; she tried to think of the other kids and to remember that her problems were shit compared to theirs.

He reached out and touched her arm. "You need to see a lawyer, Mary Beth."

"I can't afford a lawyer."

"You can if you sell the house."

"I won't sell the house if he'll get half."

"You may not have a choice."

"He's committing adultery."

"This is the twenty-first century. I think the rules are different."

"I don't have to divorce him. I can drag this on for years."

Sam seemed to think about that a moment. "Why would you want to?" he asked. "If you don't want to be married to him anymore, why would you want to drag it out?"

"To make him suffer."

He let go of her arm. "Then it seems you'll suffer, too. Why would you want to do that?"

She took a sip of lukewarm coffee. "Because I'm an Atkinson," she said. "And suffering is what we do."

"To make up for being rich?"

She shrugged. "You'll have to ask my cousin Nikki. That would pertain to her."

On the way back to Molly's room Mary Beth stopped at a pay phone and checked her messages, damn the fact that she had left the cell phone in the Lincoln. There was one message from the agent: The interested party had offered four million nine.

"Take it," the agent recommended. "She won't bother with a counteroffer." *She*, Mary Beth thought. Probably one of those new double-breasted Wall Street types who operated with a palm pilot and had split custody of the kids; who had amassed a portfolio that would have made Mary Beth's trust fund measly by comparison, if there were anything to compare. "Also," the woman added, "she might be interested in some of your furnishings."

Mary Beth perked up. Could this mean cash before the Sotheby's auction? Money for the wedding? "You can discuss that directly with her once a deal is made."

Four million nine. Four nine, less a million-dollar mortgage that she'd needed not long ago, in part to do the renovations when she'd converted Dorothy's suite into a playroom of her own.

Four million nine, less a million. Would she be willing to give half of it to Eric?

"The sooner we know, the better. It helps that the buyer is familiar with the place. You might recognize her name: it's Roxanne LaMonde."

It had been a long, tiring day at camp, the kind of day that made muscles and bones and everything ache, but felt so damn good you couldn't wait to do it again tomorrow. The kind of day that had reinforced for Nikki the choice that she'd made.

*Help is help,* Alice had reminded her. *We get it when we can.*

Shifting on the driver's seat, Nikki looked out at the landscape as it slowly changed from beach scrubs and flatland to thick, dense trees that lined the road and hugged the curves and hills, over twenty miles from its farthest tip-to-tip.

"Let's go on a twenty-mile trip," Mack had said to Nikki more often than she could recall. It was his way of saying "Let's go up-island to Philbin Beach where we can be alone with the tide."

Would he leave the island now that she had to reject him?

Was she prepared for that?

The thick trees gave way to the berry bushes and the low brambles of Aquinnah: Up ahead, the redbrick lighthouse stood on the cliffs, framed by the sun, which was lighting the sky with its day's end of orange and pink, and by the piece of the shore melting into the dusk.

Nikki was surprised Connor had chosen to stay out there: Perhaps he felt more comfortable "away" from the family that was no longer his; perhaps he wanted to work and make deals and be the business guru that he was in solitude for a change.

She turned down the dirt driveway of the up-island inn, and wondered how he would react to her proposition, and what he would expect in return.


"Nicole?"

She jumped at the sound of her name, because suddenly Nikki felt vulnerable, standing as she was in the welcoming, open foyer of the charming inn. The last time she had been there had been with Mack. They'd come for dinner in the fall, and sat next to the fireplace by the wide windows that overlooked the cliffs.

"What's wrong?" Connor asked, and of course he would, because why would he think otherwise?

"Nothing," she said and tried to smile. "Dee said you'd arrived. I wondered if we could talk."

He guided her through the oak-floored reception room to the flagstone terrace on the back lawn. She thought of the many times she and Mack had walked along the beach and Mack had looked up at the inn and entertained her with made-up biographies of those who stayed there.

"Newlyweds from New Hampshire," he'd say of a young couple standing on the terrace, holding hands and gazing at the water. "They were given a four-day, three-night package by some well-meaning friends."

Or, "A doctor and his long-suffering wife." Mack would somberly nod toward an older couple who sat outside sipping morning coffee, he reading the newspaper, she cutting a wedge of melon into bite-size pieces. "They're down from Boston. She forces him to take a vacation every eight weeks, and he hates every minute of it."

They had watched and he had invented stories as they strolled along the beach, because there was no harm and because it amused them in their sequestered little world.

"Coffee?" Connor asked. Out in Aquinnah, serving alcohol was against the ancient town law.

Nikki shook her head. She wondered what kind of story Mack would make up about her and Connor, two people nearing middle age if not already there, sitting with civility on the terrace as if they hadn't been divorced for fifteen years. Would Mack think they were getting back together?

"So," Connor said, after he signaled a waitress and ordered a cup of hazelnut coffee, "this is unexpected."

"Is it?" she asked. "You know this is where I live." She'd once heard of a theory about the first thirty seconds of an encounter setting the tone, the mood, the *air* between people for the duration of the scene or the date or the meeting. She wondered if she'd been sarcastic and if the tone would thus be tense. She wished she'd ordered coffee to take her mind off other things. "Connor," she said, her eyes traveling out to sea. "I'll get to the point. You already know that my trust fund's gone."

He nodded in that way he had of neither commenting nor criticizing, which was most unnerving, because it meant she had to keep talking.

And then she thought of Molly.

And her commitment to the kids, and the fact that she would make it happen, even if it meant going back to Connor, and to the life they'd had.

His coffee arrived.

She watched him stir in half a teaspoon of sugar and a tablespoon of milk. She remembered how that habit had made her insane, that he practically counted each grain of sugar as if one too many or too few simply would not be acceptable. It was not a major flaw, yet still, it had almost driven her mad.

She shook her head and told herself milk and sugar didn't matter. Then she took a deep breath of cool evening salt air, and said, "I've come to take you up on your offer to help."

Before he had time to respond, she launched into her story. She told him of her goals for The Rose Foundation, how she wanted to establish corporate sponsorship to take her work worldwide. "If Atkinson Enterprises is at the head of the list, it would set us up as a viable organization. And help us gain international recognition and contributions. Romania alone has nearly nine thousand AIDS kids, Connor. Imagine the good we can do with enough money behind us."

He tented his fingers in his thoughtful manner. He let her continue.

"We're already more than the camp, you know. We've been providing a few hundred kids with costly medication. I pumped my money into it because I thought the lives of a few kids were more important than my own financial gain."

He held up his hands. "Stop." He smiled. "You don't have to convince me of your good deeds. I'm not the enemy."

She laughed and rolled her eyes. "My mother's presence lingers in the air, God rest her odd, pathetic soul."

He leaned back in his chair. "How much do you need?"

*How much do you need.* Would it really be that simple?

"Twenty million to start." The figure Gabrielle had offered seemed a good place to begin.

He could have whistled or coughed or choked for that matter, but Connor was Connor so he did no such thing. Instead he said, "How about if we start with ten? Then you can let me know how you're doing raising other funds, and we can discuss more at that time."

It was all so matter-of-fact, as if he'd anticipated this

moment and thought out his response. *How about if we start with ten?* Did that mean he did not expect her to share his bed as well?

"That's it?" she asked.

He nodded.

She studied his still-good-looking face and wished she'd been a different kind of woman who'd not felt the need to divorce him. She wished she could have loved him with the ease with which she loved Mack. Life would have been much less complicated. "You're the greatest," she said, and meant it.

With a quick smile, Connor stood up. "And as much as I would like to spend all evening here, I'm afraid I have other promises to keep." He looked over her shoulder and broke into a smile. "Good evening," he said, but not to her.

Nikki turned around and saw a lovely woman walk toward them in a long white dress, a pale yellow sweater tied around her shoulders. She had short-cropped pale yellow hair and a wide smile for Connor. Her lips were painted in soft, subtle coral and her teeth were straight and perfectly capped.

He walked over to the woman and kissed her on the cheek. "Nicole," he said, turning back to Nikki, who sat in deadened silence. "I'd like you to meet Louise Garth. Louise, Nikki Atkinson, my former wife."

So Connor had not come early and had not come out to Aquinnah for peace and quiet or to make guru business deals.

Nikki stood up and shook Louise Garth's hand. "It's very nice to meet you," she said, then smiled at Connor. "Dee didn't tell me you'd brought a guest."

He laughed. "Our daughter does her best to keep us both off guard."

Nikki laughed in return, a combination of consternation and relief. She did not have to go back to Connor; she could have her money and he could have his lust elsewhere. Perhaps he had, at last, found patience for a relationship and love.

She hoped her laugh had not lasted too long. She cleared her throat. "So I'll see you both at the wedding?"

Connor smiled and slipped his arm around Louise Garth's waist. "I'm looking forward to it," Louise said with what seemed genuine sincerity. "I understand it's going to be quite a gala."

Nikki smiled again. "Oh, yes, I'm sure it will be that." But as she said good-bye and walked away, a small, surprising hole of loss began to form somewhere inside her, and she wondered why life always had to change and if she, indeed, was finally ready for it.


Her best friend had her husband, now she wanted her goddamn apartment, too.

That night, Mary Beth went home. The crisis had passed for Molly; she would stay in the hospital a few more days: Sam did not yet know when, or if, she could go back to camp. They agreed to stay in touch, though Mary Beth did not know why.

When she got home she did not check the many messages that flashed wildly on her machine; she wanted only sleep: Maybe tomorrow she'd know what to do. Alone in her king-size bed, however, she tossed and turned for hours, longing for the big, comfortable hospital chair and Sam and Molly and the small room so filled with love, longing to quell the loneliness of no one near.

It made her think of Gabrielle, abandoned as a child, alone across the ocean, with no one there who loved her, with no one there she loved to hold her hand or tell her she was pretty or to giggle with in the darkness the way she and Nikki often had, no one to share the painful things, like death and abortion and having to live up to the great name Atkinson every time you breathed.

Under her satin sheets, Mary Beth moved her hand to her flat stomach, remembering that Vineyard summer as if it were last week, knowing that if she ever contracted Alzheimer's like her mother, the abortion would be one thing that would never leave her mind.

*Get it over with,* Aunt Margaret had said, and so she had.

Dorothy, of course, had agreed, because she always deferred to Margaret, the stronger, wiser sister.

No one had ever asked if Mary Beth had cared.

No one except Nikki, who had been upset about it, more, perhaps, than Mary Beth, for Mary Beth was in denial, the place she'd spent her whole damn life because it had been easier than admitting that her father was a drunk and her mother was a weakling.

Poor Dorothy. Dot. The smiling woman who had never had a clue that life was more than debutantes and parties and white gloves and matching bags and shoes. The smiling woman who was better off with Alzheimer's than knowing that the money was all gone.

*Get it over with,* Aunt Margaret said, because a girl who had a baby out of wedlock was not welcome in society, and that would not be appropriate for an Atkinson, the same family who thought nothing of sending a seven-year-old girl off on her own and pretending it was for the good of everyone concerned.

She closed her eyes and realized how thin her life had been, hanging on to the veneer of the family name.

And that was when Mary Beth decided she would accept the offer on the apartment; she would sell it to Roxanne.

She would sell it and she would divorce Eric, the father

of the one child she had been allowed to keep because Shauna had been "legitimate" according to the rules.

And when Mary Beth had divorced him, she would work toward helping others, because it was the only thing that made sense in this greedy, screwed-up world. Maybe she'd even help Nikki: Wouldn't that be a twist?

But first, Mary Beth would have one last, sweet revenge.

It did not matter if it was the twenty-first century and the dictates were "different."

Sliding out of bed, she painstakingly dressed in her favorite Michael Kors outrageous miniskirt and transparent shirt and Ralph Lauren stiletto boots that made her feel ten feet tall. It did not matter whether the dictates were different or that it was three o'clock in the morning. She needed to look her finest: Old Mary Beth needed to let them know she was not going to make this easy. She could always burn the outfit later; in fact, she was certain she would.

Moving like a thief through her own house, she then called a cab to the back entrance so she would not see Jonathan the doorman. She knew Roxanne's address by heart, not because she went there often, but because a penthouse in Trump Tower was a hard address to forget.


"Well, well," Mary Beth said when Eric, her husband, opened the door. "Fancy meeting you here." She pushed past him and went into the foyer, the huge, white marble foyer that must be even bigger than the room where Ms. Post had stashed her gloves.

"Mary Beth," he said, which was nice, because that was her name.

"How long, Eric? How long have you been screwing my best friend?"

Just then the best friend walked in from the hall, carrying her spoiled dog, stroking its fur as if it were a penis, Eric's penis, Mary Beth supposed. She wore a floor-length silk robe: Mary Beth had been with her when she'd bought it. "About nine years," she answered.

Mary Beth nodded. She supposed if she calculated backwards she'd discover that was about the time their sex life had dwindled and she'd started seeing other men. She also supposed she could have asked when they saw each other, but she knew there would have been plenty of times—when Mary Beth was doing Mary Beth things, when she and Roxanne couldn't synchronize their schedules, when Eric made his supposed trips for his damn coin collecting, which could have been bogus for all she knew.

She felt a touch of satisfaction that she'd disallowed the last trip to Brazil.

"Why do you want my house?" she asked Roxanne, but it was Eric who answered now.

"I've always liked the place," he said. "It's home. And, God, Mary Beth, you need the money. Roxanne and I decided we'd be doing you a favor."

A favor?

Roxanne set down the spoiled dog and lit a cigarette. Then, suddenly, Mary Beth did not care about the rest. She no longer wanted cigarettes, she no longer wanted nasty habits. No more cigarettes, no more Hanks under the bed. Just Mary Beth, in person; plain, new Mary Beth.

"By the way, Eric," she said, turning back toward the door, "I cannot keep you from your daughter's wedding, but if you bring your tart, I shall serve your balls for dinner. And if you think you'll get one cent from me in the divorce, I shall sue the asses off both of you."

As she strutted through the doorway, she noticed four Elsa Peretti candlesticks standing on the marble table. She wondered if they were Shauna's wedding gift, then decided that no longer mattered, either.

# 27

Carla promised Gabrielle she would call the gendarmes or the *Polizei*, or whatever the police called themselves in Switzerland, as soon as Gabrielle left for Italy. They could not, however, get Gabrielle on a flight until Tuesday. Exhausted and bleary-eyed, they found a small hotel and slept until morning, until it was time for Gabrielle's journey to Florence, then Siena and back to Stefano.

Alone at last, Carla formulated a plan. However, it did not, no way, include the gendarmes, because she needed to see Lester face-to-face, one-on-one. She needed to tell him how many people he had hurt.

She tried to call Sam for advice. Alice told her about Molly's seizure, and said that she was recuperating fine, but they were in New York, and what in God's name was she doing in Zurich?

Carla hung up the phone and knew she was on her own, sink or swim, to find the murdering bastard on whom she had wasted her life.

\* \* \*

He was standing on the hillside with his back to her, tanned and lean and muscled from his work. He did not look as he had when first they'd met in Paris: He was polished then, dressed for the *consorzio,* Count Bonelli, not the laborer Stefano.

And yet he had the same effect now as he'd had on her then. Tiny knots formed inside Gabrielle's stomach and an ache swelled in her throat, and Gabrielle thought she'd never seen a better-looking man in all the world. The afternoon sun was behind him, splaying a glow of amber around him, a halo that outlined his body against the plump, purple grapes.

*The grapes,* Gabrielle suddenly realized. They *were* getting plump and they *were* turning deep purple. She stooped to the small row of vines beside her and touched the fruit. It had been warmed by the sun; it glistened with the mist gently sprayed upon it. She plucked a grape and popped it in her mouth. Juicy. Sweet. Dense.

*Oh, God!* She nearly cried out loud. It would be a banner year. The crops were healthy at long, long last, the vintage would be prime.

The curse upon Stefano had apparently been lifted.

"This may be the year for the *consorzio.*"

She stood up and turned from the sound of his voice. "That's good, Stefano. You deserve the best."

They stood in the sun, husband and wife, two lovers who knew well each other's curves and caresses, each other's pleasures and pains. Two lovers now unsure which way to look or how to stand or whether to touch.

*He knew your secret and he didn't tell you.* The words rang through her head followed by one word of caution: *Angelina.*

She forced herself to summon the anger over each loss and every betrayal. Her mother. Her father. Hateful Aunt Margaret.

Lester Markham.

And Stefano.

One at a time she pulled up the anger. And when she felt strong enough, she dared to look at her husband and say, "We need to decide if I shall go or stay. But first, I must see Rosa."

He did not say a word about the money or that she had come back without warning. Stefano had merely asked Enzio to call his sister and have her pack Rosa's things.

"I did not want Angelina to stay here," he told Gabrielle as Gabrielle surveyed the cupboards deciding what to cook for supper, to help Rosa believe this was an ordinary day, a happy homecoming, perhaps, not the ruse that it was. "I did not want gossip in the village that Angelina and I might be lovers, because we are not. I sent Rosa to her house so Angelina could baby-sit."

Gabrielle did not admit her doubts. She felt relieved, but wished, in part, that she was not. Her mission would have been easier if he had someone else.

But for now, Rosa was coming and Gabrielle was home. She would make a big frittata with Swiss chard and prosciutto and freshly grated Parmesan. It was one of Rosa's favorites. Taking the iron skillet from the peg on the wall, she wished that Stefano would remove his presence from the air around her.

Instead, he sat down at the butcher block. "Gabriella," he said, "I never wanted your money. I married you because I loved you."

She set the skillet on the stove more firmly than she'd intended.

"Was that why you didn't tell me?" he continued. "Did you think I'd take it from you?"

She closed her eyes. "Stefano, my money had nothing to do with you. I put it in Zurich long before we met."

"So no one would find out. Why, Gabriella? Had your family hurt you so much? Was it your way of getting back at them? By letting them think you did not need them, any more than they had needed you?"

She turned from him. Outside the kitchen window, dusk settled across the hills, its pink veil kissing the vines, blessing the rich crop. After this season, Stefano would not need her money. His family fortune would be returned; he would be free to find another woman to become his countess, an Italian woman—Angelina, perhaps, after all.

"My mother was murdered," she said with suddenness.

A heartbeat passed.

"Oh, Gabriella," he said. "I did not know...." He went to her. She stepped aside.

"Lester Markham pushed her from the lighthouse. I saw him do it. It happened twenty-seven years ago, but I only remembered yesterday." Outside the window Gabrielle no longer saw Tuscany, but the top of the lighthouse from which her mother fell in surreal, flowing motion until she hit the rock jetty and blood seeped from her delicate mouth and stained the beautiful lace collar of the beautiful white dress and the thin blue ribbon that had somehow come untied.

"Gabriella." Stefano slid his arm around her and she did not have strength enough to stop him.

"My aunt Margaret could not face the shame. So she lied to everyone and sent me away. I was seven years old."

He moved close behind her, he drew her toward him, his body warmed hers. "Seven? Not much older than our Rosa." He rested his head against hers.

"She is not yours, Stefano," Gabrielle said.

"Yes, she is," he replied, too soon to have absorbed her words. "She is the baby I watched be born, the daughter I have raised and loved. She could not be more mine if it had been I who impregnated you and not the man who did."

Gabrielle stood still, all tension drained, too limp for emotion.

He had known. He had known about her money and he had known that Rosa was not his and he had never said a word about either, and he had loved her anyway.

"I'm sorry," she said quietly.

"No," he said, "I am the one who is sorry. I am sorry we could not have been more honest with one another from the start. I guess I always knew this day would come, but I hoped it never would. I hoped we could live here in our villa, you and me and Rosa. I hoped we would never have to let the rest of the world inside."

The words could have come from her, she felt them so deeply, too. But there was still one more thing that she had to say.

"Stefano," she said. "There is something else."

He listened, not moving, as if nothing she'd say would change how he felt.

"I hope this is a banner year for the Castello di Bonelli. Because soon you will have another heir. I think I am pregnant, my darling Stefano. Perhaps this one will be a boy."

A slow moment hung in the sweet air, and then on her cheek was the wetness of his tears.

It was an elegant beige stucco mansion, parked on the edge of Zurich, with a long front walk, wide stone steps, and a wraparound plantation porch filled with pots of colorful summer flowers. It did not look like Lester's taste, but how much taste could one afford with no money of one's own?

Carla marched up the walk, thinking of her new friends and how he'd cheated them. She thought of Gabrielle—God, he had killed her mother. She did not think about what he'd done to her; she no longer could accept that she'd once loved this man.

This murderer.

This scum.

When the majordomo belonging to the Baroness von Friedberg opened the door, he said why, yes, of course, Herr Markham was at home.

Carla did not bother to congratulate her instincts: She was too filled with rage.

He would not come to the door—why would he? The majordomo returned and said he'd been mistaken, there was no Herr Markham in residence. She shoved the tuxedoed man aside and, on her square, sensible heels, stomped in the direction from which the servant had just come.


Lester stood in a big room that held several sofas and side tables and a gleaming grand piano, and had floor-to-ceiling windows with heavy drapes tied back with thick golden cords. He was next to a bar, pouring a drink.

He looked like a bum. He had not shaved in days, perhaps, and did not look at all like the man in her clippings: He looked old and dissipated and no longer handsome. There was some consolation in that.

He did not have to ask Carla how she found him. Lester wasn't stupid, and he must have known she could track him through the Swiss bank account and that the Baroness von Friedberg's estate would then be the first place she'd look. There had been too many news clippings over too many years of them "seen" together at too many fetes. Too many times Carla had cut out the baroness's face and replaced it with her own.

Instead of wondering how she found him, Lester asked, "Are you here because of Sotheby's?"

She had no idea what he meant, but replied, "Yes." She stepped into the room and looked around. He was alone, except for his glass of dark, golden liquid that he quickly drank. She thought of the champagne and the time that he had kissed her, then she pushed it quickly from her mind.

"Nice place," she said, because she realized that Lester seemed nervous and that she might be the one holding the cards. But hadn't it been that way the twenty-six years they'd been together? Hadn't she kept his life together while he had only used her?

He laughed. "I knew you'd figure out I gave them the paintings. Did they sell yet? How much did I get?"

The Manet. The Chagall. So that was it. Lester had given the paintings to Sotheby's. She was glad she'd told Sam about them, not that it mattered now. Her legs felt suddenly tired. She would have sat on a sofa, but they were made of stiff brocade and did not look inviting. "How much do you think?"

He buttoned his shirt over the white T-shirt that was pulled out from his pants. His once–Robert Redford hair was now gray and unkempt. Could he have changed so much in only a few weeks? Or had he been changing, aging slowly, and Carla hadn't noticed? "The Manet must go for eight hundred thousand. More for the Chagall."

She supposed she should not be surprised that he thought she was somehow connected to the sale of his paintings. God knew she'd kept tabs on everything else in his life. Carla sighed.

"What will you do with all that money, Lester?"

He walked to a small table that stood against the wall. He leaned against it. "First I'm going to get my own place. There's a beautiful chateau I've had my eye on at Lake Geneva."

She nodded. "I guess I hoped you'd give something back to the cousins," she said. "You cost them quite a lot."

He stood up straighter and poured another drink. "That wasn't my fault. Those goddamn tech stocks. How was I to know the bottom would fall out?"

"It was more than tech stocks, Lester. You never really knew what you were doing, did you?"

A sharp sound of voices came from out in the foyer, a staccato-quick exchange of high-pitched, angry words. In the instant it took for Carla to snap her head toward the noise, Lester darted behind the bar and pulled out a shiny black gun.

Jesus, Mary, Mother of God, it really was a gun.

"Drop it, Markham" a loud shout split the air. Sam's shout, Sam's voice. "Move back," he commanded Carla, and so she did. Sam, she thought. Thank God, Sam.

Then, in an outburst, Lester laughed. He pointed the gun into the air, not aimed at either of his intruders, just pointed outward and shaking.

"Whoever you are, you've got me," he said. "It took you long enough." Then his laughter faded and his eyes glazed with bewilderment as if he did not know what to say or what to do.

"Lester," Carla pleaded, because she needed to know. "What happened? What happened to the trust funds?"

He kept the gun pointed at nothing, but now he began to cry. It was pathetic, seeing him cry. Carla put her hand to her heart so it wouldn't dare to hurt. "I didn't mean to do it," Lester said. "I tried my best. Then the market went down and down. I tried to cover up the losses with the money that I had. The money from Margaret."

"Nikki's mother," Carla said to Sam, then asked, "But you had your own money, Lester. Your family's money."

He laughed again and wiped his tears with the back of the hand that did not hold the gun. "I never had 'family' money. I wasn't like them, Carla. I was like you, a poor slob like you."

Carla frowned. "But you knew the family..."

"I knew shit," he said, "except for *her*. Margaret Atkinson. She was my mistress for fifteen years. That's how I got my job as trust fund manager. That's how I landed my rightful place in society." He laughed again. "She was my ticket to the big time for the small admission price of my high-performance dick."

Carla winced. Margaret Atkinson was his mistress? Margaret Atkinson? And...Lester? Her stomach turned. Lester had been married...and Lester had those women, none of whom were her...but that awful woman...?

She looked at Sam and wondered if they were thinking the same thing: Could they prove it?

"You killed Rose Atkinson," Carla said abruptly.

Sam didn't say a word, though surely he must be shocked.

Then Lester laughed again. "Killed her? It was self-defense. The woman was hysterical."

Carla kept her eyes fixed on Lester while Sam slowly took one step, then another, off to one side.

"She caught us in the lighthouse," Lester continued, "Margaret and me. It was the night of the fireworks. We took the padlock off the door. Rose must have seen it was missing, so she came inside. We were naked on the floor, having sex like dogs."

Carla tried to stop herself from feeling sick.

Lester half-smiled. "Rose started screaming, and she

ran up the stairs. I chased her to the top. She thought I was going to rape her. Ha! She should have been so lucky!"

Carla winced. "So you pushed her off the balcony."

"I had to shut her up. All those people were out there..." And Lester laughed again, wobbling the gun in Carla's direction. "As for you," he said, "you were disgusting, the way you hangdogged after me all those years."

"The paintings," Sam said quickly, and Lester jerked his head—and the gun—back toward him. "The Manet and the Chagall. Sotheby's won't sell them, Lester. They don't belong to you."

"Yes!" he cried. "They're mine!"

"No," Sam said. "They traced them to the estate. Actually, they're Mary Beth's. They once hung in the house on the Vineyard. The house was left to her with all its contents."

Spit flew from Lester's mouth. "No! They're mine! That old bitch gave them to me!"

Sam shook his head. "There's no record of that. But there are photographs of the library at the house on the Vineyard, in which both paintings are visible on the walls. Dorothy Atkinson has the pictures at the nursing home."

Carla was glad of that: Mary Beth sure could use the money they would bring.

Lester looked confused. And then his body trembled. He flicked his bulging eyes from Sam to Carla, then back to Sam. He moved in front of the bar again. "No!" he cried. "They're mine!"

Sam lunged toward him and they struggled. Carla started to tremble, her fist now in her mouth, her throat making funny little noises she knew were from trying not to panic. Then the two men fell onto the floor, Lester on top of Sam. And then the gun went off.

She held her breath and waited longer than she'd ever waited in her life. And finally Lester moved off Sam and rolled onto his back. And Sam stood up and he and Carla looked down at Lester and at the bright red liquid that erupted like Mount Vesuvius from Lester's chest.

# EPILOGUE

———

The day before the wedding, Dee showed up at Camp4Kids. Sand dusted her white canvas shoes and stretch capris as she crossed the makeshift parking lot to the registration cottage. Nikki spotted her from the window, and wondered why she was there, on her mother's turf, the kids' turf.

Since their altercation at the big house, she'd had glimpses of Dee amid the comings and goings of people and cars and vans and delivery trucks that had shuttled up and down the driveway at the estate, but Nikki had decided to stay out of the way. Mack had agreed; he'd stayed at the tavern, where Nikki joined him every night.

Dee walked onto the porch. She raised her hand, then put it down, as if unsure whether or not she should knock, not knowing if this were a proper business or not. Nikki watched a moment longer, then opened the door.

"Dee," Nikki said.

"Mother. I wasn't sure if you'd be here." Her blue eyes traversed the doorway and went into the room beyond.

"May through August," Nikki replied, commanding herself to not be defensive or antagonistic. "Next year I hope we can extend it to September. The kids are great. They love it here."

Dee nodded.

"Come in," Nikki said. "Have a seat. Would you like tea?"

Dee sat on the edge of the cushion tied to an old wicker sofa. She did not answer Nikki's question, but said, "I came to say I'm sorry, Mom. I've been more than my usual rat-self lately."

Nikki sat, because it was apparent that this conversation would warrant a chair. "There's nothing to be sorry about, honey. We don't always see eye to eye; sometimes that's how mothers and daughters are." She did not mention the differences she'd had with one Margaret Atkinson.

A tiny frown line appeared between Dee's eyebrows. "I wasn't talking about us. I meant about Dad. I should have told you he was here with a woman."

Nikki said, "Oh." She crossed her feet and studied her toes. "Well, it was a bit of a shock. Something told me, however, you might enjoy that."

Dee stood up. "Maybe this was a bad idea." She headed for the door.

"Please, Dee. Don't leave."

For once, Dee didn't.

"Your father certainly has a right to see whomever he wishes," Nikki said. "I certainly don't check in with him when I date anyone."

Dee returned to the wicker without comment. "I came to ask you something else," she said, as if this talk of mothers and fathers dating and mating had grown uncomfortable. "Dad told me about your plans to expand the foundation."

That wasn't surprising, it was, after all, business.

"I'd like to help," Dee said. "I know stuff now; I'll know even more after Harvard. The truth is, Dad suggested I forget going to China and work my way around the world with The Rose Foundation. I'd like that, Mom." Then she lowered her eyes. "I want to be part of your life. I don't want to fight anymore." Then the biggest tears Nikki had ever seen splashed from her daughter's eyes.

Nikki jumped from her chair and stooped beside Dee. "Honey," she said, putting her arm around her daughter, who did not withdraw from her touch. "What is it? What's wrong?"

"Aunt Dorothy," Dee said. "Mary Beth brought her to the big house. Oh, Mom, what if something like that happened to you and we never had a chance to be friends?"

Siena was a village bathed in sepia. The famed Il Campo piazza was the center of it all—a shell-shaped sprawl of a redbrick yard, shaded only by a massive tower and rimmed by outdoor cafés and umbrella tables.

Carla sat at one of those umbrella tables sipping lemonade, wondering if her ancestors had ever ventured there in June and August for *Il Palio*, when the horses race and the people laugh and drink and feast.

Her guidebook said those things, the small guidebook printed in Italian and French, Spanish and English. It cited the Tuscan *festa* (celebration), *bellezza* (beauty), and *pici* (the delectable local pasta). It showed photos of old men and young women and olive trees and vineyards and pecorino cheese. They were pretty pictures but did not show the way things really looked; they could not add the sounds and smells and senses of driving through the countryside as she'd done that morning, or sitting in the piazza, where she now sat that afternoon.

God, she was a long way from the Bronx. She smiled,

then touched her bag where her mother's silver-framed photo was safely nestled for the trip.

Italy! Their homeland—*twice* in just weeks! She thanked her lucky stars that she'd kept up the payments on Theresa's life insurance and that it had paid out much more than the funeral had cost.

A group of pigeons flew over her; she felt as if this were a movie, a black-and-white film like they showed at the Majestic when she'd sat up in the balcony with her Good & Plenty and her dreams. If she looked to the next table, Carla felt certain that Cary Grant or Audrey Hepburn would be seated there.

And it was then—with the sounds and the smells and the senses around her—that Carla knew she would not go back to New York. Not to live. Not ever. Her mother was gone; her sons were no longer children. She'd seen them through their early years, she'd given them all she had; she had given too much to a man who had deserved nothing, nothing at all. And now it was time for Carla to have that real life of her own.

She had returned to Tuscany after Lester died; she went to Gabrielle; she told her what had happened. And when Stefano invited Carla to stay, she said, no, thank you, but that she would appreciate a good Sunday dinner from time to time.

Then she went into Siena and crafted her plan. The rest of her mother's insurance money would help her get settled, maybe in an apartment right there near the piazza, in the sun and the bricks and the sepia world, where Carla Marie Isabella DiRoma finally, thank you God and sweet Jesus, would have it all.

Mary Beth was going to pull it off. Nikki stood outside the lighthouse and surveyed the sweeping lawn and marveled that her cousin was going to host the wedding as if nothing were amiss, as if she'd not sold nearly everything but her soul within the past few weeks, as if her husband had not dumped her for her best friend and her best friend's money, as if at least four dozen cancellations had not come in at the last minute from "insiders" apparently privy to the Atkinson demise.

"Screw them," Mary Beth had said. "That will give us more room for the kids from camp. They'll love the bubble wands, don't you think?"

Mary Beth had even turned down Connor's generous offer to fund his niece's wedding, even though he was no longer married to the aunt. She seemed determined to do this on her own, to shake off her addiction to money and to things. She said she would not even apologize for the lack of truffles in the soup.

The gods seemed happy with her choices, for this morning dawned pristine, the sky the softest powder blue. Across the lawn, the white tents shaded long tables adorned with yards of festive organdy and gleaming silver servers.

Nikki smiled and breathed in the scent of ten thousand flowers, maybe more, that wafted from an exotic garden transplanted just for Shauna and her handsome, happy bridegroom.

Looking up to the big house, Nikki wondered if Mary Beth had ever known how often she had wished she could have been more like her, a woman who commanded and demanded and who always got things done. Nikki wished she could have been more like that, but that was too close to her own mother, and Nikki never could have been that; it wouldn't have been right.

"You can't fix my damn cummerbund if you're standing on the lawn," Mack shouted from the doorway of the caretaker's cottage, and Nikki turned with a smile. Last night at the rehearsal dinner, they announced to the family that their marriage would be next, but that they would do it without the tents and bubble wands.

Mary Beth had stood up and applauded. She claimed she'd been suspicious of a "dalliance" for many years.

Nikki had looked around and seen everyone smiling: No one seemed bothered that the niece and the uncle-by-marriage would soon be united. She had hugged him right there and felt ridiculous that she'd let her fears rule her actions all this time.

But now, as she began to cross the lawn toward the cottage, Nikki noticed that someone else had arrived ahead of her. She stopped and watched as Mack let his new guest into the cottage.

"I used to call you Daddy," Gabrielle said to her father as she stood inside the room, the Countess Bonelli blue-lace agate brooch pinned upon her collar, her gaze set on her father, who looked so handsome in his suit.

"And I called you Princess," he replied.

She felt the tears begin, the tears that she'd held back since she'd left Tuscany again yesterday, since Stefano insisted that they go as a family and that she finally make up with Mack. She looked up to the portrait that hung over the mantel. Her eyes stayed there a moment, her heart filled with love. Then she looked back to her father and smiled a gentle smile.

"I had a message I wanted to get to you before I left," she said.

"And that was..."

"I wanted to say I'm sorry, and that I've always loved you, Daddy."

He stepped forward and wrapped his big arms around her, and together their tears belonged to one another.

"Princess," he repeated, "I'm so sorry, too. And I'm so glad you've come home."

"It's a photo album," Mary Beth said to Dorothy upstairs in the big house, as she handed the woman in the sky-blue ensemble a large, leather-bound album. "I put it together to help you remember where you are today, and maybe some of the people who are here."

Dorothy smiled a tentative smile and turned back the pages, ever so slowly, tasting each morsel of distant recognition.

Mary Beth wanted to cry, but could not risk her makeup. Instead, she patted her mother on the shoulder, walked to the window, and looked out to the driveway. Then Shauna came into the bedroom on a cloud of strapless white *peau de soie* and crystals, flanked by the maid of honor in delicate, dusty pink.

The sight of them took a bit of air from the room. Mary Beth put her fingers to her throat and simply said, "Lovely, so lovely." Then she took as deep a breath as she could manage and gestured out to the driveway. "Your father's here."

They had not, until this moment, known if he'd have the courage to show up.

They had not, until this moment, known that if he did, would he be stupid enough to bring Roxanne? Thankfully, he was not.

Not that it mattered to Mary Beth, who turned back to her daughter and smiled once again. Yes, she thought. What mattered now was how incredibly gorgeous this bride, her daughter, was, how the skies were shining down upon them, and how she'd managed to get Dorothy there, and how beautiful her mother looked in her sundress and jacket, with the cluster of bluebells pinned to her shoulder, grandmother of the bride.

"I hope Daddy's not too disappointed," Shauna replied. Mack had offered to stand in for Eric, and Shauna had gratefully accepted.

"Are you sure?" Mary Beth asked her.

"I love Daddy," Shauna had replied, "but Mom, I'm really angry at him right now. He never even said if he'd be here. The only reason I'd want him to walk me down the aisle is if you'd want me to make it look better for your friends."

Mary Beth's eyebrows shot up. "For my friends? No, honey, please, don't do anything for them. Those days are over. Let's be who we are."

"Then I want Uncle Mack," Shauna said, and that was the end of that. "And maybe someday Daddy will understand why."

"Don't count on that," Mary Beth said, kissing her daughter's cheek. "But you can still love him, you know."


Sparkling, opalescent bubbles shimmered in the air. The guests had come by planes and boats and private yachts—they dressed in white, some with white hats and some with gloves. They filtered down the winding driveway, past the scrub oaks and the pines to the lawn that stretched past the lighthouse and the dunes and moved down to the sea. Music from the three harps drifted with the waves.

Nikki left the lighthouse and walked toward the flower-covered trellis where Shauna and Jason would take their vows. Stepping into the driveway, she heard a familiar sound: It was a Harley-Davidson coming down the driveway.

It was Sam, dressed in a navy blue suit. And in front of him sat Molly, pink-cheeked and smiling, in a frilly, peppermint-stick-colored dress. She climbed off and ran to Nikki for a hug.

"You made it!" Nikki cried. "I am so glad!"

"I'm going to be the flower girl!" Molly cried in return. "Mary Beth said if I was well enough to be here, I could be the flower girl!"

"Your friends will be so excited for you. Look, they're over there." She pointed to the section of the guest seating that Mary Beth had reserved for the very special guests—the children from Camp4Kids, who were laughing and holding crystal bottles and blowing bubbles with their sterling wands.

Molly scampered off, her pink patent-leather shoes leaving little puffs of dust.

Sam laughed. "She's so excited to be here."

"Mary Beth will be thrilled. Molly's okay?"

"She's doing great today. All we need each morning is to ask that she'll stay healthy for today."

Nikki smiled. "And you look better than you did."

He strapped his helmet to the chrome bar on his bike. "I shouldn't," he said. "I haven't come bearing good news."

Nikki wanted to ask if it could wait until later, but Sam spoke too quickly.

"I found him," he said, "with help from Sotheby's and Carla."

"You found him?"

"When I was in Punta Cana, I learned he'd only used his ticket one way. From there he went to Zurich, but I had no idea why or where. Then Carla left a message about Lester's paintings—I thought he might have tried to sell them to raise cash. I called Mary Beth's contact at Sotheby's and, can you imagine? Lester was stupid enough to leave his phone number in Zurich. It's like the murderers who carefully plan the deed, but forget to think through where to hide the body. Happens all the time."

Nikki could have made a number of comments, but she did not. "And now?" she asked.

"And now Lester is dead."

She felt no great compassion, and she was not surprised. "And our money is gone."

Sam nodded. "It's been gone for a while."

She looked off toward the wedding guests, out toward the sea. "So I'll have to depend on the Atkinson name after all," she said. She did not add that now she was also going to depend on her daughter and Mary Beth, too—what a challenge that would be! But together they could build an organization of which Rose would have been proud. Rose, she thought. Poor Rose.

"Nikki?" Sam asked. "May I ask you something about the family that's, well, sort of personal?"

Nikki laughed. "Sure, Sam. But you already know most everything about us."

"It's about Mary Beth. Do you think she could ever be interested in a blue-collar cop?" He smiled and Nikki smiled, and she looked at him and straightened his tie.

"I say give her a little time, then go for it, Sam. She could do much worse, and I'll bet she knows that."

Then they walked toward the white folding chairs, where Dorothy sat, a leather-bound photo album open on her lap.

"Guess what?" Dorothy whispered with animation to her niece. "Isn't it wonderful? Rose is here. I saw her go into the caretaker's cottage."

They sat in the shade, listening to the music, as the ceremony started.

Mary Beth walked down the white carpet aisle, with her proper, private-schooled posture, beaming this way and that to her coveted guests. No one held her arm; no one had to, for Mary Beth had enough strength to endure on her own.

Then came Molly. Radiant, glowing Molly, tossing pink and white rose petals along the bridal path. *My next portrait,* Nikki thought with a warm shiver of awe. *It will be the best I've ever done.* Her muses had returned; she could now get back to work.

And then came Dee. So elegant, so grown-up. Nikki watched her daughter and could not suppress a grin. Dee caught her eye and actually winked.

Nikki's gaze then moved to Connor, who stood in the row behind her, the lovely woman named Louise at his side. They'd said hello earlier, and this time it was okay.

Then, beyond Dee and Connor and the other guests, another couple walked toward where Nikki sat: Gabrielle and Stefano. Between them walked a beautiful, dark-haired, blue-eyed girl.

Gabrielle slipped into the row. "Sorry we're late," she whispered to Nikki. "It's Saturday. Do you know how hard it is to catch a ferry in the summer?"

Yes, Nikki knew.

"And I had to stop and talk to my father. I understand he'll be the next to marry."

Nikki flinched, but Gabrielle broke into a grin and squeezed her hand. Nikki was overcome with joy.

The music changed. Nikki wiped a small tear and turned to the aisle. Then Gabrielle leaned over and whispered, "Carla would have joined us, but she said she's never coming back."

"So Carla's never coming back. Well, neither are our trust funds," Nikki quietly replied.

Gabrielle nodded. "I know. There are other things you'll want to know, but we'll talk about them later."

And then came Shauna down the aisle, a young woman of beauty and of grace, every bit an Atkinson. Nikki sat up straight and gazed with pride at Shauna's escort, Mack, the "uncle" of the bride. His eyes quick-flashed on Gabrielle, then landed with a smile and sparks of love on Nikki, a love she now knew would endure forever, like the legend of the Atkinsons and the secrets they survived.

# ABOUT THE AUTHOR

————

Though her ancestors arrived on Cape Cod from England in 1632, Jean Stone has never, ever, had a trust fund or even some old money. She does, however, feel a special connection with the Cape and Islands. TRUST FUND BABIES is her ninth novel from Bantam, and her fifth to take place on Martha's Vineyard. A graduate of Skidmore College, Saratoga Springs, New York, she resides in western Massachusetts where she is working on her next novel.